CHOOSING HOME

A HAVEN BAY NOVEL

KATIE BECK

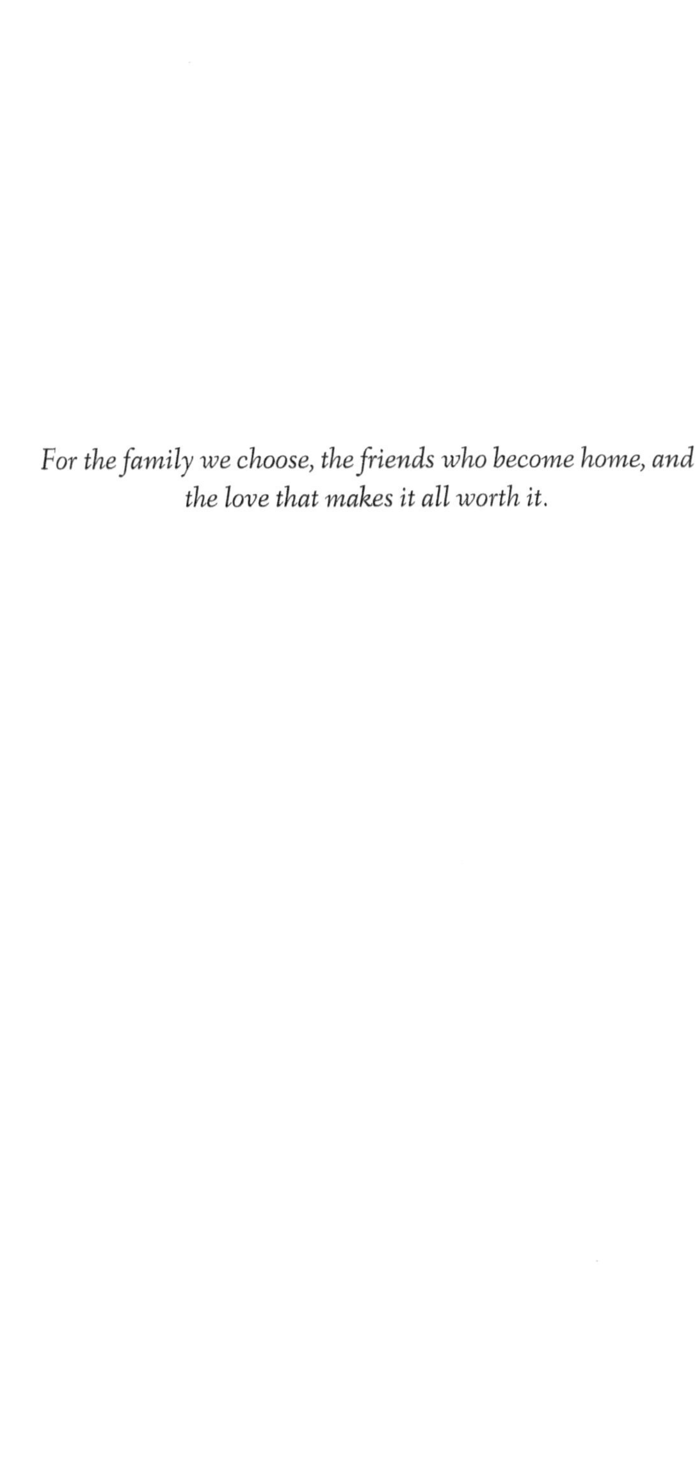

For the family we choose, the friends who become home, and the love that makes it all worth it.

There are three things every adult woman should have by the time she's in her mid-twenties: a best friend, a kick-ass outfit guaranteed to boost her confidence, and a good vibrator.

Lucky for me, I have two best friends who are my biggest cheerleaders and a drawer full of toys that make my legs quiver more than any man has.

As for the outfit, I've got that covered three times over. Some people collect records, others vintage cars. My vice happens to be cute clothes.

As army brats, my brother and I grew up knowing the importance of travelling light. For years, my wardrobe was nothing more than the essentials—until I turned fourteen, when my father's promotion to a permanent position let us finally settle into a more stable life.

You'd think that packing up your entire life every couple of years would have caused me to maintain a minimalist lifestyle after I moved out on my own, but it seemed to have had the opposite effect. The second I received my high school diploma, I packed up my baby blue

'67 Mustang convertible, Blue, and high-tailed it out of Toronto until I hit the Pacific Ocean. After emptying my savings account to rent a cute studio apartment in Vancouver, I was lucky enough to nab a waitressing job at a nearby bar called Moose's.

The day I cashed my first pay cheque, I started filling my sparse closet and every other spare inch of my apartment with second-hand clothes from the local thrift store.

Finally able to let my creative juices flow, I spent the next ten years curating a wardrobe that not only complimented my tall frame but boosted my confidence. Every piece was carefully chosen to make me feel good— both physically and mentally.

Which is why, as I pull on my favorite pair of black denim jeans with the frayed knees, my mood instantly boosts. These jeans are my favorite for a reason. They hug my subtle curves without being too tight around my waist while giving me the ideal bubble butt.

Perfect for a girls' night out.

I tuck the front of my oversized tee into my jeans and spin to check myself out in the full length mirror leaning against my bedroom wall. Satisfied, I grab my phone to shoot off a text to my friend, Brenna, who should be stopping by any minute before we head to the local bar, The Dive. There's a band playing that I've been dying to see and Brenna agreed to tag along.

She texts back that she's on her way, so I tuck my phone into my back pocket and dance my way into the kitchen to the music playing over my Bluetooth speaker. It's one of my few expensive purchases. I refuse to listen to my music on anything other than a quality speaker with the volume turned up loud.

Dipping a chip into the salsa sitting on my kitchen counter, I shimmy over to the fridge to grab a can of flavored water from inside. Most people my age start their nights off with a shot or two of tequila, working their way towards a buzz before they've even left home.

I'm not trying to sound judgy. To each their own and all that. In fact, for a long time, I used to be one of those people.

When I was waitressing, and later bartending, at Moose's, a group of us would go out after our shifts ended and stay out until the sun came up drinking and hopping from one bar to the next. In the summer, we'd hang out on patios or have bonfires on the beach. In the winter, when the hills were glazed with a fresh dusting of snow, we'd spend our days at the ski lodge drinking. Then, in the early morning, we'd crawl into bed, sleep until the afternoon and do it all again the next night. We were young and invincible with no responsibilities.

It was the best time of my life.

Until it wasn't.

I never had any problems with drinking. Still don't, to be honest. I love a good rye and Coke while the bass from the band thumps in my chest, and the carefree feeling that a light buzz brings with it.

It's the next morning that's the problem. I always used to joke that I liked alcohol but it didn't like me. The hangovers were brutal and only got worse as I got older. What started as an annoying headache turned into spending the entire next day spilling my guts into the toilet. But that wasn't the worst part.

The worst part was the "hang-xiety". That's what we would call the anxiety that inevitably follows the morning after drinking, when you're left questioning every word you said the night before.

Was I too loud?

Did I say something stupid?

Were they laughing at my joke or were they laughing at me?

Eventually, the hang-xiety got so bad that it would last for days afterward. It got to the point where the few hours of fun on Saturday night weren't worth the anxiety that lasted into Wednesday.

So, I decided drinking wasn't for me.

Don't get me wrong, I still love sipping a cold, slushy drink on a hot summer day or warming up with a shot of whisky when the cold Canadian winters bite a little too hard. But now I have a self-imposed two-drink rule. I've been known to bend that rule to three drinks on special occasions, but never more than that.

It just isn't worth it.

When I'm sober, I still get to have all the same fun as before while making sure my friends get home safe.

A muffled knock on my apartment door pulls me out of my thoughts. I turn the music down to a more respectable level. "Come in!" I call out to who I'm assuming is Brenna.

The door swings open and Brenna steps inside. She's dressed in a faded pair of jeans and flowy blue top and she's curled her short, red hair. I give her an approving whistle that makes her blush furiously.

Brenna runs the dog rescue and sanctuary outside of town where she spends most of her day covered in dog hair and dirt. She's not as into fashion as I am but I convince her to dress up as often as she'll let me. Brenna's a beautiful girl and I've seen the way her eyes light up when she checks out her reflection on nights out. She just needs to step out of her comfort zone more often.

"You look damn fine, Miss Doyle."

Again, she blushes, but she laughs this time. "Why, thank you, Miss St. James." She drops the bag that's slung over her shoulder onto the nearby sectional. Since Brenna lives outside of town and I'm within walking distance of the bar, I told her to stay over at my place tonight so she didn't have to worry about driving.

"You forgot to lock the back door again," she chastises, wagging a finger at me. She's always on me about locking up the studio. She grew up in a city like I did and has held onto the belief that if you don't lock your doors, someone is going to break in and murder you in broad daylight.

I, on the other hand, have embraced the small town life with open arms, which includes never locking your doors.

I don't bother telling her I hardly remembered to lock up even when I lived in the city.

Shrugging, I down the rest of my drink and place it on the coffee table. "It's Haven Bay. The worst that's going to happen is a raccoon might get inside."

I hit the pause button on my phone and the music stops abruptly. Slinging the thin chain strap of my purse over my shoulder, I gesture to the door.

"Alright. Let's go, chicky."

———

WHEN WE GET to the bar, the place is packed. Even though it's the end of September and the summer is fading into fall, the tourist season is still very much alive. The band is playing a Creed cover and both the dance floor and bar are crowded with people. Brenna shouts that she's going to search for a table so I make my way to the long wooden bar.

Wiggling my way through the bodies, I lean forward onto the counter, waiting to catch the eye of either of the bartenders. Eventually, I make eye contact with the owner, Rhett, who points to a bottle of my favorite whisky. I nod then mouth, "Brenna", to which he nods his understanding. He then grabs a lowball glass and a bottle from the cooler below him.

One of the benefits of living in a small town is that you get to know everything about everyone—including their drink orders. Rhett knows that I'm a rye and Coke girl, Brenna drinks just about any beer, and our friend Avery prefers vodka with cranberry juice. Rhett also knows that I have a two-drink limit and never pressures me into more, which I've always appreciated.

It could have something to do with his own limited drinking. Like me, I'd bet there's a story there, but unlike me, he doesn't seem willing to go into the reasoning behind it. If there's one thing I can appreciate, it's someone's need for privacy so I've never asked.

When most people think of me, "private" would not be the first word that comes to their mind. Sure, I've been accused of not having a filter and saying the first thing that comes to my mind. But while it might seem that way sometimes, the people closest to me know that isn't the case.

Do I like to say what's on my mind even if it can be considered a little "out there" or "risque"? Absolutely. But do I spill all my secrets and personal details to every Tom, Dick and Harry that cross my path? Definitely not.

Rhett places the drinks before me and I smile sweetly at him. "Thank you, handsome."

His lips turn up slightly and he nods as he steps away to take care of the next customer.

I pick up our drinks and turn to scan the crowd for Brenna. I find her at a corner high top table by the dance floor. As I approach, I notice she's not alone.

A preppy guy with perfect hair and expensive shoes leans over the table toward her. I know you shouldn't judge a douchebag by his loafers but there's something about him that instantly has my back up. By the way Brenna is leaning away from him, she's clearly not interested. Though it might not be as clear to the douche since he's still here.

Sliding into the chair beside Brenna, her shoulders relax at my appearance. I pass her the beer bottle and she takes a long pull while stiffly nodding along to whatever Chad or Brad is saying. He finally stops to take a breath from his ranting so Brenna jumps on the opportunity to let him down easy.

"It was great talking to you, Tad." *Damn, so close.* "But my friend and I were hoping to have a girls' night tonight. Maybe we'll see you later." She offers him a tight smile.

"Baby girl, my motel is just around the corner. Why don't you ditch your friend and we can go back there now. Have our own party." He wags his eyebrows at her suggestively and my hand tightens on my drink.

"Oh, that's, uh, a nice offer, but I'm going to have to pass. We're really looking forward to listening to the band," Brenna tries again.

I bite my tongue so hard I'm surprised I don't taste blood.

Tad, who must be missing a few brain cells, has the nerve to scoff. "These guys? They blow. And not the fun kind." He winks and it takes all of my control not to gag. "Come with me. I promise you'll have fun."

That's it.

Brenna's too polite. So even though this douchenozzle is making her uncomfortable and she's made it clear she's done talking to him, she won't want to seem like a bitch by flat out rejecting him.

Luckily for her, I have no problem being a bitch.

In fact, I rather enjoy the role.

"Okay, Chad, that's enough. My friend has said no multiple times and you're still not getting it through your thick skull. Time to go. Your right hand is getting lonely." I jerk my hand in a vulgar gesture and Brenna snickers from behind her beer.

He looks me up and down as his mouth twists into an ugly sneer. "It's *Tad*, honey. And no one asked you." He turns back to Brenna. "Come on. Let's go." He grabs her wrist and I see red.

I jump to my feet and, though Brad's got a good handful of inches on me, I step into his face, blocking his view of Brenna.

"If you ever touch my friend again without her consent, *honey*, I'll kick your balls so far inside you, you're going to need a surgical team to find them." I smirk down at his crotch then tip my head to Brenna. "Not that they'd be that easy to find now," I mockingly whisper and she lets out a loud laugh.

Tad's scowl turns deadly. "Listen here, you stupid bitch. Mouths like yours are only good for one thing and it's not talking." He takes a menacing step toward Brenna but I follow him, keeping my body between them. He glares down at me then looks over my shoulder and points at Brenna. "Whether you like it or not, I'm going to find you later, so you might as well ditch this cunt and come with me now." He smirks. "Or don't. I like it when they put up a fight."

If I saw red before, now I'm seeing the overwhelming black of Tad's imminent death. Without so much as uttering a word, I pull my fist back then let it plow into this asshole's nose. The satisfying crunch that follows makes the instantaneous throbbing in my hand worth the pain. Tad crumbles before me like the pussy I knew he was.

"You fucking bitch! You broke my nose!"

By now, every eye in the bar is on us. Wide eyes of tourists bounce back and forth from Tad's bloody shirt to my grin while the locals look on in amusement. Tad is still carrying on dramatically, calling out for someone to call the police.

Rhett pushes through the crowd toward us but stops when he sees Tad's mangled face. He lets out an exasperated sigh then turns to me.

"Really?"

I shrug back at him. "He wouldn't take no for an answer."

Rhett scowls down at Tad's bent frame, who's still whining about his precious nose. "I take it back." He rolls his eyes when Tad lets out another dramatic groan. Rhett reaches down to grab Tad's arm. "Alright. Up ya get. You're fine."

The flashing blue and red lights that pull up draw my attention away from the pathetic acting before me. One of the tourists must have called the police because it sure as hell wouldn't have been a local. Locals know we have our own way of solving things around here.

"Ah, shit," I grumble because where there's flashing lights, there's the one man who despises me more than my buddy, Tad.

And he's usually the one holding the handcuffs.

CHAPTER 2

LUKE

My head is throbbing. I should've been home hours ago, drinking a beer and watching the Jays' game. Instead, I spent the last few hours at the station, laying into some harebrained teenagers who thought it would be funny to steal a school bus and take it for a joy ride. They were pretty easy to spot—not many school buses are flying down the backroads blaring rap at 10 o'clock on a Friday night.

Catching them was another thing.

Seeing as though none of the three teens knew a thing about driving a bus, they didn't realize that turning a large vehicle at those speeds on a dirt road was probably not their best idea. The result was a school bus flying into Wayne Timmon's fenced-off pasture.

By some miracle, no one was hurt and the damage to the bus was minimal. Safe to say, I don't think any of them will be seeing the outside of their houses any time soon.

Normally, a chief wouldn't be out in the field like I was (pun intended), but in a small town, every man pulls their weight. With this being my first year as chief, I'm making sure my presence is known so the town realizes they can depend on me.

As it goes in Haven Bay, the teens weren't charged but we made a deal with Wayne to have them work at his farm fixing the damaged fence and any other chores he and the bus company deem appropriate.

One thing you learn pretty quickly as a police officer in a town as small as Haven Bay is that the town dishes out their own version of justice. It's a fine line to walk on when to enforce the laws and when to come up with an alternative.

Those teens were reckless tonight. They could've seriously hurt someone or themselves. But none of them have a history of causing serious trouble. They don't deserve to have one stupid prank affect their futures, especially when they'll be applying to colleges soon. Besides, by the looks on their faces when they were exiting the bus, they won't be pulling any more stunts like that ever again.

But I plan to watch them closely for a while. Just in case.

After the teens were picked up by their parents, I was finally able to head home. Now, as I approach Main Street, I'm dreaming of my bed when my eyes are pulled to the blue and red flashing lights at the bottom of the hill up ahead.

Groaning, I continue down the hill instead of turning toward home. Probably some tourist who had too much to drink again. I pull up in front of one of our cruisers where Officer Ethan Sharpe is standing nearby making notes. I park my pickup and, as I walk over to him, he looks up and nods in greeting.

"What do we have, Sharpe?"

Ethan shakes his head. "Assault. I'm still taking statements but from what I can gather, the bloodied guy over there made a comment to Miss St. James that she didn't particularly like. So, she clocked him in the nose." His face remains professional but I can see the twinkle of humor in his eyes. "I still have to take her statement though, which I was just about to do."

I hold back a groan. Of course it was her. Why am I not surprised?

"I'll do it, Sharpe," I say. "I want to have a few words with Miss St. James."

I stalk away before he can respond. Rounding the cruiser where Jolie is leaning against the backdoor, I'm surprised to see handcuffs on her wrists. It's not completely unheard of to have to use them but most of the time, we try to avoid cuffing anyone unless we have to. While she can be annoying and troublesome, I don't see Jolie as being the resistive type.

I look over to the bloodied man across the lot from her, who is currently recounting the sordid events of the night to a couple of women I don't recognize. Even without knowing the full story, it's obvious he's embellishing it from the way his arms are waving animatedly. When he sees Sharpe walk toward him, he stomps over, gesturing angrily at Jolie.

Ah. I have a feeling the handcuffs were less about keeping Sharpe safe and more about keeping her from clocking the greasy man again.

"Well, well. Fancy meeting you here, Chief." Her smile is teasing and playful, completely at odds with the scene around us.

She's infuriating. Does anything worry her? She's cuffed

against the back of a police car, possibly facing assault charges and she acts like we're fighting over the last slice of bacon at the diner's Sunday buffet.

Maybe it's her complete lack of respect for rules. Maybe it's the way she feels said rules don't apply to her. Maybe it's because she thinks a few well-timed winks and a flash of that killer smile of hers will get her out of trouble.

Either way, she needs to learn she's not above the law.

"What the hell were you thinking?" I demand. "You can't just walk around punching people in the face whenever you feel like it."

Her smile falls and her expression turns icy. "I know. Trust me, you should be thankful for my restraint."

Dragging a hand over my face, I bite back a sigh of frustration. I like to consider myself a patient guy; I have to be in my profession. But there's something about this woman that makes me want to pull my hair out every time I'm within breathing distance of her.

Jolie St. James has been a thorn in my side since she waltzed into Haven Bay five years ago and opened her yoga studio, Amaryllis. You'd think that a yoga teacher would be calm and peaceful, right?

Wrong.

Jolie's yoga studio specializes in what she calls "rage yoga" which apparently means a bunch of people bend over backwards (literally) while screaming and cussing.

It's jarring the first time you see it, especially if you don't know what to expect. She likes to hold them outside in the summer, which brings on its own complications. Then when it's over, Jolie hands out beers and seltzers like a goddamn bartender in the middle of a public park.

Between the noise complaints from her outdoor classes,

the open alcohol on public property, and her incessant need to spew whatever thought crosses her mind, she is trouble in brightly colored leggings.

"I'm glowing with gratitude," I grunt.

"So, now that you've decided that I'm the bad guy, are you going to charge me or can I go?" She glares at me, her scowl unwavering.

"I still need to take your statement." I reach for my notebook in my jean pocket but realize that in my frustrations, I didn't grab it from my truck.

For the love of—

I hate being unprepared. I'm a professional, for fuck's sake.

I start to lift my hands to shove them through my hair but catch myself before they reach my head. It's a nervous habit of mine, one I can't seem to quit. Officers shouldn't have a nervous tell and should always remain emotionless when on scene. So instead, I ball my hands into fists at my sides. A few minutes around this woman and I'm turning into a fucking rookie.

"Look. Just tell me what the guy did to make you so damn pissy," I snap, probably a bit more forceful than necessary. The faster I get out of here and away from her, the better.

Jolie shoots a narrowed glare at me that causes my balls to shrink up inside me.

"You wanna try that again, *officer?*" Jolie practically spits at me. I sigh. I don't know what it is about her that puts me on the offensive but I can never seem to keep my temper in check with her. Shoving it back down, I try for a calmer tone.

"You know what I meant, Jolie. What happened?"

She leans back against the car and stares back at me for

a few moments, her eyes searching mine. Eventually, the tension in her posture eases marginally.

"That dickhole knows what he did," she states simply, shrugging.

I bite off the curse that threatens to slip out, then count to five. When I think I can respond without blowing a gasket, I blow out a frustrated breath. "Fine."

"Are we done?"

Looking over her shoulder, Sharpe has calmed the hysterical man down, who is currently stomping off toward the motel down the street.

"Wait here."

I cross the parking lot to where Sharpe is standing. He finishes thanking the witnesses, tipping his hat like a regular Andy Griffith before the group turns and walks back toward the bar. He turns as I approach and reads from the notepad he's been taking statements on.

"So, the tourist's name is Tad Chesterfield. Apparently, he works for a development company and was in town for a business meeting. Came to the bar to have a drink by himself and listen to the band. Claims he approached Miss St. James and Miss Doyle where they struck up a friendly conversation. Chesterfield says he made a joke and Miss St. James took it too seriously and struck him in the nose." He closes the notepad. "Multiple witnesses claimed he was making lewd comments all night but no one actually heard the exchange between him and Jolie, except for Brenna. I kept her inside hoping that'd deescalate the situation. She's refusing to answer any questions. She said, and I quote, 'that prick got exactly what he deserves.' I convinced Chesterfield not to press charges." Sharpe smirks. "I think he was embarrassed to have been beaten up by a girl and didn't want anyone else knowing about it." He shrugs. "Either way, Jolie's free to go."

He takes a step toward her but I hold up my hand to stop him.

"Why don't you go check in with Brenna and make sure she's alright. Let her know that Jolie will be inside shortly. I'll let Jolie know she can go."

If Sharpe is taken aback by my request, he has the good sense not to show it. He hands me the keys to the handcuffs before disappearing inside the bar.

I take a deep breath before turning and stalking back over to where Jolie is still waiting, leaning against the cruiser's door, tapping her still-cuffed hands against her thighs to the sound of the music from inside. When she sees me approach, she stops and her expression becomes guarded again.

"Well?"

"Looks like you got off easy. He's not pressing charges, but I'd lay low for the next few days until he leaves town if I were you." I take the key for the handcuffs out of my pocket and step toward her. Her shoulders fall as her anger dissipates with the news.

"Trust me, Chief, there's nothing easy about the way I get off," she teases, then shoots me one of her sexy grins that always causes my chest to tighten painfully. "But that's half of the fun, right?"

Jesus.

Her comments shouldn't affect me. It's not her first time making a joke like that and I'd bet my pension it won't be her last. But her words conjure up the image of Jolie's slight frame under me, squirming and begging for release.

I nearly fumble the key that's in my hand as I try to shove the image aside but it's no use. Her perfume wraps around me like a warm hug, the sweet scent contrasting the dark, dirty thoughts that are running through my mind.

I lean closer than what's appropriate for the situation but my professionalism is the last thing on my mind as I imagine all the dirty ways we could make use of these handcuffs. I can't keep my eyes off of her mouth, the luscious, red lipstick calling to me like a siren's song.

For once, Jolie keeps her mouth shut but I can feel her breath stutter as the air around us thickens. Her wide-doe eyes are staring up at me and I bite back a groan. I feel myself harden at the thought of those big, blue eyes watching me as she wraps that sassy red mouth around my cock.

If I take one step closer, I could press myself against her and let her feel the effect she has on me. She knows it too. Her brow is slightly furrowed with confusion but there's desire in her eyes. This isn't a one-sided reaction. It would be so easy to just lean down, brush my lips against hers and...

A nearby laugh pulls me out of my trance and I glance up to see two patrons leaving the bar, walking across the street and away from us.

What the hell was I thinking?

I clear my throat then finish turning the key in the handcuffs. They fall away from her wrists and she reaches up to rub away the sting of the metal, her eyes still locked on mine. I take one last look before dropping my head and stepping away.

"You're free to go." My voice is raspy against my suddenly dry throat.

Without another word, I turn and head back to my truck. Climbing inside, I avoid the urge to turn my head and see if she's still watching me. As I pull away, I give in and look back into the parking lot.

She's there, watching me pull away. As I approach my road, I glance back in the rearview mirror to see her walking back into the bar.

Good. Better for both of us if we just forget the whole thing happened.

Whatever that was.

CHAPTER 3

LUKE

W ell, I haven't forgotten about it.

In fact, I tossed and turned all night thinking only about her—her mouth, her eyes, her curves. Every inch of her body haunted my dreams.

This isn't the first time Jolie has filled my head. I thought I had done a pretty good job of shoving those thoughts away, reminding myself of all the ways she complicates my life, all of the ways she drives me crazy. But in the dark of night, when I have nothing to distract my mind from straying, she overwhelms my thoughts.

And I hate it.

No one could be more wrong for me than Jolie St. James. She's crude, unfiltered, and a magnet for trouble.

And yet she's the first woman to pique my interest in the way she has since...

No. Not going there today.

Instead, I head down to The Dive to see if Rhett or my brother are around for a beer. Maybe take the boat out for a spin on the bay. The sun is shining and I have the day off. We've only got so many warm days left before fall comes knocking and then, all too quickly, winter will follow. I want to take advantage of the nice weather while I can.

I hop in my truck and head toward Main Street. One benefit of a small town is you're never too far from the action, which is important when the action is where I'm often needed most.

A few minutes later, I'm hopping out of my truck and walking toward the bar when I spot my brother's big, floppy-eared mutt laying on the deck in the shade. I bend down to scratch behind his ears.

"Hard life being a dog, eh, Ham?"

As if to prove my point, Ham yawns and flops over onto his back. I oblige by rubbing his belly. After checking to make sure the bowl of water beside him is still full, I pull open the door and walk inside.

Since the bar isn't open yet, Matt and Rhett are easy to spot at a high top table. Walking over, I tip my head in greeting then swipe the beer Matt just opened before he can take a drink. "Aw, you shouldn't have."

"I didn't, asshole," he grumbles, trying to grab it back but I take a slow drink before he can. Matt glares at me while Rhett snickers from beside him.

Cursing me under his breath, Matt stomps over to grab another beer. On his way back, he reaches around and attempts to flick my balls. But it's not my first day with a little brother so I block his hand, laughing.

The same way it's his job to drive me crazy, it's my job to toughen him up. If that means I get a free beer out of it, well, that's just a perk.

"So I heard there was a fight last night," Matt says, twisting the top off his beer and tossing it at my head. "Heard our little Jolie beat the shit out of some out-of-towner until he was unconscious on the floor. They say it took four people to pull her off his bloodied, unconscious body. Might be facing attempted murder charges."

Rhett chuckles while I groan. "The way gossip spreads around this town concerns me," I mutter. "How does Jolie giving a guy a bloody nose turn into attempted murder?"

Matt shrugs. "You know how it is around here. The truth isn't nearly as exciting. Better to embellish than go by the facts."

Rhett tips his glass of what I'm assuming is his usual Coke toward Matt in agreement. "Ain't that the truth. Pretty sure Dottie was starting a petition this morning at the diner to get Jolie released from jail. She conveniently didn't hear me when I told her that Jolie wasn't even arrested."

I sigh but can't help smiling at the thought of 80-something-year-old Dottie walking around the diner gathering signatures. Surely it was more about being able to spread the story to each table than it was about Jolie's supposed "justice".

Rhett continues on. "Either way, Jolie got a good jab at that slimy asshole. Apparently, he was putting the moves on Brenna but wasn't getting the hint after she told him no multiple times. Then Jolie told him to leave but instead of going, he made some creepy comment." He takes a drink of his Coke. "He's lucky I didn't hear him or he would've ended up with more than a bloody nose." His eyes flare with anger, something that's rare coming from Rhett. It's all the more intimidating because of it.

I know exactly how he's feeling because suddenly there's red creeping into my vision and my fist tightens around the bottle in my hand. To think that a creep like that was in my town harassing women makes me want to hunt the prick down and give him some old-fashioned justice.

No one fucks with my town.

"Well, as we all know, Jolie doesn't take too well to people mistreating her friends, so she hauled off and cracked him right in the nose. Perv went down like the worthless sack of shit he is." Rhett smirks. "Some tourist must've called the cops and that's when Sharpe showed up. Jolie was a little shaken up and didn't want to leave Brenna alone. Only went outside with Sharpe after I promised to stay with Brenna while she was taken outside."

I nod but the sudden buzzing in my ears makes it hard to hear what he's saying.

I feel like a piece of shit. I'm disgusted by my awful assumption about Jolie. She might put on a good front, but even Rhett saw she was shaken up by the whole ordeal.

And what did I do? Laid into her about causing trouble. She wasn't being impulsive or reckless; she was protecting her friend. I was just too blinded by my reaction to her that I lashed out and made it worse.

Fuck. I'm an idiot.

"Well, good for Jolie," Matt comments. "She's one tough cookie, that girl. Avery always says Jolie's the most loyal person she knows." He nudges Rhett with his elbow. "Obviously she's not including me in that list of people."

Even I can agree with that. Jolie St. James is a lot of things but weak is definitely not one of them.

Matt's fiancé, Avery, is one of Jolie's best friends. They met last year when Avery moved back to town after she split up with her husband. They quickly became good friends and have been inseparable since.

"Oh, shit. I almost forgot." Matt jumps to his feet, then rushes out the door. I look over at Rhett, eyebrow raised in question but he just shrugs. We're both used to Matt's strange behavior so his outburst doesn't surprise either of us.

A few minutes later, Matt comes bursting through the

door, interrupting Rhett's opinion on the Mariner's shot at the World Series. He's carrying a grocery bag and snickering to himself as he drops back into his seat. He reaches inside and pulls out two black boxes, setting one in front of each of us.

Rhett and I exchange a confused look before turning back to Matt.

"What's this?" I ask.

Matt's practically bouncing in his chair. "Open it."

I glance cautiously down at the box before me. With Matt, you never know what could be inside. It could be anything from a live snake to a dildo.

I'm going to punch him if it's the latter. Actually, I'd punch him if it's the former, too.

Rhett seems as skeptical as I am as he turns the box over at arm's length.

"Oh, for fuck's sakes," Matt grumbles. "It's not going to bite you. Just open it."

Okay, so it's not a snake. That's something then.

Inside the box is a folded piece of fabric. I pull it out and it unfolds into a pair of dress socks. But not just any dress socks. I burst out laughing, Rhett's booming laugh following as he opens his box. Matt finally lets loose the cackle he's been holding in since he handed over the boxes. Soon, all three of us are doubled over.

On the black dress socks are a bunch of pictures of Matt's head with wide eyes and the biggest, cheesiest grin plastered on his face. He looks ridiculous.

Tears stream down my face as I try to catch my breath but every time I start to pull myself together, I glance down at those stupid socks and start roaring again.

"There's a card," Matt says when he finally pulls himself together.

I reach into the box and find a white card with black cursive writing on it. It reads: *Hey, dipshit. I'm getting married. Will you be my groomsman?*

My brother's an idiot.

"Definitely worth all that work," Matt wipes a tear away as he snickers to himself. "Avery owes me five bucks." As it always does, his face softens at the mention of his fiancé. "Anyway, the card is just for show, you obviously can't say no."

I shake my head. *Typical Matt.*

"Wait, so who's your best man?"

"Gavin, of course," he says, talking about his five-year-old future step-son.

Alright. Maybe he's not such an idiot after all.

"So, Mom and Angie are throwing us a little engagement party in Mom's backyard next weekend," he tells us. "You both have to be there in your Sunday best. Mom's orders."

Avery's mom Angie is best friends and neighbors with our mom. Avery and Gavin moved in with her when Avery was going through her divorce. When Matt and Avery got engaged a couple of weeks ago, he moved in with them.

It's a little tight but Angie has MS and Avery didn't feel comfortable with her living alone. Angie's house is one level and set up well for her on days where getting around is a bit harder to manage. They're planning to build onto the house in the spring to make more room. Matt's been eager to grow their family but Avery wants to wait until after they've been married for a while.

Matt works for a construction company and is an up-and-coming artist who specializes in wood carving, so I assume he'll do most of the work on the addition himself.

Rhett and I will probably get roped into helping—not that I mind. I enjoy getting my hands dirty every once in a while.

Jolie's bound wrists flash into my mind and I can feel myself heat at the memory.

God, this girl is going to be the death of me. And now that we'll both be in my brother's wedding party, there'll be no avoiding her.

If I even want to.

No, it doesn't matter what I want. It's about what I need.

And Jolie St. James is not what I need.

"Aaaahhhhhhh PENIS!"

Well, that's a new one.

During my rage yoga classes, I encourage participants to let go of tension through groaning, yelling or cursing. Some people take that suggestion very seriously. I swear I've learned more curse words in these classes than any bar I've been to. And more often than not, it's coming from the mouth of one of my handful of octogenarian clients.

"ANGRY AREOLAAAAAA!"

Huh. Points for creativity.

I finish correcting one of my newer participant's Warrior II pose then make my way toward the front of the group. We're outside in the park behind the studio, enjoying the nice weather. Summer is hanging on by its fingernails and, as I've learned in my five years in Haven Bay, fall in Alberta can be very unpredictable. So I like to take advantage of the warm weather while it lasts.

I take my place on my yoga mat at the front of the class and adjust my body into Warrior II. My arms are stretched out in opposite directions, my legs dropped in a lunge position with my front knee bent in front of me and my body facing forward.

"Now you're going to take your left hand that's pointing forward and point it up toward the sky, letting your right hand drop and slide down your back leg. As you look up into the sky, I want you to think not just about the stretch in your muscles, but also how strong you are. I want you to focus on something that happened this week that made you feel powerful. Maybe you finally hit that goal that you've been working toward or you told your jerk of a boss where to shove his overtime." That earns a chuckle throughout the group. "Either way, focus on that moment. Now take a deep breath in, feeling your chest expand, allowing all of your strength to fill you." The collective deep inhale mixes with the song of a nearby bird. "Then, exhale all of your self-doubts. Your insecurities. Your worries. Bask in the power within you and then, from the depth of your core, let out your best battle cries."

Fifteen incoherent shouts echo through the forest. I'm thankful that the park is empty. Not that it would've stopped us necessarily, but I might have encouraged less cursing.

The locals in town know about my classes and are used to the antics. But tourist season tends to bring out a few uptight Karens who feel the need to clutch their pearls at the sound of adults letting off some steam. I've even had a few wellness checks requested from tourists who think someone is being bludgeoned in the park.

That was a fun one to explain to the police.

At the mention of cops, the image of Tad Chesterfield's bloody nose pops into my mind, bringing a small smile to my face as I guide the class into the final pose.

I'm not going to lie, punching that nutsack of a human being in the nose felt good. I don't make a habit of going around punching people on a whim, but that guy deserved the hit and more. I'm all for using your words, but when someone doesn't take no for an answer, then, well...you have to take matters into your own hands.

As soon as I saw the red and blue flashing lights from the parking lot, I knew I was screwed. Where there's cop cars, there's cops and where there's cops, there's Officer Grouchy Pants. Or should I say *Chief* Grouchy Pants since his promotion. I didn't think it was possible, but becoming Chief of Police for the Haven Bay Police Department has made Luke even more of a stick in the mud than usual.

Luckily, it was Ethan Sharpe's smiling face instead of Luke's scowling one that pushed a cloth at Tad's face, then guided us outside for questioning. Tad took one look at Ethan's uniform and started limping behind him, trying to play up his injuries.

Funny, I didn't realize a punch in the face could cause a limp.

Tad then started spewing all of this hateful, misogynistic bullshit about how Brenna and I had been fighting over him and when Tad "chose" Brenna over me, I hit him in the nose in a fit of jealous rage.

As if.

That earned him some offers of graphic threats involving his dick and a woodchipper. Not my most clever threat, but the accidental pun was a nice touch if I say so myself.

That's when Ethan was forced to slap the cuffs on me and had me stand on the opposite side of the parking lot. It wasn't my first time wearing those metal bracelets and I doubt it'll be my last.

I must say though, I prefer them on my wrists in a completely different setting. Like attached to my headboard.

I call out instructions to the class as I drop to the mat, crossing my legs and placing my hands together in front of my chest. They follow as the music from my Bluetooth speaker changes to Pink Floyd's *Wish You Were Here*. My voice is low and calm as I remind everyone to breathe slowly and quiet their minds during our final pose of the class.

I watch as one by one, each person closes their eyes, letting their bodies relax. Instead of relaxing alongside them, my muscles remain tense and my nerves are vibrating, which only pisses me off.

I blame Luke Brady.

Since our little run-in at The Dive last weekend, I haven't been able to shake this feeling of edginess. I'm wound tighter than a nun in a stripclub and I have no idea how to rid myself of all of this pent up energy. I'm a walking stick of dynamite, lit and ready to blow at any second. Only the fuse never shortens and the release never comes.

There's a sex joke in there somewhere but I'm too agitated to enjoy it.

When Luke pulled into the parking lot, I couldn't help but wish the ground would swallow me up. Not because I was embarrassed or ashamed, but because Luke has a way of making me feel like the world's biggest screw up. He acts like I'm some impulsive teenager who does what she wants, when she wants, consequences be damned.

While I admit to being a bit spontaneous in my early twenties, I haven't been that girl for a long time. These days, I'm much more likely to take my impulsive thoughts out on a carton of Chinese food than trying to ride a sled down the road attached to the bed of a truck.

Yes, it was dangerous and stupid but man, was it fun.

Speaking of stupid but fun...

Stop that. Get your head out of the gutter, Jolie.

"Alright, everyone. Great class today. Make sure you grab a drink from the cooler," I announce, pointing to the blue cooler beside the studio back entrance. "Hope you all enjoyed yourselves and leave a little lighter. Remember: you're all badasses. Don't let anyone tell you otherwise."

It's the same parting reminder I give out after every class but everyone still cheers and claps as loudly as if it were the first. People grab cans from the coolers but it's not long before people start to disperse. It's ten o'clock on a Saturday morning, so I'm sure they're running off to enjoy the beautiful weather.

Piling the Bluetooth speaker, the now empty cooler, and extra yoga mats into my arms, I make my way to the back entrance of Amaryllis. With full hands, it takes a few strategically placed hips and elbows to make it through the door, but I eventually wrestle my way inside. Unceremoniously, I drop my things onto the hardwood floor of the studio.

I start to walk away then stop. Dropping my head back dramatically, I spin on my heel and bend to clean up the mess.

I'm definitely not what anyone would consider a neat and organized person. Each time I'm faced with a mess, I have to mentally psych myself up to deal with it.

Does the mess get cleaned up? Yes. I'm an adult and a business owner and no one else is going to do it for me. But that doesn't mean I'm not going to whine the whole time.

I'm convinced people who like to clean have some sort of mutated gene in their DNA that I do not possess.

After putting everything back in its place, I'm still

vibrating with energy. I'm done with classes for the day and I'm not supposed to meet up with Avery until later, so I try some pilates to calm my nerves.

And not think about Luke.

But, as it has all week, my mind drifts to the image of Luke towering over me with a dangerous look in his eyes. Even now, I can still feel the heat pumping off of his body, can still smell the addicting scent of his cologne washing over me. And when he wrapped one large hand around my cuffed wrists?

Sweet mother of Ariana Grande. Let's just say my vibrator got a work out that night.

I was just about to offer myself up to him on a silver platter, when he had to open his big mouth and ruin the whole thing.

You're free to go.

Four little words and the illusion shattered into a million pieces at my feet. As if I was the only one affected by the moment. I'm used to Luke looking at me like he's ready to strangle me with his bare hands, but that was the first time it had been laced with sexual undertones.

I'm not sure where the sudden change came from or if it's been there the whole time, lying dormant until the perfect moment to strike. But now that it's struck, I don't know what to do about it.

On one hand, that's the most intrigued I've been by a man in, well...too long. I'd be an idiot to waste that kind of chemistry, wouldn't I? Sure, he's hot. I'd have to be blind not to notice how sexy he is. He's tall enough that he would line up perfectly with my 5'9 frame, dark features that only add to his growly persona, and a muscular body that I can't stop thinking about exploring.

Preferably with my tongue.

Great. Now I'm thinking about licking Luke's wide chest. Dragging my tongue over what I'm sure are well-defined abs, until it disappears below his waistband, brushing along his...

I clench my thighs together, attempting to ease the ache between my legs. I shake my head, willing away the dirty images that flood my mind.

What was I saying again? Oh, right. Chemistry, intrigue, blah blah blah.

But on the other, more logical hand, it's Luke. Since my first class that resulted in multiple noise complaints and Luke giving me my first of many, *many* warnings, we haven't had a civil conversation that has lasted longer than two minutes.

I'm not exaggerating. I timed it once.

He pushes buttons I didn't even know I had. He's smug, self-important and so straight-laced, I'm surprised he can get a full breath in. Luke is the complete opposite of the fun, easy-going guys I usually go for.

So why can't I stop thinking about him?

Suddenly, my phone rings from somewhere behind me. I blink back at my reflection in the studio's full wall mirror then up at the clock. I just completed an almost thirty minute pilates workout without even realizing. Apparently, that's what horniness will do to you.

Scrambling to my feet, I dash over to the other side of the studio in search of my phone. Finding it lying beside one of my portable burlesque poles, I snatch it off the floor just before it cuts to voicemail.

"Hello?" I answer, short of breath.

"Why are you out of breath? Ew, I swear to God if you were having sex..."

I laugh at the sound of my brother's voice, dramatically

dry-heaving on the other end. "That's what you get for taking almost a week to call me back. Pablo was just about to stick his..."

"Jolie Eris St. James!"

My brother, Austin, is a year older than me and plays the overprotective brother card a little too well, if you ask me. He once walked in on me making out with my high school boyfriend in my bedroom and he was about to throw poor Dean out my two-story window. I'm not sure how I talked him out of that one, but he settled for tossing him out the front door *Fresh Prince* style instead.

As much as he drives me crazy, I miss him. He still lives in Toronto and as one of the top defensemen in the NHL, I don't get to see as much of him as I'd like.

So it's fun to rile him up when I can.

"Don't you middle name me, Austin Ares. I will win that battle any day of the week, Mr. God of Blood. Don't you have a menstruation party you should be attending?" I snicker into the phone as he groans. "I was doing a pilates workout if you must know. My bed has been painfully cold lately."

"First of all, if your bed is cold, get blankets. Any Pablos in your bed will be sleeping with the fishes, capiche?" *Oh, good. He's going through his Al Pacino stage again.* "Second of all, Ares is the God of bloodlust. Use the 'm' word again and I will drive all the way to Alberta just to puke on your front step."

That's right. My mom, the folklore and mythology nut, named us after Greek gods. I'm named after Eris, the goddess of chaos and Austin is named after Ares, the god of battle and bloodlust. Either she knew our personalities at first glance in the hospital room or we grew into our namesakes. Either way, the meanings couldn't be more fitting.

I can't help laughing again. God, I miss him. "Other than threatening my imaginary boyfriends, oh God of bloody tampons..." Another round of fake dry-heaving sounds on the line. "What have you been up to, brother dearest? I saw your game last night. Nice goal, but you know you can score more goals from *outside* the penalty box than in it, right?"

This time Austin snickers back. "Oleski is a pussy. I barely touched him. Kid should learn to stay away from my goalie if he's going to play in the big leagues."

Austin got drafted into the NHL when he was 18-years-old to the Vegas Warriors where he played the first five years of his career before being signed by Chicago. Last year, much to my mother's delight, he signed a 7-year contract with the Toronto Storm. My parents now live a short thirty minute drive from his condo, which my mother uses to her advantage whenever she can. My father couldn't be bothered to visit Austin, no matter how close he lives.

We don't talk about him unless we have to.

"Alright. Whatever you say." I toss my mat into the corner, promising myself I'll put it away later then head up the staircase in the back to my apartment. We talk for a few more minutes before Austin has to leave for practice. He promises to call later in the week, though I'm sure he'll forget like always.

"Bye, Ares," I tease.

"Bye, shithead."

Dropping onto the couch, I end the call and make a mental note to check when the Storm play the Edmonton Eagles next. As annoying and overbearing as he may be, I miss my brother.

Especially since the rest of our family life is a disaster.

Checking my phone, I decide I have time to watch an episode or two of *The Office* before I meet up with Avery. It's my ultimate feel-good show and Michael Scott is the best distraction from the sudden ache in my chest.

Five minutes into the episode, I'm no longer thinking about my family drama. But as Dwight starts detailing his perfect crime, I can't help but let my mind wander to a certain grumpy police chief. So far my attempts at forgetting about that night are futile.

This is going to be harder than I thought.

That's what she said.

CHAPTER 5

JOLIE

Twenty minutes later, I'm sliding into a booth at Main Street Diner. Avery's already there, so engrossed in a book that she doesn't notice me until I scoot into the booth across from her. "Hey! Am I late?" I ask. "Have you been waiting long?"

Avery tucks a bookmark between the pages of her book and sets it aside. "Nope. It's an unusually slow day at the shop so I figured I'd take a long lunch and catch up on my reading for book club." She lets out a small laugh. "It'd be pretty bad if the club organizer didn't even read the book."

I wave her off. "If anyone is allowed to not read the book, it's you. You're a mom to a fantastic five-year-old, newly engaged, are about to start planning a wedding AND putting an addition on your house. If that doesn't earn you a free pass every once in a while, I don't know what does."

"Speaking of planning a wedding..." She digs through her bag then pulls out a small velvet box and places it on the table before me.

I pick it up, turning it over in my hands before arching a

brow at her. "You know I'd marry you in a second, Ave, but I think Matt might have some complaints about that."

Avery rolls her eyes then smirks back at me. "You couldn't handle me, J. Now open it."

So I do. Inside is the most beautiful gold necklace with a small diamond moon pendant at the center. Carefully, I lift the necklace out of the box and examine it closer.

"I got Tori the sun," she says, referring to Matt and Luke's younger sister, "and Brenna the star. Read the card." She motions to the inside of the box where I notice for the first time a small rose gold card. It reads:

THE SUN and the Moon

Like the sun, you brighten my days.
Like the moon, you protect me from the dark.
Like the stars, you guide my way home.
Together, we light up the sky.
Will you be my maid of honor?

WELL, shit.

Tears brim my eyes and I try to blink them away. I'm not usually a big crier but for a girl who didn't have many girlfriends growing up, this is a big deal to me. Friendship necklaces might seem a little cheesy to some people but I love it, not just the necklace but for what it represents— belonging. And being asked to stand in my best friend's wedding? I couldn't be happier if Ryan Reynolds walked through the diner's doors and confessed his love for me right then and there.

Sorry, Ryan. You know I love you.

"It's corny, isn't it? I told Matt it was too corny, but he

swore it wasn't," Avery rambles. "Of course, I'm taking advice from the man who thought socks with pictures of his face on them was a good gift. I can take it back—" She reaches out to grab the necklace but I yank it back, clutching it to my chest.

"Don't you dare, Avery soon-to-be Brady. I love it!" I look down at the necklace. "And I would be honored to stand with you on your wedding day." I wave at my watery eyes. "Jeez, it's not even your wedding day and I'm already tearing up. This is going to be rough."

Avery shoves at her own teary eyes. "You're telling me. I'm going to be a mess. When Gavin asked me if Matt would be his second daddy after we got married, I ugly-cried for a solid half hour. I have no idea how I'll make it down the aisle without looking like a drowned rat."

I grip her hand in mine. "Avery, I swear to you, I will never, ever, ever let you walk down the aisle looking like a drowned rat. You will look absolutely bangable on your wedding day. Matt will drop to his knees in praise when you walk down that aisle or I haven't done my job as maid of honor."

Avery snorts. "Thanks. You're the best," she says. Brandy wanders over to our table then and she takes our orders, refilling our cups before walking back to the kitchen.

I take a soothing sip of my tea. "Okay, now what's all this about socks with Matt's face on them?"

By the time our food arrives, my head is thrown back laughing at the picture on Avery's phone of Matt holding up three pairs of matching socks with his face on them. The funniest part isn't even the socks, it's the ridiculously over the top face he's making in the picture on them.

He's such a dork.

We take a break from catching up to dig into our meals.

The first bite of my cheeseburger has my eyes rolling back in ecstasy. Maybe it wasn't horniness after all. Maybe I was just hungry.

A flash of dark hair and a blue uniform catches the corner of my eye and a swarm of butterflies takes flight in my stomach. I try to casually turn in my seat to get a better look only to realize that the police officer sitting at the lunch counter has green eyes instead of brown.

I turn back to Avery, hoping she doesn't notice the weird expression in my face. She's too busy smiling down at her phone at what I'm assuming is a text from Matt. While she's preoccupied, I take a second to try and decipher the confusing feeling of disappointment settling over me.

God, I need to get laid. It's obviously been too long if I'm getting so worked up that I'm wanting to see Luke. Usually I'd be sighing in relief by his lack of presence, not disappointment.

Avery tucks her phone back into her bag and I take the opportunity to distract myself from whatever twisted reality I've found myself in.

"So fill me in on your wedding plans. I personally think you should go all out. Picture it." I spread my hands above my face, setting the scene. "Sunset wedding. You arrive on horseback, four muscular Greek gods carrying your throne to your future husband. Then Ed Sheeran will sing your first dance live and make a speech about your love story inspiring his next song, which he will mention in his acceptance speech for the Grammy he'ill obviously win for it."

Avery stares back at me, jaw dropped in shock. Her look of bewilderment doesn't phase me though. I tend to have that effect on people. "Some days I wish I knew what went on inside that mind of yours." She laughs. I join her but, in truth, some days I don't even want to be inside my own mind.

"You're not too far off though," Avery continues. "It's going to be a sunset wedding but we've decided to have it at the Silver Fox Winery in their event room. Alana is giving me a great deal since we're technically getting married in their off-season. We're still working on solidifying a date but it's going to be this spring. I keep having to remind myself that even though this is my second wedding, this is Matt's first and he deserves to do it right."

I reach across the table and cover her hand with mine. "Babe, so do you. Just because it's a second wedding doesn't mean that you deserve less than every other bride. It's your wedding day and you should have everything you want; whether it's your first wedding or your twelfth." I give her hand a squeeze. "You want a small wedding? Do that. You want the whole fricken' town invited? Do that. You want to run away and elope? I'll be your getaway car. Do whatever the hell you want, Ave, because no one's going to say 'I wish I cared more about what people thought of me' on their deathbed. Okay?"

Avery takes a shaky breath and nods. "You're the best, you know that?" She wipes away a tear. "Okay, before the water works start up again, the only other details we have nailed down so far are that Tori and Brenna are my other two bridesmaids. Luke and Rhett are the groomsmen. Gavin is Matt's best man." She points at me when I start to tear up. "Don't even start. I cried for too long about this already. I told you: I'm a mess."

As it always does, her face softens at the mention of her son. I haven't ever thought of having kids other than just an abstract "one day down the road" thought, but I hope when I have kids, I'm as good of a mom as Avery.

"One more thing. My mom and Franny are throwing us an engagement party next weekend. It's in Franny's backyard. Saturday at three. I'm assuming the way news travels around this town, once people start seeing the cars lined up, there will be some party crashers joining, so if that happens, we'll set some tables up at our house and use both backyards."

Avery and Matt grew up as next door neighbors and their moms still live next door to each other. With Matt and Avery living with her mom, I'm sure Angie and Franny are ecstatic to not only share grandchildren, but have them grow up so close, too.

I try to keep my face straight but inside, those damn butterflies start to flutter again. How am I supposed to avoid Luke at his own brother's engagement party? At his mother's house. For a wedding we're both standing in.

It's just now hitting me how much more complicated it's going to be to avoid Luke than I originally thought.

Calm your tits, butterflies. I don't want him, remember? I'm not at all affected by his sexy body or the dangerous looks he seems to save just for me. The predatory ones that resemble a lion eyeing up its meal. Or how much I want to be exactly that—his meal.

I take a drink of my water and clear my suddenly dry throat. "Sounds like fun." I mumble. I push aside my finished plate and lean forward on my forearms. "Now, for the most important detail... the dress."

CHAPTER 6

JOLIE

The second Monday of every month is my favorite day for one reason only—Book Club. When Avery took over the shop from her mom, one of the many programs she implemented was a monthly book club meeting. While I enjoy reading, that's only a portion of the reason for my excitement. The real reason is the same reason I love this town so much—the wackadoo residents.

Often enough, we spend about 10% of the night talking about books and the other 90% gossiping and telling crazy stories that you're never really sure how true they are.

A few months ago, during one of my favorite book clubs to date, Pastor Dan's wife, Sheila, told us about her time as an exotic dancer back in her college days. Before you could say "broken hip", she was giving lessons to Maeve and Dottie. That night actually ended up being the inspiration for my newest class.

Later that week, Luke got called out to Dottie's house after the lap dance she was giving her boyfriend Harold ended with his medical alert bracelet being squished between them, which alerted the police and ambulance.

Avery told me that Luke had to give Dottie and Harold a lecture on responsible, uh, "activities".

To be a fly on that wall.

Moral of the story: you never know what kind of excitement is going to come from Book Club.

Tonight has been pretty tame by comparison. Millie Loffman has only complained four times so far—a new record. Once about it being too warm outside then again about it being too cool inside. Then she complained about the meat on the charcuterie board being too salty (it wasn't) and that there weren't enough vegetarian options (there were). Avery apologized, saying she didn't realize that Millie was a vegetarian, to which Millie informed her that she was not.

See what I mean? The woman would complain that the sky was too blue.

"I'm just saying, I don't think a feces-filled pie would cook the same way as a regular pie," Millie explains from her seat across the room. Her spine is ramrod straight and her legs are crossed politely at the ankles. "So for the author to have Minny bake a pie full of feces—"

"Oh, for the love of God, Mille," Dottie grumbles from beside her. "Just say shit."

Millie shoots her a look of contempt that Dottie merely shrugs off. "—that is so similar in texture that Hilly wouldn't notice is just too unrealistic for me to believe. Not to mention the smell alone would've given her away." Millie gives a sharp self-satisfied nod as if she just single-handedly disproved the quantum theory.

I lean over to Avery. "Leave it to Millie to ruin the hilarity of feeding your boss shit-pie," I whisper and Avery covers her laugh with a cough. She leans over while someone else comments on our book of the month: *The Help.*

"Do you think it's a coincidence that Millie rhymes with Hilly?" she whispers back, referencing the bitchy antagonist that I spent the whole book wanting to punch in the ovaries. I don't even bother trying to hide my laughter. Millie shoots me a dirty look that I return with an innocent one of my own.

"I don't know about the rest of you, but I've had more than a few bosses I would've loved to serve up a pile of shit," Doug Feldman laughs.

"I have a few people in general I'd like to serve up some Minny-style justice," Sheila comments.

I snort. "Remind me not to eat any pie from the church bake sale this year."

Jessie Chapman turns, arching an eyebrow at me in disbelief. "So you're telling me there's not a single person you wish you would've taught a lesson?"

Suddenly, all eyes are on me. Looking around at the expectant faces, I'm unsure how to answer. Shrugging, I decide on the truth. "I'm sure I could think of a few. I just don't like to let things fester. If I'm not happy with how you're treating me, I'll let you know. I find that when you hold in your feelings, it eats away at you until there's nothing left."

I shrug again, unsure if I should continue, but when I look around the room, everyone seems entranced by my rant —even Millie.

So I keep going.

"It's just easier all around if you tell the person that they're pissing you off. Maybe they didn't know or maybe they didn't care. But at least you'll have your answer either way. Then you can let karma take over from there."

"Didn't you punch someone in the face a few weeks ago?" Jessie smirks over at me.

I take a sip of my Coke then smile mischievously. "Sometimes karma is too slow for my liking." There's a round of chuckles from around the room at that.

Conversations start back up and before long, Avery is wrapping up the night. After waving good-bye to the last of the group, I grab a cloth from inside the supply closet. I always hang around until everyone's gone to help Avery clean up. I'm wiping down the tables in the back when I hear footsteps approach from behind me.

"Hey, Sandy. How are you? Did you enjoy Book Club tonight?"

Sandy Sallman is the publisher of the local newspaper, *The Haven Times*. The weekly newspaper is mostly a feel-good, family-friendly publication but it's best known for Sandy's hilarious column *What's Shakin', Haven Bay?* It's basically a gossip column. Think Lady Whistledown from *Bridgerton* meets *Gossip Girl*.

In a town like Haven Bay, it's practically like waving a pail of bloody chum in front of a group of sharks. Every Tuesday morning, the locals swarm to their front porches and driveways to devour the column over their morning coffee.

Sandy smiles that warm smile of hers that causes most people to mistake her for an innocent grandmotherly woman, when in fact, she's got her ear to the ground, listening for her next story. I know better though. I like Sandy enough, but you always have to watch what you say in her presence lest it ends up in next week's paper.

"Oh, I always enjoy Book Club nights. I get half of my stories from this group," she laughs. "I wanted to talk to you about your advice earlier." My brow furrows in confusion. I don't remember giving out any advice tonight. "About dealing with difficult people," Sandy clarifies when she sees my confusion.

"Oh, that wasn't advice, Sandy. I was just running my mouth. As per usual." I start toward the next table, wiping it down with the damp cloth in my hand. "It was more opinion than advice."

Sandy follows closely behind me. "That's exactly why I need you, Jolie. You give great advice just by giving your opinion. You don't even have to try." I shoot her a skeptical look over my shoulder. "I'm serious. People are always talking about how smart you are and how inspiring your classes are. You might not realize it but people around here look up to you."

It's a nice thought but I don't believe a word she says. Sure, people like my classes and yeah, I've been known to give my opinion a time or two. But I wouldn't go so far as to say people look up to me. More often than not, people just want to hear what crazy thing will come out of my mouth next. One good thing about not having a filter is that life is at least entertaining.

With all of this flattery, I can't help but feel as though Sandy is buttering me up for something.

"I don't mean to sound rude, Sandy, but I really should get back to helping Avery clean up—"

"Wait." Sandy quickly looks over her shoulder and leans in toward me conspiringly. So much so that I find myself leaning in, too. "I have a proposition for you. I'm starting a new column in the paper. It's an advice column but without the stuffy therapist-approved answers. I want it to be real people asking for real advice. But the best part is, I want to keep the advisor's identity a secret." She grins mischievously. "Everyone loves a good mystery, right?"

"Sorry, Sandy, but I don't understand what that has to do with me."

She checks over her shoulder again, as if anyone could be eavesdropping on our conversation. Jokes on her, though; the biggest gossip in town is already a part of this conversation (and I don't mean me). "I want to offer you the job. Paid, of course."

I nearly drop the rag in my hand. She's joking, right? No one wants to hear my opinion, let alone pay me for it.

"I—"

She waves me away. "You don't have to answer right away. In fact, I want you to think about it. I need to be transparent, though. We had someone else in mind for the position but it didn't work out. After tonight, I think it must've been fate. You're a much better fit for the job. So, if you decide it's something you're interested in, shoot me an email and I'll send you more details." She continues before I can respond. "We already have a few questions ready that we were going to give the other columnist. We were planning on running the column next Tuesday, so you have just under a week to make your decision. If it's well received, we'll make it a permanent addition to the paper."

I stand there dumbfounded but Sandy doesn't seem to mind as she's already backing away. "Think about it!" She turns to walk away before quickly spinning on her heel to whisper, "Don't forget—you can't tell anyone. I'm trusting you with this secret, Jolie." Then she turns back and walks out the door, waving at Avery as she leaves.

I don't know how long I stand there for, but I must look as bewildered as I feel because Avery eventually calls over to me. My head snaps up at the sound of my name. "You okay? You look like someone just asked you for the square root of 13,978," she smiles, but I can see the concern in her eyes.

I mentally shake myself out of my stupor and offer her my best attempt at a reassuring smile. "Yeah, I'm good. Just thinking. Couldn't you see the smoke coming out of my ears?"

She chuckles but I can tell she doesn't completely believe me. Another thing I love about Avery is that she understands my need for privacy about certain things in my life and never pushes me on them. Apparently, this just became one of them.

Looks like I have some thinking to do.

Did I mention anything can happen at Book Club?

CHAPTER 7

JOLIE

One of the best lines my therapist ever told me was that I shouldn't worry so much about what other people think of me because they're too busy worrying about their own insecurities to notice mine.

I've tried to live my life by that motto as best I can, but nobody's perfect, right? And even when things seem to be going great and you haven't felt the sharp sting of anxiety's wrath in a while, that's when she sticks out a gangly leg and trips you up.

I don't remember a time in my life when anxiety wasn't a part of my everyday life. When I was a kid, I was always worrying. It was often about things that most adults don't even worry about. Questions like "what happens after I die?", "what came before I was born?", and "what if my mom died today?" constantly plagued me. It wasn't until I was a bit older and my mom took me to a therapist that I had a name for these intrusive thoughts—anxiety.

When I was younger, I liked to picture anxiety as the mean girl in school. She was obnoxious, always shoving her opinion down your throat and didn't give a rat's ass about your feelings. I named her Tiffany, after my first bully, Tiffany Chapman. Tiffany convinced the whole first grade to call me "Jolie Pee Pants" after I spilled water on my pants on the third day of class. That nickname stuck with me until the day I moved away a year and a half later.

I was fifteen when my therapist suggested I start taking anti-anxiety medication. I've been on and off them a few times since then, but I find that my mind is less chaotic and quieter when I take them. The little white pill I take every day doesn't completely keep my anxiety at bay, but it takes the edge off. It's as if it takes the tornado of my life down to a low breeze. Constant in its presence, sometimes stronger and more noticeable than others, but it's manageable. I'm not ashamed of it. I'm a big advocate for finding what works best for you and your mental health.

Some days Tiffany is this huge overwhelming presence, her words slicing me open like tiny blades, weakening me with every slice. Others, she's this laughably small figurine, barely audible against my strong inner voice. Days like today, her insults are deafening.

Why would anyone want to hear your opinion?

It's not like you have anything to say that anyone would want to hear.

How could someone like you help anyone? You don't even have a college degree.

Sandy's going to take one look at your column and laugh you right out of her office.

I drop my head onto my desk inside Amaryllis. Why am I even considering this? I'm not a writer. English might have been my favorite class in high school but that doesn't make me a writer. What if I mess it up? What if no one reads the column? Or worse—people read it and my advice ruins their lives?

This bitch in my head should get paid overtime with how many hours she's been putting into bringing my self-esteem down. Imposter Syndrome is kicking my ass already and I haven't even agreed to the job yet.

Head still on the desk, I let out a frustrated groan. Why the hell did Sandy ask me? I was content with life, running my studio and hanging out with my friends. I had stopped job hopping and the constant antsy feeling that had been plaguing me since I was a teenager had finally dulled. I was doing what I loved in a place that felt the most like home in...well, ever.

Then Sandy had to go ahead and drop this bombshell on me and that incessant antsy feeling was back.

It first started when I was sixteen and my grandpa, one of my favorite people, gave me his prized vintage '67 Mustang. My father was livid. He tried to force my grandpa to take the car back, telling him I was not responsible enough for a classic car, let alone a real one. But my grandpa was adamant, telling him, "If there's anyone who could handle a car like that, it's my Blue Jay."

A few years later, a couple months before I graduated high school, my grandpa got really sick. I was devastated. But before he passed, he gave me some advice.

"Follow your heart, Blue Jay," he said, using his childhood nickname for me, "wherever it takes you. It'll know when you're where you're meant to be."

That's the day the itch between my shoulder blades started. He passed away a few weeks later.

So once I had that diploma in hand, I packed up everything I owned and, much to my parents' chagrin, drove across the country with no job, no money and no plan.

No matter how many jobs I took, no matter where I moved, that feeling never wore down until the day I drove into Haven Bay. I took one look at the For Rent sign in what would be Amaryllis's window and something clicked into place. My heart knew I was where I was supposed to be.

So why was that pesky organ acting up now?

I lift my head off the desk, just to drop it back down, lightly knocking my head against the wood and, hopefully, knocking some sense into me.

The small chime from my pocket stops me mid-knock. I turn my head and pull my phone out to read the screen.

AVERY

It's settled ladies! We have a date! I'm getting married on April 22nd!

My head pops up at the message, a wide grin spreading as I type out a response.

JOLIE

YAY!!! (dancing emoji) (champagne emoji) (heart emoji)

BRENNA

I'M SO EXCITED! Congrats, Ave!!

AVERY

I should be thanking Jolie. I swear I never would've gotten up the nerve to pick a date if she hadn't given me that pep talk the other day.

You were right, J. As soon as I told Matt I wanted to pick a date, everything felt real. We're both so excited. I actually feel like a bride now!

WELL, shit. Way to make a girl cry.

JOLIE

> You would've got there yourself eventually. I just gave you a little push.

I'M so happy for them. If anyone deserves a happily ever after, it's Avery. I know she's excited to marry Matt—that was never the question. It was a matter of putting aside her insecurities so that she could be excited about her wedding like she deserves to be.

I'm happy I was able to help her see it for herself.

AVERY

> Well either way... Thanks.

JOLIE

> (kissy face emoji)

> Now for the important part...when's the bachelorette?

BRENNA

> OMG yes! Please tell me soon!

AVERY

> Oh god. I don't know if I should be excited or scared to see what you'll come up with.

JOLIE

> Both. (winky face)

I lay my phone down on the desk beside me, feeling so much lighter than before. Nothing like planning a bachelorette to lift your mood. But something else sticks with me—Avery's genuine gratitude for my help.

Looking into the wall of mirrors in front of me that reach from floor to ceiling, I stare at my reflection. Suddenly, realization hits me. If Avery trusted me with her problem, why wouldn't other people? I helped her so why couldn't I help other people, too? There's no law saying people have to listen to my advice anyway. If they don't like what I have to say, they can ignore it.

I straighten my spine, sitting up taller. I could help people. I could do this. I'm smart, confident (ish) and caring. I would never intentionally steer someone wrong.

I grab my phone off the desk before I lose my nerve and fire off an email to Sandy accepting the position.

Then, with a sharp nod at my reflection, I confidently strut up the stairs to my apartment. The antsy feeling is starting to feel a lot more like excitement and, for once, I'm not running.

I'm right where I'm meant to be.

CHAPTER 8

LUKE

"Really, Luke? A hole this big and you still can't get it in?"

I glare at my brother from across the lawn. He grins back at me then takes a drink of his beer. Ignoring him, I try to focus on the wood platform beside him. The large hole at the top of the board taunts me.

We're at Matt and Avery's engagement party playing Cornhole, one of the lawn games that Matt set up for the party-goers. Keith Jacobs, one of Matt's buddies from high school, is my partner for the game. We're playing against Matt and Rhett, but I haven't been able to make a shot to save my life. Poor Keith has been a good sport about losing our second game but the loss is just adding insult to injury at this point.

I've been feeling off for the past few weeks. I'm frustrated, irritable and my temper has been shorter than usual. The good thing is I know exactly what the cause is. The bad thing is that fixing it will be like pulling out my own teeth—slow, painful and will leave me aching for days.

Jolie St. James.

More specifically, apologizing to her after how I reacted that night at The Dive. I may or may not have been avoiding her since then. After I found out from Matt and Rhett what really happened, I've felt like shit for how I treated her. The woman makes it her job to drive me crazy and, because of that, I let my preconceived thoughts of her cloud my judgment of the situation. I was ready to cast her as the villain before I even took the time to hear the full story.

And that pisses me off even more.

I pride myself on being a good and fair officer. In a world where so many police officers are using their power over civilians for selfish, prejudiced, or downright evil reasons, we need to show the public that there are still good officers out there that are honorable and just.

The exact opposite of how I acted with Jolie.

Not to mention all of the unprofessional and inappropriate things I wanted to do to her against that cruiser. Push her up against it, press myself against her soft—

Nope. Not her. Not ever.

This is exactly why I stay away from her. Just her presence threatens my carefully maintained control. And I can't afford to lose control.

Ever.

"You gonna throw that beanbag sometime today or are you cracking under the pressure?" Matt smirks to Keith beside him.

"Is it just me or has engaged life made him more annoying than usual?" I mutter to Rhett beside me, who chuckles.

"Nah, you just make it easy for him. Your buttons are so tempting to push, you might as well have a neon sign over them saying *'push me'*."

I shoot him a glare over my shoulder but he merely grins back, undeterred. "Keep your shirt on, Matt, or I'll call the moms over to talk about wedding flowers."

Matt lifts his beer to me in cheers, a grin plastered on his smug face. "Go for it. In fact, I'd welcome it. I'm killing it at this groom thing, bro." He points a finger at me. "I could tell you fourteen different types of flowers right now and the time of year they're in season. I could waltz circles around you. I could tie a bow tie with my eyes closed. Any wedding planning task you throw at me, I'll hit out of the park." He mimes hitting a homerun. "I don't know why guys complain about wedding planning. Get this: next week we get to spend a whole afternoon just eating different flavors of cake. I swear I might drag this engagement out just for the fun of it."

I shake my head. Matt's all talk. He's been in love with Avery since they were kids. Life took them in different directions for a while after high school, but when she moved back to town last year, Matt was hell bent on getting her back in his life. Once she finally agreed to go out with him, there was no way he was letting her go again. As much as he jokes, I know he's desperate to get that wedding band on her finger. I'm a little surprised he hasn't already dragged her to the courthouse.

Bringing my attention back to the game, I swing my arm back and let the beanbag in my hand fly across the lawn. It hits the wooden plank with a thud and slides toward the center, stopping just before the hole.

"Oh, Lukey. Just can't seem to find the hole, can ya buddy?" Matt laughs again, nudging Keith with his elbow, who grins beside him.

"Don't worry. I'm sure we could find someone around here willing to help you," Rhett jokes. "Anyone seen

Maeve? I'm sure she'd be happy to give you some lessons." The two of them make a show of searching the backyard for the town's 80-something-year-old busy body. I narrow my eyes at Rhett but he grins back at me.

I think I need to work on my glare. Obviously these two jackasses aren't affected by it anymore.

I bring my attention back to the board in front of me, lining up my next shot. If I miss, these hyenas win and will be insufferable the rest of the night. So I try to focus. But instead of the game, my mind wanders to a pair of sky blue eyes.

Frustrated, I try to shake away the image. Tossing the beanbag toward the board, it lands even farther from the hole this time. Matt hoots with laughter and goes running across the grass. He jumps onto Rhett's back, his arms raised above his head in victory. Rhett laughs and tries to run a few feet but drops Matt to the ground instead. Undeterred, Matt continues to pump his fists and cheer from his place on the grass.

I shake my head at his theatrics. "You about done?"

Matt jumps to his feet then slings an arm around my neck. "You, brother dear, owe me a beer," he says, offering me his empty beer bottle. He tilts his head and smirks. "Look at that. I'm a poet and didn't even know it."

Shaking his arm off my shoulder, I grab the empty beer bottle from his hand. "Yeah, yeah. I'm going," I grumble before making my way across the yard to the garage.

Once inside, I reach into one of the large coolers and pull out three beers and a Coke for Rhett. Straightening, I come face to face with the sky blue eyes that have haunted my dreams for longer than I care to admit.

Jolie stands before me, her dark hair hanging over one shoulder in a long braid. She's wearing a dark green sundress that flutters in the breeze, hitting her just above the knee. My eyes wander over her endless legs before they shoot up to her face. The dark makeup makes her eyes pop and, if possible, seem even more blue than usual.

She arches a brow at me and I realize I haven't said anything yet. I clear my suddenly dry throat. "Nice day for a party."

Really? That's what you're going to go with?

I'm usually much more smooth around women but for some reason, right now my mind is blank. I want to blame the beer but this is only my second.

Maybe it has something to do with the fact that the last time I saw her, I accused her of being irresponsible and hot-headed for starting a bar fight when, in fact, she was defending her friend. Or maybe it's because that same night, I practically had her pinned against the police cruiser. Or it might be because I spent the last few weeks imagining all the inappropriate things I wanted to do to her against said cruiser.

Any of those reasons, really.

Luckily, though, Jolie seems to take pity on me and runs with my strange behavior. "It is. The sun's shining, Dottie and Maeve somehow haven't made any awkward sex jokes yet, and the love birds seem to be having a good time."

She looks through the garage window across the lawn. My eyes follow hers to where Matt has Avery alone on the porch. His arm is slung protectively over her shoulder as he leans in to whisper something into her ear. Avery turns her head to smile up at him. They look so happy that I can't help but smile watching them together.

As much as I give him shit about it, it's nice to see. Matt's a completely different guy than he was a year ago. Then, he thought the only reason anyone needed him was to make them laugh. He hid his true passion—his art—from his family because he thought we wouldn't understand that side of him.

Thankfully, Avery showed him that we'd still love him even if he wasn't always the happy-go-lucky guy he forced himself to be.

I still feel like shit knowing that my own brother felt he had to hide himself from me. He shouldn't have to tell me something like that. I should've known something was wrong. What kind of person doesn't realize how miserable his own brother is? How am I supposed to fix his problem if I can't even tell he has one?

I'm glad he trusted Avery enough to share that side of himself with, even if he didn't trust me.

Shoving the guilt away, I turn back to Jolie. Her focus is on Matt and Avery, her eyes soft and dreamy. It's a side of her I haven't seen before. The Jolie I know is more likely to be smirking or tossing an insult my way. She's confrontational and loud; there's nothing soft about her. This side of her seems younger, more innocent and the change catches me off guard.

Snarky Jolie I can handle. Soft Jolie is doing something to my chest that I'm not completely comfortable with.

I clear my throat again and it pulls her attention back to me. "Since you're here, I wanted to talk to you about the other night." It comes out more prickly than I intended, causing her to visibly stiffen.

Okay, not off to a great start.

"You wanted to talk to me or *at* me?" She arches a brow. "I seem to remember last time we spoke, it was more of a lecture than a conversation."

My frustration starts to creep up the back of my neck but I force it down. "I may have jumped to conclusions that night." My teeth clench around the words. She just waits, staring at me expectantly.

Why does she have to make this so difficult? I'm trying to apologize to the woman and she won't even let me get the damn words out.

This time, both brows shoot up but in surprise. "*May have?* You didn't just jump; you threw yourself to that conclusion head first. You took one look at me in those handcuffs and decided you knew exactly what happened."

Wrong. If only she knew what my first thought was seeing her cuffed like that...

"That's not entirely true—" I start but her humorless laugh cuts me off.

"What part isn't true? The part where you assumed that I clocked someone for the fun of it?" She steps closer until we're almost chest to chest. "Or the part where you called me 'pissy' like a temperamental toddler having a fit?"

She stabs a finger into my chest and it's like hitting a self-destruct button on my chest. My temper flares like a match to a fuse.

"Now, wait a damn minute—" I snap but she continues on as if I didn't even speak, stabbing her finger into my chest again.

"Oh, let me guess. You talked to Rhett, who was *actually* there that night and he told you what happened." *Stab.* "Is that it?" *Stab.* "Is that what has you feeling so remorseful all of a sudden?" *Stab, stab.*

Snatching her wrist before she draws blood, I pull her toward me, all thoughts of an apology flying away with the fall breeze. My scowl deepens but she just returns the glare. "Listen—"

"Like you listened to me the other night? Why should I—"

She opens her mouth to spew more of her angry rant but my blood is threatening to boil over with every vengeful word. So I do the only thing I can think of to get her to quit yelling at me.

I slam my mouth against hers.

Instantly, need explodes within me. My chest tightens and my hands ache to pull her tighter against me until I feel her tall frame pressed against me. What started as a way to shut her up quickly turns into something more.

It takes me a second to realize Jolie hasn't moved. *Shit.* I've been thinking with my dick and now I've just committed sexual assault. Just another example of how much this girl fucks with my head.

Just as I'm about to pull away, she wraps her arms around my neck, yanking me closer until we're pressed against each other. Her reaction is all the encouragement I need. I brush my tongue across her lips and when she opens for me, I dive inside. I need to taste every inch of her but I'll settle for her sinful mouth.

For now.

This is no sweet exploration. This kiss is years of pent up tension finally being released. It's desperate and punishing. She nips my bottom lip hard enough to leave a mark. I retaliate by wrapping a handful of hair around my fist, controlling the kiss. With my other hand, I cup her tight ass, giving in to temptation and giving it a rough squeeze. The movement pulls her tighter against me, my hard cock nestling perfectly between her thighs.

She rocks against me and the whimper she lets out has me answering with a groan. Any semblance of control I had is long gone as I'm lost to her sweet mouth and the sounds coming from it.

Somewhere in the back of my mind is the realization

that I have her pinned inside my mother's garage with a backyard full of people nearby. Anyone could walk in and see us.

But I couldn't give a fuck.

She claws at my shirt, scratching her nails against my chest. I'm backing her up against the wall, ready to take her right then and there when she stumbles over the cooler behind her.

I reach out to steady her but it's like a splash of cold water to the face.

What the hell was I thinking? That's easy; I wasn't. I was acting on impulse, giving in to the intrusive thoughts I've been fighting since the day she strolled into my town.

She takes a step back and her eyes go from being hooded with desire to wide with shock. Her hand lifts to her mouth as if she might feel my lingering touch.

She looks up at me, but before I can utter a single word, she spins on her heel and takes off in the other direction, leaving me standing inside my mother's garage feeling confused, guilty and horny.

What the fuck?

What the fucking fuck?

I can't seem to form any other thought other than *what the fuck just happened?*

When I went to grab a couple of drinks from the garage and saw Luke, I thought about turning around and walking away. Since that night at The Dive, I've been torn between being pissed at his stupid, self-righteous ass and being ridiculously turned on. I've made up so many scenarios of how that night could've ended and every single one ended with me being ravished within an inch of my life.

I ended up deciding to stick it out, telling myself I had to make nice for Avery's sake. It would be a long few months if her maid of honor and one of the groomsmen couldn't even be in the same room as each other.

I could do it. He's just a man.

An arrogant, holier-than-thou man with a face and body that rivals Henry Cavill's.

But a man all the same.

Why did he have to be so hot? Maybe then I could focus

on hating him instead of wanting to lick my way from his throat to his abs.

When he stood up, his chocolatey eyes and sharp jawline nearly brought me to my knees. Not to mention the way he filled out that button down shirt.

But then he had to go and ruin it by opening his mouth again.

At first, it started out innocent. I think he was even about to apologize. I almost had to check the sky for flying farm animals.

I should've known that it was too good to be true. His apology was over before it even started. Did I overreact? Maybe. But I like to think that there's no such thing as overreacting; only reacting. There's no bar set saying how much of a reaction is warranted for every single situation. Only how I feel at the moment.

And at that moment, I was pissed.

"I may have jumped to conclusions."

"That's not entirely true."

His half-assed attempt at an apology reminded me of a toddler being told to apologize. It was weak and meaningless. If you're going to apologize, have the balls to do it right.

If it was anyone else, I might've let it slide. Chalk it up to a bad experience then never think about it again. But Luke has always thought the worst of me. He's had his panties in a knot since the day I sped into town, giving me my first of many speeding tickets in Haven Bay as a welcoming gift.

As much as he doesn't want to admit it, I'm not a reckless person.

Spontaneous? Definitely. Impulsive? Occasionally. But never reckless.

Especially when people that I care about are involved. Since that list is so short, the ones on it get my complete and unwavering loyalty. Which means when threatened, this lioness protects her cubs. But never in a way that might bring them harm.

I knew once I told Avery what really went down that night, there was a good chance it would get back to Luke. I thought maybe it would make him pull the blinders off his eyes and see that I'm not actually the terrible person he thinks I am.

Apparently not.

So, I lashed out. And no, the irony is not lost on me that because he thinks I'm out of control, I acted out of control. But I can't help it. He brings out the worst in me every damn time. Even when I tell myself I won't let him get to me, he carves his way into my calm until I implode.

Just when I was about to really lay into him, he shocked the hell out of me by smashing his mouth against mine. And yes, smash is exactly what he did. There's nothing gentle or soothing about the way Luke Brady kisses. His lips overwhelm you while the rest of his body fights to control you. Every move is aimed at destroying you then putting you back together to his whim.

And the worst part is, I loved every second of it.

Fucking dick-munching shitballs. What the hell do I do now?

"Hey, you okay?"

I spin on my heel to find Brenna watching me with concern. Somehow, I made my way back to the porch without realizing. Brenna and Avery are standing with Matt and Luke's sister Tori, talking with one of Matt's relatives. They're thankfully oblivious to my freak out.

Brenna puts her hand on my arm, her worried

expression pulling me the rest of the way out of my tailspin. "Yeah, I'm good," I reassure her, plastering a tight smile on my face. She doesn't look convinced but before she can question me further, Tori leans over and mouths "help" over her shoulder.

Thank God.

I slide between Brenna and Tori to where Matt's nonna is describing in explicit detail the "wifely duties" that are expected on the wedding night.

"On my wedding night, my husband's family stood outside our door to make sure the marriage was properly consummated. And consummate we did, my dear." She gives a wrinkly-eyed wink while Avery looks like she's about to puke.

"Oh, Nonna, there you are," I interject. "Francesca has been looking for you. Something about wanting your opinion on the creaminess of the cannoli filling."

Nonna purses her lips. "I told that girl to let me make the cannolis. My daughter knows nothing about whipping cream." With that, she hurries off toward the house, presumably to give her daughter a lesson on proper baking techniques.

Avery slumps against me dramatically. "You're a lifesaver. I did *not* need to hear the end of that story."

Tori scrunches her nose up in disgust. "No one did. Not exactly the image I needed of my grandparents." She shudders then turns to me. "My mom's going to kill you by the way when she finds out you're the one who sicced her mother on her."

I shrug, unperturbed. "Sorry, not sorry. Maid of honor duties trump an angry mother-in-law."

Avery slings her arm through mine. "That they do. You're already earning your title." She looks down at my empty hands. "Didn't you say you were going to grab a drink?"

I stifle the urge to shuffle my feet. "No. I mean, yeah. I did. But then I realized I wasn't thirsty anymore. There was a line anyway."

Brenna cocks her head. "A line at the coolers?"

"Yep." I cross my arms then uncross them then drop them to my sides. "Real long one. Must've been a drink emergency."

"Drink emergency?" Tori snorts. "Is my mother trying to sing karaoke again?"

I laugh nervously. It comes out louder than I intended, earning me another suspicious look from Brenna.

Oh my god. Stop being weird.

I twist the ring on my middle finger nervously. "Must be. Either that or Maeve is on the hunt for a boy toy again."

Avery and Tori laugh while Brenna watches me carefully. Avoiding her gaze, I try for a subject change. "So, Tori, how long are you home for?"

Tori lives in Toronto working as an event coordinator for a very prestigious company. Avery told me that the last event they planned was a children's hospital gala that raised over $1.2 million. The money raised would allow the hospital to open a new oncology wing.

"Only a couple of days. I fly back the day after tomorrow. We have a charity auction coming up that requires all hands on deck. I'm hoping this will be the event to put me on the map. My boss has been waving a promotion in front of me like a carrot on a stick for years but there's no way she'll pass me up this time." She smiles confidently and I can't help but be impressed by her.

Like me, Tori left home at eighteen, but instead of wandering around like a lost dog like I did, she went out and made something of herself. Even if she's not where she wants to be yet in her career, she still has a goal and is working toward it. I wish I would've been half as disciplined when I was her age.

But then I wouldn't be where I am today. I would've never discovered my love of yoga. I wouldn't have moved to Haven Bay or started my own business. I wouldn't have met Avery, let alone be standing in her wedding.

Maybe I also wouldn't have met a certain grumpy police officer either.

I can't help but look over to where he's standing across the lawn. He's standing with a group of men, probably shooting the shit and not giving a second thought to what happened between us earlier. His posture is stiff as usual and I'd bet anything that his jaw is clenched like it always is. One of the side effects of stickuptheass-itis, I assume.

As if he senses me staring, he turns his head and meets my eyes. His face is unreadable but his eyes seem harder than usual. Is he mad that I bolted? Is it because he wanted to continue what we started? Or is he mad about our conversation? For all I know, that kiss didn't even affect him.

Even to my own ears, I can hear the lie. I felt the effect of that kiss against me. The flimsy material of my dress left little to the imagination against the feel of his hard dick between my thighs. One of the advantages of being 5'9 is that with a cute pair of wedges, it puts me at the perfect height for against the wall sex.

Not that I was planning to have sex with Luke. Or anyone, really. I'm just saying if I was...

Okay, brain. That's enough overthinking from you today.

"Is it just me or does Rhett look especially delicious today?" Tori's comment pulls me back to reality. It takes a second before I fully process what she just said but when it does, my head snaps to her in disbelief.

I wasn't sure what to expect when I first met Tori. Avery had told me stories about her from when they were kids and she sounded like a stereotypical hell-raising little sister. When Avery and I picked her up from the airport this week, the chic woman with stylish clothes and a trendy haircut who strutted out of the terminal was not the one I imagined. But today, with her jean shorts and t-shirt, drinking wine out of a red solo cup, she looks like a completely different person. Much more like the girl I pictured.

"Rhett? As in your brother's best friend? Rhett Lawson?" I try to keep the surprise off my face but I'm failing miserably.

Tori laughs. "Oh, don't even start with that. I'm a woman with eyes, aren't I? I can look at anyone I want and right now, I'm looking at Rhett." She eyes Rhett like he's a piece of red velvet cake. "I think I'll just have to go say hi. It's been so long since we last talked. We've got some catching up to do." She throws a wink at us before she bounces over to where the guys are standing. She stops beside Rhett and says something that makes him smile.

Thankfully, Luke and Matt are deep in discussion about something and don't notice the interaction between their friend and their little sister. I try to bite back my grin. I might not know much about Luke but I do know how protective both he and Matt are of their sister.

This should be fun.

CHAPTER 10

LUKE

"**I**f you don't get rid of that damn walking vagina, I'm going to take a sledgehammer to it."

"It's not a walking vagina, you uncultured swine. It's art!"

"Art, my ass. That's porn!"

I hold my hands up to stop the inevitable retort that I'd bet is on the tip of Trina Thompson's tongue. The call from dispatch came in a little after eight this morning that there was a public disturbance between Mary Benson and Trina Thompson. Since their houses are a street over from mine, I radioed in that I'd take the call.

The dull ache in my head sharpens behind my eyes. Of all the mornings to skip my morning coffee...

I resist the urge to press my fingers against my eyes and turn to Mary Benson. "Look, Mrs. Benson, I understand the statue—"

"Jeffrey," Trina puts in and I bite back a sigh.

"I understand *Jeffrey* bothers you," I say through clenched teeth. "But it's been on the Thompson property for years. Why the sudden need to have it gone today?"

Mary shoots Trina a glare then lifts her chin indignantly at me. "Well, *Dear Annie* told me that I shouldn't keep my problems bottled up. It's better to get things out into the open rather than let things fester. And that damn statue has been a thorn in my side for years. Do you know how embarrassing it is to have company over and have them walk past that...thing!" she nearly shouts, pointing a shaky finger at the cement figure in question.

Of course that damn column is behind this.

It's been three weeks since the first column was published and it's been a pain in my ass every week since. Every Tuesday, I drive around town putting out fires—both figurative and one literal.

In a normal town, an advice column would be an interesting way of getting an opinion on a problem. Then you'd take that advice with a grain of salt and come up with your own sane solution.

But Haven Bay is not a normal town.

The first week, the unknown columnist told Jessie Kinney that the answer to her husband's snoring was to consider different sleeping arrangements. Jessie took that to mean that she should kick her husband out of the house and have him sleep on the front porch.

The second week, when she told seventy year old Annie Bell that sex was a "liberating and fun experience between two consenting people that should not be shamed or judged", I had the pleasure of writing her and her partner up for indecent exposure when I caught them going at it in the parking lot of Scoops, the local ice cream shop. Did I mention they were dressed as farm animals?

I mean, to each their own. But seeing my dentist dressed in a skimpy cow costume was enough to make me want to claw my eyes out.

Now, I'm stuck breaking up a fight between two elderly neighbors over a statue that, if I'm being honest, does look eerily similar to a vagina standing in a Captain Morgan pose.

How I don't end every night with a bottle of rum is beyond me.

"Mrs. Thompson, what if I get some of the guys at the department to come down and move Jeffrey closer to your house," I offer. "Maybe in the garden? That way you could still admire him from your sunroom, but he's not visible from the street."

Trina continues to glare at Mary then crosses her arms over her chest with a huff. Finally, she drops her arms and turns to me.

"Well, it would be nice to be able to see Jeffrey from up close. As long as the boys don't mind moving it, I guess we can give it a try." She turns to point a finger at Mrs. Benson. "But if you so much as breathe in Jeffrey's direction, I'll move him right beside your bedroom window so he can watch you sleep at night."

With that, she turns and struts back to her house, letting her screen door slam shut behind her. Mrs. Benson takes a step toward me until she's practically standing on my toes. "You have until the weekend to move him or I'm getting the sledgehammer." Then she spins and retreats back to her porch.

Dragging a hand over my face, I finally let out the groan that's been buried in my chest since I arrived almost an hour ago.

This goddamn town will be the death of me.

Case closed, I walk back to where my cruiser sits along the curb. A car passes and lets out a friendly honk as I round the car. I lift my hand in an absentminded wave then throw open the door and drop onto the leather seat. Resisting the urge to bang my head against the steering wheel, I turn the engine over and pull into the street.

I take one last look at Jeffrey, standing proudly in the center of the lawn for all to see. I know art (and I use that term loosely) is supposed to be subjective but even I think the statue is pushing it. I almost don't blame Mrs. Benson for threatening to destroy him. I don't know if I could live next to something like that and not want to take a sledgehammer to it either.

Turning the corner, I cruise down the street, giving the occasional head nod to people as I pass by. With the tourist season winding down, the streets seem barren. As a town that thrives on tourism as a major contributor to the economy, tourist season is a necessary evil in my opinion. Their hard-earned cash may be the main source of many local's income, but the trouble tourists bring with them keeps me on high-alert all summer. I've spent too much time pulling out the bay's latest victim who underestimated the water's strong current.

I'm ready to get back to the calm of the winter months, where the only tourists are low maintenance hunters and skiers looking for a cheap place to lay their heads.

My stomach grumbles, snapping me back to the present. Usually I follow my morning workout with an omelet but with the early morning call to Mrs. Thompson's, I had to make due with a granola bar. Now my stomach is protesting my meager breakfast choice.

After checking in at the station and finding it quiet, I pull the cruiser into one of the parking spaces in front of Main Street Diner. I take a quick scan of the downtown as I get out of the car. Finding nothing amiss, I climb the steps to the diner, breathing a sigh of relief when I find Dottie and Maeve's usual spots empty.

Maybe if I can place my order fast enough, I'll be able to get out before they make their inevitable return. Seeing those two troublemakers is the last thing I need this morning.

Especially before I've even had a decent breakfast.

CHAPTER 11

JOLIE

Have you ever had a secret that started out as just a little raindrop that at first didn't seem like a big deal. But then as time passes, it grows and grows until one day, it's this massive, looming cloud following you wherever you go?

No? Well, let me tell you, it sucks. Big time.

What started out as just a fun little side project has turned into this gigantic secret that I'm keeping from everyone I love. It's more than a little daunting.

I honestly didn't think that the column would take off the way it has. It's been a month since I started writing and the town is up in arms over the mystery identity of *Dear Annie*. There's been a lot of wild guesses, some that I might have even believed if I didn't know the truth.

"My guess is Miss Carla. That woman loves a good story." Avery spins the straw of her iced water thoughtfully. "I could see her at her antique roll-top desk, wearing an extravagant hat with a long feather sticking out of it, clacking away at her typewriter. Like something out of an old black and white movie."

We're sitting in the diner on a Tuesday morning, having one of our regular girls' brunch. This week's issue of *The Haven Times* came out today and, as usual, the town has gone nuts with *Annie's* latest advice.

Brenna chuckles. "My money is on Dottie. Maybe Maeve, too. Those two love to stir up trouble." She turns to me, taking a sip of her coffee. "What about you?"

It's a good thing I hadn't been drinking or I might have choked. "Me?"

"Yeah," Brenna says. "Who do you think *Annie* is?"

Geez, jumpy much? Calm down, Jolie. You're going to blow it.

I shouldn't be surprised by the question; if gossip was a steak, I just served them a fat, juicy ribeye on a silver platter. But my brain is tripping over itself trying to come up with any answer other than the truth.

"Oh, who knows." I say casually, feeling anything but. I try to keep from looking either of them in the eye as I continue. "Could be anyone, really. Could be old Mrs. Creevey, for all we know." *Why did my voice just squeak?* "How do I know it's not one of you two?" *That's it. Deflect. Oldest trick in the book for a reason.*

Avery snorts. "Yeah, right. I'm running a business, raising a kid, planning a wedding *and* writing an anonymous advice column?" She leans back in the booth. "I'm tired just thinking about it." She turns to Brenna. "What about you, Bren? You've got the whole quiet and wise thing going for you."

Brenna shakes her head. "Definitely not. Not only do I not have the time or energy, but there's no way anyone would want to hear my opinion. I'm way too much of a people pleaser. I'd just tell them to do whatever they thought was right so they didn't get mad at me." She laughs.

I point a disciplinary finger at her. "You need to give yourself more credit. You're smart and strong. Why wouldn't anyone want to hear your advice? How many times have I told you: who cares what other people think if you're staying true to you. If they don't like what you have to say, that's on them, not on you."

"Thanks, J." Brenna smiles.

I smile back. "You're my friend. I've always got your back."

"Speaking of not liking what someone has to say..." Avery takes another sip of her drink. "What happened with you and Luke at the engagement party?"

I try to steel my face from a reaction. "What do you mean?" Did she see something? I thought I had hid it pretty well. Brenna might've noticed my mood change but she hasn't mentioned it, so I figured I was in the clear.

Apparently not.

Avery arches a brow at me. "Come on. One minute you were happy and laughing with Tori before you went to get a drink. Then you came back and practically had steam shooting out of your ears. Matt said Luke was ready to spit steel when he came back from grabbing beers. I might be distracted lately by the wedding, but I can still put two and two together."

I sigh. "Just the usual. Luke loves to paint me as the villain, even without knowing the whole story. Then when he realizes that there might be more to it than what his puny mind can comprehend (shocker), he offers me a half-assed apology." I shrug. "So I called him out on it. He didn't like that." *Then he kissed me within an inch of my life and now I can't stop thinking about his stupid face.* "Our usual story."

Avery and Brenna exchange a look. One I know well, seeing as though it's the same one they give every time I mention Luke. I know they think there's more to what's between us than there is. But they're wrong.

Sure, Luke's a good looking guy. Some might even consider him hot. And okay, he may kiss better than any man I've ever dated. But that was a one time thing. A mistake that I'll never make again.

Ever.

Avery takes a deep breath and I can already sense I'm not going to like her next words.

"J, you know I love you and I've got your back no matter what. I know Luke can be an asshole sometimes." I snort at that but she ignores me. "If it wasn't for the wedding, I wouldn't be asking you this. But could you at least try and make peace?" She puts her hands up in surrender when I start to object. "I get it. I know it's not only you. Matt had this same conversation with Luke. And the second we say 'I do', you can go back to being at each other's throats. But in the meantime, it would make my life a lot easier if everyone got along. You don't even have to talk to each other if you don't want—"

"Ave." I cover her hand with mine to stop her rambling. "Of course. This is your wedding. Anything I can do to make it easier on you, I'll do it in a heartbeat. Even being nice to Chief Asshat." Avery and Brenna laugh. "But seriously, I'm good. I can play nice during the wedding festivities." I smirk into my mug. "The real question is if he can."

Avery smiles. "Matt promises me Luke will be on his best behavior—whether he wants to be or not."

I sit back in my seat, wrapping my hands around my mug. "Then there's nothing to worry about. Consider it another thing checked off your to-do list."

Brandy takes that moment to walk over with a coffee

pot. "Would you ladies like anything else?" I look over at Avery who's already shaking her head.

"Sorry, ladies but I need to get back to the shop," she says, taking a few bills out of her purse and handing them to Brandy. "The lunch rush should be coming in soon and I don't want to leave Tammy to handle that on her own." She slides out of the booth, slinging her purse over her shoulder. "I'll see you guys later?"

Brenna stands beside her. "I'll follow you out. I want to exercise the dogs before the vet comes." She hands Brandy a bill and waves her away when Brandy tries to offer her change. "You coming, J?"

I shake my head. "I think I'm going to sit for a while longer. My next class isn't for a few hours and I want to finish my book for Book Club anyway." I dig into my bag to pull out this month's book.

They both wave goodbye and head for the door, chatting as they go. Brandy refills my mug with hot water and I dunk my teabag a few times until the liquid turns amber again. Then I pull my book from my bag and open it to my marked page.

This month's book is a fantasy novel that Mrs. Creevey chose. It's about a woman who is being hunted by dragon riders for unknown reasons as of yet. Enter the morally gray rider who has vowed to kill her. The sexual tension is off the charts. I'm deeply immersed in the story where the heroine is sassing the dragon rider while he holds his dagger to her throat when a blur of black catches my attention.

Luke.

Even worse, Luke in uniform.

Why is it that the first time I have to see him since the engagement party he has to have the unfair advantage of looking delicious in his police uniform while I sit in my worn yoga pants and White Stripes shirt?

Because the universe is a petty bitch who loves to fuck with me. That's why.

He takes a seat on one of the worn leather stools at the counter and pulls out a menu from the wooden napkin holder before him. Leah Morrow walks over with a coffee pot and mug in hand. She places the mug in front of him and he smiles warmly up at her. As she fills his mug, he says something that makes her laugh.

So he is capable of being a normal human being. It's just me that brings out the grumpy asshole in him.

Lucky me.

Leah saunters over to her next customer and Luke takes a sip of his coffee. Black, of course—like his soul. I snort to myself. Okay, only a little bit of an exaggeration but still.

Mug to his lips, he turns to survey the room, a habit I know all too well from growing up with a dad in the army.

Be aware of your surroundings.

Know your exits.

Determine potential threats before they can become one.

His eyes stop as they land on mine. The shift in his expression is so subtle that if I hadn't been watching him for the past few minutes, I might not have noticed it. But it's there. The slight line between his brows, the smallest of frowns pulling at his lips, the hard glint in his eyes.

Yep, lucky me.

Before he saw me, I considered ignoring him and going back to my book. But the visual reminder of his disdain for me has me singing another tune.

Before I can think it through, I stand and stroll over to where he's sitting, his back facing me again. Sliding onto the stool beside him, I shoot him my most devastating smile.

"Mornin' Chief'. How's it hangin'?"

LUKE

When I came to the diner, I wasn't expecting solitude. In a town like Haven Bay, there's no such thing as solitude outside of your own home. Even there, neighbors have been known to stop in unexpectedly for idle chit chat or gossip.

So when I feel someone plop themselves down onto the stool beside mine, I'm not overly surprised. I'm always being stopped by someone when I'm out. Rodney Jackson wanting to dissect the Eagle's game last night, Mrs. Creevey ready to complain about the weather, or even little Sam Cronheimer hoping for a glimpse at my badge. But this time I have an idea who it is, though I'm torn between hoping I'm both wrong and right.

When I glance over my shoulder, I realize I'm right. It's none other than the woman who's been haunting my every waking moment for the last few weeks.

Jolie.

My jaw clenches. Of course I'd see her today. As if my morning hasn't been frustrating enough. And just to top things off, she's wearing yoga pants that are practically painted on. The baggy band shirt she's wearing would normally be a reprieve from my frustratingly wandering eyes but it just makes me imagine what's underneath.

When did I become such a horny bastard? I don't even like the woman, yet she's the first one to cause this type of reaction in years.

Perfect.

She leans over and looks into the mug in front of me. "Black coffee, eh? Should've figured. Just like your soul."

She smiles sweetly. I swear my molars grind to dust from the tension in my jaw.

I slide the mug closer to me. "What do you want, Jolie? I don't have it in me to try and keep up with your mood swings today."

She bats her eyelashes at me innocently. "Why, what could you mean? I'm just making conversation with a friend." I scoff at the term. She ignores me. "I'm trying to play nice. Isn't that what we're supposed to be doing? For Avery and Matt?"

The corner of my lips turn up sarcastically. "You got that guilt trip too, eh?"

"Unfortunately." She picks up a napkin and starts tearing at the corners. "Nothing pairs better with your eggs than a side of guilt," she comments dryly.

My annoyance with her wanes, knowing exactly how she's feeling. My brother knocked on my door precisely twelve minutes after my shift ended with a six-pack and a pizza. I barely had my first slice halfway to my mouth when he started to lay it on thick.

"Yeah, Matt got to me last night after my shift."

More like handed me my ass. He started with explaining how Avery had been feeling nervous about the wedding. She hadn't wanted to make too much of a fuss with it being her second wedding and all. Something changed recently that had made her change her mind.

"She's finally excited about the wedding," Matt had said. "Every morning she gets up with a new idea for the decorations or the flowers or the dinner." Matt got that wistful look in his eye and the dopey grin on his face every time he talked about his new fiancé.

"You know I could care less about any of that. I just want her to be happy. It sucked seeing her second guessing herself when she was planning that boring elopement before." His face turned serious as he looked me square in the eye. "Nothing's going to mess this up for her. Not gossipy old ladies, not her ex and not her maid-of-honor and my groomsman sniping at each other every time they're within throwing distance of each other."

My brother might still be a lovable goofball, but he's fiercely protective of Avery and his soon-to-be stepson Gavin. I knew better than to argue. Besides, Avery's been like a sister to me since we were kids. I wanted her big day to be perfect as much as Matt did.

Even if that meant playing nice with the one woman who made my blood boil—both in anger and in desire.

So I relented. Much to my chagrin.

Jolie huffs out a breath. "I want to say they're being dramatic but I think the past few weeks are proof enough that they might have a point."

I scowl down at my mug. I hate letting my temper get the best of me. I try my hardest to always keep my emotions in check. As a police officer, I can't afford to give in to my impulses.

That kiss was a perfect example of how stupid that can be. Even if I can still feel her lips against mine, her tall figure the perfect height for me to...

Jolie tosses her mangled napkin onto the discarded plate beside her, grabbing my attention. "So in the interest of our newfound truce, I'm required to ask, what's got your panties in a knot this morning?"

I arch an eyebrow at her.

She plasters an exaggerated smile on her face. "What I mean to say is: what's plaguing you, my dear friend," she asks in the worst attempt at an English accent I've ever heard.

And I've watched Kevin Costner's Robin Hood.

I almost tell her exactly that, but in the interest of our truce as she put it, I bite back my tongue. "Just dealing with the crazy residents of this town. This morning, I had to hold Mrs. Benson back from taking a bat to Jeffrey." Jolie's eyebrows shoot into her hairline. "The statue, not the person."

"Ah. Sounds about right." Jolie snickers. "Did Trina throw herself in front of Jeffrey as tribute?"

The corner of my lips turn up again. Everyone in town knows Trina's love for Jeffrey. Her husband, Lenny, likes to joke that she loves Jeffrey more than him. At least I think he's joking. He's probably not far off though.

"She might as well have. Took a lot of convincing to get Mrs. Benson off the ledge but she finally backed down."

"Oh, man. I sure as hell don't envy your job. At least the screaming old ladies at my job aren't trying to take each other out over a walking vagina." She shakes her head incredulously. Leah takes that moment to stop by our counter. Most people would hear things like "walking vagina" and be shocked. Not in Haven Bay. Leah barely bats an eye and, at my nod, refills my coffee. Jolie orders a green tea. Leah quickly fills a mug with hot water and hands Jolie a tea bag then goes back to her other tables.

"I kind of don't blame Mary. I give her credit for not doing it sooner. I would've done a lot worse a lot sooner if I had to live next to Jeffrey," Jolie says. She dunks the tea bag into her mug. "What finally broke Mary?"

The grip on my mug tightens. "Apparently, she got the idea from that damn *Dear Annie* column. Something about 'not letting your problems fester' and 'getting it all out in the open' or something stupid like that." I shift my gaze to Jolie, who's stiffened beside me and is fiddling with the string on her tea bag.

She clears her throat. "Not a big fan of *Annie*, I see?"

This time, it's my turn to scoff. "Not quite."

"Why? She's just answering people's questions."

I turn in my seat to face her, our knees bracketing each other. I force myself not to focus on the spark of electricity that shoots up my leg at the contact. "She's turning the town into a circus." Jolie shoots me a dry look. "More than it already was," I correct myself. "She's got people acting like impulsive children with no consequences for their actions. A few words from her and people are willing to turn their whole lives upside down."

"Have you ever thought that maybe these people needed their worlds turned upside down?" Jolie retorts. "If people are that unhappy, they shouldn't be stuck just because they're afraid of change. If people want to be more confident, more daring, more courageous and all it takes is *a few words* for them to follow their dreams, then I'd say it's a good thing. Some might call *Annie* an inspiration."

"She's a virus, is what she is."

"A virus?!" she practically shrieks. "She's helping people, not hurting them."

"Yet. It's only a matter of time before her reckless 'helping' causes someone to lose their job, their family, or worse."

"Reckless? You make it seem like she's some selfish, shit-disturber handing out advice all—" She waves her hand around like she's trying to grasp the right word. "Willy-nilly."

I fight the urge to laugh. Willy-nilly is not a term you hear every day, especially when it's spat out like a curse word.

I shrug and lift the mug to my lips. "If the shoe fits."

Jolie grumbles under her breath then stands suddenly. "I'm late for class."

She tosses some cash onto the counter then shoves the strap of her bag over her shoulder. She opens her mouth to say more, then snaps it shut again and storms off.

I turn slightly in my chair to watch her shove through the diner door and onto the street, taking angry strides across the sidewalk toward Amaryllis.

So much for a truce.

Her behavior was odd, but not completely out of character for Jolie. Every time I open my mouth, she feels the need to argue with me. I could tell her the sky is blue and she'd have a five minute argument on how it was actually a shade of purple.

Shaking my head, I turn back to my coffee. Before I can take another drink, the radio on my chest goes off.

"Chief, we have a 314 over at the Sunny Days Retirement Residence. Seems one of the residents stole another resident's motorized wheelchair and is making a break for it down the side of Highway 18."

I groan. Well, at least I can't blame this one on *Dear Annie.* Turning the radio to my mouth, I hold the button on the side to respond. "Copy. On my way."

Shoving all thoughts of a certain dark-haired woman aside, I toss a bill on the counter then head to my cruiser.

Apparently, I have to get into a high-speed chase with a wheelchair.

THE HAVEN TIMES

pg 15 — Proudly serving Haven Bay for over 100 years. — **FREE**

DEAR ANNIE

Your local source for advice on love, life and everything in between!

The answer to this week's trivia question (pg 9) is spaghetti and meatballs.

Q.

Dear Annie,

I'm in a rut. Do you remember that Bill Murray movie where every morning, he wakes up only to repeat the same day over and over again? Well, that's my life, only with less humor and more old people.

Every morning I wake up to the same bird chirping outside my window. I hobble down the hallway to the same breakfast table, where I eat the same cholesterol-friendly meal and take the same medications at precisely 8 a.m. Then I'll hobble back down the hallway where I'll watch the same soap opera, followed by some asinine craft-hour that's been some doctor said helps to stimulate brain function.

Newsflash: most of us are pushing 90 in here. We're lucky if our bladders are still functioning, let alone our brains. That ship sailed around the time the prime minister started sending us congratulatory letters on our birthdays.

I know I'm too old for adventures. What kind of fun can an wrinkly old bag like me have anyway?

I'm not ready for this to be all that's left.

Signed,
Desperate For a Thrill

A.

Dear Desperate,

First of all, there's no such thing as being too old for adventure. Second of all, I must admit I'm dying to know if Liza is actually Horatio's long-lost sister or if she's lying to steal Simon's fortune (no spoilers!). But I can understand your frustrations.

Unfortunately, the older we get, the more routine our lives may seem— especially when you're somewhere where routine and schedules run the show.

But if you want my opinion, I say to hell with that shit (can I swear in the newspaper?)

Life is short. It might not seem like it when you're 90.

Or maybe it does, how would I know?

Either way, you only get one life. Live it however the hell you want. That advice applies whether you're 18 or 108. Never stop living your life to its full potential.

As for ideas on what kind of fun to get into, I'm your girl.

Pick a hobby that sounds like fun but you've never gotten around to trying. Take a trip to the first place your finger lands on a map. Go sky-diving (if your doctor clears you for it, of course. Please don't sue us).

Do something. Do everything.

Because when you're lying on your deathbed, it'll be a lot more fun to think of all the crazy shit you did than how many doilies you knit.

Love always,
Annie

GARBAGE DAY DELAY REMINDER

Please note that garbage pick up will be delayed next week as our favorite garbage collector is set to become a daddy on Friday. Best wishes to Daddy Simon and Mama Jordyn as she undergoes her scheduled c-section. We can't wait to meet your new bundle of joy very soon!

REC CENTRE BRIDGE SCORES

The following are the top-scoring teams in recent Bridge games at the Haven Bay Recreation Centre. Bridge lessons are available. If interested, please sign up the rec centre Mon - Fri 9 a.m to 3 p.m.

Nov. 12: North/South - 1st Sandra Moore and Terry Jones, 2nd Polly Nikolas and Rodney Coots, 3rd George and Mary Simpson.

East/West - 1st Dale McDowell and Jack Smith, 2nd Mona Monroe and Quinton Symes, 3rd Roger Tirks and Sally Fenton.

CHAPTER 12

JOLIE

I hate running.

Or should I say, I hate the act of running. I love the scenic routes. I love the endorphins that rush through my body after a long run. I love the mental clarity it gives me to keep that pesky bitch Tiffany at bay.

But the actual act of running? I hate it.

I know most runners will tell you that, after a while, a runner's high kicks in and you start to feel invincible. Your legs become numb and you feel like you could run forever.

I am not most runners.

I hate the burning in my lungs. I hate the sweat dripping down my buttcrack. I hate the way every kilometer feels like physical torture.

But I do it anyway. Every morning, without fail, I pull my whiny, sleepy body out of bed and out the back door. Then I run an excruciating 5-kilometers around Haven Bay. Sometimes, if I'm feeling brave, I'll mix it up and run through the forest behind my apartment.

When it's over, I feel accomplished and powerful. But

during? I'm so miserable, I'd punch a baby orangutan if it so much as looked in my direction.

And I mean, come on. Baby orangutans?

Fucking adorable.

Which just further proves how much of an asshole I am while I run.

I've tried listening to different playlists, audiobooks, podcasts. Anything to keep me distracted from the ache in my legs. But nothing has worked. I've just accepted that the torture I endure during my runs is worth the payoff afterward. Even if it makes me a miserable bitch and I hate every second of it.

That's called adulting.

So as I drag my tired body down the stairs of my apartment this morning, I don't even bother trying to psych myself up for this run.

My mantra today is: *Let's get this over with.*

After a quick round of stretching, I give the laces on my shoe one last tug to secure them in place then take off toward the forest. It's a rainy, chilly morning and I'm not in the mood for the inevitable conversation that comes with running through town. Even if you're running by, residents will chase you down the road just to chat. Some mornings I find it amusing, but days like this I just want to lose myself in my music and the trees.

Not literally, of course. That sounds like the start of a bad horror movie. The one where the masked man follows the woman through the woods, grabbing her when she least expects it, then drags her back to his creepy shed-like house.

Why does that sound more hot than scary?

I've been reading too many dark romances.

A movement in the corner of my eye causes me to spin on my heel, nearly taking me out in the process. I pull my earbud out and look around but find nothing but trees and bushes.

Okay, it might be hot in books but it's terrifying in real life.

I'm about to start running again when the snap of a twig behind me has me frantically spinning toward the sound. A dark figure comes racing toward me and I let out a scream, throwing my hands in front of me to punch, slap and scratch at the offender.

I might be a pansy, but I refuse to be tossed in the back of a trunk and driven to my death without drawing some blood first. Though I hate to admit it, my father taught me better than that.

"Jesus Christ, Jolie. Knock it off," the axe-murderer shouts.

"Get your serial killing hands off me, you creep! You will not wear my skin! I know Krav Maga, you sick fuck!" I shout as my fists swing toward the creepy criminal. I stomp my heel down as hard as I can on his foot and am rewarded with a curse. I'm about to thrust my knee into his groin when a hand reaches out to hold my leg in place.

"Jolie, STOP. It's Luke. Calm the fuck down."

My body goes slack as recognition hits. I look up and see that it is, in fact, Luke standing before me and not a cannibal serial killer. No longer on the defensive, he reaches up to touch a place on his cheek where a small cut is dripping blood. He pulls his fingers away and, noticing the blood on them, looks down at me in annoyance.

"Wear your skin? Really?"

I refuse to be embarrassed, so I merely shrug. "How was I supposed to know it was you? You might've been a cannibal that wanted to take a bite out of my spleen."

Head bent as he wipes the mud from my shoe off his, he

shakes his head. "That's not the part of you I want to take a bite of," he mumbles. Then his spine stiffens, as if realizing he said the thought out loud. I clear my throat, pretending not to have heard. The comment has me as taken aback as my run-in with a would-be Hannibal Lecter. But the shiver that runs up my spine has nothing to do with fear.

"What're you doing stalking around the woods at this hour?" I demand with more force than I mean to.

Luke finally looks me in the eye. He arches his eyebrow in that stupid, arrogant way that makes me want to smash a banana into his face. He looks down at his running shoes then at mine.

"Same thing as you. Running."

He's wearing loose gym shorts and a tight fitting t-shirt. The outline of his pecs and broad chest has me shifting in place. I cross my arms over my chest to keep my hands from fidgeting.

Stupid men and their stupidly hot bodies that look even hotter when they run.

I probably look like a mix between a drowned rat and a tomato, if the sweat dripping down my butt is any indication. Whereas he looks like a Greek warrior who just came in from slaying his enemy before he ravishes the beautiful handmaid.

Okay, yep. No more smut before bed. It's clearly messing with my brain.

"Are you coming?"

I choke on my saliva. Yep. Ever the elegant woman of grace and poise, I'm gasping for air at the thought of Luke Brady asking me if I'm coming.

God, I need to get laid.

Trying desperately to shove air into my lungs without, you know, looking like I'm gasping for my last breath, I bend at the waist. I'm aiming for a casual pose but by the look on Luke's face, I think I'm failing.

"Um, pardon?"

He runs his hand over his mouth but not before I see the twitch of his lips. He waves his hand toward the trail before us. "Are you going to come run with me or are you just gonna stand there sucking air like a trout out of water?"

Now, there's two things you should know about me.

First, I'm very competitive. Growing up with a brother who played hockey the way most people breathe air, it's hard not to be. Especially when I learned I could take out all of my aggression on him in the rink and not be punished for it.

The second is that I'm ruthless when it comes to winning. To me, all's fair in love, war and sport. And I'm not above toeing the line between fair play and breaking the rules to get a leg up on my competition.

Which is why, when Luke throws down that particular challenge, it ignites a fire inside of me that is completely separate from the burning in my legs.

"Run with you? I'm not sure you could keep up with me, Lukey." I smirk up at his narrowed eyes. But where there's usually annoyance, there's a playfulness I never thought I'd see directed at me. I've witnessed it between him, Matt and Rhett, with Gavin, and even with Avery. But never has it been aimed in my direction.

He takes a step closer and the corner of his lips turn up, to what I'm now discovering is his version of a smile. I swear if I ever see the man grin, I'll drop dead from shock. I'm taller than the average woman but as he leans his full frame over me, I swear I feel like a toddler. Though it doesn't stop me from straightening my spine.

"Bring it." His low voice has me feeling and thinking all

kinds of confusing things. Like how hard the forest floor would be against my back if he took me against it right now. Which is the exact opposite of what I should be thinking about a man I can't stand and who definitely can't stand me. We haven't had a conversation that hasn't ended in an argument since the day we met. He's infuriating and self-righteous and everything I hate in a man.

But he's also hot as hell and I'm only human.

To keep from offering myself up to him on a silver platter, I take off down the trail. I have the element of surprise but it doesn't take long before twigs snap behind me as his long legs eat up the distance behind me.

Usually my pace could be described as relaxed and leisurely but there is nothing leisurely about the way I push myself now.

He's close. I can feel it in the awareness that runs down my spine but I refuse to let him catch me. I will my legs to pump faster and harder until my breath is choppy and the only thing I'm focused on is my feet pounding against the uneven ground. The trail twists and I take the turn sharply, keeping Luke from passing me on the inside. His feet thunder behind me, the only sound in the otherwise quiet forest.

The early morning sun peeks through the trees but the sight is lost on me as I dodge the overgrown branches. The trail twists again and the clearing of the park opens before us. With only a few hundred meters to go, I force my aching legs to keep moving.

I feel him behind me, just far enough to keep me pushing harder. Out of the corner of my eye, I see him duck to the left in an attempt to pass me. As I move to block him, he quickly deeks right and just like that, he's beside me. I look over to see his face but he's staring straight ahead. The only proof that he realizes I'm here is the ghost of a smile on his lips. My annoyance builds but before I can let it loose, he turns his head to face me, eyes glinting with mischief. His chest is heaving and it fills me with pride to know he's working hard to keep up with me.

"What'd you think, *sweetheart?* Can you give me more?" he taunts. Then with a cocky smile, he pulls ahead of me.

Well, if I wasn't already sweating, that would've done it.

Refusing to be left behind, I give every last ounce of effort, pumping my legs harder until I'm beside him again and we're matching each other stride for stride.

Faster.

Harder.

Just a little more.

We pass the last row of trees and practically fall into the clearing at the same time. Luke bends at the waist to catch his breath while I throw myself onto the ground, heaving for air. He looks down at me in concern until I grin widely up at him. Then I burst into laughter.

Maybe it's adrenaline. Maybe it's exhaustion from sprinting the last couple hundred metres. Maybe I've finally gone insane.

Either way, I can't stop the laughter from pouring out of me. Brushing aside a tear (or bead of sweat because at this point it could be either), I look up at Luke expecting him to be staring down at me like the crazy lady I am.

But instead, he's grinning at me. And damn, if that man's smile doesn't make a sunset look like a bag of shit.

Then, as if I wasn't already blown away, he lets out a deep, booming laugh that causes his eyes to crinkle and my stomach do a funny flip.

As we sit there, laughing together like old friends, I can't help thinking there might be more to Luke Brady than I thought.

CHAPTER 13

LUKE

I haven't always been such a miserable prick. In fact, I used to be a pretty fun guy back in high school. But that was before my dad got sick. Before all the pressure, the expectations. The crushing, suffocating weight of responsibility.

Trust me, I'd love nothing more than to kick back and relax without a care in the world. To fuck around like any other bonehead my age.

But I don't have that luxury. I have a whole town to protect. A town that seems to be hell-bent on burning itself to the ground. Sometimes it feels like all I do all day is run around putting out fires. The kind that a careless teenager starts when they're left alone with a flamethrower—pointless but no less destructive.

Don't get me wrong, I'm thankful that our real emergencies are few and far between. But it's days like today, when I was called out to the senior center's knitting club to break up a fight between two elderly members, when I feel like more of a glorified babysitter than a police chief.

I shove my metal spatula under the slab of meat on the barbeque in frustration. Flipping it over, I take a long pull of my beer, hoping the satisfying sizzle from the juices touching the hot grill will soothe my troubles. The kitchen (or in this case, my back porch) is the only place that I allow myself to just go with the flow.

Feeling a little adventurous? I'll toss in a little extra cayenne to my pasta sauce. Rainy day? Beef stew on the couch will warm me up. Missing my dad a little extra? Nothing makes me feel closer to him than whipping up a pot of his famous chili.

It might not make sense to everyone, but there's nothing more calming after a long day of work than turning off the methodical part of my brain and just doing whatever feels right in the moment.

The doorbell rings through the house, loud enough for me to hear it from the back porch. Turning the burners down low and moving my burgers from the heat, I hang my spatula on the ring beside the barbecue and head back inside to the front door.

I pull open the door, only to be assaulted by a loud shout of "trick-or-treat!" before I can get a word out.

There's a group of the Avengers standing on my front step. A fierce-looking Scarlet Witch stands next to a dorky looking Iron Man. An excited Spider-Man bounces in place before me while the Hulk licks his balls behind him.

Matt lifts his mask to beam at me. "How cool is this? My first family Halloween costume. Pretty good, eh?"

Avery smiles up at him. It's pretty cute to see the three of them together like this. Or four if you're including Ham in all his Hulk-ish glory.

Matt has always loved Halloween. Every year for as long as I can remember, he made it his mission to come up with new and unique ideas for the two of us to dress up as. When Rhett moved to town, Matt jumped at the chance to include him in our group costumes. The rest is history.

Or I wish it was.

We've been the Three Stooges, Ron, Hermoine and Harry from Harry Potter, the Powerpuff Girls (don't ask), and Charlie's Angels (*please*, don't ask).

I don't mind Halloween. It's kind of fun to see what costumes he'll come up with every year. I will give him this, he's creative. But I'll never tell him that.

It's too fun to make him beg.

Gavin taps me on the leg from behind his Spider-Man mask. I bend to one knee so I'm eye-level with him.

"I said trick-or-treat, Uncle Luke. That means you're s'posed to give me candy now," he informs me seriously.

Avery gasps. "Gavin Owen Olsen! You do not demand candy. Just because it's Halloween doesn't mean—"

I lift my hand to cut her off. "He's right, Ave," I say, exaggerating what Matt calls my "cop voice". "The Constitution of Canada clearly states that any superheroes that come knocking on your door on the 31st of October and utter the phrase 'trick-or-treat' shall be entitled to compensation in the means of candy." I take a step into the house and grab the bowl of treats sitting on my entryway table. I toss a handful into Gavin's pillowcase and shoot him a wink.

"Thanks, Uncle Luke!" Gavin grins up at his mom who is currently giving me the stink eye. I shrug innocently to which she shakes her head, rolling her eyes. Gavin hops off my porch, calls out a goodbye then goes shooting off to the next house with Ham trailing behind him. Avery waves a quick goodbye then rushes after him.

Matt hangs back, digging into his own pillowcase. He

pulls out a white and red costume and shoves it into my chest. Then he pulls out a round plastic shield and passes it to me. "Here's your costume." He glares at me when I go to protest. "Don't give me any belly-aching about costumes being lame. You're lame."

He points at the costume. "Now get dressed and meet us at The Dive at nine." Matt looks over to where Avery is trying to catch up to Gavin as he runs to the next house. "Gavin should be in bed by then, or at least in a sugar coma." He grins. "I should go catch up. I'll see you tonight." He turns to jog down my walkway. "Wear the damn costume!" he shouts over his shoulder.

He takes off running, scooping up a laughing Gavin and spinning him around. Then he places him back on the ground and drops an arm around Avery's shoulder. Pulling her to him, he drops a kiss onto the top of her head and then they continue on their way down the street.

With a small smile, I close the door and turn on the porch light to signal to trick-or-treaters that my house is open for business.

No, I don't mind Halloween. I might even like it if it wasn't for the drunken idiots and troublemaking teenagers. But as it always seems to go, one person has to ruin the fun for everyone else. Which is where I come in.

That's the thing about being an officer; you have to stop the fun before it becomes a problem. Which usually means you're no one's favorite person. It's a shitty trade off to keep everyone safe—even from themselves. Even tonight, on my night off, I won't be able to let loose and have a bunch of drinks like most of the people at The Dive's annual Halloween party.

In a town this small, we take care of our own. With the next closest police station at least a thirty minute drive away, if an emergency happens and we need to call for backup, it'll be a while before anyone shows up. We're on our own out here, which means, as police chief, I'm never really off-duty.

Our town is pretty tame for the most part, especially this time of the year when we're between tourist seasons—after all of the cottagers have gone home and before the snow arrives. But I still like to stay sober on major holidays while the rest of the town is celebrating.

Between knocks on my door from trick-or-treaters, I head back to take my burger off the barbecue. Then I drain the water from the steamer and scoop a large portion of veggies onto my plate. I'm just about to dig into my dinner at the kitchen island when the doorbell rings.

After waving goodbye to the trick-or-treaters, I pass the costume I dropped onto the entryway table and pause. Lifting the costume, I hold it in front of me then burst out laughing, shaking my head in disbelief.

Matt bought me a Captain America costume but instead of the American flag suit with a star on the shield, it's red and white like the Canadian flag. There's also a large red maple leaf on the shield. I check the tag and sure enough, *Captain Canada* is printed neatly across it.

Asshole.

CHAPTER 14

JOLIE

"Brenna, quit worrying. You look hot. I wouldn't let you go out looking anything less than your best."

We're at my apartment getting ready for the Halloween party at The Dive. The trick-or-treaters have all come and gone home to devour their candy. Meanwhile, Brenna and I are applying the last of our makeup in front of the full-length mirror in my bedroom, sipping on drinks and snacking on the leftover Halloween candy.

Don't judge me. We all do it.

When Avery told us that her, Gavin, and Matt were going as the Avengers, I knew we had to keep the superhero theme going. But instead of the heroes, Brenna and I decided to dress up as villains. Just to keep things spicy.

Which is why I'm adjusting my vibrant red wig for my Poison Ivy costume while Brenna pulls at the leather jumpsuit that is her Catwoman costume.

"Are you sure this isn't too much?" Brenna asks for the fifteenth time since she put it on.

Brenna's a very modest person so when she agreed to be Catwoman, I was pleasantly surprised. When I suggested the costume, I didn't think she'd agree. Not because I didn't think she could pull it off. She's just so damn self-conscious. I'd love to know what caused her to have such a low regard for herself so I could squash the idea like a bug.

She's strong and smart. She built a successful non-profit when she was in her early twenties. She's cute and curvy and has a kick-ass sense of humor when you pull her out of her shell.

Brenna mentioned that she's been wanting to try dating so I've been trying to take her out of her comfort zone a little more. She's not naive, but she's inexperienced and I could see assholes taking advantage of that if she's not careful.

Like that fuckwad Tad tried to do.

I'm trying to help her build some confidence. If she can see her worth, then no man will be able to tell her otherwise.

"It's not too much. Nothing is ever 'too much'. Take that phrase out of your vocabulary. If you like it, who cares what other people think?" I turn to check out her costume. "You look sexy, girl. You're going to knock the socks off of every guy in the bar tonight."

Brenna blushes and opens her mouth but I spin her toward the mirror before she can object. "Look at yourself. You look stunning. But you're more than just your looks. You're smart, you're funny and you have a bigger heart than anyone I know. You own a damn business, woman! You're a badass. Start acting like it." I give her a playful smack on the arm and she laughs.

Her tension dissolves before my eyes, which was exactly what I had hoped would happen. She inspects herself in the mirror, a small smile forming on her lips as she does.

I know she has the confidence inside of her. I see it every time we're hanging out or when she's with her dogs and she lets her guard down. She keeps it buried so deep that sometimes she needs some help to dig it back up. Which I'm more than happy to help her do.

Then I'm determined to bury the hole it's been hiding in.

"Alright, fine. But I might need a couple of these to get me there." She picks up her cider and takes a sip. She sits on my colorful duvet and sways with the music pumping through my speaker.

"Whatever you want, Bren." I tip my drink back and finish the rest of the can in one gulp. Leaning over, I tap the screen of my phone to check the time.

"You just about ready? Avery said she'd be at The Dive around nine and it's almost ten to nine now."

Brenna nods and follows my lead finishing her drink. "Let's go."

Then we grab our purses and head out the door, looking every bit like the badasses we are.

———

WHEN WE ARRIVE at The Dive, the bar is already packed. A Friday night at The Dive is usually a busy place but add in a Halloween costume party and it's chaos. Reaching behind me, I grab Brenna's hand and lead the way toward the bar, scanning for Avery as we go.

As we make our way through the crowd, I take in the costumes around me. Leah Morrow and her husband, Ace, are dressed as Mr. and Mrs. Potato Head. Lenny Thompson is dressed as Captain Jack Sparrow and demonstrating his impression of Jack's famous run. A group of women that I don't recognize are dressed in men's clothing. It takes me a second to realize they are all dressed as different Will

Farrell characters. I laugh out loud at the creative costumes. Cupping a hand around my mouth, I shout to the group. "Stay classy, San Diego!" The women cheer and raise their drinks, whooping in excitement.

Finally, we make our way to the bar where Rhett is serving drinks dressed as Thor. I have to admit, he looks damn good. If there was even an ounce of chemistry between the two of us, I might flirt with him. Rhett is tall, tattooed and muscular. Mix that with his fun personality and he's definitely more my usual type. But alas, there's not even a stirring of butterflies in my stomach when I look at him. There's no spark of awareness as he smiles over at me and grabs our orders.

Oh, well. C'est la vie.

Rhett passes over our drinks. I try to thank him but it's too loud for him to hear, so he simply nods his acknowledgement. I mouth "Avery?" in question and he points toward the end of the bar where Matt, Avery and Luke are sitting at a high-top table. I lift my drink in cheers and he waves then turns to the next patron.

I hand Brenna her beer then motion for her to follow me. We duck under Buzz Lightyear's elbow and swerve out of the way of a couple of guys joined together with a white shirt dressed as a makeshift bra. Finally, we arrive at the high top table.

Avery whistles low. "Wow! You ladies look hot!" she shouts over the noise.

I toss her a wink. "Damn right, we do." I slide onto a bar stool beside her. "You don't look so bad yourself, sexy mama."

She's dressed in a bright red bodysuit and leather pants with a bright red cape tied around her waist. She styled her already wavy hair into loose curls with a matching red headpiece set on top. Her dramatic makeup accentuates her big golden eyes. She makes a damn good Scarlet Witch. By the way Matt hasn't been able to keep his hands off her since we sat down, I'm thinking he agrees.

I won't bother holding my breath that they'll stay the entire night. It's rare these days that they get night out to just have fun so it wouldn't surprise me if they went back to Matt's old apartment (now art studio) for some alone time.

In fact, I'd be a little disappointed if they didn't. They deserve it.

Matt frowns. "Um, excuse me. I'm right here. It's not easy to pull off an Iron Man costume, you know. The armor covers all of my muscles and you can't even see my beautiful face."

"No one wants to see your ugly mug anyway." Luke smirks, taking a drink of his beer while ducking from Matt's punch.

"Well, I think you make a very sexy Tony Stark." Avery leans over and kisses Matt's cheek. She goes to pull away, but he tugs her back to him to give her a longer kiss on the mouth. When he finally lets her go, they only have eyes for each other.

Yeah, they're definitely leaving early tonight.

Giving the lovebirds some privacy, I turn to Luke beside me. Taking a second to check out his costume, I snort out a laugh. "Really? Who are you, Captain Canada?" I lean toward him conspiringly. "Didn't you know, you're supposed to dress up on Halloween?"

Luke rolls his eyes but there's a hint of a smile on his face. "Yeah, yeah. I've heard it all already. At least it's not the Powerpuff Girls again."

My eyes widen in shock then I throw my head back laughing. "You're joking. You wore a Powerpuff Girl costume? No way." I snicker again at the thought of big burly Luke in a dress. "I need proof. Right now."

Luke shakes his head. "No way. This was before people had cameras on their phones. The only proof of that Halloween was burned a long time ago."

I sigh. "Boring." There's a flicker in his eyes but it's gone before I can distinguish its meaning.

I give my drink a pensive stir. "I can't decide who you'd be. Blossom was clearly the boss, which definitely screams you. But Buttercup was the badass bitch who hated everyone and I mean..." I wave my hand up and down at him, "that's got you written all over it. Bubbles is way too cutesy, unless you were doing it ironically."

He grimaces and my jaw drops. "Oh my god. You were Bubbles, weren't you?" He shrugs, but I can see his lips tipping like he's fighting a smile. "Did you have pigtails? Please tell me you had pigtails."

He looks over at me for a second as if deciding whether to answer. Finally, he sighs. "Yeah, there were pigtails." I throw my head back laughing again. "Matt thought it would be funny to make me the perky one. The wig was ridiculous but the dress was surprisingly comfortable."

I give him an incredulous look and he chuckles. "You don't think I could pull off a dress? I'll have you know these legs look damn good in a dress."

I can't stop laughing and this time, he joins me. I always forget how nice of a laugh Luke has. Probably because he keeps it tucked away, saving it for a special moment.

Like the other morning when we ran together. I'm still shocked that we managed to spend an entire run without arguing once. I mean, it did start as a challenge that he threw down. But that was the longest we've been around each other without fighting. It wasn't so bad. And—gun to my head—Luke wasn't entirely unpleasant either.

"Is that why you're not out dancing?" I ask, nodding toward the dance floor. "You forgot your party dress at home?"

"I don't dance, sweetheart." He smirks at me. "Sorry about your luck."

I roll my eyes. "In your dreams, Chief." He winks and takes a long drink of his beer, watching me over the bottle.

Whew. Is it hot in here?

"Well, would you look at that," Matt comments and we both turn to look at where he, Avery and Brenna are watching us. "Looks like the truce is working already." He grins. "Who knows? Maybe you'll even become friends by the wedding."

Luke grunts and I take a drink to avoid answering. Because as much as I hate to admit it, this new side of Luke isn't completely terrible.

Avery and Brenna exchange a look. Brenna looks like she's trying to solve a math equation that's on my face. Meanwhile, Avery is smiling triumphantly at me as if she knows something I don't. I lean back in my chair, trying to pay attention to the band and avoid both of their stares.

While Matt might be oblivious, it seems the rest of the table is aware of a shift happening.

I'm just not sure if I'm ready for it.

LUKE

"Who knows? Maybe you'll even become friends by the wedding," Matt comments casually. Then he turns his attention to the band, unaware of the bomb he just dropped on our table.

Friends? Me and Jolie? I scoff at the thought.

I sneak a look over at her. She's doing her best not to look at her friends, staring into her drink then over at the band. I can feel the discomfort radiating off of her from here. My stomach twists and I have the overwhelming urge to reach out and touch her. To offer her comfort. To say something to make her smile.

I mentally slam on the brakes. *What the hell?* Since when do I care about comforting Jolie? She's never once cared about my feelings, so why should I care about hers? We don't have that kind of relationship. We're not friends and we never will be.

So why am I suddenly leaning closer?

Conversation shifts to the wedding, but I tune it out. Instead, I'm watching Jolie. She's listening raptly as Avery goes into detail on how the venue will be set up and the flowers she's chosen. That's one thing I can't deny: Jolie is a great friend. She's attentive, loyal and fiercely protective of her friends.

Just ask that douchebag Chesterfield's nose.

I still feel like an asshole for the way I acted that night. She brings out the worst in me and I hate that even more. But there's no excuse for me assuming the worst of her. In a world where men are believed far too often over women, I shouldn't have jumped to conclusions the way I did—no matter our history. Especially as an officer.

Even though I feel bad about my reaction, I can't condone the way she went about it. Sure, in high school I would've jumped head first into a fight to defend Matt or Rhett. But you can't go around punching people in the face when you're an adult.

Just another example of Jolie's impulsiveness and complete disregard for consequences.

A loud crash from the front of the room pulls my attention away from my ping-ponging thoughts. I look up to see a stumbling Spice Girl pushing her way onto the stage beside the lead singer of the band. In her haste to climb on stage, she knocked over one of the high top chairs, causing the crash.

My back straightens as my body automatically goes into work mode. I don't recognize her as a local so she must be a tourist or someone here for the band. Assessing the scene, I watch as the woman rotates her hips beside the singer then leans in to shout along the lyrics. The singer, obviously used to drunk crowds, smiles stiffly while continuing to sing. He turns his back to her, blocking her from reaching the microphone, which stops her mid-dance.

She frowns, her arms flopping to her sides as sways on her feet. "What the fuck?" she yells over the music.

I scan the room for security. One of the bouncers is busy at the entrance checking IDs and the other is showing another patron the door.

Rhett is watching the scene from behind the bar. He's trying to push his way through the crowd to get to the stage but he's blocked in by the many thirsty bodies.

I lock eyes with him and give him a small nod before shoving aside my drink to stand. I'm only a few tables away from the stage and closer than him, so I pull myself to my feet, decision made. Pushing past the dancing bodies, I make my way to the front of the stage where the drunk woman is making another grab for the microphone. The singer blocks her move, sweeping the microphone from the stand and taking a few steps away from her and toward the front of the stage.

I have two choices: I could wait until the woman gets closer to the edge and lift her down from the stage. Or I could push my way around to the back of the stage and get to her that way.

The first would be the fastest but could spell trouble. I'm not in uniform (this stupid red and white costume doesn't count) and a random man grabbing a woman, even if to get her out of harm's way, is a fast-track to a sketchy grey area in propriety.

The second is a safer bet but I'm not sure if I trust myself to get to her fast enough before she falls off the stage and hurts either herself or someone else.

The last thing Rhett needs would be a liability claim if she fell off or took the microphone from a band member. He prides himself on providing a safe place both for people to listen to music and bands to perform in. He worked hard to make The Dive's reputation what it is today. I'm not about to let that be thrown away over a Spice Girl.

Even if that means I might get in trouble.

As expected, the woman follows the singer toward the edge. I'm just about to lean forward to make a grab for her when a bright green figure flashes in the corner of my eye.

I turn in time to see Jolie climb on top of a high top chair, then stretch one of her long legs over and step onto the stage. One hand holding onto the back of the chair for balance, she pulls herself onto the stage. How she manages to do all that in heels higher than the Rockies is beyond me.

I watch, transfixed, as she struts over to the drunk Spice Girl. I place my hands flat on the stage, intending to stop whatever the hell Jolie's planning.

Just as I'm about to heft myself up, Jolie wraps an arm around the Spice Girl's shoulders and pulls her closer. But instead of the headlock I'm expecting (because, come on, it's Jolie), she hugs the woman toward her and away from the lead singer. Then she tips her head back and belts out the lyrics to the song playing.

As most drunk people tend to do, the woman leans into Jolie as if they've known each other their whole lives and joins her in singing. Subtly, so subtly that if I wasn't watching them intently, I might not have noticed, Jolie guides the Spice Girl away from the edge of the stage and toward the steps in the back. All while continuing to sing and dance.

The song ends and Jolie and the woman clap and cheer. Then Jolie turns and guides the woman down the steps and back onto the dance floor. She then says something that has the woman throwing her head back laughing, causing her to stumble. That makes her laugh even harder as Jolie guides her back to what appears to be the woman's group of friends.

Safely tucking her away from trouble, Jolie leaves the woman with her friends and saunters over to where I'm standing dumbfounded. She notices me watching and dips at the waist in a bow. "Thank you, thank you. I'll be here all night," she jokes as she approaches.

She smiles up at me then turns beside me to watch the band, swaying to the song. I stare down at her, shock and irritation splayed across my face.

Does she even realize how badly that could've gone?

Dealing with drunk people is one of the most difficult parts of being a police officer in a small town. We don't have much in the way of crime but we have our fair share of tourists out for a good time. Rhett does a good job of keeping people from getting too out of control, but it's not always easy.

Drunk people are unpredictable and impulsive—my two least favorite attributes. There's so many ways Jolie's intervention could've ended badly. She could've somehow offended the woman on stage and ended up in a fight. The woman could've pushed away from Jolie, lost her footing and fallen off the stage. If she was injured, she might've sued The Dive. Then Rhett would lose his bar and be swimming in a sea of legal fees for years.

Somewhere deep in the back of my head, I know she was just trying to help. But you can't just act without a plan. Or at the very least, without thinking your actions through. People could get hurt as a result of that kind of negligence. I should calmly explain that to her. But instead, as I always seem to do around Jolie, I lose my cool.

"That was pretty stupid," I state, glaring down at her. The smile on her face melts instantly into a frown.

"Pretty sure the word you're looking for is 'fantastic'. Or maybe even 'thank you for doing my job for me, Jolie'." She shakes her head, turning her attention back to the band. "Unbelievable."

"What's unbelievable is how little you actually think before acting. Do you have any idea how badly that could've gone?"

She turns to face me. The look on her face is homicidal. She steps forward until we're practically touching. I shove aside the hum of awareness that runs through me from her being so close.

"As much as you like to believe otherwise, I'm not an idiot. I was a bartender for years and have dealt with a lot worse than Scary Spice over there." She laughs humorlessly. My temper spikes at the sound. "Which you would know if you bothered to treat me as anything more than the gum on your shoe. I'm a real person with real thoughts and feelings."

She spins on her heel and stalks back toward where Matt, Avery and Brenna are sitting. Even though my temper is ready to blow, I watch as her body relaxes the farther she gets from me. I give into the impulse to shove a hand through my hair. *Damn, woman.*

But as much as I want to deny it, there's a part of me deep in my gut that knows she's right. I've gone so long thinking of Jolie as a thorn on a rose stem that I forget she's not all bad. If I'm being honest, I always thought she hated me so I didn't think anything of it when I'd let loose on her. Better to let her see me as an asshole than have her realizing my secret.

Because Jolie is the one person who could take me to my

knees if she tried. As police chief, I can't afford to let anyone have that kind of control over me. No matter how much I want her. No matter how much I crave her sassy mouth.

None of that matters. So I'll continue to shove my wants and desires deep down inside me.

Like I've always done.

"For the love of Betty White, stop staring at me!"

The red notification badge on my email app blinks back at me, taunting me from my screen. That little asshole's number has been increasing steadily since I opened my laptop this morning and hasn't stopped since.

The responsible thing to do would be to sit down and go through each email until the number of unread ones are at a more manageable number.

Yeah, right. What am I? An adult or something?

Instead, the anxiety I have from watching each new email come in has me paralyzed in procrastination, delaying the inevitable.

At least half of that number has to be junk mail, right? For all I know, I have 16 unread coupons from Bath and Body Works. Or I won that hospital 50/50 I bought tickets for last week. I could be a millionaire and not even know it. But I'll never know because I'm sitting here staring at my laptop like it has rabies and is ready to pounce on me if I so much as push a key.

Okay, J. Where's your lady balls? You can do this. You don't have to respond to every single email.

Oh god, that's daunting.

No, stop that. You are a strong and powerful woman who is not afraid of an overwhelming amount of emails.

I plop down onto my couch, lifting my laptop from its place on my coffee table and place it onto my lap. Bracing myself, I open my email app and watch as another new email pops into my inbox. I scroll through the emails, deleting the junk mail as I go, which is disappointingly less than I hoped. Even after getting rid of all of the spam, I'm left with 39 unread emails.

Mother of Miley Cyrus. I groan. This is what I get for agreeing to have all of the column questions sent directly to me. Well, technically the emails are sent to the general email address *The Haven Times* created to remain anonymous. But it was my stupid idea to have both the general email and my personal email all in the same app. So now all of my personal emails and the *Dear Annie* emails fill my inbox like one big overflowing volcano ready to erupt, spewing discount codes and angry old ladies all over.

I quickly scan my personal emails, finding one from my mom checking in. She fills me in on life back in Ontario and how they went to one of my brother's games the previous night. There's a picture attached of her and my father, her grinning at the camera while he frowns next to her. She's wearing my brother's jersey but he's in a generic dark shirt.

Obviously, my father could not have been bothered to wear a Toronto Storm jersey. Risk his reputation as a tight-laced stick in the mud to support his son? Fat chance. You'd have a better chance of getting Dottie to give up sex for a month than catch my father wearing something as trivial as a hockey jersey.

I shoot off a response back to her, avoiding any mention of my father. I've tried explaining how to send pictures through texts to my mom multiple times but she can't seem to figure it out, so she continues to send them through email. My brother and I like to laugh about how technologically illiterate she is but we love her too much to say it to her face. She tries, which is more than I can say for her husband.

I click through a few more personal emails then switch to the *Dear Annie* inbox. There's a handful of emails thanking *Annie* for her advice—I like to leave those ones for last because they make me smile—and another ten or so emails asking for advice. Then there's my least favorite: the hate mail. There's only a few this week but I dread opening them every time.

There's been an outpouring of positive feedback from the column. So much so that Sandy has decided to make it a permanent feature in the paper. But like all good things in life, there's always a few people more than willing to rain all over other people's parades.

I like to call those people my haters. Makes me feel like Taylor Swift. Sometimes after a particularly rude email, I blast *Shake It Off* and dance around my living room with my middle fingers in the air. It helps keep my mood from plummeting when Joe Shmoe is calling me a nosey bitch with no life.

Hello, pot? It's kettle.

I click through the hate mail, barely scanning over the words as I delete each one. I'm not in the mood to be told off by some internet warriors hiding behind their computer screen.

I'm talking to you, peachpielover99.

I'm about to hit 'delete' on the next one when my eyes catch on two words—*find you*. Against my better judgment,

I expand the preview to show the full email. My eyes quickly scan over the content, growing bigger as I read the email again. It's short but to the point.

You better watch your back, bitch. I'm going to find you and ruin you. The way you ruined me.

Um, the fuck?

A shiver runs up my spine as I read it a third time. Usually emails from angry readers are more geared toward a specific letter or arguing about why my advice is wrong and how I should've answered. I've never had any that are intimidating or threatening.

But this email is both.

I try to shake off the feeling of unease. It's probably just an angry husband who's pissed off I told his wife that no, having to work a full-time job then coming home to cook, clean and take care of her kids while her husband naps on the couch is not fair to her.

Or maybe it's the girlfriend of the man I told that if he was unhappy working two jobs to pay for his girlfriend's shopping addiction, he should tell her.

Either way, I'm sure it's like every other angry email I've received—all talk and no action.

A loud crash sounds from outside my window and I jump in my seat, barely stifling a scream. I whirl around to peek out the window from behind my curtain. All the air whooshes out of my body in relief when I see the cause of the noise.

Jake Fenton and his brother Sam are struggling to move Jake's old dryer into the back of his truck. Looks like Jake dropped his side and Sam is reaming him out for almost scratching his truck.

Trying to calm my racing heart, I let out another slow breath. I think that's enough creepy letters for one day.

Quickly deleting the email, I force my hands to steady as I click on the next. It's from a real reader looking for advice. I let myself relax into the couch as I read.

Dear Annie,

My husband passed away two years ago this December. We were together for nineteen wonderful years and were blessed with two children. I miss him every day.

Lately, my friends and family have suggested that I should start dating again. While I know they mean well, I'm nowhere near ready to jump into dating, when the death of my husband still seems so fresh.

How do I nicely tell them that, while their intentions may be good, I'm not interested?

Sincerely,

Grieving

My eyes fall closed as I take a second to gather myself. That's the funny thing about grief. They say that time heals all, but grief is one wound that never truly heals. It will scab over, only to be ripped open again when you least expect it. Eventually it will scar, leaving behind a permanent reminder of what you lost.

All it takes is a certain smell as you pass by the bakery or a song that comes on the radio and you're taken back to the day you last felt their arms wrapped around you.

Some might think it's weird that I'm still grieving as hard as I am over the loss of my grandpa, even though it's been almost ten years. But my grandpa and I had a special bond.

Growing up, my father and I had a tenuous relationship at best. My father is a proud and strict man. He likes things to always be just so. When something or someone doesn't fall perfectly in line with his expectations, he berates them or belittles them until they eventually give in.

Enter his spirited, fly-by-the-seat-of-her-pants daughter. He tried for years to get me to fall into line, to extinguish my creative flame that he despised so much. To him, my outgoing, dreamy, and unpredictable nature was something to be ashamed of and fought for years to change.

But I wasn't my mother. I wasn't going to let him control me the way he did her.

As I got older, my house became more of a prison than a home. The more boundaries and limits my father came up with to keep me in line, the more I pushed back. If he took away my stereo for playing Eminem instead of classical music, I'd rap the songs from memory at dinner. If he told me the band shirts I loved to wear made me look like a hippie, I dyed my hair pink and wore only tie-dyed clothes for a month.

My mom was a good mom but she always had an excuse for him tucked up her sleeve, ready to pull out at a moment's notice.

"Your dad's under a lot of stress at work."

"You two don't have anything in common. It will be easier when you're older."

"He's just not sure what to do with a daughter."

My brother tried to stand up for me but he had his own battles with my father. My father put a lot of pressure on him between school and working part-time. Hockey was Austin's escape.

The only person who really understood me was Grandpa Joe. He was my mom's father and the man I was named after. Grandpa Joe was the kindest and most genuine man you'd ever meet. Even near the end, he was sharper than a whip and could tell stories that would make a sailor blush. He was my safe place, my kindred spirit and my biggest fan.

Once, our whole family went to the flea market, including Grandpa Joe. It was one of those rare days when my father and I got along. After stuffing our faces with pretzels the size of a basketball, we walked around to check out some of the booths.

I found this hideously adorable poster of an Italian Greyhound dog wearing a tophat and a ridiculously large bowtie. I instantly fell in love with it and knew exactly where I would hang it in my room. My father hated the poster and refused to buy it for me. He said it was too weird and childish, right in front of the artist. If his refusal didn't convince me to buy it, the devastated look on the artist's face solidified it.

When I went to pay for it with my birthday money, my father threatened to not let me go on my grade eight graduation trip. After an especially brutal fight that lasted the entire drive home and into the night, I came home from school the next day to that very poster, framed and lying on my bed with a note stuck on it. It read: *Stay weird, Blue Jay.*

Blue Jay was the nickname Grandpa Joe had given me when I was just a baby. He used to tell me that the day I was born, my mom handed me over to him, crying and screaming. As soon as I was in his arms, I instantly calmed and stared up at him with wide eyes. He said that looking into my blue eyes reminded him of a blue jay, full of courage and curiosity.

Grandpa Joe was the person I was closest to and the only person I felt truly comfortable to be myself around. When his health started to decline, I spent every day after school at his house. We'd play cards, watch old Western movies or I'd read to him. Sometimes I'd just listen as he told me story after story from his younger years.

One day, my mom called while I was at school and before she even said the words, I knew. He was gone. He'd passed in his sleep, she told me. Just like he always wanted.

I was devastated. The only man I respected was gone.

No more long talks from his Lazy-Boy chair.

No more life advice over the Chess board.

No more warm hugs with his lanky but strong arms wrapped around me, squeezing me tightly, never letting go first.

Most days, I'm able to think about him and smile at the memories. But every once and a while, like now, the grief runs me over like a semi-truck.

I take a deep breath then sit up a little straighter. Pulling the laptop further onto my lap, I start typing.

DEAR GRIEVING,

I want to start off by saying I am so incredibly sorry for your loss. I cannot begin to imagine the heartache you're feeling and I hope you find support during this difficult time.

Now, if there's one thing you take from my advice, I hope it's this: grief has no timeline. Grief is not linear. It's not something that lessens as time passes. Some days you can focus on the good times and smile at the memories. Others, it might feel like just getting out of bed in the morning is a huge feat.

Do what feels right for you.

If you're not ready to date, please don't feel pressured to. You're not doing yourself a service by forcing yourself into something you're not comfortable with.

Some people find grief easier to deal with when they have someone by their side. Some people find they don't need another partner and are content to have had their love story already.

And you know what? Neither are wrong.

There's no right or wrong when it comes to grieving a loved one—whether it's your husband, your grandparent, or your best friend. Grief is grief. Take the time to feel every part of it because some days you'll be able to carry it like a feather pillow and other days it'll be as immovable as a boulder.

Listen to their favorite song. Put on that jacket they used to love that still smells like them. Watch that movie you two watched together every Christmas. Do whatever it is that makes you feel closest to them and feel all your feelings.

But do it for you, no one else.

Love always,

Annie

I HIT Save on the copy of my response so I can proof it later before sending it over to Sandy. I try to scroll through some more emails but the weight of grief pulls me deeper and deeper until I can feel the tears welling up in my eyes. Shutting my laptop, I drop my head into my hands. I push my palms into my eyes so hard I see white, attempting to stop the tears from spilling over but it's no use.

A sob rips through my throat as the tears pour out of me and down my cheeks. As I've done so many times before, I wish my grandpa could see me today.

Well, not exactly like this. He'd hate seeing me cry like

this. If he saw me right now, he'd probably say something like, "No use crying over something you can't change, Blue Jay." Then he'd wipe away my tears and tell me to go outside and enjoy the sun.

Grandpa Joe was a firm believer that there wasn't anything a good drive with the windows down and the sun shining on your face couldn't fix.

He used to tell me that whenever he was missing his wife, Grandma Loretta, he'd take a drive in his old '55 Chevy and swear he could feel her sitting beside him. I never met Grandma Loretta since she passed away before I was born, but when he buckled me into his car and we'd drive around aimlessly, I believed him when he said she was with us.

Shoving aside the last of my tears, I push up from where I'm sitting on my couch and head toward the door. Stopping only long enough to grab my jacket from the rack, I check the pocket for my keys then take off down the steps of my apartment, hurrying across the studio. Yanking open the back door with a little more force than necessary, I cross the parking lot to where Blue sits waiting.

I slide onto the worn seat of my car and run my hand across the dashboard. The familiar feel of the leather sends a calming wave through my chest. I turn the key, back out of the parking space and head out down Main Street toward the county roads.

As I cross the townline, the houses give way to fields and open roads. I'm thankful I left the top down despite the weather starting to chill. It's a surprisingly warm day for November. I tilt my head up to the sky, letting the sunlight stream over my face. I bask in its warmth for a second longer before looking back to the road.

The old car is the exact same as it was the day my

grandpa handed me the keys. The only thing I've updated is the radio, which I convinced myself that my music-loving grandpa would've approved of. I turn the knob on the radio until the music mixes with the breeze whipping around me.

It's an old Sam Cook song from the 60s: *A Change Is Gonna Come*. It was a favorite of my grandpa's and I smile, feeling his presence as strongly as if he was sitting in the old seat beside me.

Luckily, mine is the only car on the dirt road. Needing to feel the roar of the engine in my chest, I press down harder on the gas pedal. Not quite fast enough to be dangerous but just enough to feel the life pumping through my veins.

As the song ends, I press a button on the radio to switch it over to my phone. I tap a button on the screen to start the playlist I made to remind me of my grandpa. Johnny Cash's deep voice croons through the speakers as *Riders In The Sky* plays. I let myself sink into the nostalgia like a warm bath. Lifting my hand, I let it float through the wind that whips past me as I drive down the dusty road.

Memories of him flood my mind. Him teaching me how to drive down a back road just like this one. Him kicking my ass at Rummy on a Saturday afternoon while my brother was playing hockey and my parents were at some work event. The two of us walking arm-in-arm through the park, waving to all of his neighbors as he showed off his "favorite granddaughter". I'd always laugh because I was his only granddaughter.

It makes me smile, realizing he probably said it just to hear me laugh.

My smile falls as the flashing lights in my rearview mirror catch my attention.

Shit balls.

I slow the car enough to pull to the side of the road, careful to keep away from the ditch below.

The police cruiser door swings open and out steps Luke. Of course, it's him. My day has been an emotional rollercoaster, so it only makes sense that he would show up now.

Before he became chief, when I'd be speeding down a back road and see those cherries flashing, I at least had a 1 in 20 shot that it would be Luke scowling down at me from above my driver's side window. Now, it seems like every speeding ticket, parking violation, or noise complaint always ends up with that damn smug face of his glaring back at me.

Once, when I complained about it to Avery, she said that Matt had told her Luke was pulling a lot of overtime, wanting to take a more hands-on approach than what the previous chief had done. Which isn't hard, seeing as though the last chief's idea of "hands-on" was going for runs to the diner and back. Chief Wilks was probably a great chief in his day, but the man barely left the station unless they ran out of snacks. He might have officially retired last winter but his level of drive had been depleted long before that.

I'd rather cut out my tongue with a butter knife than admit it, but Luke is the perfect guy for the job. Professional. Fair. Responsible. He's everything you'd want in a police chief.

To anyone but me.

With the way this man's mood swings around me, I have no idea what to expect when I see him, so I steel my spine.

He saunters up to the car. His sunglasses are covering his eyes, hiding any hint of emotion.

"License and registration, please."

CHAPTER 17

LUKE

I'm in a piss poor mood.

Two of my officers called in sick with the stomach flu that's been going around. On the same damn shift. Which is why I'm pulling a double, on my way back from a disturbance call after some rowdy tourists decided to try and do flips off of their Airbnb rental's roof and into the lake. A broken leg and a hefty fine later, one guy is in the back of an ambulance on his way to Bakersfield while the rest are packing their bags to go home.

Once they've sobered up, of course.

The owner, Tilly Green, wasn't too happy and had already given them a few warnings over the weekend. She kicked them out before the ambulance even arrived.

So when I saw that baby blue Mustang kicking up dust on my way back to town, I knew my day was about to get worse.

As I approached her car, the music that had been blaring through the speakers switched off.

Too bad. Johnny was just about to sing the ghost riders'

cry. That was my favorite part. Though I prefer to listen to it at a much more respectable volume.

I stop beside the driver's side door and peer down at her through my sunglasses. Her dark hair is wild and her cheeks are flushed from having the top down on her car. Her eyes are covered by her sunglasses but I imagine them looking just as free. The sight has me picturing her splayed out on my pillow, her cheeks flushed for an entirely different reason.

I clear my throat to shove the image aside. She frowns and arches an eyebrow at me. She must think the sound was out of impatience rather than what it was, but no way I'm going to correct her. Not only would she not believe me, I don't need her to know just how much control she has over me.

"License and registration, please."

"You can't be serious." Disdain drips from her voice as her brow arches impossibly higher.

"It's standard protocol. I'm sure this isn't your first time being pulled over, Miss St. James." I reach a hand out to her, showing her exactly how serious I am.

She scoffs then turns to grab her wallet. Then she leans over to rifle through her predictably messy glove compartment. The only predictable thing about Jolie is how absolutely chaotic she is. It only seems fitting that her car is the same way.

She turns back to me, practically shoving her driver's license, insurance and ownership into my waiting hand.

"Oh, that's right." I snap my fingers in recognition. "You have been pulled over before. Exactly seven times, if I remember correctly." I tisk at her as I examine her license. I don't know why I'm antagonizing her, but I can't seem to help myself. "Pretty expensive habit to get into. Those tickets really add up."

"I wouldn't know. Those officers of yours have never given me one. Apparently, I'm too sweet for tickets." The smile she flashes me is anything but.

This time it's my turn to scoff. Jolie? Sweet? That's probably the last term I'd use to describe her. Stubborn? Definitely. Charming? Sure. But sweet? She's about as sweet as a lemon.

"Seems like I need to have a word with my officers then." I turn her license over in my hand, hanging onto it for longer than necessary. "Flirting your way out of a speeding ticket is a little immature, wouldn't you say?"

"Not if it works." She makes a grab for her license, only for me to pull it away at the last second. She lets out an exasperated sigh then shoves her sunglasses on top of her head. "Not that I don't love our little chats, Chief, but are we done here?"

It's then that I notice the red rimming her eyes. Without her sunglasses on, her face seems paler and the pink on her cheeks looks like it's more from crying than from the wind.

My spine straightens as panic fights its way up my neck. Jolie doesn't cry. I saw a few tears escape when Matt and Avery got engaged but she's not a crier like Avery. She's tough; as immovable as a brick wall.

Whatever made her cry must be bad. My mind starts to race. I break out in a sweat. *It's fine. Everyone's fine,* I assure my heartbeat that's hammering against my chest. If something happened to Matt or Avery or anyone else, someone would've called me. Everyone in my family, including Rhett, knows to call the station if there's an emergency. The entire department knows to radio me if anyone in my family so much as gets in a fender bender. I check the volume on the radio on my shoulder. It's working fine.

The tension in my shoulders eases slightly. No one's hurt. Everyone is fine.

The panic gives way to confusion. If no one is hurt, what could've possibly made Jolie cry? I don't know much about Jolie's life but I know enough to know that she and her family aren't close. In the five years she's lived here, she's only gone back to visit her family a handful of times and they've never come here. If someone asks about them, she usually gives a vague answer then changes the subject.

Did something happen to one of her family members?

Ah, shit. Well, now I feel like a grade A asshole. Here I am giving her shit for going a few kilometers over the speed limit while her cheeks are stained with tears.

I hand her back her cards. "Is, uh, everything okay?" I'm stumbling over my words like a teenager trying to ask out a girl for the first time.

It's not that I don't know how to be empathetic: I'm not a monster, despite what some people might write on the holding cell wall. It's just that I have a lot of other qualities that I tend to lean into first.

Apparently, I'm leaning into the awkward quality today.

She looks away, brushing a thumb under her eye in a motion I don't think I was meant to catch. She clears her throat. "Fine."

I know that should be my cue to let it go. To walk back to my cruiser and let her go back to the alone time she obviously wants.

But something about the way the tip of her nose has gone pink and the look of despair in her eyes makes me want to wrap my arms around her and hold her until whatever it is that's causing her pain can't anymore.

So instead of walking away, I take a step closer to her car. She looks up at me, confusion clear in her eyes.

"Look," I start, rubbing a palm over the back of my neck. "I know I'm not your favorite person and I know you'd probably rather have Avery or Brenna or even Rhett to talk to instead of me but if you wanted to talk about it—"

She lifts a hand and shakes her head. "I'm fine, Luke. Really. You don't have to do this."

"I don't *have* to do anything," I reply dryly. "Have you ever known me to do something I don't want to do?"

Jolie smirks up at me. "What about the Captain Canada costume?" she asks in a soft voice. Despite the joking, she seems more vulnerable than I've ever seen her. It's making me feel all kinds of confusing things that I'm not going to delve into.

"Can I tell you a secret?" I ask. She nods, a small smile playing on her lips. It's all the encouragement I need to continue, despite the fact I'm basically handing her the ammunition to make every Halloween miserable for the rest of my life. I lean forward then sneak a look over my shoulder as if to make sure no one can hear me. "I actually don't mind dressing up for Halloween," I whisper, conspiringly.

"No way." She gasps. "But you hate Halloween!" I shake my head slowly. Her mouth drops open, eyes wide. "You're telling me you secretly love dressing up in Powerpuff Girl costumes and taking ridiculous pictures with Matt and Rhett?"

I smirk. "Well, I could do without having to wear a dress again but yeah. It's actually kind of fun. I just like to give Matt shit about them."

She shakes her head again, this time her smile growing into a full grin. I can't help but smile back, knowing I put that grin on her face.

"You can never tell him though," I say. "I think half of his fun is thinking he's finding new ways to piss me off."

"That's every younger sibling's goal in life," she chuckles. "Your secret is safe with me." She looks down at her hands, considering. I think she's about to make some excuse and drive away before I hear her soft voice.

"I was thinking about my grandpa when you pulled me over. He passed away when I was in high school. Something happened today that reminded me of him and before I knew it, the grief was pulling me under."

She looks up at the sky, the grin from earlier long gone. "He gave me this car. He loved to drive around listening to music at the loudest volume. I think that was partly because of his hearing loss and partly because he was an awful singer and didn't want anyone to hear him." She chuckles at the memory. "I guess I just wanted to feel closer to him and this was the only way I could think of."

She closes her eyes, her head still tipped up. I remain quiet, not wanting to break the spell we're both under. For once, Jolie isn't being sarcastic or trying to bite my head off. We're not two people who can't stand to be in the same room as each other without starting a fight. We're not putting on an act to play nice in front of our friends.

We're just...us.

I turn to lean my back against the front end of her car. I cross my arms over my chest and look out at the field in front of me. The silence between us is calm and peaceful— two words I never thought I'd associate with Jolie and I.

"My dad died when I was in high school," I finally say. "He was sick for a couple years before that so it shouldn't have been a shock but it still felt like a kick in the gut when he finally passed."

Everyone in town knows the story of my dad's sickness. The town rallied to help us out when he was first diagnosed. From helping carpool us kids to school and sports to bringing over premade dinners as he got closer to the end, the town took care of us. When we needed them, they were there, without us having to ask. Helping your neighbors is just something you do in a small town.

I don't think anyone completely understands how much it meant to our family, knowing we had a whole town supporting us at our darkest time.

I'll never forget it.

"He was close with all of us kids, in our own way. Matt and him had the workshop. He and Tori used to spend hours listening to music. But for me, it was fishing." I look down at my feet and smile. "We weren't very good. More often than not, we'd go out and catch nothing but weeds." I lift my head and look back out over the field. "But we loved it. Sometimes Matt and Tori would come along but as we got older, they stopped coming out as much. Eventually, it was just me and my dad."

The car door opens then slams shut. Jolie leans back on it beside me. She doesn't look over at me, just continues staring out at the field like I am.

So, I continue.

"One Saturday morning, my dad woke me up extra early and told me he had a surprise for me. He had already packed up the truck before I woke up, so we jumped in and drove to a secluded area. The trees were so thick, I could barely see where we were going. Eventually, we got out and walked for a long time. Just when I was sure we were lost, he pushed aside some branches. We walked out into the most beautiful clearing I've ever seen."

I remember that day so vividly. My dad could hardly contain his excitement, I could feel it vibrating off of him. I couldn't help but join in his enthusiasm. When he pushed back that branch, I don't think I've ever seen a more breathtaking sight. A small, shallow stream laid before us, trees lined on either side. It was so quiet, so serene that it seemed like if either of us talked, it might disappear.

"My dad surprised me by bringing his fly fishing gear. I had never done it before and had been bugging him to let me try. He taught me how to fly fish that day. It was the best day of my life." I feel her eyes on me but I don't turn. "From that day on, that place was ours. We never talked about it and we never took anyone else there. It was just for us."

I've never told anyone about that clearing before. Not Matt, not Rhett, not my mom. As far as I know, no one else knows it exists. I'm not sure what prompted me to tell Jolie about it and while it feels strange, it also feels kind of...right.

I sneak a glance at her. She's watching me, her eyes are rimmed red. She gives me a shaky smile.

"That's where I feel my dad the most. That's where I go when I'm feeling stressed or frustrated or when I just need a break." I let out a long breath. "So I understand what you mean about needing to feel close to them. More than you think."

Her hand is beside mine, lying flat against the car door. Acting on instinct, I lace my pinky around hers. She looks down at where our hands are connected, then up at me. There's an emotion in her eyes, almost like understanding.

I give her a small smile. Then I turn my attention to the landscape before us and feel her do the same.

I feel a shift between us. I'm not sure what it means.

But I think I'm about to find out.

THE HAVEN TIMES

Proudly serving Haven Bay for over 100 years.

FREE

DEAR ANNIE

Your local source for advice on love, life and everything in between!

The answer to this week's trivia question (pg 9) is squash.

Q.

Dear Annie,

I'm not what you would call a "spring chicken". It's been many years since I entered this world but it'll be a while yet before I'm taken out of it. I might be old, but I've got a hell of a lot of living left to do.

Which brings me to my point: there's a lot of things I want to do before I go belly up. Most importantly, to walk down the aisle to the man I've loved for nearly my entire life.

The problem is, I told him years ago that I didn't want to get married. In fact, I made him swear to me that he would never propose or I'd run him over with my daddy's beloved combine.

I thought marriage was a way for men to control their wives. Which, in my defense, was the case in my day. But now, I realize it's a way of showing the person who makes your toes curl and your heart stutter (which at this age can be dangerous), that you love them and want to celebrate that love with your friends and family. Or what's left of them.

But what if after all these years, that's not something he wants? What if he decides that it's not worth the hassle? That I'm not worth the hassle?

Saying what's on my mind has never been a problem for me, but for some reason, I can't find the words to tell him exactly what I want from him. That is, to marry his stubborn old ass.

What should I do?

Sincerely,

You're Never Too Old For Love...Or Am I?

A.

Dear Never Too Old,

First of all, I'd like to start off by saying you're never too old for love. Period. End of conversation. This I will not budge on.

Now, for the heavy stuff. I want you to know that I'm incredibly proud of you for standing up for what you believe in, in a time when it was more than just frowned upon to do so. I hope that if I ever have the chance, that I'm as courageous as you are when it comes to following my heart.

With that being said, you need to be brave again. Baring your soul to another person can be scary. Even if it's someone you know loves and cares about you, it's not always easy to be that vulnerable. When you give your heart to someone, you hope that in return, they'll protect and cherish it. But life doesn't come with guarantees and love is no different.

You have to trust that what you have with your boyfriend is stronger than your doubts and what he feels for you is more than enough.

But one thing I want you to remember, no matter how your conversation goes: You are enough. With or without your man, you are enough.

Take a chance on what you want. I think you'll regret it if you don't.

Love always,

Annie

MISS LIV'S DANCE ACADEMY HOLIDAY CONCERT RETURNS THIS WEEKEND

Miss Liv and her dancers return this weekend for a trip down memory lane with her Holiday Concert titled "Holidays from Days Past."

Tickets are $10 each and are available for sale at her studio, online or at the Senior Center front doors.

Miss Liv promises a spectacular show, with something for the entire family. "This is one concert you won't want to miss!" Miss Liv boasts.

CHAPTER 18

JOLIE

"Another excellent class, darling. My ass hasn't looked this good since I was a young woman with nipples that still pointed upward," Dottie exclaims after class ends. She and Maeve make their way to the front of the studio while the rest of the class files out the front door. God, I hope I'm as amazing as these women when I'm their age.

I moved classes indoors a few weeks ago after the first snowfall. Indoor classes are fun and give an extra element of being able to control the noise level and light in the room, but I will miss our outdoor classes. There's just something about hearing Maeve's cursing while a bird sings in a far off tree that makes everything feel right in the world.

We're deep into November now and the gray skies are filled with clouds plump with flurries just waiting to fall. We've had a few snowy days but we're due for a big storm sometime next week after which we probably won't see the grass again until March.

"Now, Jolie. I want to discuss something with you." Dottie tucks an imaginary stray hair behind her ear, flashing her extravagant engagement ring at me in the process. "It's about my bachelorette party."

Yep, you read that right. Our very own Dottie Adams is getting married.

I had an inkling that the letter I responded to a few weeks ago was from her but I try not to guess so it doesn't skew my answers. Either way, she must've taken my advice because a few days after the paper came out, Dottie's long time boyfriend, Harold proposed. And not only did he propose, but he did it with a rock the size of a glacier. Apparently he'd bought the ring decades ago. He said he wanted to be prepared in case Dottie ever changed her mind.

Adorable, right?

Word on the street is that the wedding would be next year at Silver Fox Winery but this is the first I've heard about a bachelorette party. Though I'm not surprised. From the rumors going around town, Dottie and Harold's wedding is going to rival any of the royal weddings. According to Dottie, she's going to make Meghan Markle look like the Paperbag Princess.

For any other octogenarian couple, you'd think the wedding would be enough excitement, but no. Not Dottie. She wants the full experience. Which apparently includes a bachelorette.

Please, God, don't let there be old man strippers.

The image of a wrinkly old man swinging his saggy Speedo in my face has my stomach rolling.

It's times like this when I curse my vivid imagination.

"We want to have it here," Maeve declares.

Um, excuse me? There will be no saggy balls in my studio. Not only would I have to burn the entire building to the ground afterward, but my giant mirror wall would give me way too many vantage points to see said saggy balls from.

Oh, God.

Puppies.

Sunsets.

Buddha doing a kickflip.

Think of anything other than saggy old man balls.

"Well, the first stop of the party, at least," Dottie amends and I have to fight the urge to sigh in relief.

"That sounds very interesting, ladies," I reply. "What did you have in mind? I know the rage yoga classes are your favorite. Or would you prefer something more low-key?" I thank God herself that I'll be spared the trauma of witnessing Dottie getting a lap dance.

"Actually, we wanted to arrange for you to teach a private pole dancing class," Maeve says, pointing to the other side of the studio where five of my new portable poles sit.

My smile falters for a second before I plaster it back in place.

Pole fitness classes are one of my newest additions to the studio. I've been wanting to bring it into the studio for years and finally invested in the equipment last spring. So it's not that unusual of a request. In fact, a good percentage of the participants that sign up for classes are bachelorette parties. It's becoming a popular trend, one I'm happy to cash in on.

The problem is I've never taught a pole fitness class to anyone as... advanced in age as Dottie and Maeve. I think the oldest person in one of my classes was in her sixties and was almost more limber than me.

Dottie and Maeve get around pretty well but I know for a fact Dottie has a titanium hip and Maeve's knee seizes up at the slightest hint of rain. They do pretty well in my less advanced yoga classes but pole fitness requires a new whole level of flexibility that I'm not confident these 80-something year old women have.

But I'm willing to try if they are.

Hey, you only get one bachelorette, right?

At least, at this age you do.

"I'd love to host a class for you, Dottie," I tell her. "Let me know the details and I'll work on a special program for you. We might have to make some adjustments to some of the moves but I'll make sure you still get the full experience."

Her answering grin solidifies my decision. "Oh, that's wonderful. I'm so excited!" She wraps me in a rare Dottie hug and I gently squeeze her back.

"Now that that's settled, we can make arrangements for the limo to take us into Bakersfield to the strip club after." She turns to Maeve. "Sylvia says there's a club that serves all-day breakfast beside the bingo hall, so we can have dinner there before we hit up the slots." Maeve nods along as the two of them make their way out the studio door, lost in their plans.

I shake my head in a mix of awe and disbelief. Yeah, I definitely want to be Dottie when I grow up.

My watch vibrates signaling a text. I open it to see a message from Avery asking if I'm busy. Unsure where I left my phone last, I hit the button to call her from my watch instead. She answers on the first ring.

"Sorry to bother you. You're not in the middle of a class, are you?" she asks.

I roll my eyes and take off toward the front desk in search of my phone. "That was only once and it was in a class full of locals. You shouldn't text me saying 'I need help' unless it's an emergency." Finally finding it under a pile of papers, I switch to my phone.

"I'm pretty sure the full text was 'I need help picking out a paint color'," she laughs.

Even though I know she can't see me, I cross my arms disapprovingly. "My watch only showed me the first three words. I happened to look down, saw your message and panicked. You can't expect me not to panic reading that. You know I'm fragile."

I can hear her smile through the phone. "You're right. I'm sorry."

That's why I love Avery. Since day one, she's just rolled with my punches even when most people would call me dramatic. No matter what I throw at her, she loves me through it all. We may have only known each other a little over a year but she's my ride or die. I would do anything for her.

"So, what's up?" I hold the phone to my ear with my shoulder as I roll up the remaining yoga mats. Since that was my last class of the day, I start to close up the studio.

"I need a wedding-related favor. And before you say no, I should preface this by saying there will be lots of food and drinks."

"You had me at food," I joke, pushing the rolled mats into their designated cubbies. "Whatever you need, I'm in. I already told you, anything I can do to make wedding planning easier, I've got you."

She sighs. "Thank you so much. Alana set me up with a tasting with the chef at the winery next week," Avery explains, mentioning the winery's owner and event planner. "The thing is, Matt's exhibit is coming up and he's swamped with work. I tried to reschedule but apparently they have a bunch of events coming up and don't have another opening until January. I really wanted to get the menu nailed down so I can start designing the invitations and people won't be able to mark their dinner option if we don't know the menu and—"

"Avery, breathe," I interrupt. She obliges, taking a deep breath on the other end of the phone. "It's fine. Text me the details and I'll make sure I'm available. I'm happy to help. Especially if that means I get to eat delicious food for free."

Avery lets out a relieved laugh. "You're the best. Matt's so bummed that he's going to miss out, but I told him I'd try to sneak some leftovers home for him to try. He's been working so hard between the art gallery and helping plan the wedding. Not to mention working for Taylor Construction full-time. He wants to be involved and I appreciate the help, but I can't help thinking he's stretching himself a little thin."

I turn off the overhead lights in the studio then cross the studio to climb the steps to my apartment. "Is he still hoping to cut back his hours with Buck?" Matt works for a construction company but his true passion is woodworking. He's made a pretty big name for himself in the art community and after setting up a website last year, he's selling his work all over the world.

"That's the plan. He's almost at the point where he's making enough from his art that we can afford for him to drop to part-time," Avery explains. "There's a big art collector attending his exhibit next week and Krista's hoping this will open more doors for him."

I step into my apartment, toe off my shoes and drop to the couch. "That's awesome. Tell him I said good luck. I'm sure he'll do great."

"Thanks, J. I will. He deserves for this to work out." Someone calls to her in the background and I hear her muffled reply. "Anyway, Matt and Gav just got home so I'm going to let you go. I'll text you the details about the tasting. Thank you so much. I owe you big time."

"You don't owe me anything. I'll talk to you later."

After hanging up with Avery, I can't help but wonder what it would feel like to have someone to come home to. Someone who cheers me on while I do the same for them. Someone who believes in me unconditionally.

Someone who loves me for me.

Snow is fucking stupid. It's cold and heavy and wet and serves no purpose other than fucking up my day.

I shove my snow brush into the ground beside my wheel again, trying to clear away some of the build up around my tires but I can already tell it's no use. The snow is coming down about as fast as I can clear it from my car.

I let out a frustrated groan. I'm supposed to be on my way to Silver Fox Winery to meet Avery for the wedding tasting. Instead, I'm currently stuck on the side of the road, surrounded by white, white and more white.

Avery and I have been watching the weather all week since there was a snowstorm expected to hit. When I checked this morning, the radar assured me that the snow wouldn't hit until 7:35pm, leaving us tons of time to make it to our 4pm appointment at the winery and back to town before the snow started.

The radar is also fucking stupid.

"Lying piece of liar face radar," I grumble to myself as I make one last effort to dig myself out from the snow drift that I'm stuck in. Not that I can see where I am. For all I know, I could be stuck in the middle of the road.

The snow started to fall around noon but I checked with Avery and assured her we would be fine. Then it got a little heavier. Determined not to worry the already anxious bride-to-be, I decided to leave early for the appointment. The roads were getting a bit slippery at that point but I was sure it was nothing that me and Blue couldn't handle. She might hate the snow as much as I do, but she's never let me down before.

Apparently, there are some storms that even Blue can't weather.

The storm came fast and hard, turning the grey skies white and, in a matter of minutes, the roads were covered in snow. It didn't seem to be slowing down any time soon. After driving for what felt like an hour at the slowest speed imaginable, I hit a drift and, well...here I am.

Exasperated, I give my tire one last kick before shoving open my door and sliding into the front seat. I rub my gloved hands together to thaw my frozen fingers.

Okay, this is fine. I'm stuck in a snow drift in the middle of nowhere with nothing but my winter coat and five year old Uggs. I knew I should have got my winter tires put on last week when I got my oil changed. Blue doesn't do well in the winter with snow tires, let alone on the three-season ones she's wearing now. Manny even offered to switch them for me right then in the shop but I was running late and told him next time.

Famous last words.

My brother has been bugging me to buy a winter emergency kit since he watched that Discovery show about Alberta highways in the winter and how dangerous they are. He rattled off statistics on the number of accidents that occur every year and the injuries that follow.

I'm never telling him about this. I'd never hear the end of it.

Though that kit would come in handy right now. At least I could light a flare to let other cars know I'm here. What if someone doesn't see me and comes crashing into my car? I'll be roadkill.

That's if anyone is even out in this weather. For all I know, I'm the only one crazy enough to travel in this shit storm. I'll freeze to death before anyone even finds me. It could be hours, even days before someone comes this way. By then, the coyotes will be gnawing on my frozen corpse like a Jolie-popsicle.

My heartbeat starts to trip in my chest and my breathing is coming in shorter intakes as I imagine slowly freezing to death in my grandfather's beloved car.

No need to panic. No one's turning into a popsicle. I just need to call someone. Yeah, that's it. Maybe I can get a tow to come dig me out before the roads get too bad.

I pull my phone out from its place in the cupholder and notice four missed calls from Avery. Tapping the Call button, I bring the cold phone to my ear. It barely rings before Avery answers, her voice panicked.

"Jolie! Are you okay? The snow is awful. I tried calling you to cancel but you weren't answering and I got worried."

"I'm fine," I answer, trying to keep the panic out of my voice. "Just stuck in a snow drift. I was about to call a tow when I saw all the missed calls and figured I should call you back first. I'm fine. I promise." Something catches my eye in my side mirror and I squint to try and see it through the white out reflecting back at me.

"It's hard to tell but I think I can make out headlights

coming toward me. Stay on the line with me so I don't get murdered asking this guy for help."

I watch as the car comes into view, pulling up behind me. The door swings open and I realize that the car isn't a car at all, but a truck. Relief washes over me. A truck might be able to pull me out of this mess or at least give me a lift home until I can get a tow to pull Blue out. A man jumps out of the cab and stomps toward my car.

"Don't hate me," Avery says nervously.

My forehead wrinkles in confusion. "Why would I..." I trail off as the man reaches my door.

Luke knocks on the glass and I manually roll the window down.

"Need a little help?"

LUKE

When Avery called and told me Jolie was out driving in this storm and hadn't been answering her phone, I was concerned. Driving in Alberta winters can be tricky in a regular vehicle, but in her car? It's no wonder she got stuck.

The vintage car might be beautifully maintained but it's next to useless in the snow. Especially on the back roads. I have no idea how she's made it this long with that car.

Avery called me because she wasn't sure what to do and didn't know whether to call the station, so I was the next best thing. I was off duty but I reassured her that I'd find her and took off in my truck.

Avery said Jolie was headed toward the winery before she stopped answering her phone so I followed the most likely route there. The further I drove with no sign of her, the worse the gnawing feeling in my gut became. By the time I caught a glimpse of her taillights through the blowing snow, my hands were sore from their tense grip on the steering wheel that had nothing to do with the worsening road conditions.

Throwing my truck in park, I jumped out and stomped my way up to her car. I've never felt such an overwhelming sense of relief as I did when I saw her bright eyes staring back at me through her icy window. All thoughts of worry and panic blew away with the snow and I could finally breathe through the clenching in my chest.

To my surprise, it took hardly any convincing to get her into my truck. I know how much she hates to depend on anyone but I think she realized she was in no position to argue. After explaining that there was no way I could pull her car out of the drift without causing her car some serious damage, she agreed easily. With her hand on my arm for balance, we made it back to my truck without either of us falling on our asses.

I glance over to where she has her hands raised to the vents, trying to warm what I'm sure are freezing hands. Her toque is still pulled low over her head and she has tiny icicles in her hair. Her cheeks and nose are red from the cold. The look should not be as appealing as it is.

She looks adorable.

"How long were you out there?" I ask, clearing my throat.

She shrugs, rotating her hands so the backs of her hands are facing the heat. "I think I drove for half an hour before I got stuck. Honestly, I don't even know where I am. One minute it was lightly snowing and the next, the wind had shifted and I couldn't have seen a moose if it walked out right in front of my car." She finally looks over at me. "I tried to dig myself out but I didn't have anything to dig with. I tried using my snow brush." She smiles sheepishly.

"Didn't work too well so I gave up. I got back in my car and saw the missed calls from Avery. You showed up not long after that."

Normally, I'd lecture her on the importance of having a winter emergency kit in her car, especially in one as old as hers. I'd list off all of the ways things could have gone wrong and how dangerous it was to go out during a storm.

But for some reason, the only thing that comes out is, "I'm glad you're okay".

Jolie arches an eyebrow at me. It seems to be her signature move where I'm involved. "That's it? No lecture about how irresponsible I am? No scary stories about how I could've been mowed over by a semi-truck or froze to death with only my Uggs to keep me warm?"

The corner of my lips turn up. "Seems like you just did it for me." When she offers me a small smile back, it feels like another step forward for our truce.

We sit in silence for a moment before she turns to me. "So, what's the plan? Probably shouldn't be sitting here for too much longer or you'll get stuck too."

I look out at the snow before us, assessing our options. Though it would take a lot more snow to get my truck stuck, it's not safe to be driving right now. We're far enough out of town that turning around would take too long and then getting stuck might actually be a possibility. Not to mention the hazards of other cars or wildlife jumping out at us.

I scan the horizon and pull out my phone, tapping on the GPS. Luckily, the towers haven't lost connection yet. The app loads and I realize we're not far from Silver Fox Winery.

"We're just down the road from the winery," I tell her, shifting the truck into Drive. "Let's head there and reevaluate once we're out of the storm. Worst case, we'll grab a couple rooms at the lodge."

One of the more unique qualities about our local winery is that it has a lodge connected to it. It helps keep revenue coming in for the winery year-round and it's convenient for guests who may have indulged too much during the tastings. It's one of the reasons Matt and Avery chose the winery as their wedding venue. They didn't want their guests to have to worry about getting home safely at the end of the night or finding a ride back into town.

It takes us twice as long as it normally would to get to the winery. When we finally pull into the driveway, the sun has long since set. The parking lot is surprisingly full for the end of November, so I have no choice but to park near the back of the lot. I jump out of the truck then hurry around to the passenger side to help Jolie down. She's already got the door open and is trying not to slip on the side bar as she lowers herself to the snow-covered ground. I reach out to steady her then wrap a protective arm around her waist as we slip and slide our way to the winery.

When we finally reach the entrance, I pull open the heavy glass door and usher Jolie in before rushing behind her. Once inside, I stomp the excess snow off of my boots then look down at Jolie. She's brushing the snow off of her toque, her cheeks rosy from the cold. I'm not sure if it's the chandelier above us that's giving her an angelic glow, but for a second, I can't take my eyes off of her.

"Holy shit balls. It's colder than Santa's dick out there," she rasps.

Did I say angelic?

I chuckle despite myself and she looks startled at the sound. Before she can comment though, a short woman in her fifties rushes over to us.

"Oh my goodness, you two must be frozen solid!" Alana Fox, the owner, cries as she approaches. Silver Fox Winery has been in her family for six generations. She took over as owner from her father a few years ago but still has her hand in many aspects of the business, including event management.

"Avery called to say that you might be headed this way. She said you got stuck in a drift. How awful!" She wraps an arm around Jolie's back and guides her further into the lobby. "We sent most of the staff home early when the storm started to shift but I wanted to make sure I stayed until we heard from you."

I follow behind them, trying not to shake off too much snow onto the hardwood floors as I go.

Jolie rests her hand on Alana's. "That was so kind of you, Alana. We really appreciate it."

Alana waves her off. "It's what we do." She stops before the large check-in desk. "Now, the radar shows that the snow isn't supposed to let up until tomorrow morning. I'm sorry to tell you but I think you're stuck with us tonight. I have our front desk staff checking to see what rooms we have available for you both. Once I hear from them, I'll get you your room keys."

This time Jolie wraps Alana in a big hug. "Thank you so much. You're a lifesaver. I don't think my nerves could've handled driving another minute in that storm."

Alana hugs her back. "I can imagine. Don't you worry. We'll get you settled and we'll call about a tow in the morning." She steps back and looks between us. "Now our chef had already prepared the tasting menu before he left but I'm afraid it's gone cold now. I can heat it up for you, but it definitely won't be the same."

Jolie smiles at her. "Oh, don't worry about that. I'm so

hungry, I'd eat my boot if I thought I'd be able to chew through the material." Alana laughs. " It's been a long night and I'm starving." She looks up at me and I nod in agreement. When I left town in search of Jolie, it had been too early for dinner and it was now long past then.

"Say no more. I'll have that out to you in a jiffy." She gestures to the dining room behind us. "We have a pretty full house this weekend but feel free to grab any open table you find." She spins on her heel and heads toward what I assume is the kitchen.

Jolie turns to me and shrugs. "Well, at least we'll get a decent meal out of all of this."

Her optimism used to be one of the things that drove me nuts about her. Her constant need to find the silver living seemed exhausting and pointless.

You can't show me a pile of garbage and call it art. Sometimes it's just garbage.

But suddenly her optimism doesn't seem like such a nuisance. Today was probably really scary for her. If I hadn't come around, who knows when someone would've found her? Yet here she is, still smiling and making jokes. I'm in awe of her resilience. I'm seeing sides of her that I didn't know existed, but I'm finding myself wanting to get to know.

Well, no better time like the present.

CHAPTER 20

JOLIE

Silver Fox Winery is a stunning venue and will make for a breathtaking backdrop for Avery's wedding. Like most of the residents in Haven Bay, I've been to the winery many times before for day trips and smaller events like their paint and sip nights. But I've never stayed as a guest.

The tasting room is the farthest I've ever made it inside the winery, as the rest of the venue is reserved for overnight guests and larger event attendees. Their dining area is just off the side of the tasting room and as soon as we pass through the heavy glass doors, I can tell why it's closed to the public.

The room is stunning. The walls are covered in white stone with dark wooden beams crossing above us. Tall windows stretch from floor to ceiling with an antique chandelier hanging in the middle. I imagine the currently snow-covered windows showcasing the never-ending rows of vines with incredible mountains in the distance.

Now that we're sitting at one of the tables and out of the cold, the storm makes the inside of the dining area feel cozy under the blanket of snow. There's a fire lit in the stone fireplace across the hall and the crackling of the flames adds to the ambiance.

After shooting off a quick text to Avery and Brenna in our group chat letting them know Luke and I made it to the winery safely, I take a long drink of my bottle of hard cider. The bartender was sent home before the storm hit, but Alana brought us over some drinks while we waited for our food. I'm not much of a drinker but I gladly accepted the drink. It's been a long day and all I want to do is sink into a hot bath. They're still trying to figure out our rooms so the alcohol will have to do.

For now.

I'd be lying if I said I wasn't slightly panicked. My broke ass can't afford a night at this very beautiful but equally expensive lodge. My car is probably buried under a mountain of snow by now. I don't want to even think of the damage this storm will do to my beloved car or I might break down in tears at this very table. I'm sure that would be the nail in the "Jolie is a lunatic" coffin in Luke's mind.

Oh, that's another thing. I'm stuck here with a man who hates my guts.

But here's the thing. When Luke found me on the side of the road, he didn't look like he hated me. If anything, he looked worried, almost panicked. Then when we were safely back in his car, he seemed relieved.

And the way he held onto me as we rushed to and from his car didn't feel like it was because of some truce his brother forced him into. It felt comforting and protective. Like he cared about my safety for a reason other than me being his future sister-in-law's best friend.

Since we sat down, he's been attentive and thoughtful, asking me questions about myself and my life. It doesn't seem like he's asking to pass the time either, but because he actually wants to know the answer. Like he wants to know me.

It's a little unnerving.

I always wondered what it would be like to have Luke's attention in any way other than his disdain. Now that I know, I'm not sure what to think.

Part of me wants to revel in it, soaking it up for as long as it lasts. The other part wants to hide under this table or jump head first into the snow outside. Anything to take his eyes off of me.

Because one thing I've learned about Luke today is that when he's looking at you, even if only for a few moments, you're the only thing that matters. Even when Alana came over to drop off our drinks and chat with us for a moment, he never looked away for longer than a moment, including me in every comment, every joke.

All of this attention is a complete 180 from his usual distaste for me. So much so that I can't help blurting out, "Why are you being weird?"

Luke stares at me, his beer halfway to his lips. He sets the bottle back on the table in front of him. "How is sitting here drinking my beer being weird?"

I roll my eyes. "You know what I mean. You're being all nice and charming and—" I wave my hand up and down in his direction, "unLuke-ish."

He relaxes back into his chair. "UnLuke-ish?" he asks, his lips twitching at the question. "What exactly is 'Luke-ish'?"

"You know. Grumpy, sarcastic, lecture-y. Full of insults with a stick up your rectum."

To my surprise, Luke lets out a bellowing laugh. My eyebrows shoot up. It takes a second for him to pull himself together before he responds. "Yeah, that sounds about right."

I point a finger at him. "See, that right there. The Luke I know doesn't laugh like that. At least not with me. At me, maybe. But even then you usually look at me like you've just swallowed a pickled lemon coated in vinegar. So why are you being so..." I pause, searching for the right word, "nice?"

He tilts his head as he listens to me rant, the smile on his face growing. When I stop to take a breath, he leans his forearms onto the table. "You done?" It takes a second before I nod. "Good." He leans closer and I find myself gravitating toward him. "I know you're probably confused and I get it, I've been sending mixed signals the last little bit. I wish I could give you a reason but the only thing I can tell you is that I'm sorry. I know I've been a dick to you in the past." I snort at that but luckily he just smiles. "I may have realized that you're not as awful as I initially thought."

I place a hand over my heart and gasp. I use my other hand to fan my eyes holding back fake tears. "Oh, my stars," I whisper in a bad Southern accent. "That's the sweetest thing anyone has ever said to me. You're going to make me cry."

He gives me a dry smile at my theatrics. "You know what I mean."

I drop my hands and pick up my bottle. "Luckily for you, I do. You're not so awful yourself, Chief."

We both take a long pull of our drinks, never breaking eye contact over our bottles. Alana takes that moment to bring over our meals. She places the plates before us. Piled high on the plate is a large portion of beef tenderloin covered in au jus with a side of garlic mashed potatoes and parmesan asparagus. My mouth waters as the flavorful scents hit me.

"This looks delicious, Alana," Luke says, digging into his plate. I do the same and bring a forkful of the meat to my mouth. I can't help but moan as the tender beef hits my tastebuds. Luke's eyes flash to my mouth, pausing for a second before darting back down to his plate.

Okay, well that was weird.

"Thank you," Alana replies. "I wanted to let you know that I spoke with the front desk about your rooms." She gives us an apologetic look. "Most of our staff was sent home before the storm hit. The ones that offered to stay through the storm were set up with rooms. Between that and the rest of our guests, we only have one room available," she says. "But you're in luck. It has a balcony, walk-in shower and a king-size bed."

Um, what? No. Not happening. No, no no.

"Do you have any cots available?" I ask, trying for a casual tone.

"I'm sorry, we gave our last one to a guest this afternoon."

"So, you're saying there's only one room available and there's only one bed?" Luke clarifies.

"That's right," Alana answers.

Of course there is.

Fuck.

CHAPTER 21

JOLIE

I know what you're thinking. Only one bed; how unrealistic and cliché. But as someone who worked as a front desk clerk for a boutique hotel for two years, I'm here to tell you that it happens. In fact, it happens more frequently than you'd think, especially when it comes to last minute bookings.

The tenderloin I'm chewing turns to cardboard in my mouth.

Luke and I are just starting to make peace, maybe even becoming friends. Now all of sudden I'm supposed to be sharing not only a room with him but a bed?

The universe has a sick sense of humor.

Luke seems to sense my shock and speaks up. "We really appreciate anything you can spare for us, Alana," he says. "Thank you."

Alana nods. "Absolutely. Now, if you two are all set here, I think I'm going to head to my office. Thankfully, I have a pull out couch for times like these." She leans toward our table. "Since you're friends, feel free to help yourselves to the bar. All the liquor and wine is locked up but there should be some beers in the fridge that you can help yourselves to," she says in a low voice. "And there'll be a complimentary bottle of wine in your room."

Somehow through my shock, I manage to thank her. She passes over the key to our room before heading out of the dining room.

An awkward silence lingers in her wake. We're the only people in the room and I'm not sure where to look.

Should I make a joke? Should I offer to sleep on the floor? The lodge is a four-star destination, so I'm sure their floors are clean and not at all covered in bodily fluids and—

Okay, so not sleeping on the floor. I'm sure there's other options. I've definitely slept in worse places.

In my early twenties, a bunch of our friends went to a concert. After, we went back to one of their houses to crash. There were so many people and only so many beds so I ended up sleeping in the bathtub. I could do that again.

Then I remember the pulled muscle in my neck I suffered through a few months ago from sneezing too hard. My spirit might be of a 20-year-old but my body is very much a 29-year-old. Despite being flexible from yoga and running, I think stuffing myself into a bathtub overnight might paralyze me.

Luke breaks the silence. "So, that's not ideal."

I sigh. "No, definitely not."

"Well, there's only one thing we can do," he leans forward, his face serious. I arch an eyebrow at him in question. "We need to duke it out over who gets the bed."

I laugh and he smiles. It's times like this when he gives me a glimpse into the goofy side of him that I wonder if there's a whole other man inside that I know nothing about.

"Clearly," I agree. "How else do you make decisions?"

"Don't think that because you're a woman I'm going to

take it easy on you." He tilts his head thoughtfully at me. "I'm quite the feminist, you know."

I scoff, nonchalantly leaning back in my chair. "Oh, don't worry about me, Chief. My brother was an avid wrestling fan. I was learning how to give 'Stunners' by the time I was five. Stone Cold Steve Austin would be impressed by my moves."

Luke's lips turn up at that. God, why does that little smile heat my entire insides?

"I knew you'd play dirty, sweetheart," he teases, his voice low and gravelly.

Oh, damn.

What started as a condescending nickname now has my belly flipping every time I hear it. I have no idea if he meant that to sound so hot and suggestive but, wow. His words combined with that sexy as sin voice has me imagining all kinds of dirty, filthy ways we'd play together.

I used to think Luke would be a bore in bed, all rigid and lifeless. Now, I'm afraid there's not much I wouldn't do if Luke used that voice on me.

Shit.

It's going to be a long night.

LUKE

After we finish our meals and put our dirty dishes on the cart beside the locked kitchen, we decide to head to our room so the staff can close up. Jolie grabs a few more bottles of beer and cider from the bar and we make our way down the winding hall toward the lodge portion of the venue.

We eventually find our room and I slip the keycard over the lock pad on the door. The light turns green and I hold the door for Jolie to walk through. Following behind her, I close and lock the door.

Once inside, I pause to take in the room. It's big, with 10 foot ceilings and a large patio door that opens onto a snow-covered patio. Where the wood aesthetic in the dining area is subtle, it's more prominent in the rooms. Large dark beams are widely spaced on the wood ceiling. White stones similar to the dining area create an accent wall behind the lone bed.

There it is. The object that will test every ounce of willpower I have.

The bed.

It's actually quite spacious but you could put Jolie and I in an Alaskan King and there still wouldn't be enough mattress to keep me from feeling her presence.

What she said earlier was true: I've been acting differently around her tonight. For some reason, finding her on the side of the road, frozen and clearly trying to hide how scared she was, did something to me. I tried to blame it on what Matt likes to call my Knight in Shining Armor Syndrome. But as I sat across from her at the dining table, talking and joking just the two of us, I knew it was something else.

All this time I spent trying to fight her every chance I got, thinking she was designed to drive me crazy when in reality, I was the one being a jackass. Sure, she gave it back to me just as hard, but I'm starting to find that there's more to Jolie than I originally thought.

And I want to find out more.

She haphazardly kicks her boots off, drops the bottles down on the dresser and then launches herself onto the bed. She bounces once then rolls onto her back, letting out a deep sigh of contentment as her body sinks into the comforter. Her hair is wild and splayed out on the mattress as she runs her arms over the soft material.

"This bed is heaven," she sighs. "You have to feel it. I swear I could orgasm from how soft it is."

I stand corrected. She was designed *specifically* to drive me crazy. I'm sure of it.

Knowing how dangerous it would be to lay down beside her right now, I shake my head. "I'm good."

She sits up on her forearms and looks at me for a second before shrugging. "Suit yourself, Chief."

She readjusts so that she's sitting on the bed with her legs crossed underneath her. She looks young and innocent. *Yeah, right.* I don't think Jolie has ever been considered innocent in her life. She has a permanent mischievous glint in her eye that used to make me uneasy, knowing her next move usually just creates problems for me.

So why am I now so eager to get a peek at what's going on inside her head?

"Alright. I think we need to address the elephant in the room," she announces. I tilt my head at her in question. "Sleeping arrangements."

"I'll sleep on the floor," I offer.

Her face twists into a disgusted grimace. "You're not sleeping on the floor." She holds up a finger. "First, that's gross." She lifts a second. "Second, I would feel like an absolute dick if I got this entire cloud of a mattress to myself." A third finger raises. "And third, that floor is probably covered in jizz and pee and whatever other nasty stains are lodged into the carpet."

Well I mean, when she puts it that way...

Silver Fox Lodge is a nice place and they pride themselves on providing a clean and welcoming environment. I'm sure the floor is perfectly clean.

But now I can't get the image she so eloquently painted for me out of my head.

"We're both adults," she says. "Despite what every romance book ever written might say, we can share a bed without anything inappropriate happening." She smirks and as if not being able to help herself, she adds, "I think I can resist your charming personality for one night."

The corner of my mouth twitches. I know I should be fighting her more. Sharing a bed with Jolie is a bad idea. Plain and simple. A smarter man would insist on sleeping on the floor.

Apparently, I'm not a smart man. "Fine."

Shrugging off my coat, I pick up her discarded one and hang them both in the closet. Closing the door, I turn back to where she sits on the bed looking around. An awkward silence fills the room and I find myself unsure what to do.

Before I can think of something to say, she claps her hands on her thighs and stands. "Well, I don't know about you but I want to get out of these wet jeans."

My eyes just about bug out of my head. She slowly walks over to where I stand, rooted to the ground. I know I should probably say something or stop her but I just watch transfixed as she stops before me.

She looks up at me and my breathing slows until I feel like my chest is about to burst if I don't release some of the tension. But I'm too scared that if I move, if I so much as blink, she'll change her mind. I'm not even sure if I want this but all I know is that the way Jolie is looking at me has me all kinds of fucked up. She's so close, her scent wraps around us like a blanket. She'd barely have to reach out and she'd be touching any part of me she wanted.

I need to know her next move more than I need my next breath.

She reaches up and I brace myself for her touch. But instead of my arm or my chest, she reaches over and opens the closet door behind me. Eyes still locked on mine, she pulls a white robe with the lodge's logo on it from inside. Finally, she breaks the connection and turns toward the bathroom. She starts to close the door but at the last second, looks over her shoulder at me with a confused expression before the door blocks her from view.

The door clicks shut and I let out a whoosh of air. I run a hand over my face. I'm such an idiot. Did I honestly think she was just going to strip down in front of me? Of course she was reaching for a robe. And I just stood there like a fucking pervert staring at her. Apparently, when there's even the slightest chance at seeing a naked woman, my brain shuts down and I turn into a drooling neanderthal.

I slump onto the bed and drop my head into my hands.

This is gunna be a long fucking night.

THE HAVEN TIMES

DEAR ANNIE

Your local source for advice on love, life and everything in between!

The answer to this week's trivia question (pg 9) is Chad Michael Murray.

Q.   A.

Dear Annie,

My husband and I have been married for over 20 years. We're happy together and have created a life that I love. We've never had an issue with intimacy—we have five children to prove it!

But there's some... things I've read about that I want to try. The only problem is, it's a bit out there. I wouldn't consider our sex life vanilla but this is definitely a big jump from what we're used to.

I love my husband dearly but I'm terrified to talk to him about this. What if he is disgusted by my requests and it affects our relationship? I would be mortified if he thought differently of me for it.

But I can't keep these ideas out of my head.

Sincerely,

Kinky and Curious

Dear Kinky,

From the way you describe your marriage, I can tell you have a deep respect for your husband and I'm sure he feels the same about you.

When you've been married to someone for 20 years, there are bound to be a few uncomfortable conversations.

Whether it's a mole on your buttcheek that you just can't see but are a little worried about or deciding how to have "the talk" with your kids, I'm sure you've pushed your comfort zones multiple times over the years. So why stop now?

Who knows? Your husband may have some "things" of his own he'd like to try but is too scared to bring up. As long as you both consent to it and you do your research beforehand to make sure everyone's safe, I say have fun!

Love always,

Annie

BEWARE OF PHONE SCAMS

The Haven Bay Police Department is issuing a warning to all residents to be aware of phone scammers.

A new round of fraudulent calls have been making their way around the county claiming to be bail bondsmen.

Scammers have been calling citizens, claiming that their grandchild is in jail and need money to release them.

Victims are instructed to wire money to them immediately. To make the transaction seem legitimate, victims are given a code.

No Canadian court or police department will participate in this practice.

If you receive such a call, please do not give out any personal information and report the incident to HBPD.

EUCHRE TOURNAMENT POSTPONED DUE TO STOMACH FLU

This weekend's euchre tournament will be postponed to a later date as many of our members have fallen ill.

Please stay tuned for further information regarding new tournament date.

Stay healthy and remember to wash your hands frequently to avoid the spread of germs.

CHAPTER 22

JOLIE

h my Dolly Parton. What the hell is in the air up here? This situation just keeps getting more and more insane.

I'd be lying if I said I didn't notice the way Luke's been looking at me since we got in the room. Did I make a few of those innuendos on purpose? Of course. I'm only human and pushing Luke's buttons is my favorite pastime.

I fully expected him to roll his eyes or grumble about how immature I am. What I didn't expect was the flash of desire in his eyes or the way he looked like he wanted to devour me whole as I walked over to grab my robe.

Nope, that's definitely new.

I can tell when a man is turned on and geez Louise, was that man ever turned on. I thought about making a joke once I got close enough to touch him but the second I was within arm's length, all thoughts of jokes and teasing went out the window. In fact, all thought in general evaporated faster than water droplets in a sauna.

You'd think being out in the cold, wet snow would've lessened his appeal. Nope. I'm convinced that Luke Brady could be covered in steamy, hot manure and I'd just plug my nose and dive in head first. The man oozes sex appeal and doesn't even know it. He's got that dominant, alpha male thing going for him and damn, if it isn't working for him.

I shove my wet jeans down my legs and hang them over the side of the claw-foot tub. I take a look at the large walk-in shower that's beside it and consider taking a hot shower. But the thought of being naked with Luke in the next room is giving me too many conflicting feelings, so I decide against it. Instead, I pull my sweater over my head, leaving me in my white tanktop and underwear, then shrug into the soft robe. Rubbing the luxurious material of the lapel against my cheek, I take a deep breath, inhaling the calming scent of lavender.

All things considered, there are definitely worse places to get stranded in a snowstorm.

I mean, if you don't mind a little sexual tension with your stay.

For a second when I was standing in front of Luke, I thought he was going to lean in and kiss me. I'm not sure he even realized he was dropping his head until I reached into the closet behind him. That seemed to snap us both out of whatever trance we were in. As I walked to the bathroom, I couldn't help looking over my shoulder to see his reaction. He was watching me, holding my gaze as I shut the door behind me.

It was hot and powerful and...confusing.

I wonder what he's doing out there. Is he still standing in front of the door, feeling as confused and awkward as I am? Maybe he went to sleep and I can just crawl into bed without having to talk to him. Then in the morning we can pretend the whole thing never happened.

Or what if he's out there, laughing at me? Maybe the

whole thing was some twisted joke to humiliate me. Dread fills my stomach and my knees feel like they're ready to buckle. I grip the bathroom counter tightly until I'm sure I'll feel the granite against my skin long after I let go.

No, I immediately chastise myself. *That's just that stupid bitch Tiffany talking. Luke wouldn't do that. He might not be your biggest fan but he's not cruel.*

I look up at my reflection in the mirror. In an attempt to block out the intrusive thoughts that are threatening to pull me under, I repeat the affirmations I've come to rely on.

You are strong.
 You are smart.
 You are worthy.

OVER AND OVER, I chant these words to myself until I feel steadier. I inhale deeply then let out a breath.

Much better.

Feeling stronger, I force a smile and throw open the bathroom door. Luke's no longer in front of the closet door. I take a step out of the doorway and notice him standing in front of the balcony door. Most of the glass door is covered in snow, but he's looking through a small clear section at the top. When he hears me come out, he turns, his face uncertain as his eyes search mine. I watch his gaze dip to my robe then shoot back up to my face. He swallows hard and I'm suddenly very aware of my lack of clothing.

The tension in the air is thick. I hate this feeling of not knowing what to say. Which I guess is why I spit out the first thing that comes to mind. "Let's play a game!"

Apparently he's just as surprised by that as I am

because he tilts his head slightly, the line between his brows deepening. "Game?"

Running with it, I grab a beer for him and a cider for me from inside the mini fridge. Luke must've put them in there to chill while I was in the bathroom changing. "Yeah, a game. We don't really know that much about each other, other than the fact that we drive each other nuts." His lips twitch at that and it's all the encouragement I need to continue. I climb onto the bed and sit crossed legged on the mattress. "Have you ever heard of two truths and a lie?" I ask, offering him the beer.

After a second of hesitation, he gingerly accepts the beer then drops onto the edge of the bed, one leg still on the floor with the other bent in front of him. He looks like he's ready to jump off the bed at a moment's notice, but at least he's humoring me. "No, but it sounds pretty self-explanatory."

I nod, twisting the cap off of my cider. "It is. You list off three things about yourself—two that are true and one that's a lie. Then I have to guess which one is the lie." I tip my drink toward him. "You in?"

He considers it then adjusts himself so he's facing me. "Yeah, okay."

I'm a little surprised that he agreed but I'm not going to waste what is probably my only opportunity to get a look at the real Luke. "Do you want to start or should I?"

"It was your idea, so you can."

"Fair." I lean back on one arm, thinking. "Okay, I'll start with an easy one." I look over at him and try to keep my face as neutral as possible. "I lived in Toronto for four years but I've never been to the CN Tower. My brother once dared me to eat a worm when I was nine. I don't have any tattoos."

Luke takes a drink of his beer, searching my face.

"There's no way you don't have at least one tattoo. I've never seen any, but that doesn't mean anything. You've obviously been to the CN Tower. Even I've been to the CN Tower and I've lived in Haven Bay my whole life. I want to say you'd never eat a worm but I also know you can't turn down a dare. So I say the tattoo one."

I smile and shake my head. "Nope. I've wanted to but there's never been anything I liked enough to get it done. Except for a few henna tattoos in high school, I have virgin skin."

"Then it's the worm one, for sure."

I shake my head again. "Nope."

His eyes grow comically wide. "You've never been to the CN Tower? How is that possible? Not even on a field trip?" I shake my head again. "I don't believe you."

I laugh. "I swear! I'm terrified of heights and as much as I wanted to go up, my legs wouldn't let me."

He gives me an incredulous look. "Now I know you're lying. You used to work for a ski lodge. How did you manage that without going up the ski lift?"

I'm a little taken aback that he remembered I worked at a lodge in my early twenties. I remember mentioning it to Matt once in front of Luke but I didn't know he was listening. "I wasn't an instructor so I didn't have to go up," I explain. "I used to hang out at the apres ski with all the boarders but if anyone asked, I made up an excuse."

He looks at me in surprise. "I didn't think there was anything you were afraid of. You're fearless."

I resist the urge to scoff. "I've been called many things in my life but fearless is not one of them."

He arches a brow at me. "How do you figure? You moved across the country when you were barely an adult and you've lived on your own ever since. You started a business when you were twenty four and made it a success all by yourself. That seems pretty fearless to me." He sits back against the pillows and tucks an arm casually behind his head, as if he didn't just drop a mic on me.

I didn't even realize Luke knew half of that stuff about me but I guess it makes sense. When you move to a town as small as Haven Bay, everyone knows everything about you before you've even finished unpacking. I just assumed that he wouldn't care enough to remember the details.

For the second time tonight, I'm not sure what to say. Especially after what seemed suspiciously like a compliment. "That's different," I say but he shakes his head.

"No, it's not. That all took guts. Whether you want to admit it or not, you're fearless, Jolie."

What the hell does someone say to that? He takes a drink of his beer as I stare back at him, dumbstruck. No one has ever called me fearless before. When I told my parents my plans—or lack of—for after graduation, my father told me I was being reckless and stupid. He listed off all the ways I would fail and said he gave me a month before I called him begging to come home. My mom was mostly quiet but asked me multiple times if I was sure it was what I wanted. My brother told me I was crazy in a way that only a brother could get away with. Then he helped me pack and gave me a hug before I left, telling me to call him every day until I got here.

But fearless? Definitely not.

I'm so filled with fear, half the time I don't know what's a real threat vs one I made up in my head. Hence my need for medication.

For someone who swore he couldn't stand me a few days ago, he sure isn't acting like it.

I pull the robe further over my legs. "I think that means it's your turn."

He watches me for a second then looks up at the ceiling thinking. A few moments later, he looks back at me. "Okay, got 'em."

I lean forward, my hands clasped under my chin in an exaggeratedly animated expression. Luke rolls his eyes. My reaction is a bit dramatic but I'm genuinely excited to learn more about him. He's such a closed book that it's like pulling teeth trying to get any personal information out of him. With this new side of him coming out, I'm more and more curious about the real Luke.

"My favorite singer is Lizzo. My favorite animal is a cat. When I was eleven, I convinced Matt that his fifth grade teacher was an alien in disguise and if she got wet, her mask would wash off and she'd turn back into an alien."

A laugh bursts out of me before Luke even finishes his last sentence. "Okay, the last one is way too detailed and hilarious not to be true. Your imagination is not that good to make that up on the spot." I tap my chin in mock thought. "On one hand, Lizzo is absolutely amazing. If it was any other person, I'd say that has to be your truth, but your personality *screams* black cat: grouchy, irritable and only tolerates affection for a second before biting the one giving it." I can't help but grin at the unamused look he gives me. "So I have to say the Lizzo one is a lie."

"I've never been more happy to tell you that you are, in fact, wrong," he says then smirks when I gasp.

"What! Impossible," I huff while he continues to smirk. "Wipe that smug look off your face." I take another drink of my cider and am surprised to find it already empty. I roll off the bed and put the empty bottle in the recycle bin. "Okay, so which one was it?"

I pull another cider from the mini fridge and hold a beer bottle out to him in question. He lifts his bottle to check out its contents. Seeing it's almost empty too, he nods and I pass him another beer.

"As much as it may pain you to hear, I am not a cat person. While I can appreciate their need for personal space and independence, I can't say they're my favorite."

I drop back onto the bed, sitting cross-legged in front of him. "So what's your favorite then? Dogs?"

"Nope."

"Rhino?"

"Cool, but no."

I think for a moment before pointing my bottle at him, a triumphant smile on my face. "I've got it. Gorilla. You're both grumpy, easily provoked and need to be the toughest in the room."

He cocks his head at me. "Really?" he says dryly.

I throw my hands up in the air. "I give up then."

He readjusts the pillow behind him, knowing he's torturing my impatient self by dragging this out. Then he leans back and says ever so casually, "Red panda."

My jaw drops. "Are you shitting me?"

He tilts his head in confusion. "Why would I lie about something like that?"

"I don't know. Because you're annoying and you love to screw with me." I shove at his legs that are stretched out in front of me, knocking the one on top from its casually crossed position. "There's no way your favorite animal is a red panda."

He smirks, recrossing his legs. "And why not?"

I shove his leg again and he sighs. "Because you're a big, scary cop! Your favorite animal should be something equally tough and intimidating, like a shark. Not the fluffiest, most precious animal to ever exist."

He shrugs. "Have you seen those videos online of a red panda being scared? They're adorable. They're like little teddy bears with a mask on."

Why is that the cutest thing I've ever heard? And coming from big, tough Luke?

Ugh, my heart.

Wait, what?

No. You need to shut that shit down right now, I warn my fickle hussy of a heart. I am not going to swoon over Luke Brady. If he could hear my thoughts right now, he'd probably laugh in my face then list off all the reasons why he would never date me.

I'm not being self-deprecating. I know I'm a catch. Just not for Luke.

Which is fine. As far as I'm concerned, Luke and I would make a terrible couple. Between his anal tendencies (and not the fun kind) and my lack of filter, we'd drive each other nuts. We'd probably spend our entire short-lived relationship at each other's throats.

I bet the sex would be hot as hell though. With the amount of tension between us, we'd probably end up in the bedroom the majority of the time, taking out our anger on each other's bodies. Luke would be his normal dominating self but maybe I wouldn't mind him telling me what to do so much if his hard body was above mine. Slamming into me with fervor, his punishing grip on my hips leaving bruises on my skin. Or him standing menacingly above me as he orders me to my knees and...

"Jolie?"

My eyes snap up to his. He's watching my face, his brows furrowed together in bewilderment. I'm not usually one to get embarrassed but I can feel my cheeks burning. It takes all of my effort not to lift my hands to cool them. Yeah, it's definitely embarrassment that has my cheeks burning, not the thought of Luke's head between my—

Down, girl.

Reminding myself there's no way he could possibly know what I was just thinking, I try for a casual tone when I reply. "Yeah?" I rasp.

Is that my voice? God, could I sound any more desperate?

"I said it's your turn." He looks over at me in concern. "You okay?"

"Yep," I squeak out. "All good."

I clear my throat then subtly shift away from him, putting some much needed space between us. It doesn't matter how hot the sex would be, I won't ever cross that line with him. I know exactly what happens when you hook yourself to a man like Luke. You end up with your light stomped out, your voice silenced, and your shine dulled.

Just ask my mother.

So I won't give in to this newfound intrigue. No matter how badly I want to.

I can't.

CHAPTER 23

JOLIE

By the time I've thought of my next two truths and the lie, my nerves have calmed and we settle back into a comfortable rhythm of back and forth.

I have to admit, I'm a little taken aback by how fun Luke is. Since I've known him, I've only known him to joke with Matt and Rhett. Even then, it was more sarcasm than goofing around like Matt and Rhett love to do. But this version of him is different. He's laid-back, making jokes and even throwing in a pun or two.

What's more surprising is how easily conversation has flowed between us. We may have known each other for years but this is the first time we've actually taken the time to get to know each other. And I'm finding that Luke isn't as bad as I once thought. We haven't even argued once—a new record for us.

"Cookie dough is clearly the superior ice cream," I state matter-of-factly, "and don't bother trying to convince me otherwise."

He holds his hands up in surrender. "You won't get any

arguments from me. Cookie dough ice cream has been my favorite since I was a kid."

I drop my jaw and slap my palms on my thighs. "Luke Brady, did we just agree on something? Did we just become best friends?" I don't expect him to catch the quote. There's no way Luke would ever watch a movie as crude and pointless as *Stepbrothers*.

But without missing a beat, Luke mirrors my move and shouts, "Yep!"

All I can do is stare at the man before me. Then laughter bursts from my chest, throwing my head back with the force of it. I look through watery eyes to see Luke grinning back at me. It rips another laugh out of me.

I lean back a little too far and nearly fall off the side of the bed but Luke reaches out and pulls me forward before I can go ass up over the edge. Quickly, I steady myself then look up at him, eyes wide. I expect him to make a snide remark about being a hazard to myself. But imagine my surprise when he dissolves into laughter, looking more like a boy than the 200 lb man he is. His laugh triggers my own and before I know it, we're both doubled over. I let out a very unladylike snort, which only spurs us on more.

Eventually, we pull ourselves together, wiping tears from our eyes. After a moment, Luke's phone chimes out a message and he leans over to grab it from the bedside table. While he checks his phone, I take advantage of his distraction to watch him.

He's nothing like who I thought he was. I've had more fun tonight, laughing and talking with him than I have in months. Is there something in the air around here or is it the fact that there's none of the usual stressors that cause so many of our arguments?

Either way, this side of him is unexpected but in a not entirely awful way.

He lifts his head so I quickly look away. My eyes catch on the alarm clock beside the bed and realize it's already past midnight. Damn, where did the night go?

As if my body can tell the time, I try to stifle a yawn but Luke notices. "I think it's time we hit the hay." He nods toward the bathroom. "You can go first."

I nod then pull myself off of the bed and stretch out my sore muscles. "Thanks." I walk to the bathroom, shutting the door behind me. I look into the mirror and stop suddenly. The fact I've been avoiding all night slams into me like a runaway train.

I'm about to spend the night in bed with Luke.

Oh, boy.

LUKE

While Jolie's in the bathroom, I clean up our empty bottles and deposit them into the recycle bin. After double-checking that both the front and patio doors are locked securely, I turn my phone on vibrate and place it back on the bedside table. While I know there's not much I can do while I'm snowed in, I don't want to miss any calls from either the station or my family.

I checked in with the station when we arrived. My deputy assured me that everything was under control. It's not uncommon for the winds to shift and the storms hit harder than what the weatherman initially anticipated. Winters in Haven Bay are unpredictable and when you add in the lake-effect off the bay and the fields just outside of town, road conditions can worsen in the snap of a finger.

Even the most seasoned of winter drivers can get caught in a drift when the snow gets blowing.

I reassured her that I was only a phone call away but she essentially waved me off and told me to enjoy my night off.

Yeah, right. Like I'll be able to sleep without thinking about all of the car accidents, stranded citizens and power outages this storm will cause. How can I protect my town when I'm snowed in at the lodge miles away?

I unbuckle my belt, undo the button and zipper and shove my pants to the floor. At least it's only for a night. I'm sure the snow plows will be out on the roads overnight and Alana's crew will have us cleared out by morning. I'll call a tow for Jolie's car first thing, drop her off at her apartment and be at the station before nine. Then I'll take over and work on damage control.

The bathroom door opens and Jolie walks out, her robe still wrapped around her slim body. It isn't skimpy by any means. In fact, it's actually quite modest, hitting her just below the knee. On any other woman, it would resemble more of a coat than a robe. But on Jolie, she might as well be wearing a silk lingerie set with the way my body is reacting.

I need to quit drinking. It's clearly from the beer and most definitely not from the sight of her bare legs peeking out from underneath the soft material as she walks. One thing you notice about Jolie right away is how amazing her legs are. They're muscular and go on for miles.

One of the first times I saw her, she was wearing these tight cut offs that cupped her ass perfectly. I remember being just as lost trailing my eyes up her long, shapely legs to her juicy ass. The chunky heels she was wearing looked out of place in Haven Bay as she strutted down the sidewalk like a model on a runway. But if she noticed the stares she was getting, she didn't seem to care. She stopped before me and all I could think was with those heels, she would be the perfect height for me to devour her luscious mouth without straining my neck.

That was before she opened that sassy mouth of hers. "If I broke out in song, would you arrest me?" she had asked. When I just stared at her in confusion, she replied, "You know, like that town in Footloose." I tried explaining to her that it was dancing that was illegal in the movie, not singing, but she waved me off. "Same thing. Either way, this town looks exactly like that one. Which means it must be secretly run by a fun-hating minister."

Then she gasped. I spun my head around looking for the cause of her distress. Finding none, I turned back and found her wide-eyes looking at me. "Does that make you the rebellious trouble-maker that corrupts the minister's daughter?" She scanned her eyes up and down me, tilting her head before shaking it. "Nah, you're giving off more fun-police vibes to me."

That was strike one.

Then she turned and crossed the street, disappearing into what would eventually be her yoga studio.

When she opened her studio, she started offering her screaming classes or "rage yoga" as she calls them. The number of noise complaints the station received that day from both locals and tourists had my radio going crazy. I went to her studio, planning to have a chat about by-laws and appropriate noise levels but found the lights off and the studio empty. I heard a shouted curse from the park so I rushed around back, only to find Jolie and a group of people on yoga mats, screaming things that would shock even the most foul-mouthed sailor.

When I tried to talk to her about it, she just smiled and offered me a beer from the cooler beside her.

That was strike two.

Then when I tried to explain the laws on open alcohol, she actually had the nerve to smirk and tell me to "just relax".

That was strike three.

She's been the bane of my existence ever since. The attraction from that day has always laid dormant somewhere in the back of my mind. Sure, she's gorgeous, with her long brown hair and eyes so blue they make the sky jealous. I'd be an idiot to say otherwise. But I've never crossed that line, never let myself feel more because Jolie St. James is trouble with a capital T.

So why is it that I can't keep my eyes off of her now?

She chews softly on her bottom lip, almost shyly as she slips under the sheets. Something about that look has my heart thundering against my chest. I rub my palm over it, trying to keep it from bursting through. She crawls into bed, lying on her side. Then she looks over her shoulder at me. "You gonna lay down?"

Right. Because I'm going to lie beside her.

In bed.

Together.

With her bare legs just inches from mine.

All night.

Someone up there is playing some sick, cosmic joke on me. I bet it's my dad. It would make his romantic heart sing knowing I was forced to sleep in the same bed as the woman who up until recently, I couldn't stand to be alone in a room with.

I'm not even sure when it all changed, if there was some big shift between us or if it's been slowly developing for months. All I know is one minute I'm dreading sitting on a diner stool beside her and the next, I can't stop thinking about how soft her skin would feel against mine.

She arches a brow at me and I realize I've been standing here staring at her like some creep, so I lift the blanket and slide in next to her. I try to keep as much distance between us as the bed will allow as I roll onto my side, giving her my back. I hear the flick of a switch behind me and suddenly, the room is submerged in darkness.

See? This is fine. If I lie still for the next few hours, the sun will come out, the snow will be cleared and we can get on with our lives as if this whole confusing night never happened.

She shifts behind me and it reminds me how painfully close she is. She moves again, lifting the blanket to adjust herself then settles back onto her side. I wait for a few moments and when she seems to have settled, my eyes start to drift closed. Just as I can feel my breathing start to slow, a jolt from behind me pulls me out of sleep's warm embrace.

"Would you quit fidgeting over there?" I whisper-shout over my shoulder.

She shuffles then bounces. "I can't. It's this stupid robe. I feel like I'm wrapped in a burrito. And not in a good way." *Shuffle, shuffle.* "It's making me claustrophobic."

With a sigh, I roll onto my back and look over to where she's yanking at the material, trying to free herself from its confines. The more she pulls, the more twisted the robe gets until she's swinging her arms and kicking her legs in frustration against it.

Biting my cheek to keep from laughing, I lift the blanket off her flailing body. Finally free, she stumbles to her feet beside the bed and pulls the robe off, whipping it onto the floor. Then she stomps on the pile and, just for good measure, gives it a swift kick across the room.

She turns to me, hair a mess and eyes menacing. She huffs out a breath that blows a stray piece of hair out of her face.

I swear I can taste blood, I'm biting on my cheek so hard to keep the smirk off my face. I might be inexperienced when it comes to women, but I'm not suicidal. Even I can tell when a woman is mad and by the look in her eye, Jolie is one smile, one twist of the lip away from losing her ever-loving shit.

So even though she looks like the deranged cat woman from *The Simpson's*, I don't dare tell her that. I give her a few seconds to calm her ragged breathing then ask, "You good?"

I try to keep the laugh that's bubbling in my chest out of my voice, but fail. She narrows her eyes at me in a look that makes my balls shrink up inside me. She points a threatening finger at me, as if it's my fault she was just roped up like a steer at the rodeo. "Something funny, Brady?" I hold my hands up in surrender and shake my head. "You try sleeping in that death trap. I'm lucky I didn't suffocate to death in it!"

It takes all my effort not to roll my eyes at her dramatics. She points over at the offending garment. "I'm not sleeping in that thing. Death by robe is not how I plan to go."

My eyes follow her pointed hand but they catch on the never-ending tanned skin before me. It's then that I realize just how little Jolie's wearing. With her robe gone, she's left in pale pink underwear and a white tank top.

That's it. Full stop. Nothing else.

As in, I can see her nipples through the flimsy material. And even though the room is a warm 74 degrees, the tempting pink buds are hard, as if begging for my mouth to lavish them with attention. My mouth waters as I picture leaning forward and doing exactly that until I hear a soft *"ahem"*. My eyes shoot up to an amused smile on Jolie's lips.

Caught, I quickly look away. Then I reach behind me, fisting the back of my shirt and pulling it over my head. I hand it over to her, but she doesn't take it. Seeing the hesitation on her face, I try again. "Just take it. I don't want you to be cold."

She still doesn't reach for it, her eyes bouncing between my face and the shirt, so I toss it at her. She grabs it just before it hits her in the chest. She looks down at the shirt, a corner of her plump bottom lip tucked between her teeth. My hands ache to smooth it out. Instead, I roll away from her, shoving the temptation down into the place I reserve just for her.

A moment passes before I feel the bed dip and the blanket pull up. She's quiet for a while, to the point where I'm sure she's fallen asleep. I let my eyes drift closed and the last thing I hear before sleep pulls me under is a soft, "thank you".

When I dream that night, it's of a vibrant blue jay singing a peaceful tune.

CHAPTER 24

JOLIE

A low voice pulls me out of sleep. As they always do, my eyes fight to stay closed, the soft mattress beneath me promising endless hours of comfort if I just give in to sleep. The voice mumbles again and my curiosity gets the better of me. I roll onto my back to see where the source is coming from.

Luke stands by the patio door, his head bent with a phone pressed to his ear as he paces back and forth. His face is creased with worry as he listens to the person on the other end. Then he sighs, dragging a hand down his face. His response is too low for me to hear and he hangs up. He turns to the window but there's tension in his back.

"Everything okay?" I ask, and he turns sharply to face me. There's a softness in his eyes when he looks at me, his shoulders dropping marginally. Warmth spreads within my chest.

"Sort of. I called Henry over at the garage about picking up your car," he says, talking about the only mechanic and tow truck in town. "He said the roads are still a mess, despite every plow and able-bodied volunteer being out all night. It's still snowing and it's not supposed to let up until late afternoon. The back roads leading out of the winery won't be cleared for hours yet. Apparently, since the car is tagged and you're safe here, your car's pretty low on the priority list."

My heart sinks. I knew there was a risk taking Blue out when the snow started, but she's never let me down before. I naively thought this time would be no different. I don't even want to think about the pile of snow she's under right now. I only hope the damages are minimal and inexpensive. I don't think I could manage losing Blue, too.

I sit up in bed, rubbing the sleep from my eyes. "So what do we do? Would your truck be able to make it back to town?"

He shakes his head. "Alana came by earlier to drop off some clothes from the gift shop. She told me that while they've cleared the parking lot and some of the courtyard, their snow blower won't be able to clear the road. With the snow still coming down the way it is, they can't keep up." He palms the back of his neck and slides it down his neck. "Looks like we're stuck here for a while longer."

An awkward silence fills the room. Despite our apparent friendship last night, I'm not sure how to act now. Did our truce only apply in the dark of night, when it was just the two of us? Will he go back to hating my guts the second we cross the threshold of the door?

My stomach growls. I put a hand on it as if to silence the noise. Well, it seems like we'll find out sooner rather than later.

"Should we go grab something to eat then?" I ask. He hesitates, looking down at his phone as if someone is going to call him for help at any second. "Not much we can do while we're snowed in. Might as well go grab some food."

He pauses for a second, then shoves his phone into his pocket. "Fine. I want to see if there's anything Alana needs anyway. I'm sure she could use the help."

I nod then toss back the blanket to stand, despite my sleepy body's protests. Eyes closed, I reach my arms above my head to stretch out my tired muscles.

When I open my eyes, I'm met with a pair of dark ones staring back at me. Or should I say at my legs. It's then that I realize I'm wearing Luke's shirt and my panties.

And that's it. Oh, and they're not just any panties. Oh, no.

These are my back-of-the-drawer, why-do-I-still-own-these, only-wear-on-laundry-day-because-who-wears-thongs-anymore panties.

And with my arms still raised over my head, Luke has a full view of the very skimpy piece of fabric that's barely covering my goodies.

Why didn't I just wear the bathing suit bottoms like I wanted to? This is why I make an awful adult. Most people don't wait until they're down to their last pair of underwear to do laundry. Most people throw out the underwear that they've had since college and no longer wear because they're horribly uncomfortable.

I mean, who really wants to walk around with a perma-wedgie all day?

Not this girl.

My arms drop to my side. Thankfully, Luke's shirt is long enough to cover my ass, but just barely. Luke's eyes shoot up to mine and he has the good sense to look a little embarrassed to have been caught gawking at me.

Normally, I would have no problem making a joke and poking at his discomfort. I mean, they're just legs right? Some bathing suits are more revealing than this.

But for some reason, the words are lodged in my throat. The room suddenly feels too small, the air too thick. Maybe it's because we just spent the night lying half-naked next to each other. Or maybe it's the way his eyes traveled over my skin, like a soft caress. I swear I felt it right to my core. Either way, I do what any sane person in this situation would do.

I run.

Not even offering an excuse, I hurry past him and into the bathroom, slamming the door behind me. Leaning against the door, I let my head drop back against the wood.

What is happening?

———

AFTER I BOLTED into the bathroom, the room was quiet for a few moments before there was a soft knock on the bathroom door. "I'll meet you in the dining room?" Luke asked, and I squeaked out an "okay". A moment later, the front door opened and closed.

I turn to the mirror and give myself a mental slap in the face.

What the hell are you doing? This is Luke. The man hates you, remember?

Why am I getting frazzled over him? Who cares what he thinks about me or my underwear?

Or the look of pure heat he gave me when he saw them.

Nope, pump the brakes. Not going there. We're friends and that's it. In fact, we're not even friends; we're two people who love their friends and are playing nice for their sake.

That's it. Nothing more.

Satisfied that my head's on straight, I open the door but

stop suddenly at the neatly folded stack of clothes at my feet. Bending down, I scoop up a Silver Fox Winery shirt, a pair of jogging pants, a spare toothbrush, toothpaste and deodorant. Luke must've put them outside the door for me before I left.

I can feel myself starting to smile at the sweet gesture but wipe it away.

Lock that shit up, St. James.

I hurry to dress and brush my teeth. Before I leave, I pull my purse out of the closet and pull out my medication bottle. Luckily, I'm a forgetful person so I keep my anti-anxiety medication in my purse for days when I forget to take them before I leave home. Washing the pill down with a cup of water, I pull open the room door then head down the hallway toward the dining room.

Turning the corner, the hallway gives way to the grand dining room, which is surprisingly busy for eight thirty in the morning. Alana had mentioned last night that their meals were usually served at the dining tables, but with her lack of staff, the meals would be a bit more informal and served buffet-style.

There's about twenty guests spread out across the dining room. Alana and a few of her staff are busy refilling the warmers with fresh food, clearing away dirty dishes and refilling the drink station. You'd think they'd be rattled by the lack of help, but the staff are smiling and chatting with guests as if it's a regular day. Being this close to the mountains, I'm sure they've been snowed in a time or two and have learned to roll with it.

Even the guests seem to be in a pleasant mood, given that their vacation plans have been dumped on—literally and figuratively. It's nice to see. Speaking from experience, not all customers are as accommodating as these ones. Even over something as out of the winery's control as the weather. I don't know how many times I've been yelled at by a customer for something idiotic or miniscule. I once had a customer berate me for fifteen minutes about her room being too cold. When I pointed out that each room came with its own thermostat that she was welcome to adjust, she went off about how the rooms should be set to an appropriate 82 degrees as (and I quote), "anyone who sets their temperature below 80 might as well go stay in a hostel".

Luke is standing at one end of the serving table where Alana is refilling one of the warmers. I make my way through the dining area toward them.

I wonder how he's going to play this. Will he apologize for the underwear thing? God, I hope not. Talk about pouring salt in the embarrassment wound.

We're adults. He saw me in my underwear and that's it. Let's laugh it off, then pretend it never happened. It's only weird if we make it weird.

He looks up at me as I approach, his expression unreadable. Alana looks up at the same time and smiles.

"Oh, I'm so glad the clothes fit," she says, setting the tray of scrambled eggs in her hands on the table. "I was just telling Luke I had to guess on sizes but I figured baggy clothes were better in this weather anyway."

"They fit great. Thank you for doing that. It was really thoughtful of you," I tell her. "Hopefully there's something I can do to return the favor."

She gestures to the food warmers with her serving spoon. "You can help by eating up all of this food. Grab a plate and dig in. Drinks are in the dispenser on the table to your right." She empties the rest of the eggs into the warmer then props the empty tray on her hip. "Help yourself."

Luke takes two plates from the stack before him. He passes one to me then gestures for me to go ahead of him in line. Apparently, we're acting as if nothing happened. Perfect.

"Let me know what I can do to help," he offers. "I can clear the parking lot. Or I can check out the furnace, make sure everything looks okay. Whatever you need."

Alana smiles warmly. "Thanks, Luke. I'll keep that in mind but I think we're okay right now. Our maintenance guy, Frank, lives on-site and has been keeping an eye on the furnace. The lot was cleared this morning but it'll probably need to be done again this afternoon. I'll keep you in mind then but for now, just relax."

Luke's lips turn up but there's tension in the expression. Luke's known around town as quite the workaholic. It doesn't matter whether he's on duty or not, he takes his job of protecting and serving the town very seriously. It must be killing him not being able to do anything.

When I worked at a spa in Vancouver, the other massage therapists and I used to have a name for people like Luke: a Dwayne. As in "The Rock". Because massaging them was like massaging granite—hard, immovable and with no give. There's no one I've ever met who was more of a Dwayne than Luke Brady.

The image of Luke spread out before me, while I run my hands over his hard muscles, has me swallowing a little harder than usual.

Normally, I'd poke fun at him for it, maybe make a joke about how the stick that's lodged up his ass would probably make it hard to shovel snow. But for some reason, I feel a little tug of sympathy for him. I know what it's like to have pent-up energy with nowhere to put it and it's uncomfortable to say the least.

So I take pity on him. "Can we at least help with the dishes? I'm sure you and your staff could use a break and we'd be happy to help." Maybe he'll take my offer as the gesture of good faith I mean it to be.

Alana hesitates, her eyes searching between us before relenting. "If you really don't mind, that would be appreciated. Thank you. There's a tour in a few hours and I'm sure the staff would love a break before having to set up for it." Luke's shoulders visibly relax beside me.

Alana places the empty tray on top of a cart filled with empty dishes and utensils. "Make sure you stop by for the tour. It's at noon in the tasting room." She nods to an empty table nearby. "Now, go eat. You are guests after all." Then she turns and pushes her cart toward the kitchen doors, stopping to smile and chat with a nearby guest on her way.

"It must be nice to be that calm all the time. I swear there's nothing that can shake her," I comment, shaking my head as I turn to continue filling my plate.

Luke nods, following behind me. "I assume it's a good trait to have when you run a venue." He scoops a spoonful of scrambled eggs onto his plate. "I have no idea how my sister does it. She was always the most dramatic kid. I can't imagine her calming a bride down over the color of the tablecloths."

I balance my full plate on the edge of the serving table to fill a mug with steeped tea. "I thought Tori was doing really well for herself in Toronto. Avery said she's working for one of the top event planning companies in the city." I stir a bit of sweetener into my tea. "She must be doing something right."

Luke fills a mug with black coffee then shrugs. "I guess. She doesn't really talk about it much. She's busy, I know that. Her schedule is just as crazy as mine so a lot of times we're only on the phone a few minutes before she has to rush off." We carry our plates over to a nearby table and sit down. "If I ever ask her about it, she answers vaguely and then changes the subject."

"I respect that. It's a lot of work being a girl boss, I'm sure." I stab my fork into my eggs and bring it to my mouth. Even with them sitting in the warmer, they're still cooked to perfection. Fluffy and lightly seasoned—my favorite. I already reported back to Avery on the delicious dinner from last night. If this is how their food is buffet-style, I can't wait to see how the reception dinner goes.

"How long has she been in Toronto?" I ask, taking a bite of my bacon. My eyes nearly roll back in my head. I swear if I wasn't afraid of keeling over at 40, I'd eat bacon at every meal. After the day I had yesterday, there's nothing that will cheer me up faster than a plateful of bacon. It should really be its own food group. I moan and take another bite.

I look up from my plate and see Luke watching me intensely. It's then that I'm hyper-aware of the sound that just came out of my mouth.

He clears his throat and nods. "Uh, yeah. She moved out there for college and has been there ever since."

I nod back. After that, we sit in a tense silence eating, conversation filling the room around us.

So much for things not being awkward between us.

CHAPTER 25

LUKE

I think I'm having a stroke. Or a temporary lapse in sanity. There's got to be some reason for the complete lack of control I have over my body when Jolie is around.

I did well last night. I managed to stay on my side of the bed, without an inch of our skin touching. It usually takes me a few minutes to turn off my brain every night before I can drift off. But last night it took almost an hour before sleep finally pulled me under.

It might have something to do with the fact that Jolie was lying beside me in *my* shirt. Oh, and she had no pants on.

Real funny, Dad.

When I woke up early this morning, her bare leg was draped casually over my thigh. My hand was just about to skim her soft, warm skin when my eyes shot open, realizing who that leg belonged to.

I jumped out of bed so fast, I'm surprised I didn't wake her.

I looked back at the bed I had just vacated, my heart

pumping vigorously in my chest. But the sight did nothing to help the painful cadence. She looked beautiful, her hair draped across the pillows, her long limbs strewn across the bed. It took all my effort not to crawl back into bed beside her. Instead, I grabbed my phone and placed some calls to the station.

But then she had to go and lift her arms and my world upended. Her curvy waist, those luscious thighs.

And that fucking thong. Is she trying to kill me? Thank God it was too dark for me to see that last night or I would've never fallen asleep.

"Have you ever stayed here before?" she asks, breaking the silence.

I clear my throat, hoping to erase the image of her long legs from my mind. "I have," I say, fiddling with my coffee mug. "It's a pretty popular winery and one of the only local venues so I've been to quite a few weddings here. Alana does a good job of making each wedding feel unique though, so it looks different every time I'm here." I take a drink of my coffee. "Have you?"

"A couple of small events but never a wedding." She smiles broadly. "I can't wait to see what they do for Avery and Matt's. It's going to be beautiful."

I turn to look out the ceiling to floor windows beside me. The morning sun has melted away some of the snow from the windows so you can actually see out of them. Outside, the snow continues to fall but it's more peaceful than threatening the way it was last night. Just beyond the windows is a flagstone terrace with tall wood pillars that lead out into the vineyard. Rows and rows of vines cascade down the hill, covered to protect them from the harsh winter. In the distance, a handful of snow-covered mountains line the horizon.

Winter in town, even one as small as Haven Bay, is filled with potential dangers. Icy sidewalks, slick roads, and power outages from storms are just a few of the hazards_that have the department's scanner going crazy. I've spent many snowy nights digging out some arrogant travelers from a ditch who thought they could beat the storm.

But winter in the mountains is peaceful and quiet. The world is asleep, tucked under a blanket of snow. Once a year, I take a few days off and venture up to stay at my buddy, Wade's, hunting cabin that's not far from here. He lives over in Edmonton but lets me use the cabin and in exchange, I knock out the cobwebs and clean out the fireplace. Up there, you can stand out in the open and feel like the only person for miles and miles.

In the spring, when the world awakens again, this area is the closest thing you'll find to heaven. Nothing beats the view of the sunrise peeking over the mountains while the birds soar over the budding trees and the wildlife crawl out from their winter hiding places. Add in the already picturesque views that the winery offers and it's bound to be like something out of a movie.

Yeah, springtime at the winery will make for a beautiful wedding.

But instead of saying any of that, I simply nod. "Sure will."

Jolie stabs her fork into a pile of eggs then continues to describe the details of the wedding from the décor down to the flowers. Quite frankly, I'm only half-listening to her ramble on.

Details are usually what I do best, but in this case, I have no problem admitting that I'm out of my element. I wouldn't know a candelabra if you beat me over the head with it and the only chargers I know haven't been to the Super Bowl since 1995.

So I let my mind wander to where it most often goes—work. I sneak a peek at my phone from under the table but there's no messages. It should give me comfort that the department can run smoothly without me, even during the aftermath of a snowstorm. I should be relieved that I work with such reliable and capable officers that they're able to do what needs to be done without my supervision.

But it doesn't.

Instead, my chest twists like a rag being wrung out. I shift in my chair then push a hand to my chest, trying to shove this feeling back down where it belongs. The feeling that something bad is going to happen and I won't be there to help. The feeling that my friends and family could be in trouble and I wouldn't be able to do a damn thing about it. This damn feeling that's been rearing its ugly head since I was a teenager.

Jolie quiets, her eyes following my hand on my chest. "You okay?" she asks softly. Not trusting my voice, I nod again. She gives me a look that tells me she doesn't quite believe me.

After a moment, she looks away and drops her fork onto her plate. "Well, I'm finished." She stands, plate and mug in hand. "You ready to tackle some dishes?" I nod, even though I've barely touched my breakfast. I'm starting to feel like a bobblehead at this point, unable to string together any words.

Pull your shit together, Brady.

I pick up my half-full plate and stand. "Let's do it." With that, we head over to the kitchen. Outside the door, there's a cart with a tub of soapy water and dirty dishes on top. I grab the handle and push it through the swinging door that leads into the kitchen.

It takes us a few minutes to figure out how to load the dish sanitizer but eventually we get a system going. The longer my hands are busy, the more the tightness in my chest starts to ease and I'm able to breathe deeply again.

Jolie's prattling on about some of the local gossip, nothing especially interesting that I need to comment on but enough to keep my focus on her words and not on my own thoughts.

I shove the dish rack into the sanitizer and pull the lever to close the lid. Taking another deep breath, I slowly regain my composure until I feel strong again. I revel in it, forcing it to grow with each breath.

Because strong is the only thing I can afford to be.

THE HAVEN TIMES

pg 15   Proudly serving Haven Bay for over 100 years.   **FREE**

DEAR ANNIE

Your local source for advice on love, life and everything in between!

The answer to this week's trivia question (pg 9) is peanut butter.

Q.

Dear Annie,

I'm thinking about having sex for the first time with my boyfriend. I'm a virgin, but he isn't. I know I love him and that he loves me.

He told me that he's willing to wait and that he doesn't want to pressure me into anything. It's not that I don't want to have sex; I do. I'm just nervous and not sure what to expect.

Basically what I'm wondering is: how will I know when I'm ready?
Sincerely,
V is for Virgin

A.

Dear V,

I'd be lying if I told you that every single person you have sex will be with someone you love. That's not to say you won't. You might—everyone is different.

But chances are, there will be people you sleep with that you don't love. And that's okay. Sex is a natural thing shared between two people.

But while love isn't a prerequisite for sex, there are some qualities that you should never compromise on when it comes to picking a partner.

1. Trust. When you have sex with someone without a condom, you're essentially having sex with everyone they've had unprotected sex with. You might trust your partner but do you trust their past ones? Are you 100% sure none of their partners could've lied about being clean? So wear a condom. Every. Damn. Time.

2. Respect. Unfortunately, there's people out there who will act like the perfect partner, say all the right things, do all the right things. Until they don't. Until they get what they want from you and ditch you. You're probably thinking, my partner would never do that. And I don't say this to scare you, but no one ever thinks their partner will do it. Until they do. Respect yourself and demand respect from the people around you.

3. Good Communication. Don't like what your partner's doing? Unsure about birth control methods (hint: condom)? Unsure of where you stand in your relationship afterward? Communicate, communicate, communicate. If you're scared to speak up with your partner, they're not the right person for the job.

4. Fun. With all this in mind, sex should be fun. If you're scared, anxious, doubtful or feeling guilt-tripped, the sex won't be good. It's as simple as that. There should only be one reason why you have sex: because you want to. Not because they want you to. Not because you think you have to. Not because other people are.

With the right partner, sex can be fun, exciting and make you feel like the goddess you are. Take proper precautions, talk it out, and do what's best for you.

At the end of the day, trust your instincts. If something doesn't feel right, it probably isn't.

Love always,
Annie

CLOCKS GO BACK SUNDAY

For all you old folks whose clocks don't automatically turn back, remember to turn your clocks back on Sunday.

Police Chief Luke Brady warns that Daylight Savings will not be a valid excuse for speeding so plan accordingly.

"That's it, baby. Right there." My back arches, my toes curl and my head drops back as I let out a low moan. The jets from the hot tub thrum against my back, letting them soothe my aching muscles. I sink further into the steamy water, relaxing into the seat.

After Luke and I finished up with the dishes, he wanted to check in with Frank, the maintenance guy, to see if he needed any help. When he walked away and thought I wasn't looking, I saw him peek at his phone. I think it's driving him crazy, not having anything to do.

Luke is so used to taking care of everyone all the time that he doesn't know what to do with himself when he's not needed. There was a minute during breakfast when I caught a glimpse of something in his eye. Something I've become far too familiar with.

It looked a whole lot like that bitch Tiffany.

I never pegged someone like Luke to have anxiety but I guess that's the tricky thing with mental illness. It doesn't discriminate. It can affect anyone at any time.

Luke didn't seem like he wanted to talk about it, so I

helped distract him with idle chit chat, lame jokes or anything else that might take his mind off of his spiraling thoughts. After he left, I took the opportunity to explore the lodge. The snow continued to fall so my exploration outside lasted the five minutes it took me to walk from the front of the winery terrace around to the back.

After that, I wandered around inside, offering my assistance to any staff I happened upon. All of them gave me a warm smile, but refused my offer. So, with nothing to do, I found myself in the lodge sunroom, reading a book from the shelf in a leather wingback chair where I stayed until the wine tour began.

The tour was fun but combined with the lively conversation at dinner, I was exhausted and ready for a long soak in the hot tub.

The sound of a sliding door has me opening one eye to look out over the shadowed terrace. It's a public hot tub, so it could be any of the other guests from the lodge. Having met most of them at the wine tour, I'm not worried about any creepy men slinking in beside me. Still, I was kind of hoping to just relax. My social battery is running dangerously low after spending most of the day making small talk with strangers.

Recognizing Luke's broad frame, my shoulders relax back into the tub.

"I'm surprised to see you out here," I call out over the sound of the jets. "You don't seem like the hot tub type."

Luke walks over to one of the lounge chairs under the terrace and toes off his shoes. "What does a 'hot tub type' even look like?" He reaches a hand behind his back to pull his shirt over his head.

I try to keep my head from lifting as he shoves his jeans to the floor, leaving him in just his black boxer briefs. Even though I saw him in his boxers last night, it was dark and he slid into bed seconds later, so I wasn't able to get a good look. In the glow of the setting sun tonight, there's enough light to catch more than a glimpse. And what I'm seeing is making my mouth suddenly dry.

Well, hello there, sailor.

"You know what I mean." I wave my hand aimlessly above the water. "Relaxed. Calm. Like they might enjoy sitting still for longer than three minutes at a time."

Luke slides into the seat across from me and damn if the glowing lights under the water aren't bouncing off his impressive chest. He's muscular in a less obvious way than other men, like his body is used for function rather than for show. There's a sprinkle of chest hair across his pecs that trails lower, disappearing under the water. I'm not usually a fan of chest hair but it's giving rugged-cowboy-manly-man vibes and it's really doing something for me.

He lets out a groan as he settles back in the seat. "I've been helping Frank clear snow for the last three hours. My entire body is screaming at me right now. Even my eyelids are sore. I'm exhausted, but there's no way I could sleep with muscles this tight." He twists in his seat, letting the jets hit his lower back. "Do you think Stu would give me a history lesson on bees to help put me to sleep?"

I snort a laugh. Stuart P. Flanagan, as he introduced himself before the wine tour, is a wine enthusiast, astrology buff and amateur beekeeper. He was staying at the lodge for some meteor shower that I didn't catch the name of and to visit the Whitecourt Meteorite crater. He's a perfectly nice man but could (and would) talk your ear off about anything bee, wine or astrology related if given the chance.

While we were on the wine tour, Stuart had asked our tour guide, Mandy, what species of bees were native to this area. Luke made the mistake of asking Stuart what bees had to do with wine. The result was a fifteen minute lecture on the important role bees play in pollinating the cover crops that surround the grapevines.

"Don't be mean to Stu," I scold, sitting up in my seat. "You won't be laughing when he and I kick ass in Trivial Pursuit tomorrow."

Luke closes his eyes, a small lift curves his lips. I've learned that's his version of a megawatt smile.

He's a subtle man, our chief.

"I'm sure you two will do great," he says, his smile turning into a smirk. "Maybe you can room with him tonight instead."

"Very funny," I arch an eyebrow at him and his smirk grows.

Oh yeah, did I not mention? We're staying another night. Luke called the station after the wine tour and the roads are still a mess. There was a car accident not far from here that took three tow trucks, five police officers and six volunteer firefighters to clear. Luckily, no one was hurt but the damage was enough for them to close the back roads for the rest of the day until they could clear away the debris and snow.

The more he heard, the deeper Luke's frown got. I could practically feel the tension rolling off of him in waves. After he hung up, he shoved his phone back in his pocket, grumbled something about needing to find Frank, and stormed away.

I hadn't seen him since then.

I looked for him at dinner but he was nowhere in sight. Now I realize he must've had some things to work off if he subjected himself to shoveling snow for the last three hours.

We fall into a comfortable silence, the only sound

coming from the jets. The sun has since set, but the memory of the sky ablaze with oranges and pinks while the sun dipped below the mountain tops earlier this evening is one I'll never forget.

I twist in my seat, looking out over the vineyard. I can't see very far in the dark, but the light from the terrace illuminates the first few rows. I imagine what it will be like in the spring, when the ground is dry and green, with the trees starting to fill and the flowers are budding.

I picture having my yoga mat spread out between the rows of vines, sinking into Warrior pose with the setting sun behind me. I should talk to Alana about hosting some yoga classes in the vineyard when spring comes. Maybe one of my calmer, sunrise beginner classes instead. I don't think she would appreciate me scaring off any guests. We could even offer a discount to the overnight guests while extending it to the locals as well. I'm sure my regulars would love a change of scenery by the time winter's over.

While I love rage yoga, there's something about a peaceful class that warms my heart. Being able to stretch and push your body while the sun kisses the tops of the mountains before you, surrounded by nature and its serene sounds is an opportunity I can't pass up.

I feel guilty staying at such a beautiful venue for free. Luke and I have both offered to pay for our rooms or at least our meals but Alana wasn't having any of it. I even tried to talk the front desk attendant into letting me pay without her knowing, but they refused, saying Alana had told them not to accept our money.

"It's no one's fault that you're stuck here. You shouldn't have to pay for a warm place to rest your head," Alana replied the last time I asked.

So we've been helping out where we can, doing dishes,

clearing meals and in Luke's case, shoveling snow. It may not be much, but I know it's making Luke feel better.

"Can I ask you a question?" I ask, breaking the silence.

Luke lifts his head to look over at me. He looks more relaxed than I've seen him all day, but his shoulders still hold that tension that never seems to leave him. He nods so I turn toward him.

"Why does it bother you so much that you can't help in town?"

Luke's face remains expressionless, just blinking at me. So, I do the same thing I do every time I start to feel nervous.

Ramble.

"I just mean, that's why you have a team behind you, right? If you can't trust them to handle things when you're not around, what good is having a whole department?" *Blink, blink.* "You're only one person. You can't take care of an entire town by yourself. Not even the Flash could be everywhere all at once. Especially with a town this crazy." I chuckle nervously as he continues to stare at me. "We may be small, but we make up for it with craziness."

Finally that smirk returns. "The Flash, eh?" he asks. "You don't seem like a superhero nerd but they're hard to spot these days."

I let out a slow breath. I wasn't going to bring up the subject of what I suspect was the start of an anxiety attack at breakfast. But I couldn't shake this nagging feeling that I needed to help. "My older brother was a big comic book nerd when we were younger. He still is. Thankfully he hasn't dressed up as Spider-Man for Halloween in, oh, two years now. So you could almost say he's matured."

"Hey, don't knock Spidey. Though I've always been a Batman guy, myself."

I tilt my head, assessing him. "I don't see it. Billionaire playboy with zero responsibility? That doesn't seem like you."

Luke shakes his head, leaning forward in his seat. "That's Bruce Wayne."

I scoff. "Okay, I may not be the biggest superhero buff, but even I know Bruce Wayne and Batman are the same person."

Luke shakes his head again. "That's not what I mean. The billionaire playboy is the persona Bruce Wayne gives off to hide the fact that he's actually Batman." He runs his hands over his thighs and I swear I only ogle them for half a second. Three-quarters at most.

"I guess what I like about Batman is that he could be anyone. Sure, the billions of dollars help with the gadgets. But he doesn't have superhuman powers to fall back on. He's not this perfect guy who always does the right thing. He's got flaws and makes mistakes and sometimes lets his anger get the best of him. People don't always appreciate him but he still shows up and protects the city. Even if he has to be seen as the bad guy sometimes, he still gets the job done."

My mouth is hanging open by the end of his speech and he chuckles. "What?" he asks.

I snap my mouth closed and sit back further in my seat. "Nothing. I'm just not sure I've ever heard so many words come out of your mouth at once. At least, not when there's no lecture involved." He arches a brow at me and I throw my hands up in surrender. "I'm not trying to start a fight. I liked it."

He doesn't answer, just turns his head to look out over the vines. But since I'm a glutton for punishment, I poke the bear a little more. "I noticed how you didn't exactly answer my question."

He doesn't look back at me when he replies. "I know."

I wait, but he doesn't continue. Well, I'm a lot of things but I'm not a quitter. "Look, I know we're not exactly friends but we did survive a near-death experience together—"

Luke gives me a wry look. "Near-death experience? I don't think I'd consider being stuck in a snowdrift for twenty minutes as near-death."

"So," I continue, ignoring his logic. "I think that makes us less of enemies—"

"Are you always this dramatic?" He shakes his head. "What am I saying? Of course, you are."

I narrow my eyes. "Would you shut up for half a second? I'm trying to help."

"I know what you're doing and it's not necessary. I'm fine. Sure, I wish I was down there helping with damage control. But it's not because I don't trust my team. That's my town. Those are my neighbors. They're mine to watch out for. It's as simple as that."

There's a finality in his tone that even I know not to push any further. So I let it go with a sharp nod. We fall back into silence, this one more tense than the first. The night is awake with the sounds of nature. In the distance, a wolf calls out to the moon while a nearby owl lefts out a soft *hoo.*

Eventually, Luke sighs, dropping his head back onto the headrest. "I didn't mean to snap at you," he says, more to the stars than to me. "It's just that I'm...protective. With my family, my friends. This town. I..." He runs a wet hand over his short hair. "I don't like not being there when they need me." He finally tilts his head to meet my eyes with his own solemn stare.

Understanding has me softening toward him. I know there's a lot going on inside his head, some of which I don't think he entirely knows the extent of. But I also know what it's like to not be fully in control of your thoughts, constantly at war between the rational and irrational.

Speaking from experience, I think he'd benefit from having someone to talk about it with. It can be hard to reach out to a friend or family member, not wanting to feel judged or pitied. I found my person in my therapist, Sue. I'm not sure Luke's thoughts on therapy but something tells me he's not ready for that step yet.

So I promise myself to be that person for Luke. Even if he's not ready yet, I can wait. Despite what he thinks, I can be patient. Especially about something as important as mental health.

"My favorite food is bologna," I say. Luke's head snaps up and he gives me a quizzical look. He opens his mouth to respond but I cut him off. "I can fit my whole fist inside my mouth. My dream vacation would be to go to the French Alps."

I can see the moment Luke realizes what I'm doing and watch the subtle changes in his posture that signal his relief. If there's one thing I know about Luke, it's that he likes to be in control. He needs it. Showing any hint of vulnerability would be his worst nightmare. Showing that side of himself to me probably felt like chewing steel.

So I offer him an olive branch by switching the subject, continuing our game from last night.

He sinks further into his seat, chewing his lip in thought. As he does, I try not to watch as a ripple of water rolls down his broad chest. This isn't about me drooling over the hot cop that's half-naked and dripping wet like something out of a bad porno. No matter how good he looks and how badly I want to run my tongue all over his...

Stop that. Pull your shit together, J.

"It's gotta be number three," he says and for a second, he might as well be speaking Swahili because I have no clue what he's talking about. Then it hits me.

Right. The game. The game to distract Luke and make him feel better. That game.

"There's no way someone who doesn't like heights would willingly spend time in the Alps," he continues. I shake my head and he narrows his eyes at me. "Bullshit."

I laugh, lifting my hand in the Scout's Honor symbol. "I swear. It makes no sense, I know. But I saw a video about this attraction called 'Step into the Void' online not long after I left Toronto. It's a glass box suspended 3,000 feet in the air on the peak of a mountain called Aiguille du Midi that overlooks the French Alps. I've looked up hundreds of videos on it ever since." I drop my hands into the water, letting the hot water warm them. "I was too broke back then to travel and by the time I could afford it, I was too chicken shit to ever go. I almost went a couple of times. I had the whole thing planned, even bought a ticket. But I backed out right before I was supposed to leave for the airport." I shrug, suddenly self-conscious. "It's fine. I'm sure I'll get there one day."

Why did I think this was a good idea?

Oh, yeah. Luke cut himself open to me, so I had to take a chunk out of myself in return. Well, mission accomplished.

Now all I can think about is how much of a wuss I am. I'm 29 years old, for frig's sake. If I want to stand at the peak of a mountain top in France, I should be able to stand on the damn peak.

But instead I keep letting Tiffany win. That dumb bitch has been ruling my life for so long, I forget that other people can just act on their dreams without a shadow leaning over their shoulder saying, "Yeah, but what if?"

"Then it's definitely number two. You might have a big mouth, but there's no way you can fit your whole fist in it."

I lift my chin to look over at Luke. He offers me a small smile and it gives my heart a little tug.

We're quite the tragic pair tonight.

I take the life preserver he's thrown me and roll with it, shoving Tiffany back down into the cave she belongs in.

"You're clearly a child at heart so I would bet you have the taste buds of one, too," he says.

I lift my arms to stretch them across the back of the tub. It's a casual move but one that has my chest lifting out of the water and my flimsy bra poking out from under the water. Up until now, I don't think Luke gave a second thought about what I was wearing under the water.

By the look in his eye and the bob of his Adam's apple, I'd say he is now.

And a third.

And a fourth.

His eyes drop to the water, probably trying to see if I have my thong on from this morning but the wake from the jets makes it impossible to tell.

I don't bother telling him that I borrowed bathing suit bottoms from Alana. I would've borrowed a top, too but her chest was much bigger than mine and I didn't want to give anyone a free show of the girls.

Though something tells me that Luke wouldn't have complained.

"Well, Chief. You would be wrong." I lean forward, loving how his eyes follow the movement. "Not only can I fit an entire fist in my mouth, but I can do it without gagging." And because I can't help myself, I shoot him a sultry wink.

I expect him to grumble about inappropriateness or get all awkward and change the subject. Instead, to my shock, he leans forward until his knees bracket mine. So close that his scent mixed with the tub's steam is making me lightheaded.

"Too bad, sweetheart. I don't mind the thought of you gagging around my..." his eyes dip down to my lips then slowly back up to my eyes, "fist."

Holy shitballs.

Looks like the chief came out to play.

The question is, do I want to play, too?

Luke reaches out and tucks a stray hair behind my ear that had fallen out of my messy bun. His touch sends a shiver through me.

"Cold, sweetheart?"

"Hell, no."

He grins and if I wasn't sitting, my knees would be buckling. I don't think I'll ever get used to how devastatingly sexy his smile is. The fact that he picks and chooses when to share it only makes it that much more potent.

Slowly, achingly slowly, he leans toward me, his eyes holding mine the entire time.

Suddenly, the sound of a sliding door has me pushing back into my seat, my eyes snapping up to the terrace.

"Well, hello there, Jolie. Luke." Stuart steps out onto the flagstone, shutting the door behind him. "I didn't realize you were out here, but I'm happy for the company."

"Hi, Stuart," I squeak out. *Smooth.* "Beautiful night, isn't it?"

While Stuart's setting down his towel and slipping off his shoes, I sneak a glance at Luke. He's watching me, heat illuminating his stare. I swallow against my suddenly dry mouth. Finally, he slowly sinks back into his seat, but his eyes never leave mine.

"Well, that my dear, Jolie, is the result of the geometric center of the sun being six degrees below the horizon and—"

Stu drones on about something that I'm sure is very interesting but his words are lost to me. My head is spinning and it has nothing to do with the heat from the tub and everything to do with the man sitting across from me. His intense stare makes me want to fidget in my seat.

"Have you ever been, Luke?"

I have no idea what Stuart's talking about, but Luke thankfully seems to. "Not recently," he answers, still holding my gaze. Finally, he breaks the spell and turns to Stuart. They launch into a conversation about who knows what and I take the opportunity to slide lower into the water.

I have no idea what I'm doing. But one thing is for sure: there's no way I'm going to survive another night in that bed beside Luke unscathed.

CHAPTER 27

LUKE

Stuart P. Flanagan deserves a raging case of toe fungus. Either that or a medal of honor for saving me from myself.

I can't decide which.

Before he came out onto the terrace, I was prepared to pin Jolie to the wall of the hot tub, press that long, supple body against mine and devour her irresistible mouth. I was seconds away from pulling her body to mine and running my hands all over her slick body. My hands itched to explore her curves before fisting her bun and dragging that damn mouth of hers against mine.

Then ol' Stu showed up and I forced myself to behave. Not long after, Jolie excused herself then escaped inside.

I'm trying to focus as Stuart drolls on and on about who knows what. I swear I am. But my mind keeps wandering back to Jolie. The more I think about it, the more relieved I am that Stuart interrupted us when he did.

I don't need complications in my life. I need order and stability. I don't have time to mess around with a woman who may or may not be annoyed by my very existence, depending on the time of day.

She's probably thinking the exact same thing about me. Jolie and I couldn't be less right for each other if we tried.

Tonight was just another one of her jokes that went too far. I'm sure by the time I get back to the hotel room, she'll be laughing her ass off about it.

Stuart finally takes a breath between stories and I take the opportunity to stand up. "Well, Stu, it's been great talking to you but I had a long day of shovelling snow and I'm ready to hit the hay." Water splashes as I fling my leg over the edge of the tub to the stairs.

"Can't say that I blame you. I wouldn't be sitting here with me either if I had a beautiful woman waiting in my bed." Stuart chuckles and I stop.

"It's not like that between Jolie and me," I reply but Stuart smirks as if to say *yeah, right.* "We're..." I pause, unsure what you'd qualify us as, then decide on the simplest term for the most complicated answer, "friends."

Stuart's smile grows. "The way you two were staring at each other when I came out, I'm surprised the water wasn't boiling over." He tips his head back to look up at the sky. "No friend of mine has ever looked at me like that. If they did, we sure wouldn't be friends for much longer."

Not sure what to say to that, I simply wish him a good night. I take the steps down the hot tub two at a time, grab my towel and head to the back door.

Drying my chest off as I go, I consider Stuart's comments. I naively figured that he hadn't noticed how close we were when he came out. Apparently not.

I shove open the sliding door, my shoulders screaming in protest. I wasn't lying when I told Jolie earlier that I was sore. Shoveling thick, wet snow all day will do that to you.

By the time Frank called it quits, every muscle in my body felt like lead.

Before I got in the tub, the only thing I had on my mind was a long soak in the heat then dragging my ass to bed and dropping face first into a dreamless sleep. Whenever my mind is racing like it was earlier, nothing brings me out of a spiral quite like physical labor.

Now, despite my aching muscles, my body feels like a live wire, restless with untapped energy as I make my way down the hallway to our room. My mind is racing but now in an entirely new direction.

One I'm not sure I'm willing—or ready—to go in.

I reach our room too soon, hesitating at the door. If I act like nothing happened, maybe she'll go with it and we can avoid any awkwardness.

Unless acting like it didn't happen would insult her and then I'll have to sleep next to a pissed off Jolie all night. I'm not convinced that she wouldn't shave my head in my sleep or something equally insane, so that seems too risky of an option.

Besides, just because she's not going to be my future wife, doesn't mean I want to hurt her feelings. I might be a dick but I'm not a complete asshole.

There's a difference. Trust me; I walk that thin line every day.

Talking about it is also out of the question. I'd rather stab myself in the eyeball with a sewing needle than have that conversation.

The only other option is almost as risky and just as terrifying: continue what we started. Before I even finish that thought, I'm mentally shutting the idea down.

For the umpteenth time since I met her, I remind myself of all the reasons why I can never give in to my urges when it comes to Jolie. We're too different. She's chaos on impossibly long legs, while I thrive in order. She's loud and unfiltered. I need peace and quiet. We'd never work.

There's countless reasons but the main one remains the same: it's just not a good idea. For either of us.

Refusing to stand in the hallway like a creep any longer, I blow out a long breath before turning the handle and pushing my way into the room.

I'm not surprised to see the lights are still on. Jolie's a night owl like me. When I'm on the night shift, driving around town doing my checks, I've noticed a time or two her lights are on well past midnight. It's kind of comforting, knowing that someone else is awake in the middle of the night, when it feels like you're alone with your thoughts. As someone who doesn't necessarily enjoy being in his own head some days, I appreciate being able to ground myself that way.

It's then that I realize the room is empty.

"Jolie?" I call out but there's no answer.

Suddenly, the bathroom door swings open and Jolie comes tearing out, a plunger raised above her head like a baseball bat. I raise my arm to block the disgusting make-shift weapon before she can hit me with it. "Jolie, it's me!" I shout and she stops midswing.

She lowers the plunger and lets out a breath. "Holy queso, Luke, you scared the bejeebers out of me!"

My eyes bounce between her wild hair, loose and kinked from her bun, and the white plunger that's still in her hand. If she didn't have a fecal-sword pointed at me, I'd laugh at how deranged she looks. "What the hell are you doing?"

"Me? What're *you* doing?" she demands. "Have you ever heard of knocking? I thought you were a murderer!"

"How many murderers do you know that know you by name?"

"Um, actually, seventy-five percent of women are murdered by someone they know, *chief.*" She points the plunger at me.

I knock it away from my face. "Get that thing away from me." She wags it in front of my face again, causing me to lean further out of her reach.

"Jolie," I warn. "Put that thing away before you give yourself hepatitis."

She rolls her eyes but complies, setting the plunger on the ground beside her.

Finally safe from her bacteria dagger, her comment from earlier sinks in. I grin. "'Holy queso'?"

She shrugs. "I don't like guacamole." Then she turns and walks back into the bathroom.

Well, that's one way to break the ice.

———

THIS BED NEEDS to be measured because there's no way in hell this is a king. Was it this small last night? I can feel every breath Jolie takes as if it's my own. I could probably tell you the exact distance between where her leg rests on the mattress and mine. She's one small shift away from being pressed against my back.

And don't even get me started on the temperature. It's got to be ninety degrees in here. I'm starting to sweat and it's only partly from the effort of trying not to move.

I'll have to talk to Frank tomorrow because the thermostat in this room is definitely broken.

I look over at the clock on the bedside table. The bright red lights stare back at me. 3 a.m.

I fight back a sigh. Maybe I could fall asleep if I could get the image of Jolie in the hot tub wearing that damn bra out of my head. The steam billowing around her, causing some loose hairs to stick to her cheek. The water lapping over the soft mounds of her...

Fuck sakes. Now I'm lying beside her sporting a chubby like some kind of pervert.

What did I do to deserve this? I'm a good guy. I recycle. I tip my servers. I even helped Sam Townsend's naked, wrinkly old ass out of the tub last week when he fell in the shower.

I don't deserve this level of torture.

"Luke?"

"Yeah?" I say over my shoulder.

"I can't sleep." Jolie blows out a breath from behind me. The mattress dips as she flops onto her back.

I hesitate, then roll to lay beside her. "Me neither."

She turns to switch on the bedside lamp, the sudden light making me shield my eyes for a second. Then rolling onto her side, she props her head up on her elbow and looks down at me. "Want to play?"

I nearly choke on my saliva and my eyebrows shoot up. She must realize how that sounded because her eyes widen and she throws her head back, letting loose a laugh. "A game, you perv. Two truths and a lie." She pokes me in the shoulder. "It's your turn."

I stare up at the ceiling, trying to clear my thoughts from all the ways I'd love to play with her, none of them having anything to do with the game she mentioned.

"Okay, um..." I pause, thinking it over. "I was the quarterback on my high school football team. My first job was in a hair salon. The first date I ever went on ended up in the hospital."

"Ouuu," she practically squeals. "Those are so good, I want them all to be true." She bites the corner of her lip in thought and my eyes follow the movement. Luckily, she's too lost in thought to notice before I force my eyes to hers. "You love control, so quarterback makes sense. Getting to call all the shots, everyone depending on you? That sounds exactly like something you'd love. The hair salon thing seems too good to be true. I can picture you gossiping with the little old ladies while you apply their curlers." I make a face and she laughs. "The first date thing seems like there's a story behind it that I can-*not* wait to hear."

She thinks it over for a second then pokes me in the shoulder again. "I'm going with number 2. All of that estrogen would drive you crazy, there's no way you could've worked in a salon. Barbershop, maybe. But a salon? No way."

I roll onto my side and mirror her pose. "Nope," I reply, making the "p" pop. I can't help but smile at the look of pure delight that flashes on her face.

"No. Freaking. Way." She smacks my arm with each word, nearly knocking my head off of my hand. Seems that Jolie is a hitter when she gets excited. "I need all the details."

"It's really not that exciting of a story. My mom owned a hair salon when I was growing up. All of us kids worked there as our first jobs. I mostly swept floors, filled shampoo bottles and stocked the shelves. Boring stuff. I got a job at Garcia's Apple Orchard the second I was able to." I grin at the memory. "Hauling bushels of apples by myself was a hell of a lot better than listening to gossip all day."

Jolie smiles back at me. "I get that. You'd be surprised how much gossip I hear after classes at the studio. I swear if

I let them talk during class, they'd chat the whole damn time."

"Haven Bay loves its stories."

"It's all part of the charm," she replies. "So, we've established that you were a secret hair stylist..." I poke her in the ribs and she chuckles. "Okay, so it has to be the first-date-hospital one. Number 3."

I shake my head and she smacks my arm again. This time, my head does fall off of my hand. I jokingly glare at her as my head snaps up but she ignores me.

"Shut up! Did you step on her foot so hard while dancing that you broke her foot? Did you choke on her gum while making out in the backseat of your mom's car? Did a stray sheep jump out in front of your car and you swerved to miss it but you ended up hitting a tree instead and she had to ride in the ambulance all the way to the hospital not knowing if you were going to live or die only to have a dramatic first kiss when you woke up from surgery?"

I stare at her, unblinking. "Your mind is like a carnival ride. You're giving me whiplash. Where the hell do you come up with that stuff?"

She shrugs. "I read a lot." She points a finger at me. "Now spill."

She's practically vibrating beside me with excitement and I can't help but think how adorable she looks right now. Her blue eyes are dancing, her lips slightly turned up as if her body is waiting to release the grin she's holding back.

"Alright," I start. "Well, it wasn't anything as Hallmark-y as that. I was fourteen and had a crush on Marnie Miller. She was this beautiful girl that moved to town the year before. That summer, she worked at the diner, so I dragged Matt and Rhett there every day. I used to bribe them with milkshakes so I wouldn't look like a creep going by myself.

You can get Matt to do pretty much anything if you bribe him with food." She laughs and I take a second to revel in the sound. "Anyway, I finally worked up the courage to ask her on a date and for some reason, she said yes. The town used to set up a big screen in the park and put on a movie every Friday night in the summer. We watched *A Walk to Remember* in the park then went for a walk along the boardwalk."

Jolie leans forward, hanging on my every word. Having this much attention on me outside of work would usually make me nervous but for some reason, it's making me want to drag out this story for as long as I can. She's so expressive; every thought is written all over her face. I can't help but smile watching her reactions.

"So, we got to the end of the boardwalk and I could tell she wanted me to kiss her. I leaned down and the second our lips touched, I was in heaven. Little did I realize, I was about to send her there. Literally."

Jolie's eyes get comically wide and her mouth opens slightly, fully invested in my story. I was so nervous to kiss Marnie that night. I was terrified I'd be bad at it. That she'd feel how sweaty my palms were and be grossed out. Or worse, she'd tell me she didn't think of me like that and that we were better as friends.

I can't help thinking that kissing Jolie, for real this time, would be like being swallowed by a black hole. She'd consume my every thought, every touch, every movement. She's not the type of woman you walk away from unscathed.

When did she stop being the pain in the ass yoga instructor and start being this fun, magnetic woman whose pull I'm no longer eager to avoid?

Best not to think about that right now.

"I had never kissed a girl before that night and I was scared. Like an idiot, I let it slip to Matt. He told me that the best way to be good at kissing was to wear lip balm." Jolie snorts at that. "I know. I should've known Matt didn't know shit all about women. I was taking dating advice from the guy who was in love with his best friend and didn't even know it. Anyway, I didn't have any so I snuck into Tori's room and borrowed her strawberry-kiwi lip balm. Turns out Marnie was allergic to kiwi." Jolie gasps and I nod solemnly. "Yep. Exactly. Luckily, she had her Epi-Pen but she still had to go to the hospital to get checked out."

"You went with her?" Jolie asks, slightly surprised.

My brows furrow. "Of course." She gives me a small smile. "What?"

She shakes her head softly, still watching me. "Nothing. Just...you're a good guy, you know that?"

Her praise makes me uncomfortable so I shift onto my back to avoid her gaze. "Your turn."

I feel her eyes on me for a second longer before she looks away.

"I've never had a serious boyfriend. I didn't have my first kiss until I was sixteen. I once dated a guy with a Marge Simpson fetish."

I turn my head to give her a skeptical look. "Marge Simpson fetish? That can't be a thing."

She pushes a loose hair out of her face and behind her ear. She brushed her hair before bed so she no longer looks like a deranged Hagrid. "It's a thing. Don't kink-shame, Chief."

I hold my hands up in surrender. "I'm not kink-shaming. I'm just kink-curious."

"Blue hair, green dress, raspy voice," she says as if it's the most obvious thing in the world. "Yes, right there,

Homie," she rasps in a damn near perfect Marge Simpson impression and a laugh is ripped out of me.

"I can't decide if I want that to be true or not. I can't picture you in a blue wig and green dress."

Jolie smirks. "He preferred green lingerie."

Well, fuck. That shuts me up fast. My mouth is suddenly dry, picturing Jolie in a lacy nightie. The green material of the bra pushing up her soft round breasts, the see-through material draped open over her stomach, the edges brushing over the top of her matching panties.

I think I'm starting to have a Jolie-kink. She could be dressed as Shrek and I'd still want to devour her, inch by inch.

"I'm going to say that one's true. It's too detailed and your impression of Marge was spot on, meaning you've practiced it far too many times."

Instead of looking embarrassed or even mildly uncomfortable, Jolie grins. "It is. I can also do a mean Lois Griffin from *Family Guy*. Clearly he had a thing for animated women." She sighs dramatically. "In the end, I guess I was just too much of a real woman for him."

That pulls another laugh from me. Damn, my cheeks are starting to hurt. I don't think I've laughed this much since Matt thought it would be a good idea to get frosted tips in high school. He said, and I quote, "Justin Timberlake pulls it off and I'm way hotter than that guy".

Yeah, my brother's an idiot.

I think over the last two options. Sixteen is kind of late to have your first kiss, but I also can't see Jolie never having had a serious boyfriend before. She's beautiful and fun and she's got balls of steel. She was willing to drive through a snowstorm because she promised her friend she'd be there for her. Imagine what she'd do for the man she loves.

"Number 1 is a lie," I decide.

"Nope."

I roll onto my side, narrowing my eyes at her. "Liar. There's no way you went sixteen years without a guy trying to kiss you. Did you go to an all-girls school or something?"

She shakes her head. "I went to a bunch of different schools growing up but they were all public schools. I was the new girl more often than not. We finally settled down in Toronto when I was fourteen. My brother was a year older than me and the guys I was interested in were either friends with him or afraid of him." She shrugs. "It's not like I missed out on anything. There wasn't anyone I wanted to kiss back then anyway." She tilts her head thoughtfully. "Maybe that's why I've never had a serious boyfriend before either. Never found someone that piqued my interest long enough."

"That makes sense," I say. "So, who was the lucky guy?"

"Jamie Sheenan. He was smart and funny and played on the varsity baseball team. He used to sit in the seat in front of me on the bus. We'd talk the whole way to and from school. He was a year older than me, which in high school is practically a decade older, but he never treated me differently. He asked me out one day when we were getting off the bus and I practically floated home. We went to the movies a couple of times and he kissed me in the back row during *Pirates of the Caribbean*." She sighs wistfully. "As if I needed another reason to love Jack Sparrow."

"What happened to Mr. Back Row?"

"Oh, you know. High school romances hardly ever last. He graduated a couple months later and went to some college in the States on a baseball scholarship. Last I saw on Facebook, he's a firefighter somewhere in Colorado and is married with a baby on the way." She waves absently. "C'est la vie."

It must be indigestion that has my stomach churning. I can't possibly be jealous of a kiss that happened thirteen years ago. I've never even met the guy, know nothing about him other than he used to ride the same bus as the girl I'm lying beside. But for some reason, I want to smash his nose into my fist for even looking in the direction of what's mine.

I mentally slam on the brakes. What the hell is wrong with me? Jolie's not mine. If she could hear my thoughts right now, she'd probably smash *my* nose in. We might've had a moment out on the terrace but that doesn't give me any claim over her.

I need to focus. A couple days snowed away from the real world with Jolie and my mind's starting to play tricks on me. I mean, sure. The last two nights, alone in the room with Jolie, have been more fun than I've had in a long time. No one from town would believe the number of times I've smiled this weekend, let alone laughed. Maybe it's the lack of responsibility or maybe it's the fact that no one is expecting me to be a certain way. Jolie has never had any expectations of me other than to be a grumpy asshole. It's kind of nice.

Or maybe it's the woman herself that's making me want to just let myself...be. Not having to worry about being the perfect police chief. Or the dependable older brother. I can do whatever I want because the woman across from me is doing the same thing. Until tomorrow morning when the roads are clear and we can go home, no one will ever know what happens in this room.

It makes me want to give in to what I've wanted since that first day on the street five years ago. When I was run over by the want—no, *need*—to have her. To make her mine.

Even if only for the night.

I'm in trouble.

I have no idea when it happened or what's different but somewhere in the last day and a half, Luke has changed his mind about me. And not just in a "oh, she's not as bad as I thought" way. More like "he wants to bang my head against the bedframe" type of way. And for the first time ever when talking about Luke, I mean that in the fun way.

One minute we're laughing and playing this ridiculous game for a way to pass the time and the next, he looks like a tiger ready to pounce.

It happened not once, but twice tonight. I've played this game many times throughout my life and never once have I thought of it as a sexy game. Apparently, Luke has a different opinion on that.

He shifts closer so that he's lying on his side, head propped up and looking down at me, mirroring my earlier pose. Staring up at him from my back, the move makes me feel vulnerable and small but the thrill is outweighing my nerves.

I try to think of anything to say but the heat radiating off his chest, his close proximity, and the faint smell of chlorine that's making my head spin. My mind is completely and utterly blank as all laughter from earlier evaporates in the heat between us. Even if I could think of something to say, my suddenly dry throat would make it impossible to talk.

"Do you know what I think?" he asks in a low, husky voice. I merely shake my head. I can't look away as he leans in closer. "I think the reason you made those men wait is because you know you deserve better than some incompetent asshole that doesn't know what to do with a woman as irresistible as you."

I can't blink, can hardly breathe as I search his eyes. "Irresistible?" I ask, hardly recognizing my own voice. It comes out breathy and whispered, something I'll probably hate myself for later but at this moment, I couldn't care less.

"That's right, sweetheart," he rasps. "Irresistible. You're so goddamn irresistible. Trust me, I've spent the last five years fighting against it. Against you and this damn pull you have on me." His eyes never leave mine as he leans closer until his words are like a secret whispered against my lips. "But tonight, I'm done fighting it."

At this moment, I'm every cheesy line in any romantic movie come to life. I'm not thinking about the fact that a few days ago, Luke and I couldn't be in the same room without wanting to strangle each other. I'm not thinking about how the steam from the hot tub probably has my hair looking like the rat's nest my mother always threatened it would be if I didn't brush my hair.

And I'm especially not thinking about the fact that after tonight, when the sun comes up and the roads are clear, we'll be back to our usual selves, driving each other crazy.

At this moment, in our dark hotel room, hidden away

from reality, all I'm thinking about is Luke and how he's making me feel right now.

Irresistible.

His lips brush against mine. It's not a kiss but more of a promise of what's to come. If we just give in to it. It has me lifting my head, following him as he pulls back, drawing me into him more than any kiss ever could.

Because if this little interlude is anything to go by, giving in to Luke might just be my undoing.

And I can't wait.

He brushes his lips against mine a second time, again refusing to apply the pressure we both need. "What do you say, Jolie?"

I almost give in. Almost close the distance between us that I know will kick start a night I'm not sure I'm ready for but crave anyway.

But there's a little voice inside my head that needs to clarify. I tilt my head back, letting him chase my lips. "If we do this," I say as he skims his fingers along the hem of my shirt, causing goosebumps to erupt across my skin. I try to focus, needing to get these next words out.

"If we do this," I try again, "it's just tonight." His fingers continue to explore, not daring to venture from the small strip of exposed skin to where my body is aching to be touched. I swallow hard. "Tomorrow, we go back to driving each other crazy. Tomorrow, we're nothing more than two people with mutual friends who are getting married." He slides his pinky just below the waistband of my jogging pants and I'm practically panting.

"Promise me."

Luke stares down into my eyes. His face is an unreadable mask, his only tell that he's as affected by his movements as I am are his dark, lust-filled eyes.

But I have to be sure. I refuse to give myself over to someone like Luke for anything longer than a night. No matter how different he may seem this weekend, I won't risk losing myself to someone like him.

Someone like my father.

To my relief, though, he finally gives a small dip of his chin in agreement.

"One night. I promise."

Then he slowly, painstakingly slowly, dips his head, his gaze holding mine until our lips touch.

Our kiss at the engagement party was heated, the result of our anger bubbling up until it had no choice but to boil over. This kiss is completely new. It starts out slow and exploring. He takes his time, like he's trying to memorize every stroke of our tongues, every brush of our lips. It's overwhelming, like a drug pulsing through my veins.

I can't get enough. I can't get close enough. I fist his shirt, pulling him against me. He comes willingly, but hovers just above as his hand roams over my body, almost reverently.

As much as I'm loving the feel of his hands all over me, I need to feel him against me. Everywhere. I don't want to know where my body ends and his begins.

I pull on his shirt again until he's pressed against every inch of me. I lock my ankles around his, keeping him in place then lift my hips to rock against him. His hard length presses against the thin material of my pants, teasing me with just enough pressure to make me gasp, but it's not enough.

I need more.

I need all of it.

All of *him*.

I have no idea where this desperation came from but it's

like the first touch of his lips against mine was the catalyst to my undoing.

Which might be embarrassing if he wasn't just as turned on as I am. At the sound of my breathy gasp, his grip on my hip turns punishing, like he's fighting for control.

Well, that just won't do.

If the briefest contact has me this unraveled and we haven't even taken our clothes off yet, I need him to be as desperate and out of control as I am.

I don't want neighborly Chief Brady to make love to me.

I want growly and dominating Luke Brady to fuck me.

I want him to let go and unleash that aggression that he keeps so securely caged from the rest of the world.

If we've only got one night, I want all of him.

No holding back.

With that thought, I sink my teeth into his bottom lip and arch against him, rotating my hips so that his hard cock is straining against my center. I can't resist letting out a moan as the friction shoots sweet pleasure through me.

If our mouths clashing for the first time was my undoing, that moan was his.

"Fuck, Jolie," he rasps as he tears his mouth from mine. He lifts up, sitting back on his bent knees between my legs. His dark eyes narrow down at me. I can't hold back the Cheshire Cat grin that spreads across my face as I sit up on my elbows to follow him.

"You want to play, sweetheart?" he growls. "Alright. Let's fucking play." There's a wicked glint in his eyes as he wraps his forearms under the back of my knees and yanks them in the air until I'm flat on my back. Before my head has finished bouncing off the mattress, he dives down claiming my mouth with his.

The kiss turns wild. It's everything all at once. It's

desperate yet determined. It's hurried yet worshiping. It's reckless yet persistent. My head spins as his mouth chases mine, stealing every breath from me.

He lifts slightly, keeping his mouth fused to mine until the last second when he pulls his shirt over his head. Tossing it haphazardly behind him, he settles back between my legs.

This time, his hand goes back to my waist where it disappears below the waistband of my pants. I would mentally do a happy dance if I could form any thought other than where his hand is drifting down my hip.

His hand stops and I let out a frustrated groan. He smiles against my lips and I've never wanted to kick someone in the groin while being so turned on before.

"You need something?" he asks as he traces his finger below my waist. I instinctively lift my hips to follow his touch. He drops his voice to a husky whisper in my ear. "Ask me nicely."

Despite the shiver that runs down my spine, my first thought is *fuck that*. If he thinks I'm going to beg, he's got another thing coming.

Two can play at that game.

I shake my head, refusing to give him what he wants. The corner of his lips turn up slightly and I wonder if this is actually what he wanted all along. There's always been a power struggle between Luke and I. It only makes sense that we're the same way in bed.

Avery once compared us to fire and gasoline; just as likely to consume each other as we are to combust. Little did she know, she couldn't be more right. Though somehow, I don't think this was quite what she had in mind.

I lift up to kiss him but when he starts to chase my mouth, I pull away. Dropping my mouth, I kiss my way down his neck, his chest. When I push against his shoulder to roll him onto his back, he surprisingly complies. Shifting to straddle his waist, a thrum of power pulses in my veins at the way his eyes are intently watching mine.

One of my favorite things about Luke is that his focus is always on you. Even at our worst, he never made me feel insignificant or small. The same way it is now as I cross my arms in front of me to pull the hem of my shirt up and over my head. I toss the shirt over the edge of the bed, never taking my eyes off of his.

His look of white, hot desire makes me feel regal, like a queen on her throne. Leaning into that energy, I reach behind me and unclasp my bra. Letting the straps slide down my arms, I hold the cups against my chest, keeping myself covered as I stare down at him.

"You gettin' shy on me?" His words are casual but I can feel the evidence just how *un-casual* he's feeling pressed against me. He reaches for me but I shake my head, leaning back away from him. The motion presses me further down on his hard cock and he groans. "You gonna let me see you?"

I bend forward, keeping the bra still pressed against my chest, until my lips are just a whisper away from his. "Ask me nicely, *sweetheart*," I practically purr against his lips.

I lift my eyes to his. His lust is clearly at war with his ego. It makes me smile, knowing how much I affect him.

I have no problem with a dominant man. In fact, I usually prefer it.

Now, you might be clasping your pearls and praying to the heavens right now at my lack of feminism. But hear me out.

There's something about giving yourself over to someone that's just so...freeing. To let them be in total control of your pleasure. He's not taking anything from me, I'm willingly handing it over.

It's the only time I'll ever let a man tell me what to do.

But the idea of making strong and stubborn Luke give up his control to me, has me feeling invincible.

His fingertips skim along my hips, up my waist to my ribs and back down again. Goosebumps erupt over my skin but I fight to maintain my composure.

"You think you're in charge or something, darlin'?" Luke drawls, brushing an open mouth kiss just below my ear. He works his way down my neck, across my collarbone and just above the top of my breasts. He dips his tongue below the cup of my bra at the same time he grips my hips and pushes me down on his erection.

Oh, fuck. I nearly gasp as my head tips back. He fights dirty. I knew he wouldn't give in easily but a part of me is loving the fact that he's putting up a fight for dominance.

That's fine. I know how to fight, too.

I rock my hips forward and I don't have to fake the moan that rips out of my throat. His answering groan and tight grip on my hips tells me he's as on edge as I am. We're both ready for the game to be over and take what we desperately want, but not willing to give in.

"God, you feel so good," I croon, then tip my head forward to look down at him. With that, I massage myself through the thin material of my bra, while rocking against him again. The friction against my clit and my nipples causes my mouth to part in a silent prayer.

From below me, Luke's jaw ticks and his chest heaves as he watches me use his body to pleasure myself. I smile down at him. "I bet you beg so sweetly," I comment. Then, just for good measure, I give a nipple a pinch, whimpering at the feel.

Just like that, Luke snaps. Reaching up, he wraps a hand around my throat and pulls me down to him. Before I can get out a smart remark, he claims my mouth with his, his other arm wrapping around my waist to hold me against him. The hand on my throat tightens just enough to elicit a flash of excitement straight to my core. All thought leaves my mind and I'm acting on pure need as I meet him stroke for stroke. I'm about to throw up the white flag when he rips his mouth from mine, his breaths coming in rough pants as he lets out a ragged, "please, Jolie. Please."

Oh, thank god.

What the hell have I gotten myself into?

When I promised Jolie one night, I figured it would be a release for this overwhelming tension we've had building between us all of these years—both sexual and non. Sure, it'd be fun because, let's be serious, it's Jolie we're talking about. We'd have some fun and tomorrow we'd go back to the way things were before this weekend.

But I had no idea it'd be so much more than that. I should've known that sex with Jolie would be completely different than anything I've experienced before. She's not just some girl to take for a roll in the hay.

It's a surprise to no one that I like to be the one in control in bed. There's hardly a place in my life that I don't like to be in control, except in the kitchen. So when Jolie decided to take things into her own hands, I figured I'd let her have her fun for a bit.

Little did I know, the surrender was almost as good as the fight.

And the prize?

Sweetest fucking thing I've ever seen.

Jolie straightens until she's straddling my waist again. I'm about to beg, plead, write her a damn ballad if she'd just let that bra fall. Luckily, she saves my pride by letting the straps fall down her arms. My mouth goes dry and my cock gets impossibly hard. I slide my hands up her waist, loving how her breathing quickens despite her show of bravado earlier.

This girl is a mess of contradictions; sweet yet sassy. She has a spine of steel with the heart of a marshmallow. She's confident enough to make a grown man beg yet trembles at my touch.

I can't get enough of her. I may have promised her this would only be one night but I'm gonna make sure it'll be one she won't ever forget.

My hands reach the curve of her breasts. I swipe my thumbs across her, both hearing and feeling her sharp intake of breath when I scrape my rough skin across her peaked nipples. The sound goes straight to my cock, twitching in response. She arches her back, silently urging me on.

"Does that feel good, sweetheart?"

Her head is thrown back, eyes closed as she nods. I pluck one nipple between my fingers and pull. She cries out so I do it again to the other side. This time she bucks against me and I groan as my hard cock fights to break free of my boxers.

She opens her eyes and stares down at me with regal eyes. "How badly do you want to fuck me right now?"

"So fucking bad," I answer automatically, sounding like a needy bastard but I don't even care at this point. I'd get down on my knees and beg. I'd sell my soul to the devil for a taste of her. I'd do just about anything she asked at this point.

She's got me exactly where she wants me and she knows it.

"Then show me what you're made of, *chief*," she drawls, dragging out the last word.

Yes, ma'am.

Without another word, I swing myself forward into a sitting position, wrap an arm around her waist then flip her onto her back.

I'm done with her teasing.

I'm done playing her games.

It's time I made Jolie mine, if only for the night.

I shove my boxers to my ankles then kick them off. Pausing only long enough to get her nod of permission, I yank her jogging pants and underwear off her long legs then toss them over my shoulder.

Despite my body's need to be inside her, I take a second to stare down at her, bared to me.

I've never considered myself especially possessive but the sight of her makes me want to beat my chest like a caveman.

Her hair is wild from *my* fingers.

Her chest is red from the stubble of *my* beard.

Her lips are swollen from *my* kisses.

My chest tightens almost painfully. "God, you're perfect." Her eyes soften.

The mood is suddenly too serious. It's starting to feel a hell of a lot more than one night and that scares me more than any middle of the night phone call ever has. To distract us both, I slide two fingers up and down her entrance before circling her clit.

The second I touch that little bead between her legs, her back bows off the bed with a gasp. I slide my fingers down again, this time slipping my middle finger inside her before laying my palm flat against her clit.

I pump my finger into her, slowly at first, building a rhythm. She's so responsive, so beautiful I couldn't take my eyes off her if I tried. She starts to lift her hips in time with my hand. I add a second finger and she moans. I roll her nipple between my fingers with my free hand and she cries out.

She's incredible.

My eyes dart from her face to the spot where my hand is disappearing inside her. She's getting close. Her breathing picks up speed and she tightens around my fingers.

"That's it, baby," I urge. "Come for me." A few more pumps of my fingers and she cries out her release. I keep my pace until I feel her relax below me.

Leaving her only long enough to grab a condom from my wallet, I climb back between her legs, sheathing my hard cock. She smiles lazily up at me and I can't resist kissing her again. "You good?"

"Abso-fucking-lutely," she purrs and I grin. She shoves at my arm. "Don't look so smug. It's been a while since I've been with someone, that's all."

My grin widens. "Oh, yeah?"

"Yeah." She sits up on her hands and kisses me deeply then whispers against my lips. "Now give me another."

Despite my aching erection, I chuckle. "As you wish, greedy girl." Then I tuck her against my chest. When I start to roll us, she lets out a startled yelp until I'm settled on my back. She adjusts herself until her long legs are straddling my waist.

I lift her by the hips, lining myself up. "You good?" I ask one last time because once we cross this line, there's no going back.

She nods, her eyes never leaving the spot where we're almost connected. "Yes. Please."

If it were under any other circumstances, I'd point out the irony of her now being the one to beg. But the second she sinks onto my dick, I'm lost. Slowly, she takes me deeper, inch by inch. We both groan once she's fully seated.

Fuck me. I've never felt anything so good in my entire life. She hasn't even moved yet and I can already tell this is going to be the best sex of my life.

She's so tight, so wet just for me. It feels so...right.

Refusing to think about that right now, I give a testing thrust upward. Jolie moans again but swivels her hips in return.

That's all it takes before we're setting a rhythm that feels so natural, it'd be unsettling if I could think straight.

"More...Luke...harder." She pushes out each word in a breathy cry. I'm more than happy to oblige.

I'd be worried about hurting her at the punishing pace I'm setting but Jolie's giving as good as she's taking. Every rock of her hips, every tilt of her pelvis has me seeing stars and I know I'm not going to last much longer.

I reach up and press a thumb to her clit, strumming it in a quick succession that has her shattering around me seconds later. Seconds later, I'm following behind her, groaning her name as my release goes on and on.

When it ends, I help Jolie off and to her side on the bed. After disposing of the condom in the garbage beside the bed, I take a few breaths, trying to will my lungs back to work.

Jolie moans beside me and my head shoots to her. I was pretty rough with her and I'd hate myself if I hurt her. But her eyes are closed and the satisfied smile she's wearing tells me I did anything but.

"Wow," she breathes. "Not half bad, Chief."

I choke out a laugh. "Not half bad, eh?" I comment, giving her a teasing pinch on her arm. She yelps and swats my hand away. "I like to think two orgasms would make you pretty grateful since 'it's been a while'."

She smirks up at me. "I said it's been a while since I've been with someone. Not since I've had an orgasm." She smacks a quick kiss on my lips. "My vibrator keeps me very happy."

Thoughts of all the times I drove past her apartment, late at night, comforted by the light in her window. Thinking she might be feeling lonely or troubled. Meanwhile, she could've been fucking herself, moaning those sinful sounds while she pumped a vibrating toy inside her pretty pussy.

"Goodnight, Chief," she says sweetly, knowing exactly the image she just placed in my head.

This woman is going to be the death of me.

CHAPTER 30

LUKE

The distant sound of a thud and a hissed "son of a beehive" pull me from sleep. I blink against the dimly lit room, waiting for my eyes and mind to focus.

Looking around, I roll over to the sun streaming in from the patio door. Grabbing my phone, I tap the screen. It's almost 9:30 in the morning.

Holy shit. I drag a hand over my face. I haven't slept this long since...well...ever. I can't remember the last time I slept for more than five consecutive hours. I must've really been out of it.

My mind wanders back to the night before and the reason for my great sleep.

Jolie.

I roll onto my side to reach for her but find her side of the bed empty.

That has me instantly on alert. Jolie is not a morning person. Nine thirty for her might as well be dawn. I can't imagine her willingly getting out of bed at this time, when there's nowhere urgent to be.

Another thud from the bathroom has me sitting up in bed in alarm. Before I can jump out of bed, Jolie rounds the corner, coming to a stop when she sees me.

Her eyes shoot to my bare chest and I watch appreciatively as she checks me out. "Morning," I drawl, my voice thick with sleep.

Caught staring, her eyes shoot to mine in surprise before she looks away self-consciously.

I bite back my smile at her modesty. The woman was under me (and over me) last night, screaming my name as she came and she's embarrassed now?

Well, I know how to fix that.

I make a move for her but she steps hesitantly away. My brows furrow in confusion.

"Henry called," she says quickly, lifting her cell phone as if to prove it. "He said the roads are clear and my car's been towed back to his shop. He told me to come in at some point today to discuss the damage." She winces at the last word.

I don't fully know the relationship between Jolie and her car but from what little she's told me, I know that it means a lot to her so I feel for her. "How bad is it?"

She blows out a breath, making a chunk of hair shoot up out of her face. "He says that he can fix it. I'm just not sure I want to hear the cost to do it."

I nod in understanding. Old cars are great but a lot of the parts for those things aren't made anymore. If they are, they're hard to find and come with a hefty price tag.

"Henry is the best and he's fair. If it can be fixed, he'll get it done. He won't gouge you."

She nods but there's hesitation in her eyes. An awkward silence drags out until she's shifting on her feet before me. I don't know what happened between last night and this morning but this isn't the Jolie I've gotten to know this weekend. Hell, this isn't even the spitfire I knew from before. Her guard is up and she won't look me in the eye.

My gut churns uncomfortably.

Last night might've been impulsive but it was unbelievable. At the risk of sounding corny, I feel like a whole different person.

I woke up smiling for the first time in years. There's a stupid grin on my face that I couldn't get rid of if I tried. And not just from the sex but the entire weekend. The teasing, the playfulness. The easy conversation that held no judgment or expectations.

The thought of her regretting it has me feeling like the time I bet Matt I could eat all of my Halloween candy before him and we both puked our guts out for days. At least after that, I knew that eventually I'd be able to indulge again.

I promised Jolie one night. No second chances, no do-overs.

One night. Then it was over.

Well, the night might be over, but I'm nowhere near done with her.

She pulls her coat out of the closet and drapes it over her forearm. "We should probably get going then."

Panic clutches my chest. We can't leave yet. The second we're back in town, I'm going to be nothing more than the annoying cop who gives her warnings and spoils her fun. At least here, in this secluded corner of reality, I have a chance at winning her over.

"Don't you want to grab some breakfast first?" I ask, hoping to keep the desperation out of my voice. The thought of her walking out the door right now has me grasping at straws. Anything for another day, another hour of her time.

What the hell is happening to me? This isn't me. I'm not this guy. I've never begged a woman to spend time with me in my life. Not even when I was a desperate teenager.

I don't do relationships. Not anymore. A few dates and that's it. No hard feelings because we both know we're only in it for casual. If anything, Jolie's doing me a favor by ending it now. Relationships are messy and consuming and I don't have time for either in my life.

But for some reason, with her that's not the case.

I don't know what scares me more: the thought of Jolie walking away or the thought of her staying.

She shakes her head, making the decision for me. "No, I think it's best if we just head back to town now. I've taken up enough of your time." She tries for a small smile. "Who knew a menu tasting would turn into an entire weekend? Bet you're just itching to get back to the station."

Right. The station. I haven't given it a single thought since last night. As someone who has slept at his desk before, that's unheard of. The town needs me. I should've been up at first light, calling the station for updates.

"Yeah," I mumble back.

Her eyes shift around the room, then points her thumb at the door. "I'll just go thank Alana for the hospitality while you get dressed. I'll meet you at the front in 10?" I nod, not trusting myself to keep from begging her to stay. She nods in answer then turns, pulls open the door and steps into the hallway.

The second the door clicks shut, I drop back onto the mattress. Staring up at the ceiling, I'm hoping for the answer to a question I don't even know.

My gut is never wrong. I've depended on it too many times in dangerous situations for it to ever steer me wrong.

But right now, my gut is telling me one thing while my head is shouting another.

And I'm scared that this time, they both might be wrong.

———

AFTER GETTING DRESSED, I found Jolie waiting at the front entrance of the lobby, exactly where she said she'd be. She's talking to Alana, smiling and laughing, but as I approach, I can see it doesn't quite reach her eyes. Her posture is tense and she's leaning toward the exit.

Squaring my shoulders, I give into the inevitable. If she wants to leave so badly, fine. We'll leave.

Figures the one person I've opened up to in years wants to ditch me the second they're free of me.

I stop before them. "Ready?" I grumble at Jolie and her shoulders dip in relief. It only pisses me off more.

She nods quickly then turns to Alana. "Thanks again. I really appreciate everything you did for us this weekend." She wraps her in a hug that Alana happily returns.

So, she's fine with other people. It's just me that she can't wait to get away from.

Great.

"Any time, hun. You make sure you come back up for a real getaway when the snow's gone, okay?" Alana turns, pulling me close. "Thanks for all your help this weekend, Luke. We're so lucky to have such a dedicated chief."

I pat her arm and nod. "Any time, Alana." Then without another word, I turn on my heel and head for the door. Jolie follows behind me, waving at a staff member as we pass by.

Shoving the front door open with a bit more force than necessary, I stride across the parking lot to where my truck sits. Waiting only long enough for Jolie to hop in and close the door, I throw the truck in reverse and head out down the hill toward town.

The drive back is mostly silent, except for the low bass from the radio. Jolie alternates between shifting in her seat, typing out a text on her phone and staring out the window. Looking anywhere but at me.

My impatience only grows the closer we get to town. My grip on the steering wheel has my knuckles whitening when I finally pull into a parking space in front of Henry's garage.

Jolie unsnaps her seatbelt, then pushes open the passenger door. "Thanks, Luke. I know you won't believe me, but I don't try to be such an inconvenience." She gives a sad smile. "My dad says it just comes naturally."

And just like that, I'm brought back to last night. Our whispered confessions, the way she opened up to me. The way she made me want to split myself open in return.

The pressure in my chest eases and I loosen my grip on the wheel. I can feel my temper defusing, being replaced by the same ache from earlier.

"Well, I should go. Thanks again." She steps out of the truck and onto the salted sidewalk, careful not to slip on any hidden ice patches.

She places one hand on the door to push it shut when I stop her. "Jolie." I wait until she's looking up at me before I continue. "You're not inconvenient. And anyone who thinks otherwise is a fucking moron."

She stares at me, shocked for a moment before she steps

back. She shuts the door and it takes all my effort to pull away from her.

This time, I don't dare look back in my rearview.

THE HAVEN TIMES

  Proudly serving Haven Bay for over 100 years. **FREE**

DEAR ANNIE

Your local source for advice on love, life and everything in between!

The answer to this week's trivia question (pg 9) is Sharon Osborne.

Q.

Dear Annie,

I've been dating a woman for six weeks and it's going really great. She's funny, smart, she's a horror buff just like me. So far, she's perfect for me in every way.

Last weekend, after we went to the movies, she invited me back to her apartment for the first time. She opened the door and my eyes instantly began to itch.

Turns out, she has four cats that are practically her children. Which would be great if I wasn't allergic to cats.

Being the romantic that I am, I ignored this tiny detail in the name of love and spent the entire night rubbing my eyes, scratching my skin raw and holding back sneezes.

I want so badly for this relationship to work, but I can't spend another night in Hives Heaven. I'm scared to tell her the truth because I don't want her to have to choose between me and her cats. I would never want to pressure her to get rid of the animals she loves. But I don't want to lose her before we can see where this thing takes us.

Help.

Signed,
Itchy

A.

Dear Itchy,

Unless you want to spend the rest of your life swollen and red, I highly suggest telling your girlfriend the truth.

I know that your relationship is so new, you're afraid that telling her will make her change her mind, but you also need to trust that what you have together is worth figuring this out.

Sure, this throws a hiccup into your relationship, but what fun is perfect anyway?

I then suggest you have a talk with your doctor and discuss allergy medication options. They may have some ideas that will help you manage your symptoms while still being around your feline friends.

There's lots of ways that you can reduce cat dander in the house. Vacuuming often, bathing the cat often, and keeping the cats away from certain rooms such as the bedroom may help reduce your discomfort.

Either way, I don't think keeping your girlfriend in the dark is the answer. You don't want to start your relationship off with a lie.

Tell her the truth and invest in some good allergy meds.

Sincerely,
Annie

HAVEN BAY CHRISTMAS PARADE

Dec 3rd at 6pm

CANNED GOOD DONATIONS ACCEPTED AT DINER

CHAPTER 31

JOLIE

The cold wind pushes back against the studio door as I try to shove it open. You'd think that Mother Nature would give us a bit of a break after the snowstorm last week. Instead she's been a stubborn bitch, with temperatures well below freezing and a frigid wind that stings all the way down to your bones.

And because I have the worst luck, the coldest week of the year to date is the week I don't have a car.

The damage to Blue was worse than I expected. Blue is like me; she's not made for winter weather. I usually keep my driving to a minimum in the snow, which is easy to do when you live in a small town where everything is within walking distance.

I guess a day and a half under a mountain of snow was more than she could take.

Henry listed all of the damage that was done in detail but all I remember is the sound of my bank account crying with every dollar figure he listed off. He apologized multiple times, telling me the parts for a vintage car like

Blue were hard to find but he was trying his hardest to get the best deal on them.

When he gently asked if she was worth fixing at this point, I quickly shot him down. I won't consider not fixing her. I can't. She's the last piece of my grandpa I have left. I can't let her go.

When I rejected the idea, Henry sighed but told me he'd let me know when all of the parts came in. He offered me his car, saying that he'd use one of the work trucks in the meantime but I politely declined.

Like I said, everything I need is within walking distance so going without a car for a week or two isn't the end of the world.

Except I forgot how much I hate winter.

Cursing, I give the door another shove until I'm able to slip outside. The force of the wind has the door slamming shut behind me.

Flinging flanging winter. Why do I live somewhere where the cold air bitchslaps me in the face every morning? Why don't I live somewhere warm like Australia?

Margot Robbie would never have to put up with this shit.

Then I remember the TikTok I saw last month of snakes falling from the trees in Australia.

Maybe the snow isn't *that* bad.

I tug the hood of my winter coat up over my toque, bow my head out of the wind and trudge toward the diner. Why didn't I take Brenna up on her offer to pick me up on her way? *Oh, I'm good.* I told her. *It's just down the street. The fresh air will be nice.* I scoff at my earlier naivety. *You're such an idiot, Jolie.* I chastise myself. *You could be roasting your buns on Brenna's seat warmers right now. Instead, your ass might actually fall off from the cold.*

Well, it wouldn't be the first time I've beaten myself up this week.

My mind wanders back to the one topic I've been avoiding yet consistently been returning to all week: Luke.

Luke and that heart stopping, panty-dropping, all-the-clichés-of-swooning night last weekend. The night that I will now be referring to (in my head only, of course) as The Night My Pussy Died.

Or TNMPD, for short.

Don't get me wrong; I've had good sex before. I've even had great sex before. It's not like I'm a virgin who thinks that the mediocre two pumps her man gave her was life-altering. I know the difference. And I can confidently say that sex with Luke was off the metaphorical charts.

Elite.

Sublime.

A top-tier dicking.

The only problem is, now that I've had him, I want more. I swore it would only be one night. In fact, I made him promise me that's all it would be.

But how was I supposed to know that one night would completely destroy me?

I risk whiplash lifting my head to quickly check for cars before crossing the street. Unsurprisingly, there's no one stupid enough to be out in this weather. Except me, apparently.

Cautious of black ice, I carefully walk across the street and step onto the sidewalk before the diner.

I'm not naive enough to think that just because we had sex, Luke and I are going to start getting along, despite all of the reasons why we could not be more wrong for each other. So while I'd love nothing more than to show up at Luke's house in a trench coat and nothing else, offering myself up to him like a Christmas present, I refuse to give in.

Which is best for everyone involved, I tell myself as I pull open the diner door.

Stomping my feet a couple times on the doormat, I lower my hood and look around the mostly empty diner. The diner is decorated with garland, bows and other Christmas decorations. A rosy-cheeked Santa smiles at me from his place beside the door, welcoming me inside. My eyes scan the room and find Avery and Brenna seated a few booths away. Avery waves me over and I smile.

See? Who needs spectacular, toe-curling orgasms from a sexy police officer when you have friends like mine?

I know. I heard it, too. Denial is a powerful thing.

I take off my coat and hang it on the hook beside the door then make my way over to the booth where my friends sit.

"Oh my god, Jolie! I can't believe you walked in this. I told you I would pick you up," Brenna scolds. "You're gonna end up with frostbite because you're too stubborn to accept help."

I shrug, the warm air in the diner thawing my numb face. "Oh, this? No biggie."

Avery and Brenna both shoot me disapproving glares. I sense a lecture coming so when Brandy comes over to take my order, I welcome the interruption. She places a mug of hot water and a tea bag in front of me and I just about weep with gratitude.

"Brandy, I could kiss you," I praise. "You're a lifesaver. Better yet, a finger saver." I drag off my mittens and wrap my hands around the hot mug, letting the heat warm my frozen fingers.

"That's what they all say," Brandy answers wryly.

"Until they take off with your best friend and your dog in the middle of the night and leave you with nothing but their dirty laundry to remember you by." With that, she walks off to greet another customer.

I look back at Avery and Brenna. "Real ray of sunshine, that Brandy," I comment with raised brows.

"Never mind that sourpuss. It's been ten years, you'd think she'd stop bringing up her divorce every two minutes." Avery reaches across the table to grab my forearm. "I am so, so, SO sorry that I got you stuck in a snowstorm with your mortal enemy. I'm the worst friend in the whole world and if you hate me, I completely understand."

I squeeze her hand reassuringly. "First of all, I could never hate you, so cut that out right now. Second of all, you didn't get me stuck in anything, I got myself stuck. Third, it wasn't that bad. I actually had fun, once Luke rescued me."

Avery's shoulders sag in relief. "I feel so awful. I ruined your whole weekend. At least you had Luke to keep you company."

Brenna laughs. "When you texted us saying you were staying at the lodge with him, I thought for sure I'd hear the fire trucks heading that way. No way you two could be snowed in together without all hell breaking loose."

"Matt thought maybe you two would bury the hatchet but I told him you'd be more likely to bury him," Avery says and they both laugh. I try to join in but my mind is flooded with images of exactly where Luke was buried Saturday night and it wasn't a grave. I squirm in my seat, still feeling him between my legs.

See what I mean? Destroyed.

"It wasn't that bad," I comment, trying for a nonchalant tone. "Luke's not awful when he takes off his badge."

"Not awful." Avery snickers. "Now that's a glowing review."

Brenna smiles but she's watching me carefully. I don't particularly trust that she doesn't see right through me, so I change the subject.

"So, I know I told you that Alana still let us do the tasting but there's no way I could convey how delicious it was through text." I roll my eyes upward and moan. "The tenderloin was cooked perfectly. The asparagus was fantastic. And the cheesecake?" I bring my two fingers and a thumb to my lips and kiss them. "Chef's kiss. I'm still dreaming about it."

Avery's eyes light up. "Really? It wasn't too casual? Matt was adamant that tenderloin wasn't too informal but I wasn't sure…"

That sparks the wedding conversation and I'm saved from any further questioning.

We spend the next two hours talking about everything from wedding décor and menu options to Brenna's newest idea to stir up interest with the rescue. We've already paid our bills but we don't get much time alone anymore so we're taking advantage of it.

"I was going to talk to you about this more next week when I have all of the details figured out but I guess this is as good of a lead in as any," Brenna starts, nervously. "Have you ever heard of puppy yoga?"

"Of course," I say at the same time Avery says, "No".

"It's exactly what it sounds like," Brenna explains to Avery. "You gather a group of dogs that are looking to be adopted and bring them out to a yoga class. The dogs get to interact organically with potential adopters in a low-stress environment. It's very helpful for older dogs or dogs who might get overstimulated by big meet-and-greet events."

"That sounds absolutely adorable," Avery coos. I can practically see the hearts in her eyes from across the table. She gasps and slaps the table. "You should host one at Amaryllis!"

I laugh at her excited expression then turn to Brenna. "At the risk of sounding redundant, that sounds adorable and I love the idea. Let's do it."

Brenna gives me a relieved smile. "I was hoping you'd be on board. I mean, I figured you might be but I didn't want to push it on you or make it seem like I was forcing you into something you didn't want to do. I'll obviously handle all of the organizing, the transportation and the clean-up after. You won't have to do a thing, just show up and—"

I cover her hand with mine to stop her rambling. "Bren. I love the idea. I'm excited about it! I wouldn't say yes if I wasn't. And you're not going to do all of the work. Just tell me what you need and we'll divide and concur."

Avery sets her hand over mine like some 90s kids' movie and we're making a pact. "I'm in, too. I can borrow Matt's truck to help get dogs to and from the sanctuary. I'll put up any signage at both the shop and the café and I'll share any social media posts on our pages."

Brenna smiles. "Okay. Thanks, guys. I appreciate it. We'll go over details later but I'm really happy you're into the idea."

I give her hand a reassuring squeeze before I pull mine away. "Alright, team. As much as I'd love to stay and chat all day, I've got to get home and get some work done."

I gather my things and stand to go. Avery opens her mouth but I lift a hand to stop her. "Avery, if you apologize one more time for last weekend, I'm going to lose my ever-loving mind." She wisely snaps her mouth closed. "Bren, email me the details of what all goes into this class because you know I need it in writing or I'll never remember it all."

Brenna nods. "Will do. But will you please let me drive you home? It's too cold out there to walk."

"Thanks but no thanks. I've got two feet and a heartbeat, as my Grandpa Joe used to say. I'll be fine." I pull on my coat and toss the fur-lined hood over my head. "See you guys later. Love you both." Then I head to the front and square my shoulders as I heave open the diner door.

As I trudge down the sidewalk, I wave at Matt's truck. He honks as he passes by to pick up Avery. Gavin's in the backseat and an excited "Mommy!" echoes over the wind as I watch Avery climb inside. She gives Gavin a hug then leans across the console to give Matt a long kiss.

There's an ache in my chest that I'm too scared to name. I am *not* jealous of my best friend. I'm happy for her; ecstatic even.

Would I love to have a man to come home to at the end of the day? Sure. Someone to tell all my stories to while he listens eagerly. Someone who'll agree that the driver who pulled out in front of me on the road was, in fact, an idiot. Someone that I can laugh with, make plans with and, of course, fuck me into a coma every night.

Is that too much to ask for?

A face flashes in my mind before I can stop it.

Luke.

The scene plays out despite my best efforts to force it away. Me, walking into my apartment. Kicking off the snow, I'd follow my nose to the smell of dinner cooking in the oven. Music would play through my speaker and as I enter the kitchen, Luke meets me with a mocktail and a kiss. He pulls back and grins that adorable grin that he saves just for me.

Damn it, brain. No.

Luke is not that guy. We had fun last weekend but that's it. For all I know, he's forgotten all about me and is back to being Chief Grumpy Pants.

No matter how relaxed, sweet or fun he was this weekend, I have five years worth of evidence that that's not who Luke is.

I left home at eighteen to put as much distance between myself and my father. There's no way in hell I'm going to get involved with someone just like him. There's a man out there somewhere for me but Luke Brady is not that man.

The sooner I get that through my head, the better.

CHAPTER 32

LUKE

Being a police officer in Haven Bay is never boring, especially since that stupid *Dear Annie* column started. A slow day is when I only have to break up one fight at the senior center and then untangle 6 year old Artie Mann's head from between Miss Carla's mannequin's legs.

This week, however, the entire town seems to have made a pact to stay inside and out of mischief.

It's driving me crazy.

Days like these don't come around often, so I should be savoring it by catching up on paperwork or restructuring our training manuals.

Instead, I'm driving around town in the middle of the night, practically begging someone to so much as lose their keys so I have something to do. I'd climb a tree to rescue a damn cat if I had to. Anything to distract me from thinking about *her*.

Five days. It's been five long, torturous days since I dropped Jolie off at Henry's garage and drove away. There hasn't been a stretch of more than three minutes straight when I haven't thought of her.

Her eyes. Her smile. Her fantastic tits. Her endless legs that I'd sell my soul to have wrapped around my head.

I never even tasted her. How much of a jackass am I that I had *one fucking night* with her and I didn't have my head buried between her legs the entire time?

A massive one.

I adjust myself through my uniform pants just thinking about it.

But it's not just her body that I miss. Though holy shit, do I ever miss it.

It's her. Her freely given smiles. The way she laughs with her whole body, as if there's so much happiness inside her, it has to spill out of her somehow.

But then there's a vulnerable part of her, too. One that she trusted me enough to show a glimpse of that weekend. A part that I want to shield away from the rest of the world. To protect her from any and all harm.

I'm gone for a girl who wants nothing to do with me. And to be honest, I don't blame her. I've never been anything but an asshole to her, last weekend being the exception.

I'm so fucked.

I turn onto Main Street, telling myself that it's because I need to check on the downtown strip. For all I know, someone could be robbing Jenson's Market right now. I wouldn't be doing my due diligence if I didn't make my rounds.

The fact that Jolie lives on Main Street is merely a coincidence.

I know. Stalking her isn't going to help my appeal. But I

think we've established by now that I don't make good decisions when it comes to this girl.

My car just happens to slow as I'm passing her apartment. Her lights are on, which isn't surprising despite the fact that it's ten thirty at night. I bet she'll be awake for hours still.

I imagine what she's doing. Is she a reader like Avery? Does she listen to music like my sister, Tori? Maybe she has a secret hobby like Matt did. There's a lot about Jolie that I don't know.

But I'd like to find out.

Her comment from last weekend pops into my head. About her giving her vibrator a work out. Maybe she's up there right now, legs spread wide, head thrown back. Her hand wrapped around a long vibrating toy as she plunges it inside her—

The sound of my ringtone blares through the speakers of my car and my brother's name lights up my car's dashboard screen. My eyes dart to Jolie's apartment, as if she somehow might have heard the noise and might catch me staring up at her window like a creep.

The rational part of my brain is telling me there's no way she could hear through my car and her closed window but I duck my head and speed away just in case. I aimlessly stab at the Answer button while checking the rearview mirror to make sure she isn't watching me flee away.

"H...hello?" I stammer, then clear my throat. *Way to play it cool, you stalker.* Driving a little faster than what's legal, I take a sharp turn off Main Street, trying to put as much distance between myself and Jolie's apartment as possible.

There's a pause on the other end. "Luke? What the hell was that?" Matt asks, trying not to laugh through the phone.

"Please don't tell me I just interrupted your special 'Luke time', did I?"

"For fuck's sake."

"Oh, don't act like you don't do it. Unless..." He pauses. "Well, that would explain why you've been such an asshole for the last...thirty years," Matt chokes out past his laughter.

"What'd you want, Matt?" I run a hand over my face. I'm in no mood to deal with my brother's idiotic behavior tonight.

I guess having him think he interrupted me jerking off is better than what I was actually doing—stalking his fiance's best friend.

Matt gasps dramatically from the other end and I roll my eyes. Everything's always a production with this guy. "Is that any way to talk to your favorite brother? 'What'd you want?'" he mimics. "How about 'Hi, how are you? How was your day? Here's ten thousand dollars for putting up with my grumpy ass all these years.'"

Sometimes I like to think that my parents found him as a baby with some traveling circus. That maybe his biological mother got shot out of a cannon too many times when she was pregnant with him and that's to blame for his flair for the dramatics.

There's no way I share any DNA with this knucklehead.

I don't answer, letting the long pause draw out as Matt waits me out. "What'd you want?" I finally respond. He lets out a long sigh and, because I know he can't see me, I smile.

"You're killing me, Smalls," Matt replies. "Anyway, I called because Avery and I were talking about what to do this weekend. Gavin's with his dad and it's been too long since I've spun my wife around the dance floor. So we're going to The Dive on Saturday."

I start to protest, thinking about all of the paperwork I have waiting for me at the station. I don't bother pointing out that they're not married, so she's not technically his wife yet. Last time that one earned me a punch in the shoulder. Before I can reject him though, Matt cuts me off.

"Participation is mandatory. Consider it groomsman duty."

"Groomsman duty?" I ask dryly. "How is going to the bar to listen to a band considered groomsman duty?"

"Because the groom said so. And anything the groom wants, the groom gets. Ipso facto, groomsman duty." I groan but he ignores me. "Besides, Avery feels really bad about the whole Jolie getting stuck in a snowstorm and you playing John Wayne rescuing her in your Chevy thing."

My chest constricts at the mention of Jolie. My mouth dries as images of her under me, mouth open and eyes wide as she screams my name.

Well, I lasted a full six minutes without thinking about it. Must be a new record.

I clear my throat but my voice still comes out scratchy. "Tell her it was no problem."

There's a shuffle on the other side and Avery's muffled voice. "I told you, Freckles. He loves playing white knight," Matt tells her. "You're probably still riding that high, aren't ya, Lukey?"

Little does he know I'd trade my left nut to ride that high again. For even a chance at a do-over with Jolie. To relive that entire night in slow motion so I could commit every second to memory.

Fuck, I'm in trouble.

I give a noncommittal grunt but luckily, Matt doesn't press me for details. Thank god he's so oblivious. One benefit of him being so blissed out having Avery and Gavin in his life, he seems less likely to butt into mine.

"Alright. So, I'll see you Saturday." He pauses and I know he'll wait me out all night if I don't agree.

"Fine."

"Good. Maybe we can find you a lady friend. Y'know. Give Little Luke a break from your hand for a night." Matt cackles like an old lady as I stab the End Call button on my dashboard.

"Idiot," I mutter, then turn and head back toward the station. I think my luck has run out for the night. I make my way around town, careful to avoid Main Street. It takes me twice as long but I use the time to rationalize to myself.

Maybe Matt's right, in his own roundabout way. Maybe this newfound obsession with Jolie has nothing to do with her and is actually the result of me finally breaking my dry-spell of sex.

Yeah, that's it. That's gotta be it.

Johnny Cash's low drawl comes over the radio and Jolie's bright eyes flash in my head. Her dark hair pulled high in a bun as she lounged in the hot tub. That damn bra that pushed her spectacular tits above the water, then again when she teased me and made me beg.

No, this isn't some sex-induced haze I'm wading through. This is all Jolie.

Okay. So I'm... intrigued by her. Whatever her reason for wanting to restrict it to one night was valid. Just because we had fun together, doesn't mean we could ever make a relationship work.

We're like oil and water. We don't mix.

After getting to know her this weekend, I realize I might have misjudged her. But that doesn't change the fact that we would never work long term.

She's impulsive while I always need a plan.

She's loud and showy while I prefer privacy.

She's like a wildfire, consuming everything in her path and I'm an evergreen going up in flames at the first touch. That can't be a healthy basis for a relationship.

Not that I'd have much experience with relationships. And I don't want to.

Not since Mindy.

Mindy was my college girlfriend. Her friend was dating my roommate, who had dragged me out for a beer to celebrate exams being done one night. She was sweet and funny and when she smiled, I couldn't help but smile back. We talked and laughed and by the end of the night, I asked for her number and could hardly wait to call her the next day.

We were inseparable after that. Everyone thought we'd get married after graduation and we would've, if all had gone according to my five-year plan.

Graduate. Get a job at the Haven Bay Police Department. Buy a house. Work my way up the ladder. Get engaged after a few years then have a small ceremony in town. Become Chief of Police for the HBPD. Then when we were both ready, have a couple of kids.

Mindy knew about my five-year plan and knew how important it was to me. She had the same aspirations so it seemed like the perfect fit.

But dating a police officer sounds great in theory until you're living it; especially when you're living in a small town. During the first few years, I worked my ass off, picking up extra shifts and staying late. When you're a cop in a small town, you don't just turn your head to problems when you're off-duty. If Mrs. Tidmin accidentally backed her car into Steve Stingle's garden again, I wasn't going to just walk on by without stopping to help.

After a couple of years of cold dinners, missed holidays and interrupted date nights, Mindy decided that the life we dreamed of wasn't for her anymore. I got off duty one night and came home to an empty house and a resentful note. In it, she called me codependent and obsessive. She said no self-respecting woman would stick around to play second place to a town full of "wackjobs".

So even if I somehow convinced Jolie to give me another shot, it wouldn't work.

The best thing for me to do right now is just forget about her.

CHAPTER 33

JOLIE

"Come on, you glorified twig. I'm not going to hurt you. Just come out already." It's my least favorite time of the month; the dreaded admin day.

I'm not what anyone would call "organized". Especially since I can't seem to figure out the accounting program that Avery recommended and I'm too proud to ask for help. So I'm stuck with good old paper and a pencil for calculating my expenses for this month.

My father used to tell my brother and I that the enemy of success was disorder. Then he'd dump out our backpacks onto the kitchen table to evaluate our binders for what he deemed the appropriate level of organization. When I'd inevitably fail his assessment, he'd sigh and call me a disappointment. Once, he told me that I wouldn't make a good wife because "even a housewife needs an organized grocery list".

Yep. That misogynistic asshole was supposed to be my role model. It's no wonder I high-tailed it out of his house the first chance I got.

Which is why, despite being down on my hands and knees searching for a damn pencil, I refuse to admit that I have a problem. Even if all of my writing utensils have sprouted legs and run off the edge of the table in the middle of my work.

Honestly, after looking at the estimate Henry gave me to fix Blue and my monthly bills, the pencil might've intentionally jumped.

"Aha!" I shoot up on my knees with the pencil in hand, narrowly missing rapping my head on the underside of the table. "There you are, you little stinker."

Climbing back into my chair, I pull the paperwork back onto my lap, hoping the numbers on the pages have significantly decreased since I last looked.

Nope. Still very much in the red.

I groan, dropping my head into my hands. Why, why, why, did I choose to live in a place where there's snow? I could've moved anywhere after high school. Florida, Texas, California. Anywhere where the sky doesn't take a giant dump on your car, forcing you to take out a small mortgage to pay for the repairs.

Though with my luck, my car would probably get swept away with a hurricane or be smashed by falling objects during an earthquake.

I blow out a long breath, staring at the paper until all the numbers start to blur together. Then I drop my head back between my shoulder blades. What am I going to do? I can't afford the vintage car parts needed to fix Blue and still make all of my bills this month. My credit card is already near maxed-out from Christmas shopping and I have nothing of value to sell.

I could offer extra classes to make up for it, but I need

the money now. Henry has a lead on some parts but he needs to order them quickly.

That leaves me with only one choice and it creates such a bitter taste in my mouth, I have to take a drink of my iced tea to wash it away.

I need to borrow money from my family.

I know my mom would gladly give me whatever I needed, no questions asked. But there's no way for her to get me the money without my father knowing. Which means the money would come with a lecture on accepting handouts that would turn into him belittling my job and my life choices. "Isn't it time to get a *real* job, Jolie?" he'd ask me in that condescending tone he prefers. "We can't keep supporting your habits forever, you know."

Habits. As if I'm a crackhead begging for money for my next hit instead of a successful business owner who has had a run of bad luck and needs help.

So, no. I refuse to ask my parents for help.

Which leaves one person.

Before I can chicken out, I grab my phone and hit my brother's name to FaceTime him. He picks up before I can change my mind and end the call.

"Twerp! How's it going?" Austin's cheery face lights up my screen and despite my twisting stomach, I grin.

"Twerp? Really? What are you, twelve?"

"Damn right," he answers proudly.

I roll my eyes but I can't help the tug in my chest. Austin might be ridiculously annoying but he's my brother and I miss his stupid face.

There's laughter in the background. I take a closer look at the screen. There's a wooden stall filled with clothes behind him. "Where are you?"

"Locker room," he answers casually. "Just finished

practice." A voice yells out something unintelligible and he looks away from the phone to yell. "It's my sister, you dickhead. Don't be gross."

A goofy face pops up on the screen. "Hi Jay, baby. Looking good," my brother's best friend, Chase Bozzelli, purrs sweetly. "When're you going to quit playing hard to get and accept my proposal?" He lays a hand on his bare chest, holding his heart like he's in pain. "A guy can only take so many rejections before it gets to his head."

I bite back a smile. "Oh, Chase. You know this wild filly can't be tamed." I flutter my eyelashes at him. "But if anyone could put a ring on this finger, it'd be you."

Chase gives me a toothy grin, only to have Austin wipe it away with a hand to his face. "Cut that shit out. You ever touch my sister, I'll cut off that Tootsie Roll between your legs and feed it to you."

I sigh. *So dramatic.* Glad I'm not like that.

Chase isn't bothered though and smiles at me from behind my brother's hand. He gives me a goofy wave. "Good to see you, sugar. Come see me soon, ya hear?" When Austin lunges at him, he takes off out of the frame, giggling like a little girl.

Austin stands and walks out of the locker room, his teammates catcalling me through the phone while he shouts vague threats over his shoulder. "Buncha vultures," he grumbles, opening the door to what looks like a hallway.

"So, are you calling to tell me you're coming home for a visit? It's been years since I've seen your frizzy-haired self."

I gasp theatrically. "First of all, how dare you? My hair is not frizzy. You're just jealous I took all the good genes and left you with Uncle Norm's hairline." Austin gasps back and I snicker.

"Watch your mouth, you little twerp. I have a headful of

the most luscious locks in the entire NHL. Ask BuzzFeed. They did an article on it last month."

"Second of all," I continue, ignoring his dramatics. "It hasn't been years. I saw you when you played Calgary in the spring."

"That was in Calgary though, and I only got to stay one night before we had to fly back. It's not the same." He brings the phone closer to his face so his puppy dog eyes take up most of the screen. "You know, Christmas is coming up and the team has a home game on the 22nd. You could always come for the game then stay at my place. You could leave after Boxing Day."

I love my brother, I really do. He might drive me crazy sometimes but that's what brothers do, right? And I hate being so far from him.

But if I'm being honest with myself, which I rarely am, when I left home at eighteen, it wasn't just to get away from my dad. I was running from my brother, too.

Or more accurately, my brother's shadow.

Growing up, Austin was the kid that could pick up any ball or stick and have mastered the sport in under an hour. He was naturally athletic and smart as hell. But hockey was his game.

The summer before high school, he shot up six inches and put on thirty pounds of muscle. Combine that with the hockey camp he'd convinced my parents to put him in and his place on the junior hockey team was pretty much set before training camp even started.

Don't get me wrong; Austin worked his ass off to get to where he is now. He's on the ice six days a week and in the gym seven. When he's not training his body, he's working on his mental game. He deserves every bit of his success and I'm damn proud to be his sister.

But there's only so long you can live in someone's shadow before your own light begins to dim.

It wasn't Austin's fault. He treated me the same way he always did. It was everyone else that changed.

Even before he was drafted to the NHL, the spotlight had been on Austin. People knew he'd be a star one day, so they clung to him, trying to weasel their way into his life. And when that didn't work, they'd try to wedge their way into mine.

It got to the point where I didn't know who was in my life for me and who was in it to get closer to my brother. It only got worse when he was drafted.

By that time, I was tired of being Austin St. James' little sister. I needed to just be me.

So when graduation came, I told Austin I needed to get away from my father. Which wasn't a lie, but not entirely the truth. Even though I know my brother would understand, I still feel guilty about lying.

Which is usually how he convinces me to visit Toronto —and my parents—once a year.

"We'll see, Ares," I answer vaguely.

He groans. "Alright, alright. Quit middle naming me." He slides his back down the wall to sit on the hallway floor. "So, what do I owe the displeasure of your call then, sister dearest?"

Ignoring the jab, I take a deep breath. "I need your help," I practically choke out, the words sour on my tongue.

"Anything," he replies automatically. "What'd you need?"

I let out a slow breath. It's not that I thought he'd say no; Austin would give the shirt off his back if he thought it'd help someone in need. For his baby sister? He'd give me the moon if he could.

No, it's not Austin that's the problem.

It's me.

I pride myself on being self-sufficient. I promised myself when I left home I would never want to have to ask permission for anything again.

So even though he's my brother and even though I know he would never think less of me for it, I hate asking for his help. But it's for Blue, for my grandpa's last gift to me, so I swallow my pride and explain the story.

When I finish, Austin lets out a slow breath. "Well, I'm glad you're safe, even though I'm pissed off that you went out in a snowstorm. Especially in Blue. I've been telling you for years you need an SUV, something built for Canadian winters. Maybe now you'll actually listen to me," he lectures. "Text me how much you need and I'll send it now."

Relief and guilt swirl around in my gut. "Thanks, Aus. I swear I'll pay you back every penny."

"You will not." His eyes suddenly light up and I can already tell I'm not going to like what he says next. "In fact, consider it a Christmas present. Along with a ticket to Toronto on December 21st."

I open my mouth to argue but he clicks his tongue at me. "Nope, it's done." His eyes soften. "Come on. It's only for a few days. You can stay with me at my condo. We can decorate my Christmas tree, watch bad movies, and eat too much junk, just like the good ol' days. Then we'll go see Mom and Dad on Christmas Day so they can't complain that we didn't try and then you can fly home and go back to avoiding us." He smiles to show he's joking but I feel another stab of guilt.

Because that's exactly what I've been doing—avoiding them.

"Fine." I point a finger at the phone. "But if I have to put up with our parents, you're springing for first class."

He laughs. "You've got it, twerp." Someone calls his name and he looks away for a second before looking back at the screen. "Look, I've gotta go. Text me the amount and I'll see you in a couple weeks. Love ya, kiddo."

"Love you, too."

After ending the call with my brother, I feel marginally better. True to his word, a few minutes after I text him, I get an email notification that he's transferred the money.

Well, at least that's taken care of.

It only cost me a day in hell. Otherwise known as Christmas at my parent's house.

I huff out a breath then grab my laptop and open up my emails. Maybe some *Dear Annie* work will take my mind off my troubles.

That thought is quickly squashed when I open the first email. I check the address field and again, it's to my Amaryllis email from an unknown sender. Dread swims in my stomach.

Nosey bitches get what's coming to them.

I slam my laptop shut, my heart racing.

How did they find out it was me?

Are they watching me?

Who are they?

I squeeze my eyes shut, trying to think of anything to distract myself from the growing panic that's crawling up my spine.

It takes a while before I finally convince myself that I'm safe enough to crawl into my bed. I promise myself I'll bring the emails to Sandy's attention tomorrow. She'll know what to do.

But for the first time in a long time, I remember to lock my door that night.

THE HAVEN TIMES

pg 15 — Proudly serving Haven Bay for over 100 years. — **FREE**

DEAR ANNIE

Your local source for advice on love, life and everything in between!

The answer to this week's trivia question (pg 9) is magma.

Q.

Dear Annie,

I like to consider myself a reasonable woman. I let my granddaughter listen to that stupid pop music on the radio when I drive her to school. When someone comes around with gossip, I make sure to check the facts before passing it on to the next person I see. I even have Facebook.

But I cannot hold my tongue any longer. I have something I need to get off of my chest. I know it will cause issues with someone I consider a good friend but I can no longer sit idly by and let her ruin my street. Our town is a respectable one and I refuse to let her tarnish my hard work.

Do I continue to bite my cheek in the sake of friendship or do I finally let the truth out?

Sincerely,

Reasonably Concerned

A.

Dear Reasonably Concerned,

I'm not sure what exactly your truth is that you feel needs to be shared but I can tell you this: secrets are like snowballs. The more you let them spin, the larger they grow and the harder they are to carry.

I know, I know. It's easier said than done. But I'm a firm believer that the truth is best out in the open, especially among friends.

Now that's not to say you need to tell your bestie that the haircut she adores is actually a mullet. Telling the truth does not mean you need to be mean. Take care when talking to your friend. Be respectful and you will be met with respect. Be hurtful and you might just lose that friend.

Love always,

Annie

CHIEF BRADY REMINDS YOU NOT TO DRINK AND DRIVE THIS HOLIDAY SEASON.

HANDCUFFS ARE A GREAT GIFT, BUT GET THEM ANOTHER WAY.

CHAPTER 34

LUKE

The music is too loud.

Don't get me wrong, it's good music. The band is from a few towns over and is playing mostly classic rock covers with some originals tossed in. But when I have to shout to be heard, it's too damn loud. So instead of talking, I've been listening to Matt prattle on about hockey since I walked into The Dive half hour ago.

Usually I love any chance to talk sports. Football, baseball, hockey. College or professional, it doesn't matter. I follow it all. I watch ESPN every night while I cook dinner and can recite most player's stats at the drop of a hat. I like to think it has more to do with my love of sports than it does my lack of personal life. Something I never noticed until this week. But after spending the weekend with Jolie, my life has seemed far more pathetic than it once did.

Which is why I'm hardly listening to Matt's asinine theory about the Wildcats playoff probability. My mind is wandering to the one subject it's been hooked on all week: *her*.

I've tried distracting myself. I've tried listing off all the reasons why pursuing her would be a bad idea. But it's like I went my whole life seeing in black and white until one day, someone handed me a pair of those color blindness correcting glasses. My world was a kaleidoscope of beautiful reds, blues and greens, better than anything I ever could've imagined. Only for them to snatch the glasses back and break them in two in front of me, guaranteeing that I'll never experience it again.

How am I expected to go back to the drab grey sky I was accustomed to when I've seen what a rainbow looks like?

"Where are the girls?" I ask when there's a break in the conversation. I'm hoping I sound casual but even I can hear how eager my voice sounds. Luckily, Matt somehow doesn't pick up on it. Just the mention of his future-wife has his face turning into a dreamy, gooey mess.

"They're at Jolie's getting ready," he says. "Oh, wait. Here they are now." He nods toward the door, that goofy smile he gets on his face when he sees Avery shining bright. I follow his line of vision. Avery, Brenna and Jolie are standing just inside the bar entrance, shrugging off their coats and hooking them on the bar's coat rack.

Jolie pulls off her hood, saying something to Brenna that makes them both laugh. The loud music means it's impossible to hear the sound but it fills my head just the same.

I've seen her laughing, joking and having fun hundreds of times but for some reason, this time feels like the first.

You know in those corny rom-com movies when the crowd parts and everyone else in the room dims. Then there's this almost angelic spotlight that shines only on the main character?

Yeah, that's how this feels.

What the hell is wrong with me? I'm not this cheesy

guy who becomes obsessed with a woman after only one night together.

The music ends and Matt takes the opportunity to call out, waving the girls over. Spotting him, they make their way through the crowd toward us. Avery swoops into Matt's waiting embrace and he pulls her close for a lingering kiss.

Jolie steps up to the bar beside me, brushing her arm against mine. The briefest contact of her cool skin on mine and my heart rate spikes. Every nerve in my body is alive, all focused on that one spot on my arm.

Okay, I might be that guy.

"Whew. It's colder than a reindeer's nipple out there." Jolie laughs, running her hands over her arms to chase away the chill. She catches Rhett's eye from across the bar and points to herself and the girls. He nods his understanding and reaches for a glass.

She swivels to lean her elbows back on the bar. I can't help staring down at her and the way the move pushes her chest forward. The deep V of her top has my mouth watering, remembering the taste of her on my tongue.

I take a long pull of my beer to wet my suddenly dry mouth.

Fuck sakes.

What is this woman doing to me? And why do I hope she never stops?

"Hey, Chief." She smiles sweetly up at me, her eyes bright with amusement. "How's it hanging?"

"About three inches long and a little to the left," Matt interjects then laughs at his own stupid joke.

Avery swats his arm and Brenna groans. Rhett lets out a chuckle as he passes out the drinks. Jolie laughs and the sound goes right to my cock.

I dip my head so my mouth is beside her ear. "You

weren't laughing like that when you had this cock buried deep inside you, *sweetheart*," I drawl, letting my breath tickle her skin.

Her breath catches and her eyes dilate. There's no doubt in my mind she's remembering exactly the image I've painted for her. Her eyes shoot to the others but they continue talking amongst themselves, unaware of what's happening between us. I take a drink of my beer, using the bottle to hide my smile at her disheveled expression.

Good. At least we're on an even playing field now.

Jolie blinks a few times, then takes a drink. The song ends and the band starts to play *New Orleans is Sinking* by The Tragically Hip. Jolie lights up, grabbing Brenna's arm.

"I love this song! Come on, girls. Let's dance." She turns to me. "You guys coming?"

I shake my head. "I don't dance."

Matt shrugs. "I'll keep him company."

"Suit yourselves." With that, she pulls Brenna and Avery after her, weaving through the crowd toward the dance floor.

Rhett heads back behind the bar while Matt and I watch the girls dance. After a minute, I force myself to turn away. "Not joining them?" I ask Matt, gesturing to the dance floor.

He shakes his head. "Nah. Avery's been stressed with the wedding and work. The bookmobile program starts in the new year and she's working her ass off to get it all organized before then." He leans back on the bar. "She deserves this."

"Is there anything we can do to help?" Rhett asks from behind the bar.

"Thanks, man. I'll talk to Avery and let you know. I've been trying to help out when I can but between all the permits for the expansion on the house, wedding stuff, and taking care of Gavin, there's not enough hours in a day to get it all done."

Suddenly, I feel about two inches tall. Am I really that absorbed in my work that I didn't realize my own family needed me? I feel like a dick for not offering to help sooner.

"Whatever you need, let us know. We'll get it done," I say, clapping a hand on Matt's shoulder. He nods and I feel marginally better.

The conversation changes to renovations and Matt's plans for expanding Avery's childhood home that their family will be living in after the wedding.

We're debating the usefulness of a mudroom shower when Avery and Brenna come striding through the crowd to where we're standing. We step aside so they can each grab a seat at the bar, both of them breathing hard.

"Wow, that was fun!" Brenna smiles widely.

Avery nods, grabbing Matt's beer to take a drink. She points the bottle back at him. "After I take a breather, you're joining us out there. You promised you'd dance with me tonight."

Matt takes the beer from her hand and dips his head. "Love to, Freckles." He gives her a quick kiss. "Hopefully you can keep up. I'm wearing my dancing shoes tonight."

Rhett groans, knowing how awful of a dancer Matt is. "Try not to break anything this time, eh? We just got the stage steps fixed from your last dance off."

Matt shrugs. "I can't help it if my moves are too much for you, Rhetty boy."

Avery clicks her tongue. "I don't know, Rhett. That sounded like a challenge to me."

While Matt and Rhett bicker like an old married couple

with Avery playing instigator, I lean over to Brenna. "Where's Jolie?"

"She found a new dance partner." She points through the crowd to where Jolie's dancing near the stage. Her head is tossed back laughing, one arm slung over the shoulder of some prick in a Henley and jeans. He's running his hands over her back, leaning closer as he whispers something in her ear.

My chest tightens. My vision goes red. The grip on my beer bottle tightens to the point that I'm surprised it doesn't break in my hand.

What. The. Fuck.

It takes everything in me not to storm through the crowd and rip him off her. I want to toss her over my shoulder, claiming her in front of everyone in this bar as mine.

But she's not, a voice in my head reminds me. It's the only reason I'm not doing exactly that. Because despite my caveman thoughts, I'm not some Neanderthal dragging her back to my cave by her hair.

As much as I want her, Jolie's her own woman who makes her own decisions about who or what she wants.

And she's made it pretty damn clear that's not me.

But because I'm a glutton for punishment, I continue to stand at the bar, torturing myself as I watch her flirt, dance, and laugh with that fucking asshole who doesn't deserve any of it.

Neither do you, the voice says again, and I take an angry pull of my beer to drown it out.

The song bleeds into a slower one and every muscle in my body tenses as he pulls her in close, pressing her tall frame against him. They sway for a few moments before Jolie says something into his ear. Then she untangles herself from his arms and heads toward the back of the bar.

I take another angry drink, watching as she slips around the corner to the hallway that leads to the bathrooms. I force myself to turn away from her and back to the bar. Staring down at the wooden bar, I list off all the reasons I gave myself all week why we were a bad idea.

I slam my beer down on the bar with more force than necessary.

Fuck it.

Without a backward glance, I push my way through the crowd. Rounding the corner of the back hallway, I come to a sudden stop just before crashing into someone.

Reaching out to steady the body before me, I look down to see the bright blue eyes that've been haunting my every waking thought for as long as I can remember.

CHAPTER 35

JOLIE

The music from the bar turns into a dull thumping as I shut the bathroom door behind me. Striding over to the sink, I turn on the faucet. I rinse my hands, more for something to do than anything, then yank a few paper towels from the dispenser. Drying my hands, I toss the crumpled paper into the garbage then grip the edges of the sink in each hand. Then I take a deep breath, staring down at the sink for a moment before lifting my eyes to the mirror.

What the hell is wrong with me?

When Steve approached me and asked me to dance, I was flattered but ready to politely shut him down. That was until Avery and Brenna practically shoved me at him. We laughed about my overzealous friends which turned into us doing the "get to know you" game.

You know, *where are you from? What do you do for a living? What do you like to do for fun?* That old tired dance.

Steve was nice enough and made me laugh. It didn't hurt that he knew his way around the dance floor and filled out his jeans quite nicely.

But for some reason, when he pulled me close to sway to a slow song, it was brown eyes I was thinking about, not his green. And if I'm being honest, he was too nice. In the fifteen minutes we'd been talking, he agreed with everything I said.

In other words, he was boring.

I groan, dropping my head forward. Listen to me. *He was too nice?* That's my biggest complaint? Just because he didn't argue with me or purposely push my buttons, that makes him boring?

How messed up am I?

I know that Luke is wrong for me. Since I was a little girl, watching my father walk all over my mom and then try his hardest to do the same to me, I swore I'd never be with a man even remotely similar to him.

And until now, I've kept that promise. Most of the guys I've been with have been fun and carefree, never planning further ahead than their next meal.

Luke's not that type of guy.

Luke's the type of guy who meal preps and has retirement savings. He's the kind of guy who has the next five years of his life laid out in front of him like a checklist.

Buy a house in his hometown?

Check.

Build a career within said town's police department?

Check.

Get married, have exactly two point five children and a golden retriever named Buddy?

Check. Check. Check.

Not that there's anything wrong with that. But that's not how I live my life. I'm happy in my one-bedroom apartment above my studio. I love my job and my friends. Get married? Yeah, sure. If I found the right guy. Kids?

They've always been an abstract idea. As in, maybe someday. But also maybe I'd rather just travel. We'll see how it goes.

I don't fit into Luke's nicely laid out plans.

And before last weekend, I was sure that Luke would be the type to force you into those plans, no matter how badly the fit was.

But now I'm not so sure.

The Luke I got to know at the lodge was caring and thoughtful. He was still grouchy but he also laughed easier. He was playful and funny.

I'm realizing there might be more to Luke than what he lets the world see. And that version of him makes me more anxious than the one I'm used to.

Take tonight for example. Before we came, I decided that my best course of action was to go back to the way we were before we got snowed in together. We're both adults. We could act normal. Just because I've seen him naked and had his cock inside me and he made me come so hard I saw stars...

What was I saying?

Oh, right. Normal.

So, when I saw him standing at the bar, I decided to walk right up to him and play it cool. But apparently, he had other ideas.

Hot, dirty ideas.

No. I stare back at my reflection in the mirror. *One night, remember? That's all it was supposed to be. That's all it can be.*

Luke can say whatever he wants, act however he wants but I won't give in.

I give myself a decisive nod, square my shoulders, then pull open the bathroom door. I strut down the hall and am about to round the corner back into the bar when a body slams into me, nearly knocking me on my ass.

Large hands reach out to steady me.

"Shit, I'm sor—" I look up and see Luke's dark eyes staring back at me. There's a sharp edge to him, an anger simmering below the surface.

"Luke?"

Instead of responding, he grabs ahold of the back of my neck and yanks me to him, his mouth crashing down on mine. I'm stunned for a moment, unable to think or do anything other than succumb to his whim.

He takes two strides forward, his mouth never leaving mine, until my back hits the wall behind me. The contact awakens something inside me and my hands go to his waist, pulling him closer until his erection hits my stomach. I swivel my hips, lost to the feel of him pressed against me.

He groans then deepens the kiss, hungrily chasing my mouth. We're a tangle of hands and teeth. My heart rate thunders in my chest as I meet him stroke for stroke.

The bar cheers as the band plays a fan favorite and somewhere in the back of my mind, I know this is a bad idea. We're making out in a dark but very public hallway. It's not noticeable from the bar but at any second, someone could walk around that corner and see us.

The thrill of getting caught only spurs me on.

He places open mouth kisses along the column of my neck. "We can't," I mutter while I hold his head in place.

"I know," he mumbles against my skin as his mouth trails lower.

"We shouldn't be doing this." I gasp as he rocks against me, our clothes causing enough friction to have me panting but not enough to satisfy.

He pulls my shirt to the side to kiss along my collarbone. "Tell me to stop."

But I can't. I won't. Because while my head is telling me *no*, the rest of me is screaming, *more!*

Someone laughs loudly from beside us and we spring apart just as a man staggers around the corner. Luke steps in front of me, shielding my body from view with his own.

The man stumbles down the hallway toward the bathroom, barely giving Luke a nod before he slams the door shut behind him.

Luke waits a moment before turning to face me. His chest is rising and falling in quick succession as his warm chocolate eyes stare down at me. "You okay?"

I nod, though I'm far from okay. I'm ablaze with need, desperate for something only Luke can give me. He sees it in my face, his eyes searching mine. I stare back at him, neither of us willing to move.

He looks up at the crowd behind us then back down at me. "You wanna get out of here?"

I nod quickly. "My place?"

"Fifteen?"

"Make it ten," I answer then turn on my heel. Hurrying through the crowd, I find Avery and Brenna by the bar with Matt and Rhett.

"I'm going to head out," I shout over the music, gesturing toward the door.

Avery smiles wickedly. "Things went well with Steve, I assume?"

I swallow hard but force a smile. "Yeah, he's great. But I have to get home. I have a class in the morning. I'll see you guys later."

I give her a hug then turn to do the same to Brenna. As I pull away, she arches a brow at me. "You're good?"

I smile but it feels like there's a sign hanging from around my neck that says **Going to fuck Luke** in big bold letters across it. "Yep. No problem."

Thankfully, she lets me go without any further questions and I scurry out the door, stopping only to grab my coat. I make the short walk to my studio, practically running through the back parking lot. In record time, I push open the back door and hurry inside.

A shadowy figure approaches from beside me. "You don't lock your doors."

I jolt, grabbing my heart to keep it from jumping out of my chest. "Holy fish knuckles, you scared the bejeebers out of me," I cry, swatting Luke's chest.

He continues to stare down at me intensely. "You don't lock your doors," he repeats. He says it like a statement but I answer him anyway.

"Not always. I forget sometimes." I shrug off my coat and hang it on the hook beside me. I try to take a step inside toward the stairs to my apartment but Luke blocks my way.

"You forget sometimes?" he echos.

Apparently, we're not going to continue where we left off until we clear this up so I sigh and step back to look at him. "Yeah, sometimes I remember to lock it and sometimes I forget." He looks like he's about to blow a gasket. "What's the big deal? It's Haven Bay. Nothing bad happens here."

His mouth twists into a hard line and he steps toward me until I'm staring up at him. "Bad things happen everywhere." His voice is a low growl. It should not turn me on as much as it does, but here we are. "Lock. Your. Doors." He takes a step toward me with each word until my back hits the door. "Always." With that, he flips the deadbolt behind my head. "Got it?" I nod, too stunned, and quite frankly, too turned the fuck on to form a thought.

"Good girl."

Aaaaaaand there goes my panties. Ruined by two little words.

I pull his head down to mine and our mouths clash, picking up exactly where we left off at the bar. Grabbing hold of his shirt, I try to push it up his torso but his hands grab mine, stilling them. I groan in frustration.

I swear to god, if he's stopping again to lecture on some stupid lock...

"As much as I love the idea of fucking you against the wall," he rasps, guiding me toward the staircase, "I don't need the entire town looking at my bare ass while I do it." He nods to the large bay windows that take up the majority of the front wall.

Oops. Another thing I often forget to do is close my blinds. Oh well. As hot as against-the-wall sex is, something tells me that's not Luke's style.

Oh, well. Nothing wrong with sex in a good ol' reliable bed. Much better for the knees. Another perk of pushing thirty.

We quickly climb the stairs to my apartment. Luke shoves open the door and pulls me inside. Then he slams it shut, pushes me against it and takes my mouth in a searing kiss. I shove at his shirt and this time he complies, stepping back only long enough to pull off his shirt before he's settling back between my legs.

I run my hands over his chest, reveling in the way he feels against my palms. Slowly, I drag my fingernails down his chest and he inhales sharply. He rips his mouth from mine, grabbing my hands to bring them above my head. Holding my wrists together with one hand, he trails the other hand down to my waist.

"You want it rough, sweetheart?" he growls and I arch against him as the sound goes straight to my core.

"I just want you," I pant. He closes his eyes to my words. A moment later, he opens them and they look softer than before.

"How do you want me?" he asks.

I don't even have to think. "Desperate."

A slow smile overtakes his face.

"Done."

CHAPTER 36

LUKE

When I followed Jolie into the hallway at The Dive, I didn't really have a plan. I just knew I needed to see her, be near her. Watching her dance and laugh with that jackwagon had me feeling all kinds of fucked up.

I have no right to feel this possessive over someone I slept with once and up until then, drove me insane.

But I never claimed to be a nice guy. If making Jolie mine makes me an asshole, so be it.

I give her pinned wrists a light squeeze. "Keep these here or I stop." She nods, staring back at me with wide eyes. "I need your words, Jolie."

"Yes," she breathes.

I trail my fingers down the sensitive skin of her arms and over her ribs. Her breathing turns to pants when my thumbs graze her breasts over her shirt.

My lips curve upward, knowing exactly what my teasing is doing to her. I continue down her waist until I reach the strip of skin where her shirt has risen up from her raised arms.

"Your skin is so soft," I mumble, leaning in to kiss just below her ear. "I could touch you all day." Her head turns toward me, following my mouth but I continue to place open mouth kisses along her neck. "But you're not soft, are you?"

She shakes her head, speechless for once in her life.

"No, you're tough as hell. You're a fighter." My hands drift up from her waist to her ribs, her silky shirt sliding up with them. "Just like me."

Higher and higher my hands glide along her skin until they're grazing just below her tits. She arches into me, silently begging me to touch her but I don't move them. Instead, I lift my head to her ear again and nip her lobe. "But I'm done fighting how I feel for you."

She shivers and when I lift my head, her brows are furrowed in confusion.

This isn't the time to explain. She's not ready for that talk. And quite honestly, I'm not sure I am either.

I distract us both by sliding her shirt up. She arches, allowing me to pull it up and over her head. The corner of my mouth tilts upward when she keeps her arms stretched above her, barely lifting off the door as I undress her.

"Good girl," I mumble, dropping her shirt to the ground. Then, never taking my eyes off hers, I drop to my knees.

"Do you know what I was thinking tonight while I was watching you with that asshole?" I raise my hands to unbuckle her jeans, then slowly slide the zipper down. "Watching you wrap your arms around him." I grip the waist of her jeans and peel them down over her hips. "Dancing with him." Over her round ass. "Laughing with him." Down her long legs. "Smiling at him." I lift her right calf out of the jeans and place it on the floor, then mirror the move with her left, until she stands before me in just her bra and panties.

I take a second to drink her in. Her long, dark hair messy from my hands gripping and pulling it moments ago. Her chest, deliciously pink from my stubble, rising and falling in quick succession. Her normally sky-blue eyes now a stormy gray as she watches me, waiting impatiently for my next move.

She looks exactly how she said she wanted me—desperate. Maybe if I was feeling vengeful for her teasing last time, I'd play with her more. Wind her up but never giving her what she wanted until she was begging me for it. The way she made me beg for her.

But I want her too badly to play any more games.

Instead, I slide my hands slowly up her smooth legs, letting my thumbs graze her inner thighs until she's practically panting, arching into my touch. Then I grip her panties at the hips and pull down one side.

Holding her gaze, I lean forward and place a soft kiss on her hip. "Do you want to know what I was thinking, sweetheart?" I ask against her skin. When she doesn't answer right away, I pause.

It takes her a second to focus on my words before she shakes her head quickly, her tousled hair grazing the tops of her breasts. My mouth dries, remembering the sounds she let out last time when I had my mouth wrapped around her nipple.

My entire body is wound tighter than a spring but I'm determined to do this right. To savor her the way I didn't get to last time.

I pull her panties down further, grazing my mouth along her waist as I inch closer to her center. She lifts her hips eagerly. Smiling against her skin, I drift lower, dropping her panties down her legs.

I dip my head, my mouth a whisper away from her clit as her mouth drops open in a silent plea. "I was thinking how badly I wanted it to be me," I tell her, just before I place a soft open mouth kiss against her centre. She whimpers, the contact so good and yet not enough. "That it were *my* arms you were wrapped up in." A firmer kiss. "*My* jokes making you laugh." My tongue teases her clit, making her cry out. "*My* words earning your smile." A long lick along her slit and her head falls back against the door with a muffled, "Oh, god".

"He didn't deserve you."

Her head tilts forward. "And you do?" she replies, voice hoarse.

Despite the bite of her words, I smile. That sassy mouth of hers. I hate how much I love it.

"That's the difference between me and him, sweetheart." I dip one hand to explore her pussy with my fingers, spreading her wetness as I tease her entrance. "He thinks he does." My other hand spreads her lips wide, using my forearm to keep her hips pressed firmly against the wall. "I know I don't." At the same time that I dip my head, I push two fingers inside her, causing her to cry out in ecstasy. "But I'm gonna eat this pussy anyway."

And I do exactly that.

The second I taste her, my control snaps. I told myself I would savor her, devour her until she was sliding down the door, melting into my touch and moaning my name. A slow build into a delicious fall.

There's nothing slow about the way I'm taking her, though delicious is exactly how I would describe it. But by the sounds that are coming out of her mouth, she doesn't mind it one bit.

I alternate between sucking and licking her clit while my fingers thrust eagerly inside her. I curl them to hit the soft spot inside her and she shatters, her orgasm claiming her as her walls clench around me almost painfully. I have to hold her to the door while she bucks against me, crying out my name on a sob while she rides the waves of her orgasm.

When it finally subsides, she goes slack against the door, desperately trying to shove air into her lungs. I shoot to my feet and my chest swells when I notice her arms still raised above her head, though now bent in exhaustion.

Who knew Jolie had a submissive side to her?

"Fuck, you taste so good. I almost came listening to you scream my name while you held my fingers so tight, your sweet taste in my mouth." I place a slow kiss to her lips that she lazily returns. Reaching up, I grab her wrists and lower her arms. They drop like dead weight onto my shoulders and I grin.

"Tired, baby? Should I take you to bed?" I bend, intending to scoop her up but she stops me with a hard grip on my arms.

She pulls me back to her and this time, she claims me with a kiss. I follow suit, the kiss growing urgent until she pulls her mouth from mine. The wild look in her eyes has my cock flexing against my zipper.

"Lose the pants, Chief." Then in one fluid movement, she pushes me away from her, points her toes and raises her leg to the sky, giving me the most delicious view of her, bare and waiting for me. "You owe me another."

God, I love yoga.

I strip out of my jeans in record time, stopping only long

enough to put on a condom. Then I dive back toward her, pressing her leg further into her with my chest.

The contrast of my chest hair against her silky, unmarred skin looks wrong but I can't be bothered to care. Not when my cock is lined up where it's been dying to be all week. When she's running her nails down my back, driving me fucking crazy as she moans into my mouth.

Her nails bite into my ass as she urges me closer. "Now, Luke," she demands, her voice hoarse. "Now."

Don't have to tell me twice.

Sinking into her, we both groan. Sweet heaven above, I'm convinced there's no better feeling than this right here. Not just sex, but sex with Jolie specifically.

It's everything. I have no words to describe it other than an all-encompassing feeling of completeness.

But I don't have time to dwell on that before she's rocking into me, spurring me into action. Just like that, any semblance of control I had left is gone.

"You're going to want to hold on, baby."

It's all the warning I give her before I'm thrusting into her, every sharp jut of my hips shoving her higher up the door until her feet no longer touch the floor. Her head is thrown back against the door, a chant of curses and pleas escaping her as she hangs on for the ride.

Harder. Higher. Faster. It's not nearly enough as we chase our pleasure. I can feel my release tingling at my spine. I know I'm close but I refuse to come without her. Tilting my hips, I rock against her clit. Her answering scream has me coming so hard, my vision darkens as I growl her name.

When we finally catch our breath, I help her lower her leg and pass over her clothes before discarding the condom in a nearby garbage can.

Fully-clothed, Jolie turns to me, tucking her hair behind her ear. "So," she says, dragging out the word. "That was not how I was expecting my night to end."

I smile, my chest feeling lighter than it has all week. "Really? Because that's *exactly* how I wanted mine to."

She laughs and I have to run a hand over my mouth to keep the stupid grin off my face. I'm not sure when it happened but her laugh is my new favorite sound.

I should probably go but I hate the idea of leaving right now, knowing all the things I want to say but probably shouldn't. At least not yet. Not before I figure it out myself.

There's a long pause. I'm about to force myself to leave when she smiles shyly up at me. "I usually have some Ashwagandha tea to unwind after going out. Do you want some?"

My answer is automatic. "Love some."

Her smile widens. "Do you even know what Ashwagandha is?"

"Nope."

She laughs and shoves my shoulder playfully. She ambles past me then stops to smile over her shoulder from the doorway of the kitchen. "Coming?"

Oh, yeah. When it comes to Jolie, I'm so fucked. I'd follow her into shark-infested waters right now if it meant she kept smiling at me like she is right now.

So fucked.

JOLIE

What is happening? The sudden turn of events from tonight is giving me whiplash.

"Let's go to The Dive this weekend," Avery had said. *"We'll dance, I'll buy you an apology drink. It'll be fun!"*

Somehow, I don't think making out in dark corners then getting fucked against my front door by her future brother-in-law is what she meant by fun.

My mind latches onto that one thought. Luke and I just had sex. Spectacular, toe-curling sex. For the second time this week. Against my front door.

Again, *what is happening?*

Strolling into my tiny kitchen, I don't even have to look behind me to know Luke's following me. I can feel his every move as if it's my own. My body is still humming with the after-effects from the two Earth-stopping orgasms he gave me. I can still feel his hands on my skin like a brand saying *mine, mine, mine.* I'm surprised my legs are able to carry me this far. They feel ready to give out at a second's notice.

He comes up behind me, standing closer than necessary but not touching me. My mind is buzzing, a million thoughts flying around but I can't grab onto a single one.

I've slept beside the man, had sex with him but can't think of anything to say over tea? My inner self slaps a palm to her forehead. *Get it together, woman.*

I don't bother to turn when I point to the breakfast stool tucked under my kitchen island. "Sit," I sputter.

He chuckles at my nervous behavior but follows my direction, taking a seat at the island. He leans on his forearms, clasping his hands in front of him and smirks as if to say, *now what?*

I turn and flee to the safety of the other side of the kitchen. Facing the cupboard, I take a second to get myself under control. I take a slow breath to calm my galloping heart. Why am I so nervous? This is Luke. He might be a growly bear but that's never phased me before.

Maybe that's the problem. I have no idea what to do with this sweet, attentive version of him. I'm usually so self-assured, but when it comes to him, my mind goes blank and my arms feel like cooked spaghetti noodles.

Why can't I figure out what to do with my hands?

I internally groan as I reach into the overhead cupboard and grab my jar of tea bags, pausing to turn on my electric kettle. I hate this feeling. This insecure, awkward feeling of uncertainty.

Setting the jar on the counter, I grab my favorite mugs from the hooks on the wall and place them before me, tossing a tea bag in each one. When the light on the kettle flicks off, I busy myself by pouring the water into the mugs, trying my hardest to ignore the feel of Luke's eyes on me.

Maybe if I knew what this all meant, I wouldn't feel so awkward. Was this just a spur of the moment thing? Was this because he saw me with someone else and was jealous?

Or was it something entirely different?

Grabbing a mug in each hand, I straighten my shoulders and turn back. Passing his tea over, he turns the mug to read it then laughs. "Why am I not surprised?"

I shrug, smiling. The tall black cup is one of my favorites. "I do yoga because punching people is frowned upon" is written in script lettering across it. I take a sip of my tea, turning to lean back against the cupboard beside me. "It's true."

Luke smirks. "I have a feeling Chesterfield would disagree."

I laugh, snorting at the mention of that prick Tad. "I almost forgot about him. I wonder what happened to him."

Luke takes a drink of his tea. "According to the Haven Bay rumor mill, whatever business deal he came to town to solidify went under because of what happened at The Dive. So I'd assume he's not too happy."

I can't help feeling some satisfaction from that. It

doesn't surprise me that whoever he was in business with heard about our "altercation". Everyone knows everything that happens in this town, whether they want to or not. The fact that they decided to no longer do business with him because of it is also not surprising.

Haven Bay takes care of their own.

What does surprise me is the lack of judgment or anger in Luke's tone. He almost sounds...amused? Which is strange since he was the one chewing my ass off in the parking lot after it happened. I know he technically apologized but it was half-assed and out of guilt and...well... we all know how that ended.

I tilt my head at him. "Since when are you Team Jolie?"

He pauses with the mug halfway to his lips. "Recently, I'm finding myself more and more Team Jolie." He winks and damn him, why does that make my heart flip? His face falls. "Seriously though. I know I said it already but I handled that whole situation like shit. I'm sorry. Again. I should've believed you."

I clear my throat and stare down into my mug, feeling that damn insecurity again. "Thanks," I mumble, then lift my mug to take a long drink.

The hot tea is hitting my tongue when a mischievous glint sparkles in his eye. "Though I wouldn't mind getting you into a pair of handcuffs again."

I choke, just barely keeping the tea from spraying out my mouth. Forcing myself to swallow, I cough into my hand, tears welling in the corner of my eyes at the force. Luke just grins, taking a drink of his tea like the smug jerk he is.

When I finally pull myself together, I wipe my eyes then cross my arms over my chest. "Okay, what the hell is going on here?"

He looks innocently down at his drink then back at me. "I was enjoying my tea before you started fighting for your life. Now I'm wondering if I'll have to put down my drink to Heimlich you."

I narrow my eyes. "Don't get cute with me, Brady. Answer."

He just grins back. "You think I'm cute?"

I tilt my head at him disapprovingly.

He holds his hands up in surrender. "Alright, alright." He leans back in his chair, rubbing a hand over the back of his neck. "Look. I don't know what's going on, okay? I can't stop thinking about last weekend." I open my mouth to object but he levels me with a hard stare. "And it's not just sex. Last weekend was the most fun I've had in..." he shrugs, not finishing his sentence. "I'm no good at this stuff. I'm not a relationship guy. My work takes up too much of my time for me to be." His eyes hold mine solemnly. "All I know is I can't get you out of my head. Your laugh. Your smile. The ridiculous shit that comes out of your mouth." He leans forward until his hands are almost touching mine but not quite. "I want more."

For a second, I'm stunned speechless—something I've found Luke is very good at doing. Of all the things I thought that he might say, that was not even in my top 100.

Part of me is soaring knowing that this feeling I've been fighting all week (and probably longer, if I'm being honest) wasn't one-sided. That what happened at the lodge was more than just a matter of right place, right time.

The other part of me is skeptical. Confused. Even a little bit angry because...

"I thought you couldn't stand me," I counter, my brows furrowing. "We're Luke and Jolie; Haven Bay's worst enemies. We drive each other crazy."

"First of all, I'm pretty sure Mrs. Benson and Jeffrey are Haven Bay's worst enemies," he comments and I fight the urge to smile, picturing the elderly woman trying to knock down the inappropriate statue. "Second of all, you've been driving me crazy for a long time, sweetheart, but not in the way you think."

I stare into his dark eyes, searching them for any hint of a lie. "So, what? You want to date me? You want us to go from wanting to throttle each other to being star-crossed lovers? How would that even work?" I know I'm starting to spiral but this makes no sense to me. How can so much change in one week?

"There's no way we could make a relationship work," I continue. "We're too different. I'm a fly-by-the-seat-of-my-pants dreamer and you're Mr. Responsible." I start to pace as I work through my thoughts. "Maybe we could make it work for a couple of weeks but long-term? We'll end up hating each other by the end of it and our friends will be the ones to suffer." I stop suddenly and whirl back on Luke. "Our friends! Matt and Avery are getting married in a few months. I refuse to ruin her wedding because our relationship failed and now we can't even look at each other from across the aisle."

Luke arches a brow at me. "You haven't even agreed to go out with me and we're already broken up and destroying my brother's wedding?"

I throw my hands up in exasperation. "You know what I mean."

He stands and slowly rounds the counter like one might approach a skittish animal. "Breathe," he demands. I force air into my lungs. "We're not even sure what this is yet and you've decided it's going to fail." He takes another hesitant step toward me. "You haven't even told me what you're feeling."

I close my eyes, trying to gather my nerve. What *am* I feeling? Could I actually...like Luke? The guy whose job it is to stomp out my creative flame? Whether it's my out-of-the-box yoga classes or my column, he's always trying to stifle my ideas. Though admittedly, the column one is inadvertently, but still. It could never work.

I'm about to tell him exactly that when I open my eyes to find him much closer than he was a moment ago. My head tilts back as I look up into his suddenly serious face. He dips his head slightly, barely a few inches, but it's enough to cause the air to stick in my chest.

Instead I say, "I feel it, too."

He looks down at my mouth and I swallow hard. "Aren't you curious?" he asks as his eyes slowly drag over my face. I nod slowly. He lifts a hand to push a stray hair behind my ear. "Give us a shot, Jolie," he mumbles. "If we fuck it up, then at least we know for sure."

I take a deep breath, trying to block out my thundering heart and think rationally. "We can't tell anyone," I say. He leans back, his eyes mixed with confusion and what almost looks like hurt. "At least at the beginning," I add quickly. "Until we figure out if there's anything to this. I don't want to hurt anyone." *Myself included.*

He doesn't answer for a moment. It feels like the world has paused as I wait for his answer. Finally, he nods. "Fine."

We're silent for a moment, just watching each other.

"What now?"

He smiles wickedly. "Now, it's time for my midnight snack." Then he scoops me up, throws me over his shoulder and carries me out of the kitchen.

By the time we get to my bedroom, my laughter has turned into moans.

This might be my best idea yet.

CHAPTER 37

LUKE

"Control your stick, you overgrown gorilla, or I'm tossing your keister in the box."

"I'll control my stick when you start controlling yours. This isn't the ballet; quit trying to crack my nuts."

"As if I could hit something that small. Sherlock Holmes couldn't find those acorns if you drew him a map."

"The only map you need is one to the back of the net. Have you even scored once this game? Rhett's back's getting sore from carrying your team."

It's Thursday night and Matt, Rhett, Gavin, and I are in Matt and Avery's basement playing mini sticks. Rhett and I are on one team and Gavin and Matt are on the other.

For all you non-Canadians, the game of mini sticks is exactly what it sounds like— mini hockey sticks that are about a fifth of the size of a real stick. It's mostly played by kids, or in our case, grown men who act like kids.

I take my time, rolling the foam Spiderman ball back and forth with my stick. "You're a lot of talk for a guy who rides more pine than a witch on Halloween," I taunt from my kneeled position on the floor.

Matt growls then lunges for the ball but I twist my back to him, sliding it away. He gives me a shove but I lean into him, keeping the ball just out of reach.

"Children," Rhett mutters from the net. "I'm surrounded by children."

I ignore him, holding my brother back with my forearm as I slide the ball back and forth in front of me with the other hand. I'm about to turn when Matt calls out, "Gav!" and jerks his head toward the net.

Gavin lets out a whoop from the other end then races forward on his little legs. He taps his stick on the carpet, calling for the ball. Matt knocks the ball from my stick, sailing it over to Gavin, who easily accepts the pass before taking off toward where Rhett is kneeled in the opposing net.

Gavin dekes to the left, making Rhett dive to the side. Before Rhett can recover, Gavin slides to the right and slaps the ball into the open net. Rhett lands on his side, burying his head in the carpet while Gavin comes running over to Matt, who lifts him off the floor in victory.

"Heck yeah! That's what I'm talking about." Matt sets him back down on his feet, raising his hand for a high five that Gavin eagerly returns. "Excellent deke, my guy. You're going to be ready for the big leagues before you know it."

Gavin beams. I drop my head back and pretend to look frustrated. "Come on. This kid's killing us. You're only winning because Sidney Crosby over there is sniping goals left and right while you ride his coattails."

Obviously, I'm kidding. I love playing with Gavin. It's hard to believe this energetic, spunky kid was too scared to say a peep a couple years ago. Now I can hardly keep up with the kid and he's slinging chirps like he belongs in the NHL.

"It's okay, Uncle Luke. Winning isn't everything," he tells me sincerely. When I'm on my knees like this, we're almost eye level so he puts a hand on my shoulder and looks me in the eye. "It's better to make sure everyone on the team is having fun than worry about the score." He pats my arm sympathetically. "As long as you tried your best, that's all that matters."

This frickin' kid. I bite back a grin, keeping my face solemn as I nod. "Thanks, Gav. That's pretty smart."

He beams over at Matt who shoots him a thumbs up and a nod. "Matt taught me that."

As much as I give my brother shit, he's an amazing dad to Gavin. It doesn't matter that he's not biologically his; Matt loves that kid more than life itself. It was weird at first seeing my idiot little brother as a father figure, but now I couldn't imagine it any other way.

"Gavin!" Avery calls from the top of the stairs. "It's time to get ready for bed. Say goodnight."

Gavin's shoulders drop so I reach out to ruffle his hair. "Good game, kiddo. You kicked our butts out there. Next time, you're on my team."

Gavin's eyes light up and he grins. "Deal." He wraps his tiny arms around me and squeezes then runs overs to do the same to Rhett. "'Night, Uncle Luke. 'Night, Uncle Rhett."

Matt stands and puts a hand on his shoulder. "Come on, buddy. I'll come tuck you in." He leads Gavin towards the stairs then tips his head over his shoulder at us. "Beers are in the fridge. I'll be back in a few."

I let myself fall back onto my ass. "Gotta hand it to him. The kid's got skills."

Rhett nods then drops to the floor with a grunt. "When

did we get so old?" he complains from where he lies on his back. "We used to play mini sticks for hours in your mom's basement then go out and play ice hockey on the pond 'til dark. Now, half an hour on this carpeted floor has my knees screaming."

"Hell if I know," I answer, resting my bent elbows on my knees. "My back feels like it'll snap in half if I move the wrong way right now."

Rhett turns his head to look at me. "You grabbing the drinks?"

I stiffly turn at the waist to where the fridge sits across the room and groan when I realize how far it is. "Rock, paper, scissors?" Rhett heaves an arm up, raising his closed fist to me. I mirror the move and we pump our arms three times.

"Aha!" Rhett smacks his closed fist onto my two fingers, effectively crushing my scissors with his rock. I groan but slowly climb to my feet. *Man, when did 32 start feeling like 92?*

"Hey, so where'd you go the other night after the bar?" Rhett asks as I hobble over to the fridge. Thankfully, my back is turned so he doesn't see my grin. It's the same one that's popped up every time I think about that night.

I still can't say I'm sold on the whole "secret dating" thing but I get where she's coming from. We're two very different people with almost too close of a friend group. That's not even taking into consideration the meddling town. The first time we so much as hold hands in public, there'll probably be a group of little old ladies planning the wedding. Either that or they'd be dividing up the town into teams for when we break up.

They'd all be Team Jolie and I wouldn't even blame them. No one wants the police chief on their team.

Yeah, it's definitely best that we keep this between us. At least for now.

"Just home," I answer, avoiding eye contact by ducking my head into the fridge and pulling out a can of Coke for Rhett and two beers for Matt and I.

I gesture toward Rhett with the Coke. He sits up and snags the can mid-toss. "Funny. Your truck was still in the parking lot at midnight." He raises his eyebrows accusingly at me from over the can.

"Walked home." I shrug, popping the tab of my beer can and taking a casual drink. "It's illegal to drink and drive. Didn't you know?"

"Yeah, see I thought that, too. But I served you and you only had two beers all night." He points the can at me. "And when I locked the doors at two, your truck was gone."

Shit. It's been less than a week and our big "secret dating" ploy is already starting to fall apart.

Leave it to Rhett to see right through my lies. The guy's always been observant as hell. I tried to convince him to be a cop when I was enrolling in college but he refused. Something about what people get up to being their own business.

Seems he's thrown that philosophy out the window when it comes to my business.

I take another drink while I scramble to think of an excuse just as Matt comes tromping down the stairs. Relieved, I toss him a beer and ask, "All good?"

Matt nods, smiling. "All good. Gav was pretty wound up from the game but nothing a couple Spiderman books and cuddles with Ham couldn't fix. He was out like a light before the end of the second book." He pops the tab on his beer and takes a drink. "What'd I miss?"

Before I can answer (and hopefully change the subject),

Rhett cuts in. "Luke was just telling me where he went after the bar on Saturday."

I shoot him a glare but Rhett just smirks. People always say he's the sweet one, but they don't know him like Matt and I do. The asshole loves to screw with us.

Exhibit A.

"So, if your truck was still in the lot at midnight but was gone before two, seems to me you must've gone somewhere nearby for a couple hours first before you went home." Rhett tips his head, tapping his finger against his chin. "Now what could someone be doing for two hours in the middle of the night that doesn't require driving?"

Matt throws his hand in the air, eagerly waving it like a preschooler.

Rhett points to where he's bouncing around. "Matt."

Matt leans forward, talking into an invisible microphone. "What is 'getting laid', Alex."

Rhett pretends to check his cue card. "That's correct!" Matt jumps around like he just won a million dollars, shaking my shoulders as he cheers wildly.

"Cut it out, blockheads." I shove at Matt, knocking him into Rhett, who pushes him away.

"Hey!" Matt complains, then rights himself. He pushes Rhett's shoulder, who's unaffected by the move. Rhett takes a step toward Matt, who's bouncing on his feet, fists raised like a boxer. "Float like a butterfly, sting like a bee," Matt mumbles, dipping and weaving his head.

"Enough, Ali," I say, shaking my head at him. Matt stills and turns to me but not before Rhett smacks him upside the head then ducks behind me.

"Sure, hide behind the nympho," Matt says.

I groan. "I'm not a nympho."

Rhett pops his head out from behind me. "Yeah, pretty sure the term nympho is specifically for women."

Matt cocks his head. "Huh. What's the man version then? Nymphe? Nymphite?"

"Nympholio?" Rhett offers.

"Would you two shut up?" I shout. "I didn't sleep with anyone!"

They both stare blankly at me for a second before Matt tilts his head to Rhett. "Me thinks the nympholio doth protest too much."

I toss my hands over my head, groaning in frustration as I drop onto the couch behind me.

"It's alright, Lukey." Matt flops onto the couch beside me, slinging an arm around my shoulders. "You don't have to lie to us. I think it's good you finally got the monkey off your back." He leans in conspiringly. "You gotta drain the old snake with someone other than your hand every once in a while."

Rhett nods from his seat in the chair beside us. "Healthy, even."

Matt snaps his fingers and points at Rhett. "See!" He leans back on the couch. "You don't have to tell us who she is—though my money's on tourist because you haven't dated a local girl since—" he snaps his mouth shut, cutting off the rest of his sentence.

But I know what he was about to say. Not since Mindy.

Usually just the mention of her would put me in a foul mood. But Jolie's not Mindy. And what I have with Jolie isn't even close to what I had with Mindy.

I weigh my options. I can either continue shutting them down, though they'll keep bugging me until they get an answer they like. Or I can let them believe whatever they want to think. I don't have to confirm or deny anything. You heard them; they think it was some one-time-thing with a tourist. Some woman I met in a bar, hit it off with, then went back to her cottage and had a fun, consensual but solitary night with.

Not like they'd believe me if I told them the truth anyway.

So I nod.

"I knew it!" Matt leans forward to give Rhett a high-five then puts his hand in front of my face. I glare at him for a second, then think *what the hell?* and slap my hand against his.

"That's my boy!" Matt cheers and I can't help the tilt of my lips.

As weird as it sounds, it's kind of nice to celebrate. Because honestly? Dating Jolie, even in secret, is turning out to be the best thing I've done for myself in a long time.

Just then, the door to the basement swings open and Ham, Matt's giant mutt, comes tromping down the stairs with Avery following behind him. Her hands are full with a tray full of snacks that Rhett jumps off his chair to take from her and places it on the coffee table.

Avery drops onto the loveseat beside us. "Alright, what'd I miss?" My eyes dart from Matt to Rhett, trying to telepathically threaten them both to keep their mouths shut. I might be able to fool these two buffoons but Avery's smarter than both of them put together. She might figure it out and then Jolie will kill me for outting us to her best friend.

"Just talking about hockey," Matt answers as Rhett nods his head, grabbing a chip to dip into the salsa. I fight the urge to sigh in relief. I should've known they'd have my back. They always do.

"Well, enough talk, girls," Avery leans forward and

grabs a Nintendo 64 controller off the TV stand then gestures around the room. "Let's play some Mario Kart. Whose ass am I kicking first?"

I point at Rhett who points at Matt who shakes his head and leans back in his seat. "No way, man. She kicks my ass every night at this. It's someone else's turn."

Avery stares back and forth between Rhett and I before I sigh. "Fine. I'll do it." I switch seats with Rhett so I'm closer to the controller while Avery starts up the game.

"Get ready to eat my dust, Brady," Avery taunts.

"Alright, Owens. Show me what you got," I toss back.

And she does. Six games later, my ass has thoroughly been handed to me.

"That's my wife!" Matt cheers from the couch as Avery flies past the finish line. She jumps to her feet, doing the world's most embarrassing victory dance, complete with the running man. Matt jumps up from his seat to join her. Even I have to admit they make the most a-dork-able couple.

Yeah, Jolie was right. This group? This crazy, funny, meddling family? It's worth keeping secrets for.

THE HAVEN TIMES

pg 15   Proudly serving Haven Bay for over 100 years.   **FREE**

DEAR ANNIE

Your local source for advice on love, life and everything in between!

The answer to this week's trivia question (pg 9) is Louis Armstrong.

Q.

Dear Annie,

I've lived in Haven Bay my entire life. When all of my friends were moving away for college, I was one of the few that stayed behind, choosing to drive back and forth to school instead.

Whenever anyone asked why I didn't live on campus, I had a list of excuses ready:

"My family needed me at home."

"With my work schedule, it didn't make sense to live so far away."

"Think of all the money I'm saving!"

But none of those things were what was holding me to Haven Bay. My parents would have managed just fine without me. I could have found a job closer to campus.

The truth is, I was scared. I'd never lived anywhere other than Haven Bay and essentially starting over scared the crap out of me.

The idea of living in a building with a bunch of strangers was terrifying. Having to climb out of my shell and make friends made me want to throw up.

So I didn't. And I can't help but feel like I missed out on what could have been the best years of my life.

Now, four years later, I've been offered my dream job. The only catch— it's in Calgary. And while my head is screaming at me to stay home where it's safe, I can't help but wonder if this is my second chance to leave the nest and finally experience life outside of this small town.

What should I do?

Signed,
Stuck

Dear Stuck,

Leaving your comfort zone, no matter what that might look like to you, is always scary. I mean, there's a reason why we call it the

A.

comfort zone. It's like your bed after a long day of work—it's warm and comfortable and safe.

It's predictable. And as humans, that's the most comforting thing in the world.

That being said, there might come a time when your comfort zone might feel more like a cage than a bed.

I'm a firm believer that growth happens when we're uncomfortable. And all those things about new places that seem scary at first, can turn into the best thing for you.

Those new, intimidating people who live in your building? They could be the best friends you ever had.

The big, busy streets filled with strangers rushing by? You could do your best thinking out there.

There's something to be said about just being another body in a big city that's freeing. You're no longer worried about what your neighbor will

say if they see you ordering takeout for the third time this week. You can just be yourself. Or even better, you can find out who your true self is, without the added pressure of expectations.

I can't convince you to leave the nest. I can't tell you that you'll love the city because you might hate it. You might move there and decide that Haven Bay was where you were meant to be.

But you know what? At least you can say you tried.

Ultimately, the decision is up to you. But no matter what you decide, I hope you don't let your fear be the main reason behind your decision.

Sincerely,
Annie

CHAPTER 38

JOLIE

LUKE

How's your day going?

JOLIE

Well, my alarm didn't go off again this morning.

LUKE

Didn't go off or you slept through it because you sleep like a dead person?

JOLIE

I'm ignoring your extremely unflattering yet possibly valid point.

LUKE

A beautiful dead person. Like the Jennifer Aniston of dead people.

JOLIE

Better.

And then the diner was out of cinnamon buns when I got there.

LUKE

Completely unrelated to the fact that you slept in and it was probably eleven when you got there.

JOLIE

Completely.

LUKE

Continue.

JOLIE

Then Mr. Kingsen got stuck in Bow pose during my afternoon class and it took two people to get him out of it.

LUKE

I don't know what a bow pose is but I feel like I probably don't want to see my old Little League coach in it.

JOLIE

You don't.

His shorts were not long enough for that.

I didn't know butt cheeks could be so hairy.

LUKE

Well, now my lunch is ruined.

JOLIE

Join the club.

LUKE

How about I swing by the bakery after my
shift and pick up some cinnamon buns.

JOLIE

That's really sweet of you.

LUKE

I can think of a few places I'd like to lick
that frosting off of your body.

JOLIE

Aaaaand there it is.

I'm not sure what I was expecting to find the first time I walked into *The Haven Times* but the calm, laid-back environment in the three room office building wasn't it.

I guess I was thinking there would be more chaos, like in the movies. Newspapers everywhere, people yelling out headlines to each other while phones ring in the background. People racing back and forth from their computer to the press. Loud machinery that spins and spits out the paper at the end all neatly folded and ready for some paper boy with a tweed Herringbone cap to scoop up for his corner spot.

Okay, so maybe the only thing I know about newspapers is from the movies. But they must have gotten the inspiration from somewhere. Well, it wasn't from a small town newspaper, I can tell you that.

The room is quiet except for the radio playing from a speaker somewhere and the occasional phone ringing. There's four desks arranged around the room with filing cabinets behind them. Behind each desk, the newspaper's full-time employees sit, tapping away on their keyboards and staring at their screens.

Sandy waves me over to her desk in the far corner of the room. "Mornin' sunshine. I wasn't expecting to see you here."

I smile back. "Good morning. Hope you don't mind me stopping in." I look around the room again. "I don't mean to sound ignorant, but where's the big press and the piles and piles of newspapers?"

Sandy laughs. "It's about 100 kms from here at our printing press." She takes in my confused look. "We have a printer that we deal with who prints our papers for us. We send them the digital files on Monday morning and they print and deliver us our papers early Tuesday morning. Then we distribute them around town."

"Ah. That makes more sense." I nod. "I guess I was expecting a big chaotic production in here."

Sandy sits back on the edge of her desk. "It used to be pretty chaotic years ago when we used to set the pages by hand. But going digital keeps things a bit more streamlined. Though it can get crazy when there's a big news week or trying to squeeze an advertiser in at the last minute."

"That makes sense."

Sandy crosses her arms. "So what can I do for you, Jolie?"

I look around the room, suddenly realizing how quiet the room is. "Can I talk to you in private for a minute?"

"Sure." She pushes off the desk. "Let's take this into the interview room."

She leads me to a small room off the main area and closes the door behind us. There's a round table in the center with four chairs around it. The rest of the room looks like it's being used as a makeshift storage area with a few boxes lining the far wall and a giant dog costume leaning against the other.

"Geez, way to ruin the illusion, Scoop," I sigh. The newspaper's mascot, Scoop, is a big bloodhound dog that wears a detective's hat and trench coat. His catchphrase is that he's "always sniffing out stories".

It's cute and the kids love him, though his eyes are a bit demonic sometimes.

Sandy laughs, taking the seat across from me. "What can I say? We're low on space and Scoop's the laziest employee we have." It's my turn to chuckle. "Alright, so what brings you in, Jolie? I thought I told you that you could just submit all your columns through email so we could keep your identity a secret."

I bite my lip to keep from smiling. She makes me sound like a superhero or something.

Yoga teacher by day, advice columnist extraordinaire by night. Able to answer your questions in a single bound.

"You did, and I'm very thankful for that. It makes this whole process that much easier." I take a deep breath, knowing how this is going to sound but also knowing it needs to be said. "I'm having a little trouble with backlash, though. Hate mail specifically."

Sandy leans forward, linking her hands together. "I'm real sorry about that, Jolie. Unfortunately, there's always someone wanting to complain that the sky's too blue or the puppy was too cute. We get backlash from the town all the time."

I sit up a little straighter at that. "Really? You're a small-town newspaper. What could people possibly complain about?"

She leans back in her chair, smiling. "Take your pick.

'The torrential downpour that lasted seventeen hours got my paper wet.' 'I don't care that there was a blizzard, my paper was late.' 'There was a spelling mistake on page 12 and I just had to call to let you know that it was extremely unprofessional and you should be ashamed of yourselves.'"

I scoff. "Those can't be real."

Sandy smirks. "Oh, I'd love to say I made those up but those are all very real complaints we've gotten. And that's just in the last month." Sandy shakes her head. "Some people have nothing better to do than point out the flaws in others, instead of working on fixing their own."

I nod in understanding. "Ain't that the truth." I lean forward and drop my voice a little. "That's not exactly the type of hate mail I meant. I mean, I do get that kind as well. But recently I've gotten a few emails that seemed a little more angry. Almost vengeful."

Sandy reaches a hand out in concern to cover mine. "Are you okay? What do they say?"

"'You better watch your back', 'mind your business'. Nothing overly scary but just a little...escalated, I guess you could say, than the occasional 'you suck' type of emails I've been getting since we started." I shrug, feeling a little self-conscious now. "Now that I say it out loud, it doesn't seem as scary. It's just—" I drop my voice again to a whisper so no one outside the room can hear me. "They're not to the *Dear Annie* email. They're coming to my Amaryllis email."

"I'm sorry this is happening to you, Jolie," Sandy says, rubbing her hand over my arm in reassurance. "I just don't understand why they would be going to your studio email unless someone somehow figured out it was you behind the articles." Sandy's quiet for a moment, her lips pursing as if she's deep in thought. "And you don't recognize the email addresses they're coming from?"

I shake my head. "I've done a little research online and from what I could find, the emails were set up as a 'burner' account. I've tried a couple of those IP address location websites but it always comes up as somewhere in the middle of the Pacific Ocean."

Sandy hums thoughtfully. "Well, we have a tech company that we sometimes deal with in the city when our computers go all haywire. Maybe they have an idea on how to track who's sending the emails." She tilts her head in concern. "If you want to take a break from the column for a while, I'd understand completely."

I shake my head. No way I'm going to let this jerk run me off. I might be a chicken shit but as Luke pointed out, I have balls of steel. "Thanks, but I'm good."

We both stand to leave but Sandy pauses at the door, hand on the doorknob. "I think we should report this to the police. That way we have something on record. Just in case."

"In case I end up chopped to pieces in the bay one day?" I joke, but Sandy doesn't smile.

"I can call Luke today if you'd like," she offers.

Oh boy, that should go over well. Two weeks of secret dating and he's already getting phone calls about the trouble I'm in.

"I appreciate that, but I can call him." I force a smile. After waving goodbye to Sandy, I head back to my apartment, where I'm sure Luke is already waiting for me. Dread coats my stomach the closer I get.

Maybe if I distract him with cinnamon bun frosting, he might not blow a gasket when I tell him about the emails.

Hey, a girl can dream right?

<hr>

I push open the back door to my studio to find Luke, Dottie and Maeve standing inside. My heart races as panic hits.

What are *they* doing here?

I mean, based on the paper bag with the bakery's logo on it in Luke's hand, I know what he's doing here. But Dottie and Maeve were definitely not invited to what we had in mind.

Ew. Intrusive thoughts, intrusive thoughts.

Before my brain can come up with any visuals that might scar me for life, I plaster on a smile and step through the door.

"Did I miss the invitation to my own party?" I joke.

Dottie doesn't bother to unwrap her arm from around Luke's bicep as she turns to face me. "Oh, Jolie, honey. We were just telling Luke about our plans for the bachelorette. Lucky for him, we're only going to be in town for the first part of the night while we do your class. Then we're off to Sin City!"

Maeve leans toward me. "She means Bakersfield, not Vegas."

"Ahh," I say, nodding my understanding. "Well, I feel honored that you've included Amaryllis as part of your big night."

Dottie waves me off with her free hand, never letting go of Luke's arm. Meanwhile, he looks like he's trying to disappear into the woodwork. "Oh, honey, your class is practically the main event. Aside from the strip club. Naked men will always win." Her eyes light up. "Unless you'd be willing to bring in—"

"No way," I say at the same time that Luke growls "absolutely not." I shoot him a questioning look. He levels me with a hard stare back.

Alright, then. Looks like we have some talking to do before we get to the cinnamon buns.

Not that I would've let Dottie and Maeve bring naked men into my studio anyway, but I'm not sure why he thinks he gets a say in what happens in my business.

Dottie sighs dramatically. "Well, in any case, Maevey and I just wanted to swing by and make sure everything was all set for Saturday night. The front door was locked but everyone knows you never lock the back door." Luke stiffens beside her but Dottie either doesn't notice or doesn't care. "So we figured we'd try your apartment but you weren't home. We were just walking out when Luke popped in for that—" She scrunches her nose at Luke. "What'd you call it again?"

He clears his throat. "Annual business inspection."

"Right!" I snap my fingers and point at Luke. "The annual business inspection. That was today," I squeak out. I slap my palm against my forehead. "Must've slipped my mind. I'd forget my head if it wasn't attached to me." I laugh awkwardly.

Maeve and Dottie stare at me like I've spontaneously grown three heads. Which of course, increases my rambling. "The other day, I'm lying in bed thinking how I feel like I forgot something and I'm thinking and thinking and thinking but nothing's coming to me until Frieda—you know Frieda Rieder from Doc Watson's office—calls to tell me I missed my dentist appointment. Though maybe that was my brain's way of saving me from a day of getting holes drilled into my head." My laugh sounds hysterical even to my own ears but I can't tamp it down. "Am I right?"

Thankfully, Maeve's phone rings, and I breathe a sigh of relief when she reaches into her purse to answer it.

She checks the screen. "It's the limo company, Dot," she

says before stepping away to answer it. "Hello? This is Maeve. No, the glitter gun was mentioned in our contract, you can't renegotiate now. Hold on." She puts a hand over the speaker and gestures to Dottie. "We have a problem."

Dottie finally lets go of Luke's arm to hurry over to Maeve. "Let me talk to them." She reaches out a hand to grab the phone then turns back to me. "Sorry about this, dear. We have to go. But I'm sure whatever you come up with for the bachelorette will be fabulous."

With that, she turns and storms out the back door, grumbling about "what's a bachelorette without a glitter gun" before she starts talking into the phone.

Maeve follows behind, waving goodbye as she goes. "We'll see you Saturday, Jolie. Nice to see you, Luke."

The door closes behind them and the room is enveloped in silence.

I turn back to Luke. "Whew. I don't even want to know what they're planning to do with a glitter gun."

He stalks forward, eyes intent, until he's standing inches away from me. "You left your door unlocked."

I hold his gaze. "Looks like it, seeing as though you were just in here with Haven Bay's version of the Golden Girls."

His stone-cold expression doesn't change. "If I went upstairs to your apartment right now, would your front door be unlocked?"

My body wants to shift under his intense scrutiny but my brain prefers an alternative method to fight-or-flight.

Instigate.

I take a step closer, lifting my chin so I'm as close to eye level with him as I can manage with our height difference. "I'm not sure how that's any of your business, *Chief*."

Luke's eyes flare to life. If he was a cartoon character, there'd be steam coming out of his ears to the point that his head might actually explode on his shoulders. But there's the smallest ember of something else burning in his eyes. Something that has my insides heating and my breath shallowing.

Desire.

Looking back, maybe this was why we fought so much. We might have driven each other crazy, but deep down, there was always this undercurrent of chemistry between us. It was simmering just below the surface until the heat became too much and was forced to boil over.

"The second you came all over *my* cock," he growls and it has me clenching my legs against the growing need, "it became my business. Your safety is my business."

I'm sure later, when I've had time to rationally play back this conversation in my head, I'll get all fluttery and swoony over that line. But right now, the only thing I can hear is the challenge in his voice. Him trying to claim me. Him thinking that just because we slept together, that gives him any sort of say over my life.

"If we're going to make this whole seeing-each-other-in-secret-sort-of-dating thing work, there's one thing," I tell him, raising a single finger in front of his face, "you need to get through that thick head of yours: you do not own me." I pause to let my statement sink in. "No one will ever own me." My voice drops. "Except me."

We stand like that for a moment, Luke's face stoic and unreadable, mine hard and determined. Finally he steps back, letting my lungs rush with air again. "Understood."

My shoulders sag slightly as the tension leaves my body. I nod once, suddenly feeling a little awkward for letting that last little bit slip out.

We started this...thing between us a couple of weeks ago with no expectations; just to see where things go. We haven't talked about anything of substance since then. I'm not sure either Luke or I are ready for this serious side yet.

We signed up for fun and sex, not feelings and vulnerability.

"So, how did the rest of your day go?" Luke asks as he turns toward the stairs. He looks over his shoulder at me, tilting his head in invitation.

Just like that, the tension in my shoulders returns. This was not how today was supposed to go. It was supposed to be a quick check in with Sandy to keep her up to speed, to which she would have an answer for my creepy emails problem. One that didn't involve me spilling my secrets to my very new and very protective...fuck buddy? Lover?

Ew, no. Definitely, not lover.

Boyfriend?

That might be worse than lover.

Well, whatever he is to me, I have a feeling he'll be a lot less of it after I tell him about *Dear Annie* and the not-such-a-fan mail.

Might as well rip the bandage off now.

"Actually, now that you mention it..."

LUKE

"**S**o, now I may or may not have some internet warrior trolling me."

I'm sitting on Jolie's large sectional, my forearms on my knees with my hands clasped tight between my legs. Listening to her try to diminish the fact that some wackjob has been threatening her for the past several months.

My hands clench at the thought of her sitting at home, scared and alone. While some soon-to-be-dead man walks around thinking he's got some sort of power over her. Only when my fingers start to turn purple do I loosen my grip.

Jolie goes silent beside me. She doesn't look scared or even worried, which pisses me off even more. Doesn't she know how this could end? Harassment cases—because that's exactly what this is—are not to be taken lightly.

Sure, sometimes a stern talking-to from someone of authority like a police officer is enough to scare the perpetrator off and that's the end of it.

Sometimes it isn't.

But if it goes unreported, the chances of the perpetrator

just spontaneously stopping the threats on their own is slim to none. And in some cases, by the time the police are involved, it's too late.

I shoot out of my seat and begin to pace around her small apartment.

"So, let me get this straight. You've been receiving threatening emails from a burner email for months. The emails have been coming to your work email, not the email assigned by the paper for your column."

Oh, right. Because the woman I've been seeing is also the cause of my entire town being turned upside for the last several months. Almost forgot that part.

"And not once did you think to report this to the police?" My tone comes out slightly more accusatory than I intended but the thought of some unstable asshole thinking they can scare my woman makes me want to ram my fist into a wall.

Because no matter what Jolie thinks, she's mine.

I don't mean that in a creepy, possessive asshole way. She's mine to protect the same way this town is mine. I might not be able to define them yet, but I have feelings for her. Feelings that are growing every day. I care about her and her safety, which is why hearing Dottie say that everyone in town knows she keeps her doors unlocked made me physically sick.

If she's not going to protect herself, I have no problem doing it for her.

She finally looks up at me, the fire from downstairs back in her eyes. "Look, I'm not some bimbo in a horror movie who ignores all the red flags practically smacking her in the face before she gets butchered by her stalker. This was only the second email I received and I told Sandy about it right away. She wanted to call the police but because we're...

involved," she stumbles over the word, "I told her I'd do it. Of course, she doesn't know that's why I wanted to handle it myself." The corner of her mouth lifts. "What with the whole secret dating thing and all that," she adds wryly.

She's making light of the situation because she feels uncomfortable. I can feel it radiating off her. Whether it's from the topic or the lack of label on what we're doing, I'm not sure. She didn't seem uncomfortable when she described the emails. Only when she brought up our relationship did the change in her happen.

As soon as we figure this bullshit out, I'm going to let Jolie know exactly what being with me means.

"Fine. So now that you've told me, how do you want to handle this?"

Her eyes shoot to mine in surprise. I know what she's thinking because it's written all over her face. She didn't think she'd have a say in what happens next. That she'd tell me about the threats and I'd demand she stop the column.

A part of me would love to do that. To shelter her away from any hurt or pain. To find whoever this pathetic weasel is who thinks he can scare her into submission and pummel him into the ground.

But stifling any part of Jolie, especially her creative side, would be like keeping a blue jay from singing. The mountains don't try to hide the sunrise; they strengthen it, giving it more time to shine.

So as much as I want to keep Jolie safe, I won't risk taking away what makes her *her*.

"Isn't that your job?" she asks, clearly confused by my question.

I stop pacing to take a seat beside her. In a comforting move that surprises even me, I take her hand in mine. "It's your life, Jolie. If you want to keep writing your column, we'll find a way to safely do that until we can figure out who's sending the emails."

Her face softens with relief. "But I'd also like your permission to do some digging into other areas of your life. I don't want to assume that because it started around the same time as the column, that they're related."

Her back straightens and she pulls her hand away. I let her because I sense she needs a minute to process the idea of me digging into her life.

I used to think Jolie was an open book; that you didn't have to look too hard to know everything there was to know about her. Hell, you didn't even have to look, sometimes she'd just yell it out for you.

But I'm quickly learning that there's many parts to her. Some parts of her life, the more superficial parts, she's willing to tell you anything you'd want to know.

Her favorite colour? Green, obviously. What she ate for dinner last night? Probably left over stir-fry from her dinner with Brenna the day before. How she lived above a strip club for a few years in Vancouver? I think everyone in town knows that story.

But the nitty-gritty? The reasons she is who she is? Those are the cards she keeps close to her chest. I'm not even sure if she's shown them all to Avery or Brenna.

She eyes me nervously from where she stands above me. She's careful to keep the coffee table between us. "What makes you think it could be about something other than the column?"

I shrug because honestly, I'm not sure. "It could be the column. The timing would make sense. But I want to have all our bases covered. Starting with checking in on our buddy Chesterfield."

To my surprise, she scoffs. "You think Tad is still that butt-hurt?"

"Honestly, I have no idea. But I'm not willing to leave your safety to chance." I might be showing my hand a little bit by saying that, but I don't care. I would never be able to forgive myself if something happened to her because I didn't check into every possible lead. Even if that means I have to call in some favors from my contacts in neighboring departments. "I'll make some calls tomorrow."

She nods, looking down at her hands. "Thanks," she mumbles.

I have a feeling asking for help today was harder for her than she made it seem. Someone as self-sufficient as Jolie doesn't accept help easily, let alone willingly ask for it. These emails must've been bothering her more than she let on.

I can't wait to get my hands on the person who made her feel this way and make them feel every ounce of pain they've caused her.

Reaching out, I lift her chin with my finger until she's looking me in the eye.

"Don't thank me. Just let me help you."

She gives a weak attempt at a smirk. "I'll try."

I hold her eye contact for a second longer then drop my hand. "Why don't I go toss those cinnamon buns in the microwave? You should put on that vampire show you like." I stand and grab the bag from the bakery off the coffee table.

I don't quite make it to the kitchen before I hear her quiet "wait". I turn to find her looking down at her hands again, twisting one of the rings on her fingers nervously until she finally looks up at me. Her mouth is twisted like her body is trying to physically hold back the words she's trying to spit out.

"There's something you should know." She takes a deep breath. "I haven't had any issues with this for years. Not since I first moved to Vancouver at least. So while I don't think it has anything to do with the emails, it's still a possibility."

I wait silently, letting her work through it.

"Okay, let me start over." She takes a deep breath and looks me in the eye. "My brother is Austin St. James." She pauses expectantly. It takes me a minute before the name sinks in.

"As in the star defensemen for the Toronto Storm, Austin St. James?" I ask, trying to keep the awe out of my voice. Jolie nods. "Oh, wow. Um...wow."

She sighs. "Yeah. That's the usual response. Followed by every question from 'what was he like as a kid' to 'can you invite him over for drinks sometime?' Or my personal favorite, 'can you get me tickets to a game?'" She rolls her eyes. "The number of friends I've dumped because they became obsessed with my brother..." She shrugs again. "That's why I don't tell anyone about him anymore. It's easier to figure out if someone's interested in being friends with me for *me* when you take away the alternative option."

There's a vulnerability in her voice that I've never heard before. It makes me want to reach out and hug her, but I know she'd hate my sympathy.

I can't even imagine what it was like, growing up with a brother in the spotlight. Even though she moved away after she graduated, I'm sure her brother's name has followed her like a looming shadow since way before then.

The stories she told me at the lodge about guys using her to get to her brother are starting to make sense. Star athletes are practically royalty, especially if they have a chance at making it big. It's no wonder she took off the second she could. Austin St. James was the number one pick overall when he was eighteen. He became a household name not long after that and his career isn't slowing down any time soon.

She's watching me, waiting for my reaction. She's used to people using her to get to her brother, never knowing whose friendships were genuine. No wonder she has a hard time letting people in. And why she's so unconditionally loyal to the small list of people she does.

I find myself really wanting to be included on that list.

I lift one shoulder. "Eh, I've always been more of a Bozzelli guy."

Her answering smile is like the sun peeking out through the clouds after a storm. It starts small, so small that you can hardly see it. Then the warmth from its light spreads until you can feel it all the way to your bones.

"Chase would probably love you for saying that," she says, grinning now. She gets up, crossing the room to stand before me. Then she reaches up to hold the nape of my neck and pulls my head down to hers. She takes my mouth in a slow, sweet kiss that goes on forever. By the time she pulls away, I swear I could lift a damn semi truck.

She hums, smoothing a palm down my chest. My eyes stay locked on hers, accepting whatever the hell she's willing to give me. Her hand dips lower until she grabs the bag of cinnamon buns from my hand. Never breaking eye contact, she whispers in a low voice laced with sex, "I seem to remember a certain promise involving your tongue and a lot of frosting." Holding my gaze, she walks backward toward her bedroom, stopping just inside the doorway. "Time to pay up, Chief."

Then she disappears into the room, the sound of a bag crinkling the only thing I hear as I tear off my clothes and race after her.

JOLIE

"Do nipple tassels come in different sizes? 'Cause my left nipple is a little more pancake than Timbit, if you know what I mean."

Dear, lord. I don't get paid enough for this. "Unfortunately, yes. I do know what you mean, Dottie." I fight the urge to laugh. Though most of the guests at Dottie's bachelorette are from Haven Bay and are used to her antics, this is still my business and I need to remain professional. "And I think that question is something you're going to have to Google."

I clap my hands together to get the attention of the studio full of women. "Ladies! I think we're about ready to get started if everyone could please find a pole and stand beside it."

Twelve women ranging in ages from twenty-five to eighty-something gather around the poles. All of them are familiar faces, including Avery, Brenna, Miss Carla, Maeve and of course, the woman of (dis)honor herself—Dottie.

"Alright. Welcome to pole fitness!"

Dottie leans over to Maeve and whisper-yells, "Sounds about right since I'll be fittin' Harold's pole—"

"Let's get started!" I interrupt loudly as a few people chuckle nearby. I tap the screen on my phone to start my playlist. Hip hop pumps through the overhead speakers causing cheers and dancing to start throughout the studio.

Over the next half an hour, I take the class through various beginner moves from a simple inside step to a front hook to an extended fireman.

For the first few moves, the women are a bit hesitant and awkward. All except Dottie and Maeve that is. Apparently, all those yoga classes they've been taking have paid off because women their age are not usually that flexible. Not to mention their energy levels.

"I told you we should've worn our booty shorts, Maeve," Dottie yelled out after her third attempt at the fireman spin. "The velvet on these track pants don't have enough give."

By the end of the class, most of the women are smiling and confidently spinning around the pole. Some of the braver participants even attempt a few more complicated moves like a sunwheel and a skater hold, though not many can hold the latter. But the enthusiasm is there and that means more to me than skill ever will.

"Alright, that's all for today!" I call out as the last song ends. "Let's give ourselves a big round of applause. You all did amazing!"

The women cheer and clap. Before I can step away from my pole, Dottie calls out above the noise. "So, Jolie. How good are you on one of those things?"

"Well, the person who certified me lets me teach classes, so I like to think I'm not bad," I joke and a few people chuckle, including Dottie.

"Show us!" someone shouts from the back, which gets the rest of the class cheering along. I narrow a glare at Avery but she just grins back. She knows I can't turn down a challenge.

"Alright. You want to see what I can do?" They all cheer. "Fine. One more move." I hold up a single finger to accentuate my point.

I cue up the music again from my phone and the speakers come to life. Grabbing the pole above my head with my right hand, I lift my right leg, bending my knee so that it's pressed against the pole. Bringing my left hand up beside my right, I flex my foot and place it against the pole. I pull myself up and the crowd hoots and hollers as I swing my left leg around and hook it securely behind my right foot.

I take them through a few of my favorite, more advanced moves; several of which have me upside down with only a leg keeping me from falling to the ground. Spinning and turning, I give them my best that would make a Vegas showgirl proud.

The room erupts into cheering, clapping, and cat calling. I laugh, untangling myself from the pole then sliding down to the ground. Once my feet hit the floor, I curtsey for my adoring fans.

"That's one strong coochie," Maeve comments.

"Bet she could open a jar with that thing," Dottie agrees.

"How many Kegels do I have to do to be able to do that?" Fifty-something year old Chelsea Tavares asks.

"I can't even tie my shoes without peeing myself. If I try that, you'd be cleaning a puddle off the floor," mother of four Janis Colson says.

A loud honk comes from outside the studio and I turn to see a limo bus parked out front. A man in his forties dressed in a suit waits at the bottom of the steps.

"Woo! Ride's here!" Dottie hollers. "Grab your clothes, ladies, and let's skedaddle. We've got prime beef steak waiting for us." She winks dramatically. "And I don't mean the dinner."

The women take turns thanking me then grab their change of clothes and head outside.

Avery and Brenna come scurrying over to where I'm spraying disinfectant on a pole. "Oh my god, that was so much fun," Avery says, bouncing up and down on her toes beside me. "I felt like some kind of Greek goddess." She strikes a pose in her oversized t-shirt and biker shorts, her messy bun flopping to one side of her head. "Do I look like I could be a goddess?"

"Hell yeah, you do."

"Avery was killing it, whereas I looked more like a baby giraffe on roller skates," Brenna jokes.

Avery laughs, nudging her arm. "You did not. You did great." She turns to me. "Are you going to start making pole fitness a regular thing? I would definitely sign up for more." She looks over at Brenna.

"I could *maybe* be persuaded to do another class." Brenna grimaces at my pole. "As long as I don't have to do whatever the hell you just did." She leans away from the pole like it might bite her. "That routine might kill me if I tried it."

I snort a laugh. "It wouldn't but it takes a lot of practice. If you wanted to get there, you could learn."

This time is Avery's turn to snort. "Yeah, okay. We'll leave that to you." She lightly smacks my shoulder.

"Speaking of which, how did I not know you could do that?"

I walk over to the next pole, spraying disinfectant on the rag. "You don't know everything about me, Future-Mrs-Brady." I toss a mischievous smile over my shoulder at her as I wipe down the chrome.

"Oh, don't I know it," Avery teases.

Dropping my arm, I turn to face her. "What's that supposed to mean?"

Avery shrugs. "I just mean that you're a pretty private person when it comes to your personal life."

"Which is not a bad thing," Brenna quickly amends.

"Not at all," Avery adds. "Everyone's entitled to their privacy." She lifts one shoulder again. "There's just a lot we don't know about you, that's all." She smiles. "I guess that's just weird in Haven Bay."

I force myself to smile back. The conversation shifts but I can't help thinking about what they said. I've always valued my privacy; even before my brother became famous. But I never thought anything of it. People don't need to know every detail of my life, especially the hard parts. Janet from the grocery store doesn't need to know that my father was a controlling, manipulative old man who tried to change me my entire life.

But Avery and Brenna aren't strangers. They're not going to judge or pity me for who I was or what I went through. Avery and Brenna have had their own demons to deal with.

Avery's father walked out on her and her mother when she was really young and hasn't heard from him since. Then Avery was married to a narcissist for over a decade. Luckily, her ex has changed his ways and things all worked out, but she went through a lot to get to where she is now.

Brenna's parents got divorced when she was really young. Her mother has been out living her "best life" ever since, leaving Brenna's dad to raise her on his own. Brenna said she'll go months without hearing a word from her mom then she'll just pop back in, expecting Brenna to put her life on hold to welcome her back with open arms. Luckily, her dad is as steady as they come. He's even one of her full-time employees at the rescue.

Either way, they're very aware of how complicated families can be. So why have I never confided in either of them? Even now, I'm still keeping them in the dark by hiding my sort-of-relationship with Luke from them.

Why do I do this to myself? I isolate myself, keeping everyone at arm's length then I wonder why I feel like no one sees the real me. When in reality, I never give them the chance to.

I open my mouth—to say what, I'm honestly not sure. But no matter how hard I try, I can't get the words to form on my tongue. So I snap my mouth shut, turning back to the pole, but not before I see the sympathy in their eyes.

"What do you say we go grab an ice cream from Scoops before we head home? All that dancing has me craving a chocolate fudge brownie sundae," Brenna asks, hooking her arm through mine. I'm not sure if she's offering as a distraction, but I'm thankful for it either way.

"That sounds good," I agree, feeling the tension in my body dissipate.

Maybe soon I'll be able to tell them everything. About my dad, my brother, and my grandpa. It doesn't seem like tonight will be that night but hopefully soon.

Between the three of us, we get the rest of the studio cleaned up quickly. We head out the front door, turning off the lights and closing the door behind us. I take a few steps to follow behind, then turn back to lock the front door.

Luke can be an overprotective asshole but he might have a point about locking my door.

Not that I'll ever tell him that.

LUKE

I'm restless. I'm never restless.

The hockey game plays in the background but I'm not paying attention to the commentator's voice as I shuffle around the kitchen.

My day started with a wake up call at 4 a.m. for a multivehicle accident just outside of town and it didn't slow all day. Seventeen hours later, you'd think I'd be ready to fall face first into my bed, but my mind is buzzing and I can't seem to sit still.

I could lie and say I don't know why but I know exactly the cause: a pretty brunette with eyes the color of the sky.

Since I was so busy today, I didn't get a chance to talk to her more than the occasional text. Which should be fine. When I first started as a rookie and was working crazy shifts, I used to go an entire 24 hours without talking to Mindy. After a long day, I'd crawl into the spare room bed because she used to complain that I'd wake her if I came to ours. Then I'd be up before the sun rose to be back at the station before her alarm went off at seven.

Now I'm crawling out of my skin because the handful

of texts we sent each other throughout the day aren't enough. I just saw her last night for fuck's sake. I shouldn't be this invested in a relationship that no one even knows exists.

My phone vibrates from its place on the marble island behind me and I practically dive to grab it. Her name lights up the screen and I don't bother fighting the smile that breaks out on my face.

I'm pathetic and I don't even care.

JOLIE

You up?

LUKE

It's not even 10 p.m...

JOLIE

Smartass.

Want to come over?

I'm out the door before I can hit Send on my reply.

I told you: pathetic.

It's a quick drive over to Jolie's house but I park down the street in the public parking lot like she requested. I don't like sneaking around but in a town this small where people love to talk about whose car was parked where last night, it makes the most sense until we're ready to go public.

Around the back of the building, I pull on the heavy metal door and am pleasantly surprised to find it locked. I shoot off a text and a few moments later, Jolie unlocks the door and ushers me inside.

She starts to walk away but I stand firmly in place, staring at her until she stops and looks back, confused. I tilt my head toward the door and realization hits her. She rolls her eyes, stalks over, and makes a big production out of flipping the lock in place. Then she gestures to the lock in a move that would make Vanna White proud, making me smile.

"Good?"

"Much," I mumble, then hook a finger in the waistband of her leggings, pulling her to me.

She comes willingly, a smile tugging at her lips. Once she's pressed against me, I lift my hand to cup the back of her head. Dipping my head, I kiss her slowly and deliberately. One touch of her lips to mine and all the stress from today melts away. I tighten my hold in her hair, tilting her for better access as she moans softly.

As badly as I want to take things further, I didn't come here to rip her clothes off. Well, not *just* to rip them off. I plan to. But not until later.

I slowly ease us out of the kiss, unable to resist placing a couple quick kisses against her lips as I lean away. She smiles up at me, a dreamy look in her eye and I'm trying really hard not to think how much I'd love to have that smile greeting me when I get home every night.

No. Too much, too fast. This relationship is doomed, remember? Even if we don't end up killing each other like Jolie predicted, there's no way anyone would willingly be with me, knowing my whole life is my work.

Sure, other cops might make it work but those are the guys who put their time in and clock out at the end of the day. I'm never fully off the clock and I don't want to be. How can I effectively protect my town if I'm not willing to leave date night or Thanksgiving dinner when there's an emergency?

I can't. And no woman would willingly tolerate that. They might think they can do it, but in reality, it's too much.

But damn. If there was ever a woman who could do it, it would be Jolie. She's tougher than steel and her heart is solid gold.

"How was the rest of your day?" Jolie asks, pulling me from my thoughts.

"Long." I drop my hands so they're linked at the small of her back, holding her to me as she wraps her arms around my neck.

"People in the diner were saying the crash on 88 was pretty bad this morning. I heard it was Jack Hillman and a couple of the kids in one of the cars. Was everyone okay?" Concern is written all over her face and for some reason, it causes a rush of warmth through me.

In the back of my mind, I know people care about Haven Bay and its people, too. As much as the town jokes about emergencies making for good gossip, we take care of each other.

Like when Gavin fell off the dock last year and Matt had to dive in after him to pull him out. I don't think Avery or her mom cooked dinner for a month. Matt said their freezer was stuffed full with casseroles and other premade dinners from neighbors who had heard about the accident.

"The other car was a tourist who got checked over by the E.M.T.s at the scene, but Jack and the kids had to go to the hospital to be checked out. The kids were just for precautionary reasons but if I was a betting man, I'd say Jack has a pretty good concussion. He hit his head pretty hard off the window."

He's lucky that's all he got. Or should I say, the tourist is lucky. Some kid in his early-twenties coming to meet his buddies for a weekend away and driving way over the speed limit to get there. Combine that with sharp bends and trees blocking his view, he veered a little too far left.

Jack, who was taking his kids to a hockey game a few towns over, didn't see the other car until the last second. He managed to swerve out of the way, but the move landed him in a ditch on the other side of the road. Thankfully, there was no other traffic and the car landed relatively smoothly on all four tires.

The kid in the other car at least had the good sense to stop and call for help. It could've been a lot worse, which I made sure to remind him while I was writing him up. The most lengthy part was blocking traffic long enough to get Jack's SUV pulled out of the ditch.

"Well, I'm glad everyone's okay. How are you feeling?" Jolie's eyes search mine with concern and I feel an unfamiliar tug in my chest.

I'm not used to people asking about me after a call. Usually people are more interested in the sordid details than how those details might affect the person who witnessed them. The call this morning was definitely on the milder side of things I've seen but it's always nerve-wracking getting the call and not knowing what you're walking into. Especially when there's kids involved. Add in the fact that about 95% of the time, it's someone I know that's in danger.

I don't think my nervous system will ever get used to the feeling of walking up to a scene, not knowing if I'm about to find the lifeless body of the woman who cuts my hair or the kid I babysat in high school.

"Fine," is all I can manage. I clear my throat then look

over her shoulder toward the dark studio. "How was the bachelorette?"

Jolie snickers. She steps back and I try not to think about how empty my arms feel without her in them. She takes my hand, leading me further into the studio. Once out of the hallway, the moonlight illuminates the room enough through the zebra blinds that there's no need for lights.

"Um, Jolie?" I can see her smiling from my peripherals but my focus is on the dozen or so stripper poles set up around the room. "What kind of class did you say you were teaching again?"

I finally look down at her. She's grinning up at my wide-eyed expression. "I didn't."

"You teach pole dancing?" I ask incredulously.

She swats me in the chest. "Don't be such a prude. It's called pole fitness." She takes a few steps backward toward the nearest pole. "It's really popular and a killer workout."

I smirk. "I know another pole you could work out on." She tips her head wryly and I chuckle. "Oh, come on. You practically handed me that one."

She shakes her head, making a tsk-tsk sound. "Never knew you and Matt had so much in common with your bad jokes."

I glare back at her. "You take that back right now. I am way funnier than that dork."

She just shrugs, then reaches out to spin slowly around the pole.

"I think the only fair way to determine the validity of your previous statement is with a demonstration," I say, using what Jolie likes to call my "cop-voice".

She arches a brow at me. "You think so, eh?"

Jolie dressed in a crop top and leggings, spinning around on a pole? I nod enthusiastically. "Absolutely."

She smiles, leaning her back against the pole. "Alright. Only if you do something for me."

This time it's my turn to arch a brow at her. "I don't think I'm flexible enough to pole dance, sweetheart."

She laughs and the sound is so light and happy, I briefly consider the pole. "Not that," she assures me. "Brenna and I are hosting a Puppy Yoga class. She wants a low-stress environment where dogs who might have a hard time with the busyness of normal adoption events can meet potential adopters. It's next weekend." I hesitate and_she quickly jumps in. "You don't have to adopt one. Brenna's nervous no one will sign up, so I was thinking maybe the police department might let us put up some posters at the station and on their social media page." She smiles hopefully. "We've got some up around town and Brenna and I are both posting on ours but the more exposure the better so..."

I bite my cheek to hold back my grin. She's adorable when she's nervous and by the way she's rambling on, I can tell she thinks I'll tell her no. As if there's any chance of that. I'd stand naked wrapped in bacon in front of a pack of wolves just to watch her wrap those long legs around that pole.

I know, I heard it. Sue me.

I pretend to think about it. "Deal."

She smiles, then nods toward the chairs lined up under the large window at the front of the studio. "Might wanna pull up a chair then, Chief. You've earned yourself a_show."

I grab a chair and bring it closer to where Jolie stands in front of the pole. She's stripped out of her leggings, leaving her in just her bikini panties and crop top. I drop the chair in front of her, watching her stretch. My eyes bounce between her and the mirror that covers the wall behind her, showing off her every angle.

I nod at her leggings discarded on the floor beside me. She rolls her eyes. "I can't grip the pole with leggings on. I already changed out of my shorts and I don't feel like going back upstairs. Don't get excited."

I lean back in my chair, spreading my legs into a relaxed position. "Too late."

She shakes her head, smiling, then taps her phone. A low, sensual song fills the air through the overhead speakers, but it only adds to the mood. I lean forward in my seat as Jolie grabs the pole and takes a few steps around it.

Then she lifts herself up and swings her legs until she's in an upside down split, her legs spread wide toward the ceiling. Then she brings her legs together, wrapping them around the pole above her head.

I lean forward, ready to jump from my seat to catch her at a moment's notice because there's no way someone can hang upside down from a pole with just their thighs. But somehow she does as she continues to spin around.

One arm slides down, her other gripping the pole between her legs. She lifts one leg, bending it so that her toe is almost touching the back of her head before straightening both legs again in an upside down split.

I can't keep my eyes off her. Between the complex moves she's doing, the muscles on her back, legs, and arms, and the fact that she's doing all of this while she continues to spin around the pole has left me completely transfixed.

I knew Jolie was strong; I've seen her in her classes and I've run beside her through the forest. But this is a whole other level of strong. This is strength and art combined. It's sexy, but not in the way I was expecting. This is raw strength and emotion.

My hands itch to touch her, to smooth my hands along

her muscled legs. To feel the strength rippling beneath my hands. To test that flexibility.

The music slows and she swings her leg around to grip the pole again, pointing her other foot straight as she dips her head low, her arm stretching above her head. The look on her face reminds me of a ballerina, stoic as she loses herself in the moves, the music.

She spins horizontally a few more times before she reaches up, dropping her legs to the floor. She turns and ambles over to me, breathing heavily. As she gets closer, there's a sheen to her skin from the exertion and damn, if that doesn't turn me on even more.

"So, that's the gist of it," she says, a shy smile playing at her lips. "There's obviously a lot more to it and those moves are pretty advanced. I usually do more upbeat songs for beginner classes and bachelorettes." She clasps her hands together in front of her then lets them go to tug at her shirt. "That was just something I've been practicing for fun."

She finally looks me in the eye, her confidence from a moment ago gone. I have no idea where this insecure version of Jolie came from but I hate it. She clearly enjoyed being up there, so what happened between then and now?

I don't know if it's someone else's voice in her head tearing her down or her own, but the look on her face as she fidgets in front of me uncomfortably has my temper spiking.

She makes a move to grab her leggings off the floor.

"Stop." The command is sharp and rough. It stops her in her tracks. I wait until she's looking me in the eye before I lean back in my chair, spreading my legs wider. "Come here."

She watches me, a little unsure. The fact that she hasn't handed me my balls for telling her what to do is proof enough of just how off-kilter she's feeling.

She has nothing to feel self-conscious about. I'm still blown away by how mesmerizing she was up there. I intend to wipe any doubt she has lingering inside her head until she sees herself exactly the way I do.

I arch a brow at her and the look has her moving toward me, the corner of her bottom lip tucked between her teeth. When she's close enough, I grab her hand and pull until she's perched sideways on my leg, her legs tucked between mine.

"Do you know how fucking sexy you looked up there?" I mumble, brushing my nose along the column of her neck to her ear. Her mouth parts and her breathing changes to shallow pants. I run my hand over her bare thigh and her back arches at my touch. It takes her a second to answer, so my hand stills until she blinks a couple times, shaking her head slightly.

"You were amazing. Breathtaking." My hand continues its ascent up her thigh to her hip then across her waist, playing with the fabric of her panties. "And not because of some teenage horndog's fantasy of a stripper."

"Exotic dancer," she breathes and I have to bite my lip to keep from smiling. My fiesty girl is still in there somewhere, she's just buried under some twisted insecurities.

That's where I come in.

"Exotic dancer," I repeat. My opposite hand trails along her spine and under her shirt, making it ride up on her stomach. "You were sexy because of how confident you were. How powerful you looked. You looked like a siren, beckoning stray sailors to her without even sparing them a glance."

My right hand tightens in her hair at the nape of her neck as my opposite hand dips a finger just under her panties. "A goddess observing the mortals below." I pull my hand down, tugging her hair back just enough to keep her focus on me and my words. "A queen surveying her subjects."

My tongue glides along the outer shell of her ear and I hear her sharp intake of breath. "That's exactly what you are, sweetheart; a queen. Regal. Brave." My teeth graze her lobe and a shiver runs down her spine.

"Powerful."

I raise my head at the slight shake of her head, her brows furrowed as if trying to hold onto a single feeling. She doesn't believe me, that voice in her head contradicting my every word.

My frustration grows. How this woman can think she's anything short of incredible has me wanting to hunt down any person who's ever made her feel less than and wring their throats.

With one hand, I push her legs forward and spin her so that she's straddling my lap, her back pressed against my chest and facing the mirrors in front of us. She leans her head back against my shoulder to steady herself from the sudden movement.

While she's distracted, I lift her legs so they're draped over my thighs. Her long, muscular legs spread wide so her panties are barely covering her pussy. I have to force myself to keep my hand from moving as I hold her thigh with one hand.

Her dark hair is tousled from her routine on the pole, a part of it stuck on her parted lip. I tuck it away from her face, letting my fingers skim her soft cheek then down her neck. I wrap my hand around her throat, not applying any pressure but holding her still so she's forced to watch her reflection in the mirror. Her back arches slightly at the feel of my hand on her throat and I can feel my hard cock pulsing against my zipper.

So, Jolie likes breath play, eh? I file that information away for later. Right now, I'm focused on one thing and one thing only: her confidence. Or rather, her sudden lack of.

"Do you know what I see when I look at you, sweetheart?" I rasp into her ear. She shakes her head, eyes glazed with lust.

"A woman whose heart beats for the people she loves." My hand dips to her clit, rubbing it in lazy circles. "A fighter who'd destroy anyone who tried to hurt those people."

I slowly strum her clit and she whimpers from her spot on my lap. "Someone who was brave enough and trusted herself enough to not only leave behind the only life she's ever known to build a new one across the country, but to build a business from the ground up and turn it into a success." My hand travels under her shirt, lifting her sports bra just enough to squeeze and massage her breast.

Her eyes are everywhere in the mirror. On my hand between her legs to my hand under her shirt to my mouth that's alternating between kissing her neck and whispering in her ear. I can feel her heart racing under my palm.

Good. Mine's been doing the same thing since our first night in the lodge and it hasn't slowed since.

"Tell me, sweetheart. What are you?" I drawl, meeting her gaze in the mirror.

Her head tilts back, resting on my shoulder as she climbs toward that peak. I pinch her nipple, pulling her focus back to my question. "A queen," she rasps.

"Damn right," I praise as she rocks over where my dick is straining against my jeans. "And every queen deserves a throne." I press my mouth against her ear. "Now sit on yours."

I watch her in the reflection, leaving the choice in her hands. I can see the warring emotions on her face. Holding my breath, I hope my words will drown out the ones I can see fighting to be heard.

All of a sudden, her eyes harden with determination. Without a word, she tilts her hips up in invitation. I help her lift so she can slip her hands beneath her. She quickly unbuckles my belt and jeans, then tucks a hand into my jeans and pulls my dick out from its confines. Nudging aside her panties, she notches my cock at her entrance. I wait with baited breath as she holds my gaze in the mirror.

Then, as if I couldn't get any harder, she fucking smirks before dropping her hips onto my waiting cock, taking my entire length in one go.

We both groan and I swear my eyes roll back in my head. Neither of us move for a second, letting Jolie adjust. Finally, her hooded eyes meet mine. She rolls her hips at the same time that I lift mine to thrust into her. She gasps and the noise goes straight to my cock.

She leans forward, sliding her legs off my thighs and down to the floor. She braces herself, one hand on each of my thighs as she rocks her hips forward. I grip her hips, holding her against me as she continues to rock me against her G-spot.

I can't keep my eyes off her. She looks every bit the queen I described her. "That's it, sweetheart. I'm yours. Use me." I thrust upward and she moans. "Take anything you want. It's yours."

She throws her head back, her nails biting into my skin. It spurs me on, meeting her thrust for thrust. I reach around to find her clit. With two fingers, I strum it, taking her higher as she cries out.

"So good," she whimpers. "So fucking good."

Once, twice more she rocks her hips before her orgasm rips through her. Her moves stutter and I take over, thrusting up to drag every ounce of pleasure out of her. She's still coming when I follow behind her seconds later, groaning her name.

She slumps back against my chest, both of us breathing heavy and slick with sweat. When I finally catch my breath, I kiss her shoulder, meeting her hooded gaze in the mirror.

"*My* queen," I declare. To my fucking delight, she nods.

THE HAVEN TIMES

DEAR ANNIE

Your local source for advice on love, life and everything in between!

The answer to this week's trivia question (pg 9) is pancakes and eggs.

Q.

Dear Annie,

My husband and I have been together for four years and married for one. We recently decided that we wanted to start our family and after a few months of trying, we became pregnant with our first baby.

My family is quite large and this will be grandbaby number six for our family but the first grandbaby on my husband's side. To say that my mother-in-law is excited is a HUGE understatement. Since we announced our pregnancy, she's been dropping off gifts constantly and already started renovations on turning one of their guest bedrooms into a nursery for the baby to stay in when we visit.

All of the attention has been very appreciated and I am so happy that our baby will have grandparents that are so involved.

That was until my mother-in-law made an off-hand comment the other day about being in the delivery room when the baby was born.

Thinking that she was joking, I sort of laughed it off, but she was serious.

I told my husband that I was not okay with his mother being in the delivery room when the baby was born. I planned to have my husband and my mother in the room with me, because she was a nurse for thirty-five years and I feel better having her with me.

My husband was supportive of this decision until his mother got so upset that she began to cry when he told her we didn't want her in the room. He's torn between wanting to keep his mother happy and respecting my wishes, but now he doesn't understand why my mom can be in the room, but his mom can't.

I don't want to start any family drama, especially during what is supposed to be the happiest time in our lives. But I refuse to give in on this.

Sincerely,
Pregnant and Peeved

A.

Dear P&P,

Congratulations on your new addition! You're absolutely correct—this is the happiest time of your life and you deserve to soak up every second of it.

I must say though, when I read your email, it took every ounce of willpower not to throw my laptop across the room. After rage typing out about six different responses, only to delete them because my editor would not let me publish such language, I finally ended on this.

This time is about you and your husband and your new bundle of joy. No one else. End of story.

I completely understand the urge to keep the peace but I have to strongly discourage that. I don't know your mother-in-law personally (or maybe I do, who knows?) but I do know manipulative behavior. And your MIL is giving lessons on manipulation right now.

The fact that she threw a fit she didn't get her way tells me all I need to know about her.

You need to set boundaries now, before this baby is born. If you don't, this behavior is only going to escalate.

Rules about screen time? Not at Grandma's!

Mom said no to buying you a cell phone for your birthday? Guess who bought you one instead!

See what I mean?

As for your husband, tell him to grow some balls and stand up to his mother. Then tell him if he'd like to be spread eagle, naked in front of your family and push a watermelon out of his body for all to see, then be your guest. Until then, he can't relate.

Set your boundaries now and stick to them.

Sincerely,
Annie

MISSING:

Little Liam Ford is missing his furry friend, Hamilton.

If seen, please call Liam's mom, Pam at 123-456-7890.

Does not answer to his name. Does not come when called.

He's a hamster.

CHAPTER 42

JOLIE

"**W**ell, aren't you just the most handsome boy I've ever met," I croon into the ear of a six year old Greyhound named Roland.

It's the afternoon of the Puppy Yoga event and Brenna and a couple of her staff just dropped off the second carload of dogs. The name is a little deceiving since most of the dogs that are here are over the age of three years old but, as I told Brenna, all dogs are just big puppies.

"Roland is a sweetie," Brenna agrees, as she fills a few water bowls along the far wall of the studio. "He used to be a racing dog. A real champion from what I hear. But as he got older, he started to slow down so his owner contacted the rescue to see if we'd take him in. Which we obviously did."

I run an affectionate hand over his flank. "Well, who needs that dumb old owner, eh, Rollie." I drop a kiss on the end of his snout. "We'll find you a new family who will spoil you for the rest of your days."

His trusting eyes look back at me and I swear he smiles. He turns his head into my face and nuzzles my cheek.

Oh, come on. My heart just imploded.

"Alright, I think that's everything." Brenna stands then looks around the room. "There's baggies filled with homemade Santa dog treats and bones on the check-in counter for participants to take and give to the dogs. There's a few puppy pads in the corner for any of our younger and more excitable pups who are still in training."

She points to the rolls of paper towels in the corner. "I brought cleaning supplies so any accidents or drool can be wiped away. I'll be in the back surveying the dogs for any signs of distress or to let them out to pee but otherwise I think we're all set."

I finally tear myself away from Roland's side. "Perfect. I've tailored the class so that it'll be a lot more floor and core moves to keep participants at eye-level with the dogs. I'm sticking to beginner poses so that we can focus on a safe environment for the dogs rather than trying not to trip over anyone attempting a complicated move."

Brenna nods her agreement. This is far from her first adoption event but it's our first collaboration like this. We were both pleasantly surprised by how many people signed up, especially after Luke posted the flyer on the police department's social media. He even rallied together some of his officers and a couple volunteer firefighters from the station next door to film some content for the event with a couple of the dogs.

Hot first responders and dogs—who could resist?

Brenna said they had an influx of interest in not just the event, but the rescue in general. Because of the great reception she's received, she and Luke are planning to collaborate more in the future.

Speak of the handsome devil...

The door swings open and Avery, Matt and Luke come

walking in the studio. As they call out their greetings, ten dogs of varying sizes and breeds scurry over to inspect the new arrivals. The jingling of the bells on their Christmas-inspired collars makes the whole scene quite the production.

"We wanted to come early in case you needed any help setting up," Avery says, quickly shrugging off her coat, throwing it on the floor beside her as she drops to the floor. "Hi, babies! Oh my goodness, you are just so precious." She looks up at Matt as a small black curly-haired dog licks her face. "Can we keep one? Please?"

Matt laughs, grabbing her coat from the floor to hang it beside his on the coat hook. "As much as I want to say yes because *lookatthisface,*" Matt says, dropping down beside her to rub the face of the energetic dog that's turned away from Avery and is now licking Matt's hands, "we can't. Our house is already too small for four people and two dogs." The dog looks up at him with adoring eyes and I can see Matt's turn into hearts. "Quit looking at me like that, Freckles. It's not my fault! I'm trying to be responsible." He turns a pleading face to Luke. "Luke, tell them I'm being responsible!" Avery turns, holding the black dog's smiling face against her's and gives Luke the most pathetic puppy dog eyes I've ever seen.

Luke shoves his hands in his gym shorts' (halle-fucking-lujah) pockets. "Keep me out of this," he grumbles, sidestepping around the crowd of dogs. He stops before me and the slight crook of his smile has my knees threatening to give out.

Stop that. He was just in my bed less than twenty-four hours ago. Doing deliciously dirty things to me, might I add. You'd think I'd be able to see him without physically swooning.

"Hey," he says in a low voice.

Apparently not.

"Hey." I smile back and for a second, I feel myself leaning toward him.

"J, is it okay if I put the donation sign on the front desk or would you rather it be somewhere else?" Brenna asks from the front of the studio, snapping me from my trance.

Remembering where we are and who we're surrounded by, I take a step back while adjusting my ponytail. "Yeah, that's fine," I call out, my voice cracking which causes Luke to smirk. When everyone is distracted, I reach over and pinch his arm.

Flinching, he pulls his arm away, rubbing the spot. Then he narrows his gaze and whispers, "You're gonna pay for that." I grin, knowing there's nothing he can do to me in front of our friends.

This is the first time we've been around them since our... *arrangement* began. Suddenly, I can't remember how I used to act around Luke before. Back when I would tease him and push his buttons on purpose, knowing it would piss him off but he'd never do anything. Now I tease him knowing *exactly* how he'll respond. At least in private.

I'm nervous someone will catch on and call us out, effectively ruining this little bubble we've created for ourselves. Then we'll have to decide if we want this to turn into something real. And if we make it real, that's when real life will fuck it all up.

Better to keep hiding it. At least for now.

Besides, it's kind of hot keeping our relationship a secret. There's something to be said for "don't get caught" sex.

I haven't looked at the waiting area chairs the same since.

I'm so thankful that Luke didn't force me to talk about my sudden change in behavior after I danced for him last week. I went into that routine thinking I'd show him a few moves, then strut over to him confidently and make him beg for more.

Luke begs so sweetly.

It started out fine, losing myself to the song like I usually do. But I'm not sure if it was the call with my brother, convincing me to come home for the holidays or knowing that in a few short weeks, I'll be seeing my father again. Either way, my mind started to wander.

I started thinking about what my father would say if he knew that I taught pole fitness classes. How he would react seeing me up on that pole, despite how much fun I was having or how good I'd become at it. The awful names he'd call me. Or worse, the look of disappointment and disgust on his face afterward.

Then as that bitch Tiffany likes to make them do, my thoughts started to spiral. What if Luke looked at me with that same look of disgust? He'd seemed different lately but what if he was more like my father than I thought? Would he scoff at my moves, calling me awful names like a hooker or a slut like my father did when I cut my band tee into a crop top for a music festival?

By the time my feet hit the floor again, my mind was ping ponging with different scenarios, each more humiliating than the last.

Because no matter how hard I try to tell myself his opinion doesn't matter to me, I'll always be the little girl wanting her dad to accept her for exactly who she is.

Which is why, even though we just started dating, I'm starting to realize how much I like Luke and how badly I wanted him to do the same thing.

"Who's that little cutie?" Avery asks from her seat on the floor, surrounded by dogs. She points to the corner of the studio where a tiny, older gray dog sits shivering, watching the commotion near the front. The dog is nearly hairless, except for a few patches on her head, ears and tail.

"That's Cleopatra," Brenna answers. "Cleo for short. She's seven years old and very..." She trails off, searching for the right word, "particular. Watch."

Brenna reaches into her pocket and pulls out a treat. She takes a few steps closer to Cleo then crouches to the ground, reaching the treat out to the little dog. Cleo sniffs the air near the treat then turns her nose up at Brenna and spins away from her.

"Cleo," Brenna sings, dragging out the name. "Want a treat, honey?"

I swear to god herself that if dogs could roll their eyes, Cleo just did. Then she gets up and struts in the other direction, hopping gracefully onto a stack of yoga mats in the corner and lies down like it's her own personal throne. Even when she drops her head, she continues to glare over at where we stand.

"Wow," I remark. "I can feel her judging me from here."

Brenna sighs. "Yeah, she's a tough one. We take her to events like this to keep her socialized but she couldn't care less. She's good with other dogs; she just doesn't trust people. Some adopters have shown interest in her but if anyone gets close enough, she either stalks off or bares her teeth." She gives Cleo a sad look. "She's given my crew at the rescue a few good nips. They affectionately call her Jaws. But unfortunately, no one wants a dog who doesn't want them, so it's been a long road for Miss Cleo."

As if realizing we're talking about her, the little dog rests her head on her crossed legs, eyeing us warily from her perch. Her tiny body shakes and if I didn't think she'd bite my hand off, I'd go cuddle her.

Just as I'm considering if I could get away with having one of my fingers bitten off and still manage a peacock pose, the bell above the door rings out. Between the five of us, we grab leashes to hold back the dogs while the participants hurry inside.

The only dog that doesn't budge is Cleo, who watches hesitantly from her pile of mats.

I'll win you over yet, Miss Cleo.

LUKE

"Now with your left leg extended, we're going to bend your right knee and cross it over the left," Jolie instructs as she demonstrates from the front of the room. "Then you're going to twist at the waist, placing your right arm on the outside of your right knee. Left arm is straight behind you and you're going to face the back wall." My muscles protest with the stretch as I try to follow her instructions.

I've always prided myself on being in shape. I have to be to do my job effectively. But even in high school, I worked out four times a week and played sports year round.

But sitting here on this yoga mat, twisting, turning, and contorting my body into positions that shouldn't be humanly possible, I'm starting to rethink my strength.

My only saving grace is that my brother is doing just as badly. He's currently using both hands to maneuver his bent leg over his straight leg. He tosses me a pained look over his shoulder then mouths, "my poor nuts" causing me to snort out a laugh.

Luckily, this class is pretty laid back so I don't have to

worry about interrupting the quiet. Most participants are more focused on the dogs than yoga.

It seems like there've been a handful people who have met their canine matches—including Avery. If I was a betting man, I'd say she will be leaving today with another pooch to add to their crew. And by the look on Matt's face when that curly-haired black mutt trots over to lick his chin, I'd say he's on-board.

Jolie stands from her place at the front, continuing to talk us through the stretch. As she walks around the room, she guides us into our next few poses. She doesn't have to talk for me to know exactly where she is in the room. It's as if there's a magnetic force pulling me to her, making me hyper-aware of her every move.

It's times like these where I wish we were just a regular couple. From the second I walked in the door, all I wanted to do was wrap my arms around her. To feel her melt into my touch like she always does. And the fact that I can't is driving me nuts. At this point, I'd settle for a strong fist bump. Anything to feel her skin against mine.

But I promised her we would keep this a secret until we figured out what exactly *this* was. Except I know what this is. I know exactly how hard I'm falling for the tall brunette who's been haunting my every thought for longer than she realizes.

And that scares the shit out of me because I've seen how our story ends and it isn't with a happily-ever-after. It's resentment and guilt and a long, angry letter left on my kitchen counter.

But for some reason, even knowing all of that, I find myself wanting to hope that it'll be different with us. That Jolie might not mind the long hours and I could handle stepping back a bit from the station. I could try being home on time (or close to). I could let go of the reins a little and give my deputy a little more of the responsibilities she's been begging me to give her.

For Jolie, I could try.

"Now you're going to slowly tuck your legs underneath you into a kneeling position. Then sliding your hands along the mat, you're going to let your heads drop between your arms." I do as she says even though my body buzzes with anticipation as I feel her getting closer. "Your forehead is going to rest against the mat and you're going to let your eyes fall closed, continuing to focus on your breathing." I let my eyes fall shut and am not at all surprised when her smile is what I see first.

Was it ever this way with Mindy? Was I ever this lovesick puppy who would stretch my body into a fucking pretzel and probably humiliate myself to do so just because a woman asked me to?

I know the answer to that question before I can even finish asking it.

Hell, no.

With Mindy, we liked and respected each other. We had the same goals and the same ethics. We had fun together.

But looking back, it was never like this. I didn't think about Mindy while I was at work. I never craved her presence. I never missed hearing her voice when we'd gone too long without talking like I do Jolie's. Even if it's for her to call me on my bullshit.

Everything's different with Jolie. *I'm* different with Jolie.

As if I summoned her, she walks up behind me. Like it

always does when she's near, my heart picks up speed. She stops beside my mat. My heart nearly trips over itself when I feel her palm slide up my back. "You're going to want to lean into this stretch, feeling it along your lower back and through your hips," she instructs for the class.

Everywhere she's touching me, I've seen her do the same to countless other participants. But there's something intimate about it. Especially when she leans forward and whispers just loud enough for me to hear, "You're going to want to stretch for what I have planned for later."

Fuck. My throat bobs and my hands curl into fists on the mat. I will not get a boner in the middle of a yoga class. Especially when the material of my gym shorts will leave nothing to the imagination.

"Great. Looking good, everyone," Jolie praises and I can hear the smile in her voice.

Oh, you'll pay for that one, sweetheart.

"Now we're going to hold this pose for a few moments longer, focusing on our deep breathing." She continues to talk but I'm too busy trying to distract my imagination from all the sinful things she might have in mind for us.

Dogs. We're here for the dogs, I remind myself. Taking a few calming breaths, I start to relax. Just as I finally release the tension in my muscles, there's a brush of hair against my bicep. Turning my head slightly, I peek under my arm to see a small gray body cowering near me.

It's the little dog Brenna was talking about earlier. Clara? Chloe? Cleo? Yeah, that's it. The little three pound diva with the leopard print collar.

But I thought Brenna said she was a real hell-raiser. The little dog creeping closer to me doesn't seem so bad. In fact, by the look in her eyes, she seems...scared.

I don't move a muscle as she inches closer and closer until her tiny shaking body is pressed against my arm. Then she shocks the hell out of me by giving my sweaty skin a small lick before she tucks herself back into a little ball.

I let her stay like that for a little while, skipping the next few poses so I don't spook her.

It's not until Jolie has us sit up in a cross-legged position that I finally move. To my surprise, Cleo doesn't move from her spot beside me. She merely lifts her head and watches me change positions. When she's sure I'm not going far, she stands up and curls back into my side, this time beside my leg.

Testing her, I drop a hand to the mat, far enough away from her that it's not threatening but close enough that she could come to me if she felt like it.

She lifts her head again, watching my hand warily. I continue to follow Jolie's breathing exercises, keeping one eye on the little dog beside me. Just as I'm about to bring my hand back, Cleo crawls over to me and drops her head onto the back of my hand.

"Good girl, Cleo," I whisper.

When the class ends, people start to stand and pack up their things. I'm happy to see almost all of the participants head to the front desk to fill out adoption applications.

Cleo jumps up with the commotion and scurries back over to her place in the corner. Her eyes dart around the room and she drops to a defensive position as people and dogs mill around the room.

I hesitate for a second, then slowly approach her. Taking a seat a few feet away from where she's cowering, I study her closely.

"It's okay, girl. No one's going to hurt you," I say in the

same low, calming voice that I use when dealing with potentially hostile suspects. She lifts her head and sniffs the air toward me. "That's it, honey." She moves closer as I mumble my encouragement. Finally, she takes a hesitant step into my lap, then drops her head onto my leg.

Knowing she could still decide to take a chunk out of my skin, I slowly brush two fingers over her back. Her body tenses for a second before finally relaxing into my touch. My chest fills with pride. She trusts me, even if just for a second. Cleo blinks up at me, her eyes scared and wary but also with the slightest glimpse of hope. She lets out a long sigh, then closes her eyes. As if she's tired of being miserable all the time.

"Me too, Cleo," I whisper as I continue to pet her.

Finally, the crowds clear and Brenna's employees have picked up the tired dogs to bring them back to the sanctuary. She had explained at the beginning of the day that all applications would be vetted after the event and once approved, adopters would be able to pick up their dogs later this week.

Shadows darken the wall in front of me and I look up to see Jolie, Brenna, Avery and Matt looking down with varying expressions of wonder and happiness.

"She likes you," Jolie whispers, smiling down at us.

"Better yet, she trusts you," adds Brenna, her expression nothing short of shocked.

"I think you've found yourself a dog, bro." Matt grins.

I open my mouth to correct him. I don't have time for a dog. Dogs require love and attention and patience; all things I've proved I'm not able to give. But then her little body shifts against my leg, nuzzling closer into my skin and I know none of that matters.

To Cleo, it doesn't matter that I'm a grumpy asshole who has minimal patience and a short fuse.

She trusts you, Brenna's words echo in my head. I look down at her little body, small enough to fit in the palm of my hand.

"Yeah, I guess I did."

JOLIE

"So, just as I'm finishing emptying the bottle of dish soap onto the slip-and-slide, our elementary school principal comes walking around the corner of the hallway. Caught me red-handed. Conveniently at the same time that Miss Avery here had to go to the bathroom and left her post." Matt shakes his head, side-eyeing his future-wife. "Worst look-out ever."

After Puppy Yoga, Avery and Matt invited us all back to their house for dinner with Gavin and Avery's mom, Angie. I don't think I'll ever get tired of seeing the four of them together. They're the perfect little family and my heart always cheers whenever I see them together. I'm so happy for my best friend and the life she's built.

After dinner and bedtime routines, we piled into the basement to munch on snacks and watch the hockey game. Since it was a slow night, Rhett left the bar in the hands of his manager and came by with some appetizers from his kitchen.

Normally, I don't like to watch my brother play in front of people in case they make the connection between our last name. But lately I've been thinking more about what Avery said about keeping my life private. I think it's time to open up to my friends—at least in pieces.

Avery's mouth drops open, fighting back a laugh. "I have a small bladder and you know it. It's not my fault you weren't faster with the soap." She drops her voice a few octaves. "'It has to be evenly distributed to get the perfect effect,'" she imitates him, causing everyone, including Matt, to burst into laughter.

"Of course, no one believed me that it was *your* idea to put a slip-and-slide down the school hallway as a graduation prank," Matt complains, putting an arm around Avery to pull her into his side. "It's a good thing you're cute, you know that, Freckles?"

Avery reaches up and pats him on the cheek lovingly. "And it's a good thing you're so easy to frame." Matt pokes her in the ribs and she laughs. "Man, that slip-and-slide really flew. Too bad you were too busy being stuck in detention to enjoy it."

Matt reaches for her again but she jumps off the couch just in time. "I'm going to go check on Gavin quick. Does anyone want anything while I'm upstairs?"

We all shake our heads and she makes her escape.

Brenna turns to Rhett and Luke. "So, while Matt and Avery were off causing trouble, what were you two doing?"

Rhett drops a handful of tortilla chips onto his plate, then scoops up a spoonful of dip. "I didn't move to Haven Bay until I was fourteen. I lived down south before that." Dunking a chip into the dip, he pops it into his mouth.

When he doesn't offer up any more information, Brenna turns to Luke. "What about you?"

Luke sits further into the couch, one arm draped along the back with his foot crossed over onto his knee. He looks relaxed, something I've only ever seen him be when he's with his friends. It makes me grateful that I'm now included in that group of people.

He shrugs. "I had some buddies that I hung out with in high school. Mostly guys I played sports with growing up." He leans forward and grabs a jalapeño popper from the coffee table. "Our family had a rule that once you hit high school, you got a part-time job helping at my mom's salon. Cleaning, inventory, answering phones. I'm a year older than Matt so while he was pulling his grade eight graduation prank, I was probably sweeping hair into the garbage."

Brenna points back and forth between Luke and Matt. "You're only a year apart? Your poor mother."

Matt grins over his beer. "Yeah, Dad used to joke that I was Luke's first birthday gift, even though we're thirteen months apart."

Luke smirks. "They were a bit more careful after that. Until Oopsie-Tori came along five years later."

Matt grins at Luke. "Then it was off to the chop-shop for poor Dad." He mimes scissors cutting with his fingers and Luke and Rhett both cringe.

"That's funny. My brother and I are just over a year apart too," I comment. Luke watches me carefully, knowing how secretive I am about my family. I give him a slight nod letting him know it's okay.

"You know, I don't think you've ever mentioned you had a brother before," Matt says, grabbing a handful of chips to drop into his mouth. "What's he do?"

I take a deep breath. *Here goes nothing.* "That." I point at the TV to where my brother's flying down the ice on a breakaway, the commentators going wild in the background.

Matt's brows crush together in confusion. I can see the

wheels turning in his head as he looks at the TV then back at me. Rhett looks over at me then at Matt then at the TV. Brenna just looks lost.

I can feel Luke's eyes on me in concern but I refuse to look at him. Matt opens his mouth to say something then snaps it shut again. His expression would make me laugh if my stomach wasn't twisting with nerves.

Finally, he opens his mouth again. "Are you saying your brother..." he trails off, pointing at the TV.

"Austin St. James is your brother?" Rhett asks slowly, as if working out a difficult math problem.

I nod.

"So, wait. You're telling me your brother plays for the Toronto Storm. And this is the first time you're saying anything about it?" Matt practically screeches.

Honestly, it's not the worst reaction I've ever heard. Though it might be the loudest.

"Yep," I confirm, trying to act nonchalant.

"What'd I miss?" Avery calls as she hurries down the stairs. "What's making Matt's voice go all squeaky?"

Matt snaps his mouth shut at that. "My voice does not *squeak*," he replies, clearly offended.

"Jolie's brother plays for the Toronto Storm," Brenna puts in. She seems unfazed by this revelation which, truthfully, she probably is. And I love her for it.

"Austin St. James is your brother?" Avery asks and again, I nod. "Huh." She turns to the screen, which happens to be a close up of Austin from the penalty box.

Typical Austin, I muse.

Avery turns back to me. "Huh," she repeats. "Yeah, I can see the resemblance."

Rhett nods. "Yeah, the eyes. You've both got those big blue eyes," he remarks.

Luke stays quiet, watching me with a small smile. As if he's proud of me. My chest warms. Truthfully, I'm proud of me, too.

Only Matt keeps staring at me wide-eyed, like he's sitting beside Beyoncé or something. "So, your brother is Austin St. James."

"Yep."

"Like, first-round draft pick, star defensemen for the Toronto Storm. That Austin St. James."

"Yep."

"Can you get him to sign my jersey?"

Avery smacks his arm. He grabs it defensively. "What? It's not like I'm asking for tickets. It's just an autograph. If I had a famous brother, I'd get him to sign stuff for my friends." He tilts his head at Luke. "Instead I'm stuck with Andy Griffith over there."

Luke looks like he's about to lay into Matt so I step in instead. "Sure, Matt. I'll ask him to sign your jersey." Luke looks at me out of the corner of his eye and I smile.

In all honesty, a signed jersey is the least of my worries. Most people treat me differently when they find out who my brother is. Some use me for tickets or to get close to him. But I know none of my friends would ever do that to me. Which is why my chest feels lighter now that my secret's out. Brenna smiles at me and Luke shoots me a wink.

I thought telling my friends about my past would change how they see me, but I was crazy to think this group would treat me as anyone other than myself.

The conversation changes and I settle back into the couch. After a minute, Matt and Rhett start to argue over a call on TV so I get up to grab a water from the fridge in the downstairs bar. A few seconds later, Luke walks up beside me, leaning against the fridge. "You good?"

I nod, smiling. "Yeah, I'm good."

He turns. "That was really brave of you to open up like that."

My smile widens. "Thanks. I'm glad I did. I feel lighter. Free."

His lips tilt up in a small smile. "I'm glad." He reaches out to brush a hand down my side. I lean into his touch, wishing we were alone so I could really feel him against me.

A cheer comes from the other room, breaking the spell. I take a step back. Luke frowns but doesn't say anything.

"So, you adopted a dog," I say, smirking up at him.

"Seems that way," he answers, shaking his head. "Guess I'll have to make a trip to Bakersfield for some supplies tomorrow. Want to join me? We could grab some dinner on the way back."

A slow smile spreads across my face. "You asking me on a date, Luke Brady?" I tease.

"Damn right," he answers in that low, commanding tone of his that makes my insides clench.

I look over my shoulder to where our friends are busy watching the game. Seeing that they're preoccupied, I step closer and give him a soft kiss on the mouth.

"I'm in," I whisper against his lips before pulling away. The sudden grin he gives me has my heart doing backflips.

We're heading back to the living room when Matt calls out to me. "You know, you're not the only person here with a famous family member, Jolie."

I flop down into the oversized recliner. "Oh, yeah? Who's that?"

Matt puffs his chest. "Luke." Luke scoffs to which Matt glares at him before turning to me. "You're looking at Bakersfield High School's talent show winner of 2009."

Avery groans as Luke sighs and grumbles, "not this

again". Rhett leans forward with a finger in the air. "Co-winner, if you please."

Matt tips his head forward in a bow. "Apologies, my good sir." He turns back to me. "My buddy Rhett here and I won the talent show."

By the looks on Luke's and Avery's faces, I can tell this is going to be good so I lean forward, egging him on. "And what, may I ask, was your talent?"

Rhett grins proudly. "We lip-synced *It's Tricky* by Run-DMC."

"They had a whole dance and everything," Avery scoffs, rolling her eyes.

"Oh, this I've got to see," Brenna chimes in as Luke groans from beside me.

"I don't think you know what you're asking for," he grumbles.

"Show us! Show us! Show us!" I chant and Brenna joins in.

Matt eagerly jumps from his seat. "What my adoring fans want, my adoring fans get." Rhett stands, elbowing him. "Ouch. I mean, *our* adoring fans." They step in front of the TV, hands crossed in front of them with their heads bowed.

"Hit it, DJ," Matt announces. When no one moves, he lifts his head and tilts his head at Avery then at the remote.

"Oh! Right. Sorry, hon." She hits the mute button on the TV then grabs her phone. Turning the volume up, she rests her phone on the coffee table as the first few notes of *It's Tricky* start to play.

Matt lifts his head, perfectly lip-syncing the beginning of the song as he widens his stance, his arms stretched and dipping as he raps the first verse. A second voice comes over the speaker and Rhett lifts his head to start lip-syncing as well.

Avery, Brenna, and I have tears rolling down our faces as we watch the two jump around, dipping around the living room and attempting to breakdance. When they lean in on either side of Luke's face, rapping and throwing their hands up like wanna-be gangsters, I'm wheezing from laughing so hard. Even Luke is chuckling as he shoves them away.

When the song ends, they take turns bowing while we applaud and call for an encore.

Matt flops onto the couch beside Avery who gives him a loud kiss on the cheek. Rhett lands beside Luke, tapping his cheek. "Don't I get one too?" he jokes. To all of our surprise, Luke grabs his face and gives him a big smooch on the lip then pushes Rhett away. "Don't say I never give you anything." Luke smirks. The rest of us burst into laughter at a wide-eyed Rhett.

I grab my phone from my pocket and fire off a text.

JOLIE

Do I have some competition?

Luke's phone vibrates on the arm rest beside him. He checks the screen, tips his lips up, then taps out a response.

LUKE

Don't worry, sweetheart. His lips have nothing on yours.

But maybe you should refresh my memory, just in case.

Better yet, maybe you should just sit on my face.

I bite my lip to keep from laughing at the phone.

JOLIE

Well, that escalated quickly.

But I'm not saying no.

LUKE

That's my girl.

How long do you think we have to wait
before we can make an excuse and leave?
I want to feel your pussy on my face.

WELL, *then*. That's one way to get my attention. I squirm in my seat.

"Jolie?" My head snaps up to look at Avery. "I asked if you had any Christmas plans."

I clear my throat, trying to clear away the thoughts of Luke's head between my legs. "Um, yeah. Actually I do. I'm flying back to Ontario next week to spend a few days with my brother before Christmas dinner with my parents. I'll be back on the 27th."

Luke stiffens beside me but I pretend not to notice. I realize now that I may have forgotten to mention that little detail to him. Mostly because I've been debating whether or not to go since I made the deal with my brother.

My phone vibrates and I take a second before looking down at it.

Luke

Want to talk it out?

This time I can't hold back the smile.

"WELL," Luke says, leaning forward. "I should get going. I have the early shift tomorrow." He waves his goodbye then heads upstairs. Moments later, my phone vibrates again.

―――――

"So, were you planning on telling me about your trip home before or after you boarded the plane?" Luke asks, tracing a finger over my bare shoulder.

I groan, turning my head into his chest. "I thought maybe all the sex distracted you from that little detail."

He chuckles softly. "It was great sex, but not amnesia-inducing."

He's right. It was great. After Luke left, I waited an appropriate twenty-three minutes before I made some excuse that I don't even remember now, then drove as fast as Blue could go with her new engine and snow tires.

I made it to Luke's house with one minute to spare. After parking my car in his garage, I barely had a chance to knock before he was swinging open the door and yanking me inside. His mouth fused to mine the second I crossed the threshold and he didn't lift his head once as he walked me back to his room. Then he took his time making good on every single one of his promises.

We've been lying naked in his bed for who knows how long, barely talking. I always thought that being truly comfortable with someone meant that you could talk about anything and everything. That there were no awkward silences. But I'm quickly learning that it's the opposite; being comfortable with someone means that you don't feel the need to fill the silences. You can sit together and just be present.

I sigh, tracing patterns on his stomach with my finger. "First of all, my home is in Haven Bay, not Toronto. Second of all, it's not that I purposely didn't tell you about my trip. To be honest, I've been trying to figure out a way out of it since I made the deal with my brother."

Luke rubs a thumb over the knuckles of our entwined hands. "I thought you and your brother were close."

"Oh, we are. I'm excited to see Austin. It's my parents that I'm dreading seeing." I huff out a breath. "My relationship with my parents is...complicated."

Well, if that isn't the understatement of the year. Doing your taxes is complicated. Trying to have a secret relationship with your best friend's brother-in-law in a town as small as Haven Bay is complicated.

My relationship with my parents? That's downright disastrous.

Luke remains silent, his thumb continuing its soothing glide over my knuckles, grounding me while I gather my thoughts.

"My father and I have never had a good relationship. He's been in the army for forty years. I don't know if it's because of that or just his personality, but he believes that everyone should fall in line with what he wants." I drop my voice to imitate my father. "'Little girls shouldn't be so loud, Jolie.' 'Bright colors like that attract the wrong kind of attention, Jolie.' 'Your room is for sleeping and studying, not for hanging obscene posters on the walls, Jolie.'" I roll my eyes. "I was twelve and it was a Spice Girls poster, not a Playboy magazine."

"Please tell me you hung up a Playboy just to prove him wrong," Luke says above me and I smile.

"Nah. I should've though. But that was just the beginning of our strenuous relationship. The harder he tried to turn me into his perfect image of what a daughter should be, the harder I fought back. When I moved out after high school, he gave up trying. Now he resorts to making snide comments about my life choices, as if owning a yoga studio is the equivalent of owning a brothel." I laugh humorlessly.

As much as I've come to terms with the fact that my relationship with my father will never change, it doesn't soothe the sting of rejection. I force back the tears that are threatening to fall.

"What about your mom?" Luke asks quietly after a moment.

I swallow past the ball of emotion in my throat. "My mom and I get along fine, when we leave out any mention of my father. From what my grandpa told me, my mom was a lot like me growing up. She loved to paint and dreamed of traveling around the world." I smile despite myself. "She used to make up songs with my brother and I that were so awful and off-key, but we loved it."

My smile falls. "I'll never understand why she married him. She walks on eggshells around him, always putting aside her wants for his. It's like she let him strip away the best parts of her until there was nothing left from before but the shell of who she once was." I shake my head. "I don't understand that kind of love. I don't think I ever will."

Luke's quiet for a second then he mumbles into my hair. "That's not love."

I raise my head to look up at him. "What?"

"That's not love," he repeats, firmer this time.

He brushes a stray hair out of my face. "My mom loved to paint. Every Sunday, she'd set up a canvas, get out her paint supplies and paint all morning."

I smile up at him. "I didn't know Franny was an artist."

"She wasn't. She was awful. Couldn't paint a straight line to save her life. She painted a bowl of fruit once and it looked like a cat threw up a hairball on the canvas." He chuckles. "But every Sunday afternoon, she'd bring us into the back room and show off her latest creation. And every single time, my dad would act as if she just painted the Mona Lisa. Then he'd build her a frame and hang them all around the house."

He looks down at me. "When you love someone, you don't try to stifle their flame. You tend it. You protect it."

I lie there for a while, thinking about what he just said. I can't help but wonder what it would be like to be loved by Luke. If he'd protect my flame, instead of trying to stifle it the way my father always had.

I'm not sure what to think now. If that's all true, if Luke isn't as similar to my father as I thought, then that means every reason I have for assuming this relationship will fail is wrong.

Which would mean no more sneaking around, no more secrets. We'd be a real couple.

I'm not sure how I feel about that.

To distract myself, I adjust my position so I'm up on my forearm, looking down at him. "You know, that means I'll be gone for five days. That's five whole days you won't be able to touch me, taste me." I trail my hand down his waist and under the covers. "Are you going to miss me?"

"Maybe," he replies. His cock stirs to life beneath my hand, proving how full of shit he is. "Not as much as you're going to miss me."

"We'll see about that." I slide my body down until I'm situated between his thighs. I drop my head, taking just his head into my mouth. "I think after one day, you'll be begging me to come back."

Luke makes a strangled noise, his dark eyes searing into mine. "You think so, eh?"

I take him farther into my mouth, until his tip hits the back of my throat. I swallow past the urge to gag and he groans. "I know so." I drag my tongue along the underside of his cock then hollow my cheeks.

His sharp intake of breath has me brimming with power as I take him deeper and harder. Just as I can feel him start to pulse against my tongue, he shoots forward, pulling me off of him. Then he's flipping us so that he's hovering above me. He rocks his hips against me, his hard cock slipping inside and I moan.

"Look at you. So eager for me," he comments, his voice low and husky. "I think you'll be the one missing me."

"Wanna—Ah!" I start to respond but the words die on my tongue as he thrusts into me in one deep motion. He pulls out all the way then thrusts back deep inside, hitting that spot that makes my toes curl.

I open my eyes and see his smirking face looking down at me. He knows exactly what he's doing to me. *Game on.* I hook my ankles around the back of his thighs and tilt my hips, deepening the angle. I sit up onto my forearms, taking his mouth in a possessive kiss. After a moment, I pull away slightly.

"Wanna bet?" I ask breathlessly against his mouth.

"What?"

"Wanna bet that you'll miss me more?"

He leans forward, until my knees are pressed against my chest. "Bet me anything you want, sweetheart." My mouth drops open at the new angle and his lips tilt upward as he watches my eyes glaze over. "We both know who's going to come out on top here."

I can feel my orgasm building, but I can't resist the challenge he dangles before me. With a shaky hand, I press against his chest and immediately he leans back, his brow furrowed in confusion. While I have him off-kilter, I swing my leg over his hip and push him onto his back.

"Me," I pant. Then with both hands pressed against his stomach, I straddle his waist, dropping myself onto his hard cock in one fluid motion. Luke groans at the same time I cry out. He holds my hips in a punishing grip, urging me on as I ride him harder, faster until I fall over the edge, Luke calling out my name as he follows.

CHAPTER 44

LUKE

"**B**rady," I bark into the phone. There's silence for a second, then the person on the other end chuckles.

"Damn, who shit in your cornflakes this morning?" The tension in my shoulders eases slightly at the sound of Detective Wade Riorson's voice.

"Riorson. Nice of you to finally get up off your ass long enough to call me back," I say by way of greeting.

He scoffs. "Some of us have real work to do, Brady. Pull over any horse and buggies lately?"

I grin at the good-natured ribbing. "Not since this morning."

Wade and I were roommates in college together and graduated from the academy together. He's a detective now and lives in the city with his wife and two daughters.

When Jolie told me about the threatening emails she received, I called Wade first thing the next morning and asked him to check in on Tad Chesterfield as a favor to me. So far, my own investigation has come up dry so I'm anxious to hear what Wade found.

"Now, I know you love hearing my voice," Wade continues, "but I've only got a few minutes so I'll cut to the chase. Your boy Chesterfield has found himself in some hot water since he left Haven Bay. I made a few calls and found out he's no longer employed with the Ramco Group. Apparently, that deal he lost in Haven Bay wasn't the only one he'd messed up, so his boss decided that was the last straw and let him go. I tried calling his landlord..." There's some ruffling papers in the background as if he's checking a name. "Jay Peters. I made up a story about dropping off a package and needing to verify the address. Anyway, apparently Chesterfield's visiting family in Seattle and is expected to be out of town for the next few weeks."

I make a few notes, stopping Wade every once and a while to clarify spelling of certain names in case I decide to double check anything. Then after a few minutes of shooting the shit, Wade gets called away.

"Listen, when all this quiets down a bit, you should bring that girl of yours for dinner sometime. Margot and the girls would love to see you."

I start to correct him that Jolie's not my girl, then stop. "Will do, man," I say instead. "Thanks for your help."

I put my phone back on my desk then turn my attention back to my computer screen. Before Wade called, I'd been reading through all of Jolie's *Dear Annie* articles, looking for any indication of a disgruntled reader.

Even though *Dear Annie* has been a thorn in my side since the first article was released, before today I'd never actually read one of her articles. Now that I have, I have to admit they're great. And I'm not just saying that because I'm sleeping with *Annie* herself. Jolie's advice is thoughtful and insightful without overstepping. More than once I've found myself getting lost in her words.

I feel like I owe Jolie an apology—maybe multiple. It's not her fault that her crazy readers took her perfectly normal advice and twisted it to suit their agendas.

I should know by now that the only people to blame for the wacky actions of the people of this town are themselves. I've said it before and I'll say it again until the day I die: Haven Bay is not like most towns.

And as much as our residents love to drive me crazy with their off-the-wall shenanigans, I wouldn't change a thing about them.

I mean, I could do with less senior nudity.

A lot less.

In fact, none would be ideal.

My phone rings indicating an incoming FaceTime call. There's only one person who would be FaceTiming me at this time of night so I jump from my seat to close my office door. I tap my phone screen to accept the call, grinning.

"Missing me already, sweetheart?"

Jolie's face fills the screen. Her hair is thrown up in a messy bun and she's wearing an oversized t-shirt and sweatpants. It's dark wherever she is and I can just make out the outline of white countertops and cupboards. She mentioned that she was staying at her brother's apartment so I'm assuming it's his kitchen she's standing in.

She smiles and rolls her eyes as she grabs a bowl off of the counter. "You wish," she teases, walking through the kitchen to flop down onto a couch. "I figured I should give you a call so you don't cry yourself to sleep tonight." She smirks, tossing a couple kernels of popcorn into her mouth.

"Projecting, are we?" I quirk a brow at her and she laughs.

"Your fancy cop-talk doesn't impress me, Chief."

I lean back in my chair, smiling. "I'll just have to try

harder next time then," I reply. "What're you still doing up? It's past midnight there. Aren't you tired from the flight?"

She adjusts so that she's leaning into the corner of the couch, her knees tucked into her chest. "It's quarter after twelve but with the time change, my body thinks it's only ten. My brain's going to be wired for hours still."

"How's your brother? Was he excited to see you?"

"Yeah, he was. You'd think he played football instead of hockey the way he tackled me at the airport," she says dryly. "Then we went for dinner at this pub he's been telling me about near his apartment. He has an early skate tomorrow so he went to bed not long after we got home."

I arch a brow at her. "No Michelin-starred restaurants for the St. James siblings?"

She scoffs. "Austin is the pickiest eater I've ever met. He practically lived off of chicken fingers and Kraft Dinner until he was in college. I'll be lucky if I can convince him to eat grocery store sushi with me this week, let alone at a five-star restaurant."

I make a face at the phone. "Grocery store sushi? Really?"

"Hey, now." She points an accusatory finger at me. "Don't be yucking my yum, sir. Some of us are ballin' on a budget."

"Sir, eh?" I wag my eyebrows at her. "I kind of like the sound of that."

Even in the dark, I can see the blush on her cheeks. "Easy, tiger. My brother's in the next room."

"He's sleeping," I answer, only half-kidding.

It's been less than a day and I'm already counting down the hours until she's back home in my arms. I don't know how I'll be able to last four more days without her near me. And I don't mean just sexually.

Though that's gonna suck, too.

"Anyway, horndog. What's new since I left?"

"You mean in the..." I check the clock on my wall, "thirteen hours and six minutes since you left?" I stroke my jaw in thought. "Well, we elected a new mayor, solved the centuries old case of Simon Wendelman's missing gold tooth. What else..." I snap my fingers. "Oh, and there was a duel in the town square a few hours ago. Babs Piden shot her sister Clarice in the foot over the last bowl of chocolate pudding." I wipe a pretend bead of sweat from my forehead. "It's been a busy day at the station."

Jolie shakes her head, but she's grinning back at me. "Smartass."

We talk for a bit longer, filling each other in on our days. Jolie tells me about the obnoxious teenager that she made friends with on the plane and I fill her in on family dinner at my mom's.

When she asks me if I'm ready to pick Cleo up from the rescue tomorrow, I shrug. "I think so. I've got everything set up the way you showed me."

Sunday morning, Jolie and I drove to a pet store in Bakersfield and put a dent in my credit card over what Jolie deemed "puppy essentials". An hour later, I was loading my truck up with a gem studded collar and leash set, a fluffy pink dog bed and pink matching bowls with "water" and "food" written in fancy handwriting on them.

When I pointed out that Cleo probably can't read the bowls to tell which one is which, Jolie shot me an exasperated look and grumbled what sounded like "uncultured man" before pushing the cart further down the aisle.

"Make sure you send me a picture of her as soon as you get the collar on her. I hope she likes the memory foam dog bed we picked out. I still think the fleece one might've been better," she worries, chewing the corner of her lip.

I almost point out that dogs used to sleep on the hard ground for thousands of years and made it out just fine, but keep my mouth shut.

"So, remember my buddy, Wade Riorson with the Bakersfield PD?" I hate to spoil her good mood but she asked me to keep her updated about any leads with the emails.

Jolie nods. "You asked him to look into Tad." Her face turns serious. "Did you hear back from him?"

"Yeah, he just called before you did." I fill her in on everything Wade told me about Tad losing his job and going to Seattle.

"So, that doesn't really prove anything. He could be sending emails from anywhere, even Seattle," she points out.

"He could be," I agree slowly. Worry crosses her face. "Or he could be partying it up in Seattle and hasn't given you a second thought, other than an embarrassing thing that happened while he was on a business trip. Either way, he can't do any physical harm from Seattle." She nods, worry still evident on her face.

"Listen. We're going to find out whoever is sending these emails and I'm going to personally make sure they never get within a hundred feet of you," I assure her. "I won't let anything happen to you, sweetheart. I promise."

She searches my eyes on the other end of the screen then gives another slight nod.

"Good. But I have an important question you need to answer for me first," I say, my voice low and serious.

She nods. "Sure. Anything."

My lips curl into a wicked grin. "What color panties do

you have on?" I wink at her stunned expression before she throws her head back laughing.

"You scared me, asshole!" she cries, an adorable snort breaking through her laughter.

We stay like that for a long time, laughing and talking. My shift has long since ended and my phone is nearly dead, but I can't tear myself away to say goodbye. It's not until Jolie yawns, her eyes starting to droop that I finally give in.

"I think it's time for you to hit the hay."

She starts to protest but it's cut off by another yawn. I chuckle. "You were saying?"

"Fine." She stands up, carrying her phone toward the guest bedroom.

"Wait," I say and she stops. "Did you lock the front door?"

She rolls her eyes. "Yes, it's locked."

"Show me."

"You're ridiculous, you know that, right?"

I don't say anything until she walks to the front door and turns the phone so I can see the padlock on the door. She turns it back to her face. "Happy?"

"Very," I answer, smiling.

"Goodnight, Chief Ridiculous."

"Goodnight, sweetheart."

"So, who's the guy?"

I force myself not to react as I continue chopping the pepper on the cutting board into thin slices. "What guy?" I ask, keeping my eyes on my work.

Austin leans over my shoulder and nabs a pepper off the cutting board, popping it into this mouth. "The guy you were on the phone with last night until four in the morning."

"It wasn't four a.m." It's a sad attempt at deflecting and I know it.

He's always been supportive of me. If I told him it was none of his business, he'd let it go and never ask about it again. If I told him I was having a secret affair with my best friend's brother-in-law, he'd be the last person to judge. My brother's no saint himself, if the tabloids are anything to go off of.

So why do I care if my brother knows about Luke?

But deep down I know why. Because Luke's not some dirty little secret. Not anymore, at least. If there was any doubt of my growing feelings for him before I left Haven

Bay, it's long gone now. No matter how much I tease him about it, I miss him. That fact was solidified last night when I kept coming up with reasons to keep him on the phone.

We spend practically every night that he's not on duty together, whether it's at his house or mine. I didn't realize how much I'd gotten used to having him around until he was no longer a short drive away.

Even after we hung up, I tossed and turned for another hour before I was able to fall asleep. I woke up this morning groggy and miserable. Then I flipped over my phone and saw the good morning text from Luke and I practically danced out of bed.

When did I become this girl?

I'm not the girl whose mood is based around a guy's attention. I pride myself on never being that dependent on someone else.

So what's happening to me?

"Jeez. I didn't think it was that hard of a question," Austin jokes when I take a little too long to answer. He grins, swiping another pepper from the cutting board and popping it into his mouth.

I spin on my heel and punch him in the shoulder. Hard. "First of all, don't listen in on my conversations, you creep. Second of all, steal my peppers again and I'll chop your fingers off and feed them to your piranha."

Austin rubs his shoulder, his mouth hanging open offended. "First of all, it's *my* apartment. If you don't want to be heard, talk quieter. Second of all, I don't own a piranha."

"Keep stealing my peppers and I'm going to buy you one just so I can feed your fingers to it." I point my knife at his hands. He has the good sense to tuck them behind his back.

"Crazy woman," he grumbles under his breath as he slumps over to the kitchen island.

"What's that?" I call over my shoulder, waving the knife in the air so he can see it.

"Nothing, you maniac," he huffs from his stool. "You know my hands are insured for over a million dollars, right?"

I wave a hand over my head. "Keep your insurance money. I'll do it for free."

"Does your boyfriend know about your homicidal tendencies?" Austin asks, grabbing an apple from the fruit bowl and taking a bite. I swear he hasn't stopped eating for more than twenty minutes since I arrived. How he's still so jacked, I'll never understand.

In my next life, I want to come back as a pro athlete.

I finish chopping the vegetables, slide half into a bowl, then dump the rest into a second bowl. Inside each bowl, I've arranged peppers, chickpeas, cucumbers, Kalamata olives and feta cheese. The timer beeps and I yank open the oven door to pull out two chicken breasts that I found in Austin's fridge this morning. After adding the chicken into the bowls, I finish by drizzling Greek dressing on top.

"I never said he was my boyfriend." I walk over to the island and slide a bowl toward Austin. He eyes it suspiciously like it's a snake ready to strike. I roll my eyes at his theatrics, then make a show of taking a forkful into my mouth.

Satisfied that I haven't poisoned his lunch (the day is still young), my brother digs into the bowl as if he hasn't already eaten three meals today and it's barely noon. "Why not?" Austin asks, genuinely curious. "Is he a douche? Do I have to kick his ass?"

"Maybe I'm just using him for his body."

Austin drops his fork like it's covered in manure. "Ew.

Well, there goes my appetite. Thanks for that." He pushes the bowl aside, his face twisting in disgust.

So dramatic. "You know I'm a grown woman, right? I've had sex before. Many times actually. In many different positions. In fact once, I was upside down in this—"

"Why couldn't you have been born a guy? Or a lesbian. I could've handled a lesbian. I would've made a great wingman." He shakes his head miserably. "Wouldn't I?"

I pat his arm sympathetically. "You would've made a great wingman, Ares."

He grins. "Yeah, I would've." He pulls his bowl back to him, apparently forgetting about his earlier lack of appetite. "I'd like to point out that you never actually denied that he was your boyfriend." He smirks over his bowl.

I sigh. "Yeah, I know."

"You wanna talk about it?"

"No."

"Good. I didn't really want to hear about it." He ducks as I hurtle my fork toward him. "I'm kidding, I'm kidding," he laughs. He finishes his lunch off with one last mouthful then brings his now empty bowl to the sink, giving my shoulder a squeeze as he passes me. "But seriously, you know I'm here for you if you change your mind."

Emotion clogs my throat. "Thanks, Ares."

He groans at the nickname. "What will it take you to give up calling me that?"

I pretend to think it over. "Get me out of dinner tomorrow with Mom and Dad."

He shakes his head as he walks toward his bedroom. "Hell, no. If I have to be there, so do you."

"I hate you!" I call after his retreating body.

"Love you too, twerp."

Despite the looming dinner with my parents where

there's guaranteed to be fighting, shaming and yelling involved, I can't help feeling happy that I decided to come back. My brother is one of my favorite people and I forget just how much I miss him until I'm around him again.

"JOLIE!" He yelps like a little girl from the other room. "Did you seriously fucking Saran Wrap my toilet seat? There's piss all over my feet!"

I grin into my bowl.

Yeah, there's nothing like family at the holidays.

CHRISTMAS DINNER AT MY PARENTS' house is like something out of a movie: if the movie was a psychological thriller about how far a person can be pushed before they murder their entire family.

Austin and I have been watching a lot of true crime in our downtime.

We arrived at my parents' house at exactly five-fifteen, as per my mom's instructions. My parents' cookie-cutter colonial house is modern and well-kept in a neighborhood that could've been used to inspire the movie *The Stepford Wives.*

If it hadn't been for their Lexus in the driveway, I might've got lost. I wonder how many people have stumbled home from a cocktail party after too many drinks and walked into the wrong house.

Not that either of my parents would ever overindulge at a party. Or be invited to a party, to begin with.

"So, Jolie, how're you doing? What've you been up to lately?" my mom asks as she delicately spears a carrot with her fork.

Fucking the grumpy cop that, up until a few weeks ago,

drove me nuts. Oh, and he railed me against my bedroom door the other night, making me come so hard I thought I went blind for a second.

"Oh, you know. Keeping busy with work." I take a bite of squash and turn to my mom. "We actually just put on a very cool event at the studio. My friend Brenna owns the dog rescue in town and was looking for some fresh ideas to get adopters meeting dogs in a low-key environment. So we organized a Puppy Yoga adoption event." I smile down at my plate. "There were so many great dogs that got adopted. Some that had been there for years," I add, thinking of Cleo and Roland.

Roland was adopted by the Reids, a married couple of empty-nesters who were ecstatic to bring him home. I was so happy for them when Brenna told me the news, I actually teared up a bit.

Then there's Luke who has sent me a ton of cute pictures of Cleo settling into the house all day. I'm excited to get back to the apartment to FaceTime them.

"Oh, that sounds like such fun!" my mom exclaims.

"It sounds like an insurance claim waiting to happen. Did you even think of all the potential hazards of having a group of wild dogs in your place of business?" My father shakes his head disapprovingly. "Really, Jolie. Any sane *businessperson*," he spits out the word, like it's laughable that I could be considered a businessperson, "would have taken more than half a second to think about the risks. Did you even consider what might've happened if someone was bit?" My father throws the accusation at me and it hits true, knocking me back a step.

"Yes, I did. Which is why Brenna has insurance with the rescue for those types of things. Not that I don't trust my friend, but as a *business owner*," I say, accentuating the words, "I also spoke with my insurance broker who checked my plan and ensured I was covered." I take a slow breath, trying not to let him get to me. "Brenna has run tons of these events and nothing has ever gone wrong. She knows what animals to bring and how to maintain a calm environment."

My father scoffs. "Well, it's your business you're putting in jeopardy. I'm just saying, if you think reminding half-naked people to breathe will pay the bills when you're being sued because little Johnny got attacked by a wild animal, you're an idiot."

Every muscle in my body tenses at the criticism. There's a clanging from the other side of the table and I look up to see Austin standing, glaring down at my father. His chest is heaving and he's gripping his fork so hard, I'm surprised it's not bent.

"Something to say, son?" my father asks, barely acknowledging Austin's outrage. He takes a drink of his water, peering over the glass as if daring him to say something.

"Austin," I warn in a low voice. My brother looks back at me and I subtly shake my head. *I'm fine*, I mouth and it takes a second before he stiffly nods. Austin looks over at my mom, who's trembling like a leaf. He slowly lowers himself into his seat then picks up his drink and takes a long pull.

There's nothing I'd love more than to lay into my father. To call him out on all of his bullshit comments about my mom, my brother and me.

Austin did once. A long time ago, right before I left for Vancouver. My father was raging on and on about how I was throwing my life away by taking a year off before going to college. About how ridiculous he and my mom would look to their friends, having a daughter who would be selling herself on the streets within a year.

My brother snapped. I've never seen Austin so angry, so bloodthirsty. And I've seen him in some pretty gruesome fights—both on and off the ice.

Austin got up in my father's face, telling him how he should be proud of me and how smart I was to do what I wanted instead of what was expected of me. "Despite what a piece of shit father she had," Austin snarled at him.

He never saw my father's fist coming until it cracked him across the jaw.

Austin would've pummeled him into the ground, wouldn't have stopped until the years and years' worth of resentment was out of his system. And he would've enjoyed it as much as I would've.

If it wasn't for the sound of my mom crying, begging them both to stop.

Austin and I comforted my mom while my father stormed away, mumbling about "ungrateful children" before slamming his office door shut.

Austin and I made a pact that day that we'd keep things civil for my mom's sake. But we never forgot the look in my father's eyes when one of us stood up to him.

Fear.

"Austin, it's nice that your team has some time off over the holidays," my mom says, breaking the awkward silence. "I'm sure you could use the break."

My father scoffs. "Yeah, must be awful spinning around the ice all day, fighting off women. Oh, I forgot, your hand probably cramps from all the autographs." He chuckles at his own joke.

Austin's face drops and I can feel him deflate. As much as my father pisses him off, Austin still thinks he'll change one day. That he'll realize what he's missing out on and act like a normal father.

My anger sizzles beneath my skin as I watch my favorite person in the world shrink because of the one person who's supposed to lift him up.

"So, what've you been doing with your time off?" My mom tries again, passing a bowl of mashed potatoes to him. One look at her and my brother softens.

He piles some more mashed potatoes onto his plate. "Well, Jolie and I have been hanging out the last couple days, decorating my Christmas tree and—ow!" He shoots a glare at me that I gladly return as I move my foot from his shin. *What the hell*, he mouths.

My mom turns to me like a puppy who's just been kicked. "I thought you said you couldn't get a flight in until last night." I swear to god if I thought I could get away with stabbing my butter knife into my brother's thigh right now, I would.

"I was supposed to but, uh, there was a last minute flight that became available this week. So I came a little early to surprise Austin. For his birthday." I'm scrambling. I can feel her sad eyes on me as I fumble my way through the lie.

Austin has the decency to realize his mistake and jumps in. "Yeah, great surprise. For my birthday. So surprised!"

He's an awful liar.

"Austin's birthday is in February," my mom comments, her brows furrowed in confusion.

"That's why it was such a nice surprise!" Austin practically yells and my parents stare at him in bewilderment. Using our sibling telepathy that I haven't needed since high school, I shoot him a look. *Chill the fuck out. You're making it worse.*

He turns apologetic eyes on me. *I'm trying. I'm sorry.*

"Yeah, well, between Austin's hectic schedule, my work

schedule ramping up and Avery's wedding not far away, I wasn't sure when the next time I'd see him was," I say, slicing into my ham and popping a piece into my mouth, more for something to do than anything.

"Oh, yes. Avery's wedding. When is that again? I'd like to send a gift," my mom asks excitedly.

"Oh, you don't have to do that, Mom," I say at the same time my dad grumbles, "Absolutely not."

My mom's smile falls. "I just thought it would be a nice gesture, seeing as though our daughter is the maid of honor. I'm sure they'd appreciate a gift card for a couple's massage."

I look at my father for the first time tonight but he's staring down at his ham, angrily sawing at the meat. He points a forkful of ham at my mom. "You'll do no such thing. We don't even know these people and you're spending my money on them. With the way young people today get married at the drop of a hat, I bet they'll be divorced before that gift card expires."

"Of course, dear," my mom mumbles, eyes cast down and her smile long gone. It hurts to watch her spark stomped out in front of me. She doesn't even bother to argue anymore.

"That's enough." I slam my hand down on the table and my father looks me in the eye for the first time since I sat down tonight. "I'm so tired of you walking all over everyone, thinking we'll either scramble out of the way of your fat boot or be smooshed."

I shoot to my feet, not knowing what I'm doing but knowing I have too much adrenaline running through my veins to be still.

"Austin is an amazing athlete. He works harder than anyone I know. He's at the gym seven days a week and when he's not there, he's sleeping, eating, or on the ice. His whole life is hockey and you'd realize how much it means to him if you'd take your head out of your ass every once and a while."

"Excuse me—" my father starts but I don't let him continue. This is years in the making and I've got a lot to say.

"My friends are amazing and have accepted me in a way my own parents never could. They don't call me flighty or impulsive or reckless. They don't tell me I'm going to be a hooker one day because I decided college wasn't for me. They support me and love me." My voice threatens to crack, but I refuse to show any weakness right now.

Not in front of him.

"Avery and Matt have a better relationship than you've ever had with anyone in your life. You treat Mom like shit. You stifle her creativity and you manipulate her until she's hardly a shadow of her old self. Everyone hates you—including your own damn kids. And you couldn't give a shit!"

My father slowly rises from his seat. "You will not curse at me in my own house," he commands, his voice thinly veiled with rage.

I throw my hands up. "Are you fucking kidding me? That's what you got from all of that? Not that you're a shitty parent and husband?" I let out a humorless laugh. "Figures. I knew coming back here would be a mistake but I did it for Austin and Mom."

I smile, but it's an angry, vicious smile. "I've wanted to say this to you since I was seven years old and you took away my Pokémon cards and replaced them with Barbies. When you threw out every brightly colored shirt I owned when I was fourteen and replaced them with pastels. When you tried to keep Grandpa from giving me his car." I lean over, staring into his cold steel blue eyes that are nothing like mine. "It's you that's not good enough, not me. Not Austin. Not Mom. You. We don't need you. You're nothing but a poison in our lives, draining the life out of us. But only if we let you."

I stand up straight, pushing away from the table, refusing to take my eyes from his. "I'm done letting you."

I look over at Austin, who's grinning so wide, it's all I can see. He stands with me and nods.

I turn to my mom who has silent tears streaming down her face. I go to her, crouching down beside her and grabbing her hands. "Come with us, Mom. You have to see that he's not going to change. He's been chipping away at you for years. You're so much better without him." She cries harder. "You could come to Haven Bay. You can stay with me. Please, Mom."

She shakes her head, the tears falling harder. She looks up then. "Things don't have to be like this. He didn't mean it. He loves you both so much, he just doesn't know how to show it. He loves us."

Any hope I had of my mom leaving with us vanishes. Disappointment seeps in and I can feel my adrenaline starting to wane. Austin must see it because he's at my side a second later. "Come on, Jo. Let's go."

I stand and grab my purse as we start toward the door. Austin stops and turns to my father, his face deadly serious. "If you even think about taking this out on Mom, I will come back here and end you."

Our father has never been physical with any of us, except that one time with Austin, but I feel better knowing the threat is out there. My father doesn't acknowledge it, just continues to stare that cold, hateful glare at us.

We close the front door to my mom's crying and my father slamming his office door. We walk silently down the steps to my brother's car. We're quiet for a while as we drive back to the highway, the radio playing some rock song in the background.

Austin pulls onto the highway then reaches over and taps the screen of his phone. *A Boy Named Sue* by Johnny Cash fills the car, the same one my grandpa used to sing along to while my brother and I laughed about the idea of a boy named Sue.

There's a lot that needs to be said. What we're going to do about my mom. How the backlash of my outburst will affect her. How we're going to handle it when she inevitably reaches out, making excuses for him. At least I get to go home in a couple of days. Austin is stuck here with them, my mom's guilt trips only a short car ride away.

Instead, we sit quietly, letting Johnny Cash's deep and calming voice take us back in time to before things got so damn complicated.

When you're a kid, your parents are your first role models as to what love looks like. As you grow up, you assume that that's how love should be.

But Luke's right: what my parents have isn't love. At least not the healthy kind. People who love each other don't treat each other the way my parents do. My father would never tear my mom down the way he does if he truly loved her. He'd never make her cry, never force her to choose between her own children and her husband.

My mom thinks she loves my father but how can you ever truly love someone who forces you to hide who you are? Who treats your children the way my father treats us?

No, Luke's right.

That's not real love.

Austin turns to me offering me a small smile. "Merry Christmas, twerp."

I smile back at him. "Merry Christmas, Ares."

THE HAVEN TIMES

Proudly serving Haven Bay for over 100 years.

FREE

DEAR ANNIE

Your local source for advice on love, life and everything in between!

The answer to this week's trivia question (pg 9) is Halifax.

Q.

A.

Dear Annie,

My daughter and I have always been close. With two older brothers, she's always come to me about her problems and her exciting news. So when she decided that she was going to take a year off from school and travel Asia with her friends, she didn't hesitate to share her plans with me.

Or should I say, lack of plans.

My daughter is smart and has a good head on her shoulders. But sometimes she can be a bit naive. She sees travelling the world as a TikTok vacation complete with magical lands and extravagant accommodations.

I'm trying to bite my tongue when she talks about it but I can't just sit by and watch her make such a big mistake.

How do I convince her that her plans are a mistake without her hating me for ruining her fun?

Sincerely,
Worried Mom

Dear Worried Mom,

I know you're concerned for your daughter's safety. What mom wouldn't be?

But there's a difference between being concerned and being controlling.

One big part of becoming an adult, one that I've learned quite well over the years, is that you're bound to make mistakes. There's no way around it, that's just life.

But let me ask you this: do you think the trip is a mistake because she hasn't planned enough or because it's not what you would have chosen for her?

If it's the first, that's easy to deal with. Help her plan. She's young so you're probably right when you say that she's getting most of her ideas from TikTok. But that's where you come in. As her mother (not her friend), you should be guiding her while supporting her dream. Help her find out the best and safest spots to stay without going broke.

Show her how to use a map, show her how to manage her money so she's not out of funds by the first week. I guarantee this will bring you closer and strengthen your relationship.

But if it's the second reason, I have a hard message for you.

This is her life, not yours.

Just because you think travelling around the world instead of going to college is a mistake, doesn't mean it is. This could be the best thing that ever happens to her. She could discover a passion during this time that could change the course of her entire life.

You have no idea because none of us do.

At the end of the day, she's going to do what she wants to do, whether you approve of it or not. Don't ruin your relationship by trying to be right.

No one's ever going to thank you for telling them they were wrong. It just doesn't happen.

So instead of turning what could be something she'll

remember for the rest of her life into a scary life lesson, help her make it the best it can be.

You're a good mom. The fact that you're worried about her proves that. But there's only so long you can hold their hand before you need to let go and let them live their own lives.

Show up for her, Mom. It'll mean more to her than anything you could ever say.

Sincerely,
Annie

HOLIDAY BAKE SALE A HIT

The Lady Swans would like to thank all of the volunteers, participants, and patrons of their annual holiday bake sale.

With your help, the Lady Swans raised over $1,200.00.

The money raised will be donated to this year's charity recipient The Haven Bay Food Bank.

CHAPTER 46

JOLIE

"Josie. Josie!"

I look around the coffee shop at the two other people standing beside me. "Jolie?" I clarify, stepping toward the counter.

"Sure." She shoves the cup into my hands and turns back to start making the next order.

I lift the cup to my nose and sniff before taking a hesitant sip. Realizing the order is right, I take a longer drink then head for a table in the corner of the cafe. While I wait, I pull out my phone and tap on Luke's name. A second later, he picks up.

"Morning, pretty lady," he drawls.

"Are you talking to me or Cleo?"

"Don't even get me started," he groans. "You'd think that dog was eating from a silver spoon at Brenna's. Everything I do is wrong. I tried three different types of dog food before she'd eat, even though Brenna swears she was eating the first brand at the rescue."

"She's particular." I bite my lip to keep from laughing. "How'd you end up getting her to eat?"

"Well, I'm not gonna let her starve," Luke grumbles. "She kept looking at my chicken so I cut her up some pieces and mixed it into her kibble."

"Uh huh. And where did she sleep last night?"

"You should've heard her in the kennel. She was crying so loud, I thought the neighbors would hear."

I'm barely holding back my laugh now. "Mhmm. Where did she sleep, Luke?"

He mumbles something I can't make out.

"What's that?"

"In my bed, okay? She slept in my bed." I finally let out the laugh I've been holding in. "You should've seen her shivering in that little cage. She was scared. And that bed you got her was not thick enough. It was like sleeping on a brick!"

"Wow," I say, dragging out the word. "I never thought I'd see the day. Luke Brady's gone soft."

"Well, that's not a visual I need about my brother," a voice says from behind me. I spin in my seat to see Tori Brady standing behind me, a to-go cup in one hand and a muffin in the other. She points at the seat across from me and I nod quickly.

"Look, I gotta go. I'll talk to you later." I hang up before Luke can respond. "Hey! I didn't see you come in." I stand quickly, bringing her in for a hug. She warmly returns it, then takes a seat across from me. "Don't worry, that wasn't what it sounded like—"

Tori holds her hands up, cutting me off. "Nope, I don't wanna know," she replies. "What my brothers do in their spare time is none of my business."

I'm about to correct her again when she keeps talking. "Thanks for meeting me. Since I'm not able to make it back for the bachelorette, I wanted to make sure Avery got this in time." She hands a black gift bag across the table.

I lift an eyebrow as I take it. "Is this one of those famous Brady pranks where I give this to Avery in front of all of her friends and family and it's actually a hot pink dildo?"

Tori laughs. It's funny, I never noticed the similarities between her and her brothers until I started seeing Luke. But the sound of her laugh, the way the corner of her eyes crinkle; it's pure Luke.

"No, I promise." She smiles. "You can check the bag if you want."

I tuck the bag away under the table. "Nah, that's okay. I'll wait and be surprised with everyone else." I take a drink of my tea. "It sucks that you won't be able to make it back for the bach next week."

Tori picks off a piece of her muffin and pops it into her mouth. "I know. I had it booked off for months but at the last minute, my boss decided she needed me for a fundraiser that's the same weekend. I tried telling her I'd help with the set up the night before then fly out early the next morning, but she insisted I needed to be there for the entire event," she explains, clearly frustrated.

"That's really shitty of her. And you couldn't tell her no?"

Tori huffs out a humorless laugh. "You don't tell someone like Simone Bianci no. Not unless you want to flush your career down the toilet."

"Ah." I nod in understanding. "I'm sorry."

She stares down at her muffin, picking it apart angrily. "Yeah, well. It is what it is. Hopefully she'll finally give me that promotion she's been hinting at for the last couple years." She lifts her head and smiles. "Then it'll all be worth it."

I smile back then lean forward. "I hope you don't mind me saying this, but you look...different than when I saw you in Haven Bay. Not in a bad way," I quickly amend, "I just mean, you look so..." I wave a hand over her body and to my relief, she laughs.

"Professional?"

"Yes! I would've walked right by you if you hadn't come to me first."

It's true. The Tori I met in Haven Bay was cool and relaxed with her cropped top and cut offs. A little bit wild. The Tori sitting across from me is polished from her sleek ponytail to her tight pencil skirt to her designer heels. I don't even want to know how much those shoes cost.

Actually, yes I do because I want a pair in my size.

"Yeah, I understand," she says, playing with her coffee cup. "In Haven Bay, people know me as the wild child Brady girl. The impulsive, fun girl who got caught driving her mom's van when she was fourteen." My eyes widen and she smirks. "My mom wouldn't take me to see a concert two towns over because it was a school night. So I took myself." I laugh at the image of Tori stealing her mom's minivan when she probably could barely reach the pedals.

"Then when I left after high school," Tori continues, "I recreated myself and became this professional, driven, perfectionist." She shrugs, looking out the window of the busy city street. "I guess I have a hard time figuring out which one is the real me: the wild child or the career woman."

She looks back with a sheepish smile. "I bet you didn't expect a little psychological analysis with your breakfast, did you?"

I look down at my tea, thoughtfully. "You might not believe me, but we're not that different. I was also a wild child but my wild streak continued into adulthood. My father always hated it and tried to shape me into something else because of it." I look up at her with a sad smile. "He still is."

Tori reaches across the table to give my hand a sympathetic squeeze. "I get what my brother sees in you," she says.

My eyes widen in surprise. "Oh, I...we're not.."

She chuckles. "You don't have to worry. I won't say anything if you don't want me to. I figure if you were being open about whatever it was that was between you, I would've heard about it from my mom or Avery by now."

"How'd you know?" I ask, not denying it but not exactly admitting anything either.

She leans forward in her seat. "Please. I saw you go into the garage after him at the engagement party and you both came out looking hella horny." My jaw drops. "A little confused. But definitely horny." She shrugs while I still gape at her. "I figured you'd either had a fight or a quickie. You talking to him when I walked in confirmed it."

I think about denying it, but honestly, it's nice to have someone know. Someone who knows Luke and I and can give me a (partially) unbiased opinion without worrying about the entire town knowing a minute later.

So, I tell her everything. And I mean, everything. The fighting, our first kiss, being snowed in together, the back hallway of the bar. Okay, maybe not everything, but the sister-of-the-guy-you're-sleeping-with-approved highlights.

"We decided to keep it a secret but now we're over a month into this and it's...really good." Not sure what to do with my hands as I pour out my secrets, I fiddle with my coffee cup lid. "I guess I'm not sure if the only reason it's going well is *because* it's a secret. Do I even want to go public? This could still all end in disaster. I told you what my dad's like. What if we end up like my parents?"

Geez. For someone who had trouble opening up to her friends and family a week ago, I sure have no problem unloading on someone I've only talked to a handful of times. I suddenly feel like bolting into traffic and finding the nearest taxi, but something has me glued to my seat.

Tori stays suspiciously quiet and it only makes me fidget more.

Finally, just before my heart claws its way out of my chest, she responds. "I think comparing your relationship with Luke to your parents' is a disservice to both of you." Her head tilts sympathetically. "I know you've got some shit to unpack with your parents and I don't know the whole story, so who am I to say what's what. But I know my brother. And while he's a Type A control freak with overprotective tendencies," she smirks and I can't help but chuckle at her description, "he's not manipulative. He might like to have control but he's not controlling. He would never try to change who you are at the heart of things."

I'm still fidgeting in my chair, unsure how to respond. Luckily, Tori continues before I can attempt to fumble together my thoughts.

"And even if he was some piece of shit who tried to turn you into something you're not, you would never let him. You need to trust yourself more. I barely know you and I already know that any man or woman who tried to force you into anything you didn't want to do would have an easier time convincing Dottie to go to a nursing home."

I laugh but her words continue to ping-pong around in my head.

All this time I've been doing everything in my power to do the opposite of what my parents would do, avoiding any man who reminded me even slightly of my father. Making drastic, life-changing decisions—like moving across the country—because I knew it was something my mother would never do.

Could it really be that simple?

People can't change me, can't control me if I don't let them.

My father couldn't do it, though he tried for years.

And deep in my heart, I know Luke would never control me. He'd never even try.

But there's a small part of me that is still scared. How does someone trust another person that much? How do you trust yourself?

It happens all the time to people a hell of a lot stronger than me. Look at Avery. She might've been young when she fell for her first husband but you'd never think someone as strong as her would end up in a toxic relationship.

Who's to say that I'd be as strong as she was and leave before there was nothing left? Hell, it's in my DNA.

I realize I've been quiet for too long so I force a smile and grab the black bag from beneath our table. "I appreciate the kind words. I hate to trauma dump and run, but I'm supposed to meet my brother soon. It's my last night and he wants to do something special. Which to him probably means takeout and a Lethal Weapon marathon." We both stand and I wrap her in a hug. "It was great seeing you." I turn to leave then stop. "Um, do you mind not telling anyone about...you know...all this?"

Tori mimics zipping her lips. "Your secret is safe with me. Though if you're interested, I vote you give your relationship with Luke a shot. You'd be good for each other."

I can't think of anything to say so I just nod. We stand

and head for the door. Tori gives me a quick hug then waves goodbye as she strolls down the sidewalk.

The cold winter air takes my breath away as I turn to head in the opposite direction. I pull the zipper of my coat up higher, tucking my chin into the collar as I make the short walk back to my brother's apartment.

Maybe the cold air will clear my head enough to give me some answers.

LUKE

"**S**hut up, you piece of shit. I heard you the first time."

My kitchen is full of thick black smoke as I grab the fire blanket from under my sink and toss it onto the flaming pan. I probably look like a lunatic right now, waving my dish towel under the fire detector as its screams fill the kitchen. Cleo is standing on the arm of the couch, her high pitch yapping backing me up as I curse out the stupid alarm.

I hate burning food. I'm an excellent cook and I pride myself on my cooking abilities. People who take as much pride in their food as I do, don't burn it.

The alarm finally halts, though its shrill sound still echoes in my head, causing my already splitting headache to worsen.

Tonight was supposed to be a romantic night-in with Jolie on her first night back from her visit with her family. If this was a normal relationship, I would've picked her up at the airport, maybe surprised her at the terminal with flowers and a bag of those peanut M&Ms she loves so much.

But this isn't a normal relationship and someone might see us driving home together and ask questions. Instead, she's driving back from the airport alone in her car that she left in the overnight lot.

At this point, I don't give a shit about other people's opinions. All the reasons we had for keeping this a secret have gone out the window for me.

I'm sick of not being able to touch her in public.

I'm sick of not being able to bring her a blueberry scone because I was thinking about her in case someone's in the studio and questions why I'm there.

I'm sick of pretending I haven't been thinking about her every second of every day since that damn kiss in the fall. Even before that, if I'm being honest with myself.

I know she's not ready to go public—I can tell by the way she hides her car in my garage or insists that I park in the public lot a block away.

But I also see the way she looks at Matt and Avery with a longing that has nothing to do with either of them. The way she stands a little closer to me when we're out with our friends. The way she makes excuses to stop in at the diner when she knows I'll be there.

She wants this relationship just as much as I do. But for some reason I can't figure out, she's holding back.

Jolie's like a stray kitten, craving affection and shelter but she's just as likely to take off in the other direction if you make any sudden movements. So I won't rush her.

But that doesn't mean that I can't coax her out from her hiding place.

Mind made up, I scrape our charred dinner into the garbage can and toss the burnt pan into the sink. "Be back soon, Cleo," I call over my shoulder. She barely acknowledges me from her spot on top of the stack of pillows on the couch as I grab my keys and coat, and then lock the door quickly behind me.

Fifty-eight minutes later, I'm standing in front of the airport baggage claim that the woman at the desk said belonged to Jolie's flight. People start filing out of the terminal so I strain my neck, trying to catch a glimpse of her tall frame and chestnut hair.

Finally, I spot her walking out, chatting with an elderly couple. They laugh at something she says then take turns giving her a hug. The corner of my lips turn up. Leave it to Jolie to make friends on a four hour flight.

The couple walks away, waving as they go and I take a second to watch Jolie.

She's dressed casually in leggings and an oversized Toronto Storm sweater. Her hair is tossed haphazardly into a bun on the top of her head while she adjusts the straps of her backpack.

Her head lifts and I can tell the exact moment when she sees me in the crowd. She stops midstep, staring at me with an unreadable expression. My gut twists uncomfortably and I fight the urge to turn around and leave.

I should've asked her first. Maybe she doesn't want me here. It was presumptuous of me to assume she'd be happy to see me. I'm not her boyfriend. I probably look like an obsessed stalker—

The wide smile that spreads over her face slams down any negative thoughts I might've had. In fact, the sight of her rushing toward me erases all thought from my mind. She jumps into my waiting arms, claiming my mouth in a kiss that borders on inappropriate for an airport welcome.

After not nearly long enough, she pulls away, smiling up at me. "What're you doing here? I thought I was meeting you at your house."

I lift a shoulder, unable to hold in my smile. "I wanted to see you."

Her smile turns devilish. "So, you missed me so badly that you couldn't wait an extra couple hours for me to drive to you?"

My face turns serious. "Yeah, sweetheart. I did."

Her expression softens and she places a short kiss against my lips. "Good. Me too."

JOLIE

"Who would you most want to share a jail cell with?" Brenna reads the card aloud then picks up the six cards in front of her.

"So, that's one vote for Franny and five votes for Jolie," she says and the roomful of women erupts into laughter.

Brenna, Tammy, Franny, Angie, Avery and I are in Avery's living room for her bachelorette. We're playing a game Tammy brought where you ask the group a question then vote for who you think best applies to the question. Some of the answers have been pretty tame while others... well, let's just say I'm glad my mom isn't here for this. Luckily, Angie and Franny are both pretty open-minded and fun or else the penis crown I bought Avery would be completely inappropriate. We'll just have to make sure to get rid of the penis decorations before Gavin comes home from his dad's tomorrow.

That would be an awkward conversation I wouldn't want to have.

My mouth drops open in surprise. "Me? Why me?"

"Because you'd kick anyone's ass who tried to shank me," Angie jokes. I have to laugh because she's not wrong.

"Alright, alright," I reply, reaching for my pink mocktail. "You've got me there."

The game comes to an abrupt end half an hour later when Franny's voted most likely to host an orgy.

"On that very graphic note," Angie teases, standing up from her place on the couch. "Time for gifts!"

We all cheer, as Angie and Franny grab the gift bags we hid in Angie's bedroom. Avery, the sweetheart, is trying to refuse them but we ignore her.

"I know you said you didn't want a bridal shower but you have to let us spoil you a little bit," Angie says, as she drops three large bags and a wrapped box in front of where Avery sits on the couch.

"If it makes you feel better, just think of them as Christmas presents," I tell her, sliding onto the couch beside her.

"Then that means I get to give you presents, too," Avery points out, but I quickly shake my head.

"Your friendship is gift enough." I bat my eyelashes, making her laugh.

She mimics gagging. "Gross. I'll accept these gifts if you promise to never say anything as corny as that again."

I throw my head back laughing. "Deal."

Avery finally relents and sets to work opening the gifts Angie and Franny place in front of her.

Brenna's gift is a blown up picture of Avery and Matt from their engagement session in the fall.

Tammy's gift to Avery is a full-service spa day at Silver Fox Lodge.

My gift is a star map of Matt and Avery's wedding date using a constellation prediction website. After witnessing the breathtaking view of the stars in the vineyard, I knew I wanted to capture what is sure to be the most magnificent view on their wedding night.

Franny's gift to Avery is the earrings that she wore on her wedding day. "But what about Tori?" Avery asks through watery eyes.

Franny smiles through her own teary eyes. "I have my necklace earmarked for her. But I promised myself my earrings and bracelet would go to my future daughters-in-law. Your dress wouldn't suit a bracelet so I thought you might like these. But I can show you the bracelet if you'd prefer it instead. Or you might have your own earrings in mind..."

Avery silences her with a hug. "The earrings are perfect. I love them. Thank you."

By the time it's Angie's turn, the room is laced with emotion. Avery swipes under her eyes before taking the envelope that Angie hands her. She slides a thumb under the flap and unfolds the paper inside, her expression unreadable as her eyes read over the page. Her eyes widen as she reads it again, her expression turning into one of shock and bewilderment.

"What is it?" I ask, unable to hold in my curiosity.

Avery stares up at her mom, her eyes watering again as Angie stares back at her calmly. "She gave us the house."

Varying gasps and "oh my god" erupt around the room. The only person who looks unsurprised is Franny; which I'm assuming means she knew about her best friend's plan. A smiling Angie hasn't taken her eyes off her daughter, who's alternating between staring at her mom and down at the paper in disbelief.

"Mom," Avery finally manages, "you can't do this. This is your home. You worked so hard..."

Angie places a hand on Avery's knee. "I worked as hard

as I did so that I could do something like this for you one day." She gives her knee a squeeze. "You're building your family and you need a house to do that in. I know we were planning on expanding anyway but now it's officially yours." She smiles, brushing a stray tear off Avery's cheek. "You can keep it and expand or you can sell it and buy something you both want. Either way, it's yours to decide."

Avery leans into her mom's hand. "I know I can speak for Matt when I say there's nowhere we'd rather live than right here with you."

"Oh, thank god," Franny mumbles under her breath. Avery and Angie laugh. "Sorry, but I'd miss you all way too much. Besides, I'm too old to break in a new neighbor."

Avery smiles, turning back to give her mom a hard look. "But I don't care what you say, you're staying with us—no matter where we are. We wouldn't have it any other way."

Thankfully, Angie's MS has been slow progressing. Most days, you'd never even know she had it. But I know Avery worries about the future and doesn't want her mother living alone. Avery and Angie have already had many conversations about Angie's living arrangements, so Avery's comments aren't a surprise.

"You drive a hard bargain, daughter of mine." Angie smiles back.

Once the tears have been wiped away, I lean forward to grab Tori's gift bag from the floor and pass it to Avery. "This one is from Tori."

Avery reaches into the bag and pulls out a glossy blue book. *Bakersfield High* is written in script along the top. She stares at it in wonder, running her hand over the cover.

"It's a yearbook from my freshman year in high school," she announces. "How did she get a hold of it?"

"Some of Matt's stuff must've got mixed in with hers

when she moved out," Franny comments, peering over Avery's shoulder.

Avery flips open the book, carefully leafing through the pages. She points out pictures of her and Matt, Matt and Luke, her on the softball team. Suddenly, she bursts into laughter. We crowd around her to see what's got her so worked up.

It's a photo of what looks like a young Matt and Rhett. They're dressed in black baggy coats with thick gold chain necklaces and black bowler hats. "That's from the talent show. When they dressed up like Run-DMC and lip synced *It's Tricky*." We all laugh at their ridiculous outfits.

She continues flipping through the pages until she gets to the back of the book where there's various messages printed in messy handwriting. I scan the page over Avery's shoulder, reading the funny and sometimes unoriginal messages printed there.

I stop when I see familiar handwriting—Avery's. I read aloud the message.

Matt

No matter what life throws at us, thanks for always being my constant. You'll never know what your friendship means to me. Whether it's being my pranking guinea pig, telling me a lame joke to make me laugh or giving me a shoulder to cry on, you've always been there for me. I hope you always will be. To quote Squints, "For-ev-er!"

Avery

If there were ever even the slightest doubt that Matt and Avery weren't destined for each other, that would've squashed it.

———

A FEW HOURS LATER, I'm all bundled up in my winter coat and toque as I walk along the sidewalk, staring up at the snowy star-filled sky.

It's a surprisingly mild night for the last few days of December so despite Brenna's many offers to give me a ride home, I decide to walk the short distance from Avery's house to my apartment. As I meander along the sidewalk, the twinkling lights of the Christmas decorations smile down on me. Even though Christmas is over, the town keeps the lights hung until the end of January, saying the decorations are a mood booster during the dreary months of winter.

Nights like tonight have me feeling so grateful that I decided to take a chance on myself so many years ago by leaving home. Luke's words from our first night at the lodge echo in my head: *Whether you want to admit it or not, you're fearless.*

It sure as hell didn't feel that way at the time. I was a scared, naive teenager who thought she had the world by the balls. I smile, shaking my head. Little did I know what I was getting myself into.

But like Luke said, it was brave. Impulsive, maybe. But still brave.

I wish I could go back and hug eighteen-year-old me, alone in that small apartment in a new city. Tell her everything turns out just the way it's supposed to.

My phone vibrates in my pocket. I pull it out to see another text from Luke. They decided to throw Matt's bachelor party the same night as Avery's so they're all uptown at The Dive. Somehow, they managed to convince Mr. Responsible Luke to let his hair down.

He's been drunk texting me all night.

LUKE

I miss yiu

I grin down at my phone. I can already tell by his texting that the poor guy's going to be hurting in the morning.

JOLIE

How ya feeling, big guy?

LUKE

Terrible. Matt made me do another shotski with them.

I snort. A shotski, for anyone who doesn't live within walking distance of a snow hill, is a long ski with four or five holes cut out in the middle of it to hold shot glasses. The idea is that five people line up, then tip the ski at the same time, each drinking down a shot from said ski.

It's ridiculous but a tradition in snow-loving towns like ours.

Yeah, he's definitely going to feel that in the morning.

LUKE

I miss you.

And Cleo.

What do you think she's doing right now?

Seeing as though Cleo has exactly three hobbies which include eating, sleeping and glaring at anyone who dares walk past her, I'd say she's not exactly missing her owner.

But for some reason the two have formed a strange people-hating bond so I don't dare break his heart by telling him that.

JOLIE

I'm sure she's missing you too.

LUKE

You should come pick me up.

I want to see my girls.

My heart tugs involuntarily. *My girls.* Why does he have to be so adorable? I had planned to go home, throw on a dirty audiobook and maybe work on a few questions for the column before hitting the hay. But how can I resist him when he's saying things like that?

LUKE

Please?

I bite my bottom lip but it does nothing to stop the grin from breaking out on my face.

JOLIE

Fine. Let me go home and grab Blue.

I go to put my phone away but it vibrates again before I can.

LUKE

My truck's better in the snow.

I roll my eyes at that. Even when he's drunk, he's still concerned about my safety. But since getting Blue would take another ten minutes, I concede and turn toward The Dive.

JOLIE

Be there in two.

By the time I get to the parking lot, Luke is leaning

against his truck. Even from here, I can see the slight sway in his body, proving how drunk he is.

"How did you convince them to let you leave like this?" I stifle a laugh as he leans forward to push off the truck and nearly falls forward before catching himself.

"Told them I was getting a ride home with a *friend*," he mumbles, spitting out the last word like it personally insulted him. I raise an eyebrow at that but don't question it.

I look toward the bar. "And they're not all out here to see what kind of *friend* picks you up at one in the morning?"

Luke hands me the keys to the truck and stumbles over to the passenger seat. I open the driver's side door and, despite my 5'9 frame, have to pull myself into the truck. Once seated, I look over to where Luke's head is leaned back against the headrest, eyes closed.

"Nope," he says, letting the last syllable out with a pop. "Only told Rhett I was leaving. Made him promise not to tell anyone."

That makes sense. Rhett might give him shit from time to time, but he's a good friend and even better with secrets.

Including his own.

I turn out of the parking lot and before I'm even fully on the road, Luke's softly snoring beside me. When I pull into his garage a few minutes later, it takes me nearly double the time it took to drive here to get him awake and out of the truck.

Finally inside, I shut the door behind us and start removing my toque while Luke stumbles back to the garage door and turns the lock. I shake my head, smiling.

Apparently, some things are so ingrained that even alcohol can't dull them. Like safety.

"Cleo!" Luke calls as he wanders down the hall. "Cleo, baby. Where are youuuu?" He sings the last part like a children's show character and this time I have to laugh. He's so damn cute when he's drunk, I can't handle it.

He gasps as he turns the corner into the living room and hurries over to where she's perched on top of a pile of pillows—her signature spot.

"Hiiii baby!" He drops to his knees in front of her, running a loving hand down her back. "Daddy missed you. Did you miss me?"

Daddy?! Oh, god. I'm never going to let him live that one down.

But to my absolute shock, Cleo licks his hand, her scrawny tail wagging excitedly as Luke showers her in praise. It's only when he starts to sway on the floor, leaning his head against the couch as a pillow do I step in.

"Alright, *Daddy*. Time to get up." I tug on his arm a few times and luckily, he takes the hint and helps me pull him to his feet.

"You want me to be your daddy, sweetheart?" Luke smiles devilishly but it's ruined by the slur in his words. I figure I have five minutes max to get him to his bed before he passes out completely. Poor guy's become a lightweight in his old age.

"Oh, honey. You couldn't be anyone's daddy right now." I pull him along toward the bedroom, turning off the lights as we go. When we step inside the bedroom, Luke lets go of my hand then drops like a falling tree onto the mattress. He rolls onto his back and moans.

Not knowing exactly what type of hangover Luke might be looking at in the morning, I search through his ensuite bathroom for a couple of ibuprofens, a glass of water and a garbage pail. Placing them all beside him, I turn to go.

"Where do you think you're going?" Luke mumbles from the bed. I thought he was asleep.

"Home," I whisper, knowing he's seconds from falling asleep.

He shakes his head then opens his arms to me, eyes still closed.

"It's fine, Luke. I can walk home."

He doesn't bother answering or dropping his arms. He merely opens and closes his hands, gesturing for me to come closer.

Despite everything, I smile. "Fine." I take off my sweater, leggings and bra then pull on one of Luke's shirts from his dresser. I climb into his bed but before I can settle in, he wraps his big arms around me, pulling me into his chest. Then with a content sigh, he promptly falls asleep, leaving me staring at the ceiling wondering what this growing feeling in my chest is.

And how scared I am to find out.

THE HAVEN TIMES

Proudly serving Haven Bay for over 100 years.

FREE

DEAR ANNIE

Your local source for advice on love, life and everything in between!

The answer to this week's trivia question (pg 9) is Arizona.

Q.

Dear Annie,

I've always wanted to own my own business. I've spent my whole life working for other people, building up their own dreams wondering when I would get the chance to follow my own.

Well, I'm done waiting. I'm ready to jump into the world of entrepreneurship. The only problem is my husband is not onboard.

I should preface this by saying, my husband has always been extremely supportive. He even took a break from his career to stay home with the kids so that I could go back to school. Whenever I talked about pursuing my dream of owning my own business, he has been nothing but encouraging.

Until I brought it up last week about quitting my job and giving my dream a real shot. Then he started asking questions and pointing out flaws in my plans

When I told him I thought he'd be happy for me, he hesitated before telling me he didn't know if it was a great time. We got into

When I told him I thought he'd be happy for me, he hesitated before telling me he didn't know if it was a great time. We got into a big fight and I'm honestly not sure where we stand right now on the topic.

I'm heartbroken and confused. He's always been so encouraging of my dreams, so his sudden change of heart has me bewildered.

I really don't want to do this without him but I'm hurt that he doesn't believe in me enough to support me.

Do I do this without him? Or do I give up my dream?

Sincerely,
Devastated

A.

Dear Devastated,

First of all, I want to start off by saying I'm so proud of you for wanting to follow your dreams! This is such an exciting time in your life and I'm sorry that you didn't get the reaction that you expected from your husband.

With that being said, I don't think either of you are in the wrong here.

Let me ask you this, did you communicate effectively with your husband that this was something you were interested in doing soon or was it always a "someday" dream? If you never gave your husband any indication that this was a short term goal instead of long term, he may have been blindsided by this decision.

As someone who is prone to both impulsive decisions and outbursts of anger when people don't agree with those decisions, I can understand where both of you are coming from.

Quitting your job is a big deal—especially if you have a family to think about. Now, I don't say this to sound condescending as I'm sure you've given it a lot of thought as to how you would make ends meet during the beginning stages of starting a business. But I think that it's worth repeating.

This doesn't just affect you, it affects your whole family. There's a lot to unpack here that I'm not sure I can fit on one page so I will say this. Communication is key. Always, always, always.

Taking your emotions out of the equation, did your husband have valid points as to why he didn't think it was a good idea? Is he concerned about money? Is he concerned about taking on the majority of the workload while the business gets set up? Is he concerned about the added stress that comes with starting a business?

Or does he just not like change?

My suggestion to you is for both of you to sit down in a time where emotions are set aside and to discuss the logistics of your business plan together. Maybe once he goes over your plan, this might give him some peace of mind. If not, dig deep to find out the source of his unease.

If the time isn't right to follow your dreams, for whatever reason, please know that doesn't mean you won't be able to in the future.

Sincerely,
Annie

CHAPTER 48

JOLIE

The smell of bacon is the first thing I notice before I've even opened my eyes. The second is that I'm alone in Luke's bed. I finally pry my eyes open to the sun streaming in through the window beside me. In his drunken haze, Luke must've forgotten to pull down his blackout blinds.

Speaking of...

I sit up and look around the room. Luke's nowhere in sight. I half expected him to be in the bathroom puking his guts out by how drunk he was last night. But the bathroom is also empty.

It's then that I notice the faint sound of music playing from outside the bedroom door. I climb out of bed and, in just Luke's shirt and my underwear, follow the music into the kitchen.

I stop suddenly at the threshold of the kitchen, shocked by what I see.

Luke Brady cooking at the stove—*singing*. And it's not just any song he's singing. Lizzo's *Good as Hell* is pumping through the Bluetooth speaker on the island while Luke sings every word perfectly. Even Ariana Grande's part.

Did I die last night? Is this what heaven looks like?

Luke turns and spots me. Without missing a beat, he dances over to me and, using his spatula as a microphone, sings about doing a hair toss and checking his nails.

"What're you—" My shock gives way when he passes the "microphone" to me. I only hesitate a second before grabbing the spatula from his hands and joining him in belting out the song.

If anyone walked in on us right now, we'd probably look like a couple of lunatics, me bouncing around, shaking my ass while Luke twists his hips. But I can honestly say that singing and dancing around the kitchen with Luke has got to be the most fun I've had in a long time.

I can't help but marvel at how easy it all feels.

Natural.

Could this be what a real relationship with Luke would be like? Sunday mornings spent laughing and eating breakfast together, dancing around the kitchen and singing Lizzo?

Shouldn't it be more complicated than this?

The song ends and *The Night We Met* by Lord Huron starts up. Luke immediately grabs my hand, singing along as he pulls me close. Just as quickly, he spins me forward, my hand clasped in his as tugs me back into him. My heart flips in surprise as he dips me low.

My answering laugh is light and carefree as he smiles down at me.

"I thought you said you don't dance," I tease.

"I don't," he answers solemnly. Then he lifts me back up and pulls me close. Together, we sway to the music as one slow song bleeds into the next. I'm not sure how long we stay like that, dancing in his kitchen, but one thing I know for sure.

I'm in love with Luke Brady.

Shit.

———

AFTER MY EARTH-SHATTERING REALIZATION, I somehow managed to keep the panic at bay long enough to finish the delicious breakfast Luke made for us. Not long after, he was called into the station, despite it being his day off, and Sandy sent me a text asking to meet her at the office later this morning. Luke gave me a lift on his way to the station, where I made sure to duck out of his truck at the corner so no one would see us. I walked the rest of the way to the newspaper office.

Since it's a Sunday, the office is locked so I knock on the glass door. A few moments later, Sandy unlocks the door. "Sorry about that. I came through the back and forgot to unlock the door. Come on in."

I follow her into the interview room. "No biggie. How was your holiday?"

Sandy takes a seat across from me. "Good. We stayed at my daughter's house in Red Deer for the week. As much as I'm going to miss the grandkids, it's nice to be back home in the quiet." She laughs. "How about you? I heard you flew home to visit your family."

I force a tight smile at the mention of my parents. "It was nice. But like you said, it's good to be home."

"Well, I'm happy that you were able to make it out. Christmas without family doesn't feel like Christmas." She smiles warmly. For a moment, I think about what it might be like to have a normal family holiday. Where you're not tiptoeing around, trying to keep the peace. Only for the whole thing to end in a fight anyway.

"I'll just jump right into why I wanted to talk to you so we can both go back to enjoying our Sunday." She crosses her hands in front of her. "I had an idea yesterday that I couldn't get out of my head. I want to do a grand reveal of *Dear Annie.*"

Sandy continues, despite my shocked expression. "I know you signed up for this thinking it would be anonymous so if you don't want to do it, we can keep going the way we are.

"That being said, I think there's pros and cons to both sides. Some might be more inclined to write in a letter, not knowing who's on the other end. You also don't have to worry about being hounded while you're out, being asked for advice while you're eating at the diner or something like that." She leans forward in her seat eagerly. "But I also think there's some benefits to putting a face to the name. I think there's a certain level of trust that you gain when you know the person behind the article. You're a well-liked member of the community. People trust and respect your opinion. That's why I asked you in the first place.

"If we decide to do this, I'd like it to be a live event. A big reveal of *Dear Annie* with a live Q&A. You'll be given a list of the questions ahead of time so you're not just making up answers on the spot but they'll be read in front of the crowd."

I'm silent for a second, absorbing her rapid-fire reasoning. I mull it over, weighing the pros and cons.

It would be nice to get this secret off my chest. I hate feeling like I'm lying to my friends. I'm not worried about people bothering me on the streets. I'll just tell them to write it in a letter for the paper. Or for any persistent people, I can do my best on the spot. This town already doesn't respect boundaries—this should be no different.

But what if people are disappointed when they find out it's me? People might think I'm unqualified—which technically I am—to give out advice. What if I give someone bad advice and they hate me forever because of it?

My head is spinning with the possibilities—both good and bad—when Sandy squeezes my hand.

"I can hear you freaking out from here," she comments, smiling. "We don't have to do anything you don't feel comfortable with. If you decide this isn't what you want to do, I'll forget about the whole thing and we'll continue on like we have been."

I know she's right. Sandy's nothing if not fair. If I told her no, she'd never bring it up again. But while the word is on the edge of my tongue, I can't seem to spit it out.

Do I want to do this?

Could I do this?

"What if people think I'm not good enough?" I blurt out instead.

Sandy surprises me by shrugging. "Fuck 'em."

A laugh bursts out of my chest in surprise. In all the years I've known her, I've never heard Sandy curse before.

Is it really that easy though? As much as I try to live by the philosophy of, "don't let someone's opinion of you matter", I can't help thinking what people's reactions will be when they find out who's behind the columns.

"You're good enough, Jolie. You're more than good enough. Anyone who thinks otherwise is a twit." I smile at that. "But trust me when I say, this town thinks the world of you. You can do this." She releases my hand and sits back in her chair. "Take the week to think about it and get back to me. If we're going to go through with the event, I'd like to do it two Sundays from now so I'll need to book the rec center."

She stands and though my mind is still reeling, I do the same. She walks me to the door where I promise to give her an answer by the end of the week. Then I'm out on the sidewalk, mulling over the idea.

Could I do this? Is this something I want to do? I wish I could ask someone's opinion but the only people who know about my alter persona are Sandy and Luke.

Maybe I could call Luke and talk this out with him. Despite being against the column in the first place, he knows this town better than anyone. Besides, I think he's starting to come around to *Dear Annie*. It helps that the craziness has calmed down a bit since the column first came out.

I did hear about another break out from the retirement residence last week, but I like to think that one wasn't because of me.

"Jolie!" I turn to see Avery hurrying across the street toward me.

"Hey, I didn't expect to see you up already. I figured you'd be in bed for hours still." It's only ten but when I left, Avery, Angie, and Franny were still going strong with the drinks.

"I went to bed not long after you all left. My mom and Franny were up until who knows when, so they're both passed out in my mom's room still."

I smile at that. Angie and Franny have the best friendship. Even in their fifties with their own chaotic lives, they make time for each other. Their wine nights are known to end in sleepovers. Franny's live-in boyfriend, Pete, has had to tuck them into bed on more than one occasion.

"Want to grab brunch at the diner?" Avery asks. "Matt's

still sleeping but I left him a note so he might end up there later, too."

"Definitely. Let me stop at my apartment quick to grab my purse and then we can go."

Avery falls into step beside me as we make the short walk back to my apartment. She tells me how Rhett practically carried Matt through the door about an hour after the girls left. It seems like Luke wasn't the only one feeling good last night.

To my relief, she doesn't mention anything about Luke, making me think Rhett kept his promise.

Which should be good news. So, why do I feel disappointed?

Thankfully, we arrive at my studio so I don't have to dive too far into that rabbit hole. I pull out my keys to unlock the door but find that the door is already open.

That's strange. I could've sworn I locked the door last night.

All thought trails off when I push open the door and look around my studio. Or should I say what's left of it.

It's a war zone. Chairs are strewn about, poles are lying haphazardly all around the studio. Yoga mats are shredded to pieces on the floor as well as my towels. Not a single piece of equipment is where I left it the night before.

But the worst is the wall of mirrors. One section is smashed to pieces, a chair lying on its side beneath it. Someone must've used the chair to smash the mirrors. A message is spray painted across the only unmarred section with the words, "**BITCHES GET WHAT'S COMING TO THEM**" in big, dripping red letters.

I'm numb as I look helplessly around the room.

Someone broke into my studio while I was gone. I locked the door; I know I did. What if I had been home? If

Luke didn't text me, I might've been. Whoever did this could've walked up those stairs and found me in my apartment.

My apartment. My eyes dart for the closed door of my apartment. Did they go inside my apartment? That's my place. My safe space. And someone might've been inside it.

The more I look around the room, the more I think about someone forcing their way inside. My heart pounds inside my chest. Harder and harder it drums until it's the only thing I can hear. My hands start to tremble and it feels like all the blood has drained from my body. I stare at the threatening words until they start to blur. And though my mind is spinning with every "what if" imaginable, one thought stands front and center among the rest.

"Call Luke," I manage to croak out to Avery.

Then everything goes black.

CHAPTER 49

LUKE

I swing my truck over to the curb, slam the gear shift into park, and I'm out the door before the tires stop moving. I take off at a run, not caring that this technically isn't a parking space and I may or may not be blocking a driveway.

The only thing that matters is waiting for me on the other side of Amaryllis' big white door.

When Avery called me, my back stiffened. We're relatively close but we're not call-each-other-on-the-phone-just-to-chat close. So when I saw her name light up my phone, I was already on alert.

Then she told me that Jolie's studio had been broken into. She'd barely finished her sentence and I was out of my office, barrelling toward my truck. I didn't even stop to tell anyone what happened or call for backup.

All I could think about was getting to Jolie.

I've never driven so fast in my life. If anyone had driven like I just did on my watch, I'd have thrown their ass in lockup and had their vehicle impounded.

One of the perks of being chief, I guess.

I shove open the door, my eyes scanning the room quickly while barely registering the destruction around me. My eyes finally stop on Jolie sitting in the opposite corner of the room, bent over with arms around her head and her forehead against her knees. Avery's sitting in front of her, trying to calm her down, but even from here I can see Jolie's head is in another place.

I rush to them, gently nudging Avery aside as I kneel before Jolie. "Hey, sweetheart," I say in a low, soothing voice that surprises even me. "It's me. Luke."

If Avery's shocked by my tenderness, I don't even register it. My entire focus is on Jolie, who's continuing to rock on her heels. Her breathing is coming in short, sharp intakes and her head is still tucked between her knees. Her hands are in her hair, her fingers opening and closing on her scalp.

She's having a panic attack.

As a police officer, we're trained to deal with these types of situations and how to help someone through them. But it's different when I feel every panicked heartbeat as if it's my own. Every helpless whimper is like a sledgehammer to my chest.

My head retreats back to a cold night, the first time I used that training...

I shove that all aside and focus on Jolie. My steady hands slowly reach up to her arms. There's tension in her muscles, her entire body like a live wire. "Jolie," I try again. "I'm here. You're safe. I won't let anything happen to you. I've got you." My hands rub gentle but firm circles up and down her arms, grounding her to the here and now.

"Breathe with me, Jolie. Exactly like I do. In." I take a deep, slow breath through my nose and to my relief, she copies it, though her head is still tucked into her arms. "And out." I purse my lips and slowly release the breath through my mouth as Jolie lets out a shaky one of her own.

"Good. Now listen to my voice. Can you hear the birds chirping outside? Those damn birds are always waking me up when I stay here. Hear 'em?" No response. "How about the furnace? Not as cold outside so it's taking a break, but I can hear it humming. Do you hear it?"

She gives a small nod and I take it as encouragement. "Can you lift your head for me? Look only at me." Slowly, she lifts her head. She starts to turn but I use one finger to tilt her face back to me. "Don't look anywhere but at me. Right in my eyes." She does as I say, her normally bright eyes now stormy and frantic. "Good. Now, tell me three things you see."

"Your eyes." Her eyes lock on mine for a second before they roam over me. The panic in her eyes slowly starts to subside. "Your mouth. Your hands."

I smile and the small tilt of her lips is like the sunrise after a storm.

"There she is," I mumble, gently brushing away the hair falling into her face.

There's a knock at the door that has Avery clearing her throat. "I'm going to just—" She points a thumb at the door, then hurries over to let in a couple of officers. I turn back to Jolie who's still watching me, her eyes now drooping low, exhaustion etched on her face.

"Alright. Time to go."

I help her to her feet. She sways slightly when she stands and I have to fight the urge to pick her up and carry her out the door. The only thing that stops me is the fact that she'd probably throttle me later for it.

She's too proud to ever lean on someone like that.

Instead, I tuck her under my arm and guide her toward

the door. I pause in front of the two officers who just walked in. "Take Miss Owens' statement then mark this off as a crime scene," I say to the officers, Boyd and Henricks, who nod in understanding. "I want photos, perimeter checks, all of it." Another nod. "I'm taking Miss St. James to get settled. We'll take her statement later." My tone leaves no room for questions but they both nod anyway.

"She can come back to my place," Avery offers.

"What do you want to do?" I ask Jolie, ignoring the confused look from Avery.

Jolie hesitates a second before she looks over at Avery. "I'm going to go to Luke's," she whispers, then reaches out to hug Avery. She whispers something in her ear that has her relaxing slightly.

Avery pulls away but levels a stern look at me. "Take care of her."

I nod solemnly. She steps back and I take that as her approval to lead Jolie out the door.

"Okay, sweetheart. Let's go home."

JOLIE

For the second time today, I wake up in Luke's bedroom. This time, the blackout blinds are drawn low and there's no music coming from the other side of the door. More importantly though, the bed beside me isn't empty like it was this morning.

Luke's arm is wrapped protectively around my waist, keeping my back pulled tightly against his chest.

It takes me a second to register what happened, but when it does, it's like a floodgate opens and the memory of today comes crashing down on me.

Talking with Sandy.

Walking to my studio with Avery.

My studio. My throat tightens, remembering the utter wreckage that was left of the business I spent so long building on my own.

One night and my dream, my livelihood, was destroyed.

What the hell am I going to do? I don't have the kind of money it's going to take to fix the studio. And after borrowing from Austin to fix Blue, there's no way I could ask him for any more.

My breathing quickens as panic starts to climb my throat but before it can get a firm grip, Luke's pulling me up into a seated position.

"Hey, hey," he mumbles soothingly, as he rubs a comforting hand down my back. "You're safe. Focus on my voice, Jolie. You're safe. Everything's fine."

My throat is too tight to talk so I look around the room, grounding myself. Something I learned from a therapist years ago and has brought me back from the edge more times than I can count.

A memory flashes of Luke doing exactly that when he found me at the studio, mid-panic attack.

"Thanks," I rasp, my voice still thick with sleep and emotion. It makes me cough, and a glass of water is immediately pushed into my hand. I drink down the whole thing then pass it back to him.

"You don't need to thank me," he mumbles.

My eyes shift to my hands. "I meant for earlier." When he saw me at my lowest, my vulnerable point and pulled me out of it.

"I know," he says. "Me too."

I nod sharply, not looking up from my fingers. I can count on one hand the number of people I've ever let see my anxiety take control of me like that. While I'm not ashamed of it, I don't go around broadcasting my vulnerabilities to every person I meet.

"Hey," he says softly. He tucks a finger under my chin and lifts it until my eyes meet his. "It happens. To more people than you think."

My eyes search his. "Have you ever...you know..." I wave a hand in my general direction. His brows furrow slightly. "I mean, has that ever happened to you?"

His hand drops to my lap and he lets out a long breath. I remain quiet, watching him fight through whatever internal argument he's having with himself. After a moment, I reach over and interlace our fingers. He stares down at them, tracing them with his gaze.

Finally, he says in a quiet voice, "Twice."

I school my expression so that it's unreadable, not wanting to scare him off when he's opening himself up this way. But he doesn't even lift his head, talking to our hands instead.

"The first time was after my dad died. My mom doesn't know this, but I watched her be pulled into a tunnel of depression. I didn't know at the time that that's what it was, I only knew that I was the man of the house now and it was my responsibility to protect her and my younger siblings."

He runs his opposite hand's fingers down my arm, causing goosebumps to erupt in their wake. I didn't grow up here, so while I know the details of Luke's dad and his sickness, this is the first time I've heard of Franny also being sick.

"One day after school, I went to my mom's shop to work my shift before I'd go home and start dinner for us until she got home from work. She was always at the shop when I got there after school, but one of her employees said she had gone home sick." He shakes his head slightly. "She went back to work too early after my dad died. Said she wanted to be normal again. But it wasn't normal. Nothing was.

"So I went home to check on her, thinking I should be there to take care of her. When I walked in, she was asleep on the couch. I tried to wake her but she wouldn't wake up. I thought the worst." He pauses, swallowing hard. After a moment, his voice is thick and raspy when he continues. "I felt helpless. My one job was to protect her and I'd failed."

I squeeze his hand hard and he finally looks up at me. His eyes are red rimmed and pained but he holds my gaze.

"What happened?" I ask after a moment.

He tilts his lips up slightly. "She woke up not long after. She got hit with a bad cold and had taken some medication that knocked her out. But for those few minutes, she looked so still, so lifeless..." He shakes his head. "I lost it. I ran to my room and slammed the door shut. It felt like being swept away by a tornado, grasping desperately at anything but unable to hold it. Unable to catch my footing. I could barely stand by the time it was over. It was probably mere stubbornness that it didn't take me out at the knees."

My heart aches for him. He was just a teenager who'd lost his dad and was terrified to lose his mother, too. Feeling the weight of protecting his mom, his siblings. It only makes sense that he'd want to protect his town, too.

"The second time was after responding to my first fatal accident. Family of four hit by a semi truck." He takes a deep breath then says in a low voice, "Only the dad and the truck driver survived. I barely remember coming home after."

He doesn't say anything more after that so I just sit with him, holding both of his hands in mine. After a minute, the tension slowly leaves him. Only then do I ask him a question that's been bothering me since our first night at the inn.

"Have you ever seen someone for your anxiety?" I ask softly, using the same tone he used with me at the studio.

He shrugs, still looking at our entwined hands. "Sort of. After my dad got sick, my mom had each of us kids go to meet with a counselor and then again when he passed. But it was mostly about grief and coping. I didn't like the idea of spilling all my secrets to a stranger."

I imagine a surly teenage Luke sitting in a therapist's office, refusing to talk despite how badly he was hurting inside. From the way he explained it and the way he's refusing to look at me, I can tell he doesn't open up about this part of himself often—if ever.

I want to thank him for trusting me enough to open up, but I know that would just make him feel awkward and probably shut down more. Instead, I snuggle into him, and pull him down to lay beside me. Tucking my head into his shoulder, I trace my finger along his chest.

"The first time I had a panic attack, I didn't even know what a panic attack was. I was ten and we were on our first ever big family vacation. My parents drove all four of us from Toronto to Disney World. By some miracle, my father and I were getting along. We even went on a couple of rides together." I smile to myself at the memory. It was a good day, one of the best in my childhood.

Until it turned into one of the worst.

"My father and I were getting off a ride and were supposed to meet my brother and mom at a nearby food stand. Somehow, I lost him in the crowd. One minute he was there, and the next he was gone. At first I didn't panic. I knew what I was supposed to do if I got separated from my parents: go to the spot we had designated to meet and wait until they found me. So I went off to find the spot."

I swallow hard, remembering what came next. "Only I couldn't find the food stand they told me to meet them by. I knew what it looked like but it wasn't where it was supposed to be. There were too many people, too much noise that no one noticed me. I started to panic. My father would be so mad when he realized I wasn't behind him. Then I started thinking about all the warnings he'd given my brother and I about bad people taking kids when they wandered off. Suddenly, the people who I was supposed to go to for help all looked like the villains from my movies."

Even after all these years, I remember the feeling of being so scared and helpless. Like I'd never see my family again. The tightness in my chest, the way my heart tripped over itself as panic crawled up my spine. Luke runs a reassuring hand up and down my back.

"Eventually, an employee found me curled in a ball beside a garbage can and radioed security. My parents were there not long after that. My mom was relieved but my father was furious. I don't think he said a word to me the rest of the trip."

Luke's hand tightens into a fist against my back but he doesn't say anything, for which I'm thankful. Today was heavy enough. I don't need to add my daddy issues on top of everything.

"I've been dealing with anxiety for as long as I can remember, but for the most part I keep it in check with therapy and medication. But every once and a while it takes me by surprise and I remember I don't have as much control as I thought."

Luke pauses then rolls me onto my back, hovering above me as his eyes bounce back and forth between mine. "Listen to me. You are strong; one of the strongest people I know. What happened today doesn't change that. Nothing can change that." I stare up at him, transfixed by him. "You hear me?" I nod. "Good."

Tearing my gaze from his, I stare up at the ceiling. I haven't thought about that day in the amusement park in years. Part of me wonders if I blocked it from my memory on purpose. It was one of the first big arguments my father and I had gotten into. The first time I realized that my father wasn't the hero that everyone outside our family thought he was.

But for once, I don't feel ashamed thinking about that day. I don't feel embarrassed for letting my mental health take over my body. I feel...love.

Love for that little girl with her head tucked into her knees as her body shakes and her breathing quickens. I wish I could reach out and give her a hug. Protect her.

And then it hits me.

Tiffany isn't some stuck up bitch who's spitting hateful words because she's a miserable asshole who loves to see me suffer.

She's just a scared little girl who's lashing out, trying to protect me in the only way she knows how. She doesn't need my anger or my shame; she needs love and patience. She needs me to hug her, sit with her while she feels all her big feelings and know that no matter what, she's safe.

For the first time in my life, I understand her.

I turn my head to Luke, who's watching me carefully as I work through this revelation. The acceptance on his face has me swallowing hard. "Will you kiss me right now?" I whisper. "Please?"

He hesitates for a second. I'm lost in the pull of his eyes, so much so that I almost don't notice his slight nod. He closes the distance between us, his mouth taking mine in the softest, sweetest kiss I've ever had. It's so different from any we've shared before and it makes my heart ache.

He starts to pull back but I wrap my arms around his neck, keeping him close to me. "Jolie, we shouldn't. You—"

I silence him with a finger to his lips. "Shh. I'm done talking tonight."

With that, I bring his head down to mine again, giving us both a much needed distraction.

At least for tonight.

CHAPTER 50

LUKE

You don't fuck a girl that just had a panic attack. I know that. You know that. The friggen pope knows that.

But apparently someone forgot to mention that little fact to my dick.

The second Jolie's lips meld to mine, every insecure, anxious, angry thought leaves my head. I'm not thinking about hunting down the spineless piece of shit who destroyed Jolie's studio. Or how terrified I was to find her shaking in the corner. Or the fact that for a second, I could see myself in her fear-clouded eyes.

All of that melts away and I'm left with a fire inside me that's continuing to build with every stroke of her tongue, every tilt of her hips.

But even as my head swims with desire, there's a tiny voice in the back of my mind.

"Jolie," I rasp, pulling my mouth from hers. "Are you sure?"

She takes my face between her hands and stares into my eyes. Her eyes are a glacial blue—focused and determined.

I push away the memory of her foggy eyes staring up at me merely hours ago and focus on her looking up at me.

"Help me forget," she whispers. "Please, Luke." Her voice breaks on my name and it's my undoing.

Gently cupping her jaw, I seal my mouth back over hers, pouring myself into the kiss. I let her feel everything inside me; every feeling I'm not ready to name but in my heart, I know is true.

It's slow and purposeful; every brush of my lips lingering on hers. Something is shifting between us and I can tell she feels it, too. She can't stop touching me, running her hands along my back, my shoulders, my biceps. Everywhere she touches leaves a trail of goosebumps in her wake.

Bracing my forearm on the bed to keep from crushing her with my full weight, I shift to run my hand down her side. When I reach the hem of her shirt, she arches her hips and lets out a little gasp as my fingers tease the skin beneath. The sound shoots right to my dick, causing it to swell against my sweatpants.

Everything she does drives me wild. Her smile, her laugh. Even when she hands me my ass. Maybe even especially then.

But these sounds, the ones she makes when we're alone, are my favorite. Her breathy moans, her surprised gasps, her desperate cries. They all belong to me.

She's mine.

The thought echoes in my head as my hand dips below her waistline. It's a fact I can't ignore anymore. I feel it with every breath I take and every ache in my chest when she's not around. She's captured a part of me I wasn't quite sure still existed.

She arches into my hand, shoving at her leggings

awkwardly but my body blocks her. She growls her frustration and I smile against her lips. I love that she wants this as much as I do.

I sit back on my knees, tugging her leggings the rest of the way off before discarding my own clothes. As soon as she tosses her shirt over her head, I drop back between her legs to take her mouth once more. My hand presses between her legs, finding that magic spot and circling it over and over until she's a panting, writhing mess below me.

"Please," she whimpers.

I'm more than happy to oblige.

She's so wet that my finger glides easily inside her, so I quickly add a second. A small gasp slips from her lips but I devour the sound. She rocks her hips against my palm as I leisurely thrust my fingers in and out. Lifting my head to watch her, I continue to drag out her pleasure.

Her lips fall open and her eyes lock with mine. I can feel her clenching around my fingers. She's getting close.

Within seconds, her orgasm pulls her under and I watch as her eyes glaze and a soft cry breaks from her lips. I continue to work her over, drawing every ounce of pleasure from her. Before she can come down from her post-orgasm high, I line myself up and push inside. Her walls clench around me again, pulling another cry from her.

Normally, this would be when one of us would take control, picking up our pace until we were chasing wildly after our release.

But it seems like neither of us are in a rush this time, both of us wanting to savor the journey instead of racing toward the finish line.

I take my time slowly plunging in and out, in a rhythm that seems so natural it feels like we've been doing this forever. She clings to me, her legs wrapped around the back of mine as she meets me thrust for thrust.

Eventually, her breath catches and her mouth drops open, but her hooded eyes never leave mine as her second orgasm claims her. She whispers my name in a plea and it sets off my own release. I can't help dropping my head to kiss her, like I can't possibly get close enough to sate this need for her.

Finally, we part, breathing heavily, still watching each other. A small smile plays at her lips and I return it with one of my own.

Slowly, I shift onto my back, pulling her along with me until she's tucked into my arms, head resting on my chest. She sighs contentedly.

I wish I could freeze this moment forever. In my arms, she's safe. Nothing can hurt her while she's with me.

It's then that I realize just how much Jolie means to me. Because, while I love my town and would do anything to protect it, I would burn the entire thing to ashes if it meant keeping Jolie safe.

Let's just hope it doesn't come to that.

JOLIE

When Luke and I finally dragged ourselves out of his bed, he demanded that I sit at the island and relax while he fixed us something to eat.

It's kind of nice being catered to, though I hate the circumstances that lead to it. Luke has cooked me dinner before—and a lot fancier meals than the grilled cheese before me now—so I know it's not because of my panic attack earlier.

I know in my head that panic attacks don't make me

weak. I know that. I wholeheartedly believe that mental illness is not something to be ashamed of.

But no matter how much I tell myself that leaning on Luke doesn't make me weak, I can't help but tell myself that this is how depending on someone starts. One minute he's making me dinner and the next, I'm asking permission to go out with my friends.

It's a slippery slope and I'm not sure I have my footing.

"So, what did Sandy have to say this morning?" Luke asks, dipping his grilled cheese into blue cheese sauce. Like a psychopath.

My mouth contorts in disgust as he takes a bite of the sandwich. He notices and rolls his eyes, then takes an exaggerated bite just to watch me gag. I move my plate away from him, just in case any of his revolting colored mold sauce tries to make its way onto my plate.

"She wanted my opinion on doing a live reveal for *Dear Annie* at the rec center in a few weeks," I reply, dipping my grilled cheese into the pile of ketchup on my plate.

Because I'm a normal human being.

"What'd she say when you told her no?" Luke asks, taking a drink of his water.

My sandwich pauses halfway to my mouth. My brows furrow as I turn to him in disbelief.

Umm...come again?

He's munching away on his disgusting sandwich, completely unaware of the bombshell he just dropped.

"Why would I tell her no?" I try to keep my voice even despite my temper starting to bubble.

That gets his attention. He angles himself toward me, his expression mirroring mine but for a very different reason.

"Jolie," he starts, as if he's calming a skittish deer.

I toss a hand up, stopping him mid-sentence. "Unless your plan is to piss me off, I'd rethink using that condescending tone right now."

His mouth twists, his temper clearly being held onto by a thread, but he manages to keep his voice calm when he tries again. "Your studio was just broken into and vandalized. You've been receiving threatening messages for months," he says through clenched teeth. "Clearly someone is after you. So you'll excuse me if I think putting yourself on a literal stage for them to get to you would be an obviously bad idea."

The blood rushes to my ears as my temper boils. My fingers tighten on the sandwich until I have to drop it onto my plate to keep from smashing it entirely.

Relax. Take a breath.

Somewhere in the corner of my mind, I know that Luke's only trying to protect me. But all I can hear is my father's voice, chastising me for making another stupid decision. A choice I wasn't even sure I had made yet, until I was told yet again how I was making the wrong one.

"Well, bad idea or not, it's my mistake to make, isn't it?"

"This isn't like choosing the wrong paint color for your bedroom, Jolie," Luke says dryly. "This is your safety you're gambling."

"You don't think I know that?" I snap.

I'm an idiot. I knew this would happen. I was stupid to think that any relationship, especially one with someone as stubborn and controlling as Luke, would end in any other way. Expecting me to trail along behind him like a well-trained puppy on a leash, waiting for my next command.

Well, that's not happening.

Not to me.

We're quiet for a moment. Watching each other. Measuring the other up.

To my surprise, he breaks first, dragging a hand over his face. "Shit. I'm sorry," he mumbles. "I'm sorry, Jolie. I shouldn't have said that." He grabs my hand. "I just want you to be safe. I *need* you to be safe."

I sit quietly, torn. My heart wants to believe him. That he would never control me like that.

But my head isn't so sure.

"You said it's not for a few weeks," he says softly. "We can talk about it another time."

He watches me, waiting for my response. I give him a small nod and his shoulders relax. He leans forward and kisses the side of my head.

"Want to watch a movie? Avery brought over some of your stuff." He gestures to a couple tote bags on the chaise behind me. "I asked her to grab your skin stuff. Figured you'd want to shower and I didn't want my discount soap irritating your skin." He picks up our plates and carries them to the sink.

Despite my temper still sizzling beneath my skin, I'm starting to soften. He told Avery to grab my skincare products? He remembered that I have sensitive skin? I wasn't even sure he was listening when I complained about his lack of soap options the last time I slept over.

But he remembered. And not only remembered but cared enough to make sure I was taken care of while I'm here.

Confused beyond measure and unsure how to respond other than a quick "thanks", I grab my totes and duck into his bedroom.

After changing into one of my sweaters and pajama

pants and washing my face, I shuffle back into the kitchen. The smell of popcorn stops me at the island.

Luke has the lights turned down low and a bowl of popcorn sitting on the coffee table with a couple glasses of water. The man in question is tucked into the corner of the sectional with a large blanket covering his lap.

As if the whole scene wasn't adorable enough, Luke's leaning over, adjusting Cleo's pillow. Then he dips his head, whispering something into her ear that has her licking his nose. He gives her a quick kiss on the head then leans back into his seat.

Dammit. Why does he have to be so frickin' adorable?

I walk toward him and he turns as I enter the living room. He lifts up a corner of the blanket in invitation so I slide in beside him. Draping an arm over the back of the couch, he hits play on the remote.

Halfway through the movie, I have no idea what's happening on screen, other than there's a war brewing between the two motorcycle clubs. Tensions are high and violence is imminent.

If that's not one giant metaphor for the war between my head and my heart, I don't know what is.

Alright, universe. I hear you loud and clear.

I have no idea whose side I'm on, but I have a feeling there won't be any winners here.

———

THE NEXT WEEK goes by eerily quiet. I stayed at Luke's house for a few days while the police (and by police, I mean Luke) investigated my studio. When the investigation turned up empty, I decided to go back to my apartment.

Luke was less than thrilled about my decision, doing

and saying anything to try to convince me to stay with him. But I think he realized that the harder he pushed me, the harder I was going to push back. So he eventually relented. But not before installing a brand-new security system in the studio and at my apartment.

Overboard, yes. But it was the only way to convince him not to camp out in front of my studio every night for the foreseeable future. So I let him do it, promising to pay him back every cent for it. He grumbled under his breath something like "in your dreams", but that's one thing I won't give in on.

I can't.

Despite the fact that I have a studio that needs extensive repairs, equipment to replace, and exactly $153 in my bank account to do it all with, I can't let someone have that kind of control over me.

Oh, and I have nowhere to hold my classes until the repairs are done so for the time being, I have no income.

Happy New Year to me.

"What's got you thinking so hard this early in the morning?" Avery jokes, as she slides into the booth across from me a few days after I moved back into my apartment.

"Oh, you know. How I'm a broke ass bitch because my only source of income was destroyed by some psychopath with a vendetta against me." I shrug nonchalantly. "Just a typical Wednesday morning."

Avery's face morphs into one of worry. "I'm assuming that means the police haven't found anything yet then."

I shake my head. "No. I'm not sure they will. We're a small town with small resources. They dusted for prints but they'll have to send them away for analysis. Who knows how long that will take."

"I'm so sorry you're going through this," Avery

comments sympathetically. "I just don't understand why someone would target your studio like that."

Right. Because Avery still has no idea that I'm *Dear Annie*. Because I'm a shitty friend who keeps secrets since I'm too scared to open up to people.

Well, I guess telling her now is better than her finding out with the entire town during the live reveal in a few days.

I'm still debating if agreeing to that was a good idea or not.

"Well, we have a few theories..." I reply, unsure exactly where to start.

"Is it because of your brother?"

I shake my head. "Unlikely. No one here outside of our friends knows who he is and even if they did, the message they wrote wouldn't make sense." I chew on my bottom lip. "It might have something to do with that guy from The Dive that I punched a few months ago."

I look over my shoulder to make sure no one is listening but the diner is fairly empty today. Sandy doesn't want the big surprise ruined so we're still keeping it quiet. Even so, I lean forward and lower my voice. "Or they might be targeting me because of what I wrote in the paper." Avery blinks at me, confused. "As *Dear Annie*."

"You WHAT?" Avery shrieks.

I hush her then wave away the few diners who've turned to look at the commotion. "Wedding stress," I assure them. They chuckle and turn back to their coffees and conversations. I spin back to Avery. "Damn, Owens. Be cool."

"Sorry, sorry," she whispers. "And here I thought you secretly hooking up with Luke was going to be the most surprising thing you've done this week." She blows out a breath. "Geez, girl. How many secrets have you been keeping from me?"

I wince. "I didn't mean for it to be that way. I just...it kind of happened...and then—"

Avery reaches over and grabs my arm, silencing me. "You don't have to explain. I've told you before: you're allowed to have your privacy. I just don't want you to think you can't talk to me about things. I know I've been busy with the wedding but I'm never too busy for my friends."

"It's not that. It's not your fault. This is my issue."

"I just hope you know that you can always tell me anything, even if I've been a bit distracted lately," she tells me, her voice thick with emotion.

Of course Avery the empath would think this is her fault. She's the best friend a girl could ask for and despite her worries, always makes time for me in her busy life. It's my fault for keeping secrets.

Well, no more.

I smile. "I do. I promise."

"Sorry I'm late," Brenna calls as she hurries over to our booth, sliding into the seat beside me. "What'd I miss?"

Avery raises her brows and tilts her head at Brenna. *Subtle.* I roll my eyes at her theatrics but nod. A sly smile spreads across Avery's face as she leans toward Brenna.

"Jolie and Luke have been secretly playing hide-the-zucchini," she reports proudly.

Brenna shrugs off her coat, undisturbed. "Oh, I know. For a few months now."

I spin in my seat and stare at Brenna in shock. "How did you know?" I whisper-shout at the same time Avery practically shrieks, "You knew and didn't tell me?!"

Brenna shrugs. "I mean, you guys weren't exactly discreet about it. I swear there were times when I thought you were just going to start banging on the table in front of everyone."

I open my mouth then snap it shut. I'm genuinely at a loss for words. So much for being stealth.

"Who else knows?"

Brenna plays with her straw thoughtfully. "I'm pretty sure Rhett suspects something but I think it's more of a general wondering than knowing. Matt's clueless, if that makes you feel any better, Avery."

"It doesn't." Avery huffs. "Well, did you know she's also *Dear Annie?*" she asks, triumphantly.

I spin back toward her. "Avery!"

"What? No!" Brenna stares at me in surprise.

"I'm sorry!" Avery says. "She took the surprise out of my Luke secret. You were going to tell her anyway." She bats her puppy dog eyes at me. Now I know where Gavin gets it from. "Please don't be mad."

I groan because she's right. I would never tell Avery without telling Brenna. They're both my best friends.

"I'm not mad, you fool. Put those eyes away before they stay like that," I complain and Avery laughs.

"Okay, wait. Rewind to the *Dear Annie* thing." Brenna makes a circle with her finger. "Tell me everything."

I do my best to recap the last four months of my life, leaving nothing out. I tell them about Sandy approaching me after book club, the threatening emails that started out harmlessly, how they may or may not have become something much more dangerous and the live reveal of *Dear Annie* planned for in a few days.

"So, now Luke thinks that whoever broke into my studio is the same person who's been sending me those emails. He's convinced that they're going to come after me again and that I'm offering myself up to them on a silver platter by doing this reveal." I roll my eyes at the ridiculousness of it all.

But when I look over at Avery and Brenna, they look anything but amused.

"I can't say I blame him," Brenna comments. "If the person I loved was about to put themselves in danger like that—"

"Whoa, whoa, whoa," I interrupt. "No one said anything about love. Luke doesn't love me."

"I was there after the break in. The man flew across town and practically broke the door down to get to you," Avery points out. "I saw the way he looked at you. Like it physically pained him to see you like that. Not only that, I saw the way you looked at him. Luke was the first person you asked for when you were in trouble. And it's not because he's a police officer," she chides. "Because even when you were too scared to think clearly, you knew you needed him. You knew he'd come and that he would protect you."

Avery sits back in her seat, thoroughly pleased after her mic drop. Brenna just nods beside me.

I look down at my hands, suddenly feeling too exposed. Is she right? Am I that transparent to everyone?

I know I love Luke. I've known it since that day in the kitchen. But loving Luke doesn't mean everything will end happily-ever-after. Look what happened the other day. We're not even officially a couple and he was already trying to control me.

I mean, he apologized and has been notably quiet on my decision to go through with the reveal.

But who's to say it won't happen again?

"What if that's not enough?" I ask, my voice a foreign, trembling sound to my own ears.

Brenna slips an arm through mine. "Then you'll still be you."

I drop my head on her shoulder and blow out a long, shaky breath. Maybe she's right. Maybe love—real love—is that simple.

But am I brave enough to find out?

THE HAVEN TIMES

 Proudly serving Haven Bay for over 100 years. **FREE**

DEAR ANNIE

Your local source for advice on love, life and everything in between!

The answer to this week's trivia question (pg 9) is Beetlejuice.

Q.

Dear Annie,

My best friend and I have been friends since the first grade.

We do everything together and have no secrets from each other. We went to the same high school and had planned to be roommates in college next year.

The last few weeks though, she's been acting strange. When I text her, it takes her hours to respond and when she does, it's usually only a few words. I've asked her to hang out and she always makes up an excuse as to why she can't.

I've tried asking her what's wrong and if I did something to upset her. She keeps saying that everything's fine but I can't help but think she's lying to me.

My other friends say to let her be, that if she wants to talk, she'll reach out eventually. The idea of just sitting around waiting for her doesn't sit right with me but I don't want to push her away further.

I don't know what to do but I miss my best friend.

Sincerely,
What did I do wrong?

A.

Dear WDIDW,

I can't speak for your friend because I don't know the circumstances that lead to this change but I agree with you, it seems strange.

That doesn't mean that it has to do with you though. Maybe she has something going on in her personal life that she's trying to navigate. Maybe you unintentionally upset her and she's not ready to talk about it yet.

Either way, my best advice is for you to let her know that, while you don't know the cause of her change in behaviour, you're always there for her if she wants to talk about it.

Unfortunately, there's not much more you can do than that. The ball is essentially in her court on this one, which I know doesn't help your current distress.

And for that, I'm sorry I couldn't be more help.

So instead, I'll leave you with a piece of advice my grandpa gave me years ago: friendships are like farts. If you have to force them, it's probably sh*t.

Sincerely,
Annie

HUSBAND FOR RENT

My husband is handy, clean and respectable. He can build, repair or demo just about anything.

For $20/hr , you rent my husband to do just about anything (but not that). Call Erin at 555-123-3456.

HELP WANTED

Looking for experienced plumber to come to my home and check out a suspicious sound coming from my downstairs bathroom pipes.

Sound has been going on for multiple weeks and sounds similar to a rodent trying to claw his way out of a pipe.

Some experience with animal control would be an asset. As would experience working with ghosts, if needed.

Please call 123-456-8748 if interested in the position.

HAMILTON, WHERE ART THOU?

Hamilton the hamster is still missing.

Hamilton enjoys carrots, water and running on his wheel. He also enjoys long walks on the beach and long, hot bubble baths.

If you or anyone you know has seen this white and grey furry friend, our little Liam would sure appreciate you calling.

Call or text Pam Ford at 123-456-7890 for fastest response.

Reward: $15.00 raised by Liam himself.

CHAPTER 51

LUKE

I'm losing control. I've barely eaten, slept or showered in days. I ended up bringing Cleo to the station because I felt too guilty leaving her alone all day. But I knew the station was where I needed to be right now. So she's set up with a pillow on top of one of my office chairs, growling at anyone who comes into my office.

Honestly, I've been having the same reaction when anyone dares to bother me. I've been so immersed in Jolie's case, the entire department is scared to come into my office unless it's an emergency.

They're trained professionals. You wouldn't think they'd need me holding their hands just to do their damn jobs.

My ringtone blasts and it takes all my effort not to throw it across the room.

"Brady," I bark into the phone.

"Always the charmer," Wade comments dryly.

If I didn't need his help, I'd hang up on him. I don't have time for this shit. Not while the guy who destroyed Jolie's studio is walking around free.

"Where is he?" I growl.

"Not where he's supposed to be," Wade answers. I asked him to look into Tad again after the break in. My gut is telling me that this guy has something to do with what's going on with Jolie. And if there's anything I trust in this world, it's my gut.

"I did a little unofficial digging around and paid a visit to his apartment," Wade continues. "Or what was his apartment. Big "For Rent" sign on the front. Called the landlord pretending to be interested in renting it. I asked him a few questions about the previous renter and buddy sang like a canary." Wade chuckles. "He really didn't like this Chesterfield guy. Seems like he was just waiting for an excuse to kick him out.

"Anyway, guy's been MIA for the last six weeks or so and hasn't been making his payments for months before that. Doesn't have any family close by as far as I can find." He sighs. "Without a warrant, I can't do much more than that."

My gut twists as I sit up straighter in my chair. Chesterfield was behind the break in at Jolie's studio; I'd bet my pension on it. But where is he now? And what's his next move?

"Sorry, buddy. I know that's not what you were hoping to hear."

"No," I grumble. "It's not. I appreciate you looking into it though." I'm about to hang up when he stops me.

"Listen, man. I don't want to overstep here..."

"Then don't," I snap. Unfortunately, Wade's used to my moods and ignores me.

"Asking his landlord some questions is one thing..." He hesitates.

"Spit it out, Riorson."

"I'd just hate to see you throw your career away over this." I'm about to lay into him when he continues. "But if the roles were reversed and it was Margot this guy was fucking with... well. Let's just say there wouldn't be anywhere this guy could hide where I wouldn't find him."

I nod, even though I know he can't see me. He promises to let me know if he hears anything more and I thank him before hanging up.

I appreciate Wade's concern but I don't give a shit about my career at this point. They can drop me down to parking duty for all I care. Hell, I'd work as a bouncer for Rhett at The Dive if it meant Chesterfield never came into the same area code as the woman I love again.

Because if there's one thing I've realized from this whole thing, it's that I'm in love with Jolie. I feel it with every breath I take and every ache in my chest when she's not around. I want to protect her. And not in the same way I want to protect the people of this town. I'm quickly learning that if I had to choose between saving Jolie and Haven Bay, I'd gladly toss my badge into the bay if it meant that she was safe.

But the best part is, she'd never ask me that. She knows what this town means to me and she understands my need to protect it. Because she loves it just as much as I do.

Which is why, now that I've had some time to think about it, I understand her wanting to do this live reveal.

She's spent the last three months—even longer before the article—helping the people of Haven Bay. She deserves the recognition, though I know that's not why she's doing it. The way she sees it, it's another way for her to be there for her town. Another way for her to prove she's worth more than what her piece of shit father thinks of her.

I know I fucked up. I knew it the second the words

came out of my mouth when I told her not to do it. And even though I apologized, I can feel her pulling back. She needs space and I'll give it to her.

For now.

But there's one thing she needs to know: I'm going to fight for my girl.

I'll never stifle her, never even consider hiding her away again. Jolie is strong, a warrior in her own right. She doesn't need someone like me, but damn if I'm not going to try and convince her to keep me around anyway.

I love that woman. I just hope she'll choose to love me, too.

I just need to show her that what we have together is worth the risk.

JOLIE

"You're not going to puke, are you?" Sandy takes a hesitant step away from me. "I don't handle puking well. Sympathetic puker and all that."

I take a few steadying breaths, shaking my hands to try and get rid of my excess nerves. Exhaling through pursed lips, I try my best to ignore her.

Hot tip: if you want to distract someone from puking, don't repeatedly talk about puking.

"I could find a bucket for you if you want." Her head swings left then right, searching the small hallway outside the rec center's gymnasium.

"I'm fine," I tell her. "Let's just go over the order of operations one more time." I don't need the refresher. We've already gone through it multiple times and it's not that complicated. I'm more so asking to distract Sandy, who's bouncing so hard on her heels it actually might make me sick. Her mix of excitement and nerves is giving me whiplash.

"At two o'clock on the dot, Harvey's going to shut the gym doors," she says, talking about the paper's graphic designer. "Then I'll go up and set the stage, build the anticipation. I'll give Harvey the signal when it's time and he'll come get you for the grand reveal." She waves her hands in the air like a magician revealing her trick. "You come in. Applause, shock, "oohs" and "aahs". You can do a quick hello and introduction. Then we'll jump right into the questions."

I nod, shuffling my feet. "Okay."

"I'm going to go check with Harvey. I'll see you out there."

Why am I so nervous? As a yoga instructor, I'm used to being in front of a class. I doubt that many people will even show up. I'm sure it'll just be a handful of nosey old ladies with nothing better to do on a Sunday afternoon. When I went for my certification, we had to lead a class twice the size of what I'm sure this crowd will be. This is no big deal.

So why do I feel like bolting out the back door right now?

Tiffany's been trying to rear her ugly head all day, whispering horrible comments in my ear since before I opened my eyes this morning.

No one cares about your opinion.

People are going to be so disappointed when they see you walk out on the stage.

What makes you think you're qualified to give anyone advice? You can't even get your own life together. You're hiding from Luke because you're too scared to deal with your feelings.

That last part might have a tiny bit of truth to it. I

wouldn't say I'm exactly hiding from him. He's been preoccupied with work and I've been busy fighting with my insurance company, so we haven't had much time to connect more than a few late night calls. When we do, we're both too tired for anything longer than a brief Facetime before I nosedive into my bed.

I might be a chicken shit, taking advantage of our busy schedules to avoid him, but I know I can't hide forever. And to be honest, I don't want to.

I miss him. I miss lazy Sundays and rapping in the kitchen with him. I miss teasing him out of his grumpy moods and I definitely miss the way we fit together so perfectly in bed.

I miss *us*.

So, he made the mistake of assuming I would make a certain decision. I might've been a *tad* touchy on the subject anyway. The second he showed even a hint of controlling me, I lashed out like a wolf backed into a corner.

Was he wrong in his approach? Definitely. But Luke's not used to having to concede control. He's used to having an entire department that follows his every order without argument.

Besides, he was just trying to protect me. And his gruff, prickly exterior is one of the things I love most about him. He's too much fun to tease because of it. And I get the added bonus of being one of the few who sees his soft side.

The gymnasium door opens a crack. "Two minute warning," Harvey whispers.

Okay. You can do this. Don't listen to Tiffany. Even if there's three people in the audience, you've got just as much of a reason to be here as anyone.

Before I know it, Harvey is swinging open the door. I square my shoulders and lift my head, feigning a confidence

I almost feel. I cross the threshold but nearly trip when I see the crowd inside. Every seat is filled, with a handful of people standing along the sides.

"And here's our *Annie* now. Also known as Haven Bay's own Jolie St. James!" Sandy calls excitedly into the microphone from the stage. Applause breaks out and I almost jump at the sound.

So many people are here...for me? I mean, I know they didn't know who they were coming for when they came, but they're applauding. And not polite, golf applause but whistling and hollering with excitement.

I duck my head to hide the tears threatening to spill over. Jogging up the stairs, I cross the stage, waving awkwardly at the crowd. Sandy's clapping along with the audience as I approach. When I get close enough, she leans in to give me a hug then whispers, "you've got this" in my ear. She steps back and takes a seat in one of the chairs behind me.

I smile at the crowd, hoping it comes off more real than it feels. "Wow. What a welcome. You guys sure know how to show a girl a good time." Laughter ripples through the audience. "As most of you know, my name's Jolie and I own Amaryllis Yoga Studio on Main." *Or used to, if the insurance company won't cough up the money to fix it.* "But I also go by another name and that's *Annie*."

"Hell yeah, you do!" comes a voice from the back that I recognize as Matt's. This time my smile is genuine as I see Matt, Avery, and Brenna in the back row giving me variations of thumbs ups and waves.

"Before we get into the questions, I want to just say a quick thank you to all of you who have written in or read my responses. Thank you for trusting me enough to share your problems with. You'll never know how much that means to me." Another round of applause. "Since you've all been so transparent with me, I figured it was only fair that I returned the favor. So here I am. No more secrets."

Sandy steps up to the microphone and takes over explaining the process. Those who had been previously selected by Sandy to read their questions aloud would line up in the center of the aisle. One by one, they can ask their question into the microphone, I'll give a short response then move onto the next question.

"And as always, anyone looking to remain anonymous, please send your question to the paper's *Dear Annie* email."

Sandy gestures to Harvey, who's standing in the center of the aisle with ten to fifteen readers ready to ask their questions. He switches on the microphone and we begin.

For the next hour, reader after reader steps up to the microphone and reads their question. The first few questions I stumble through, trying to swallow back my nerves. But I quickly find my groove and time flies until the line is empty.

By the time Sandy takes the microphone back to wrap things up, I'm tired, my feet hurt, and I would do dirty, shameful things for a glass of water. But I can't keep the smile off my face. I feel light. Like a weight has been lifted that I didn't even know was weighing me down.

"Now, there are refreshments at the—" Sandy pauses as Harvey hurries toward the stage. She leans down, listening for a second then straightens. "I'm being told that there's a last minute addition to the lineup from a reader in the audience," she explains. "He's in desperate need of advice and is asking if you'd be willing to answer one more question." She turns to me.

Curious, I nod. "Absolutely."

My stomach bottoms out when Luke stands from

somewhere near the back of the room and ambles toward the microphone. He looks ridiculously handsome in his dark jeans and navy blue shirt with the sleeves shoved up to his elbows. He stops in front of the microphone and pulls a folded piece of paper from the back pocket of his pants.

My heart thrums in my ears. *What is he doing?* He didn't tell me he was coming today, though I was hoping he would. Hope starts to blossom in my chest—for what I'm not even sure.

He still hasn't looked at me.

Why hasn't he looked at me?

"Dear *Annie*," he starts, reading from the paper. "A few months ago, I got snowed in with a woman who hated my guts. Little did I know, that weekend would be the start of something neither of us saw coming. You see, *Annie*, this woman who used to love driving me insane has become the woman I can't get out of my head. She's loud and funny. She works harder than anyone I know. She's smart... sometimes too smart for her own good." He smiles down at the paper and I can't help but mirror it. "She's not afraid to tell you exactly what's on her mind. She's tough as nails. She's strong...so strong I don't think she even realizes. She's got this heart that's so pure and loyal that it beats only for those she loves. She's a wild lioness, always ready to protect.

"But here's the problem. I messed up. I tried to keep her safe, but ended up unintentionally caging her instead. And by caging her, I unknowingly tried to keep her from being the woman I fell in love with."

My heart falters and it's like all the oxygen is sucked out of the room.

Did he just say love?

Luke loves me?

I can feel the fresh set of tears shimmering on my lids,

but I don't want to look away, don't want to even blink in case I miss even a nanosecond of this moment.

Finally, he lifts his head to meet my gaze. It's then that I see the dark circles under his eyes. He looks exhausted. But there's something else in his eyes: vulnerability.

"So, my question is this, *Annie*. How do I fix this? Do you think she'll ever forgive me? Because I can't imagine my life without her in it. Without her smile, her laugh. Her smartass jokes." He smirks and I let out a watery laugh. "Because I love this woman, *Annie*. Every sarcastic, loud, unfiltered, beautiful, brave, scared part of her."

He lowers the paper to his side, his gaze never leaving mine. A few people start to whisper, others sniffle with emotion but I don't hear any of it.

I'm only focused on one man and he's staring at me like I'm holding his whole heart in my hands.

If only I have the courage to accept it.

I float down the stairs of the stage then stride over to where Luke's standing. He smirks down at me, a challenge in his eyes. But there's something else there. Something I never thought I would see on Luke Brady's face.

Fear.

He's scared that I won't accept his apology. That I won't take a chance on us.

That I won't choose him.

People tell me all the time that I talk too much. I've been hearing it all my life. Luke has joked many times that I always have a comeback for every occasion. But even I know that sometimes words aren't enough and you have to let your actions speak for you.

Which is why I reach up, hook my hand around the back of his neck and drag his head down to mine. I kiss him long and slow, smiling against his lips when he wraps an arm around my waist, pulling me closer.

Only when the crowd erupts into applause and cat calls do we pull apart, both of us grinning.

"Guess we're not a secret anymore," I comment.

"You never were!" A voice calls. I turn to see Dottie smirking from the second row.

"What'd you mean?" I ask, confused.

"Did you really think we wouldn't notice your car pulling into Luke's driveway every night?" Greta Norton, Luke's across-the-street-neighbor, calls out from behind me.

"Or how Luke bought your favorite breakfast snack and drink order every morning?" Marta Vale, one of the servers at Main Street Diner, snickers.

My mouth hangs open in shock. I don't think I've fully understood the saying "stunned speechless" until this moment.

Here we were thinking we were being so clever, hiding from everyone. Meanwhile, the whole town knew and were making bets behind our backs.

Well, except Avery, of course. And Matt by the look on his face.

"This damn town," I grumble.

Luke chuckles. "What'd you say we give them something to really talk about then?" He smiles devilishly then surprises me by dipping me low. Then he kisses me and I forget about every person in the room but him.

I love Luke Brady and I don't care who knows it.

JOLIE

"As long as you don't make me wear puke brown," I joke, switching my phone to speakerphone, "I'm sure I'll love whatever color you choose."

Avery's laugh fills my room. "I promise no puke colors."

I pull my old, worn Banff sweater over my head and pull my hair out onto my shoulders. Yanking open my front hall closet, I drop to my knees, digging through the disastrous pile of shoes, purses, hats and anything else that wouldn't fit in my bedroom closet.

Avery called to arrange a date and time to go dress shopping. She refused to make a big deal out of buying her wedding dress, but we convinced her to make a day out of it by agreeing to pick out our bridesmaids dresses at the same time. So, next week, Avery, Angie, Franny, Brenna and I will be driving into the city for a girls' day.

"Question," I ask, my voice muffled from my head being buried in the closet. "What type of shoes do you wear when someone tells you to 'dress comfy and practical'?"

"Inside or outside?"

"Outside, I think," I answer, tossing one of my winter boots over my shoulder.

"Luke wouldn't really say where. He said it was a surprise."

Avery groans. "I hate that. Guys don't understand the amount of stress they put on us by making something a surprise."

"Exactly!" I exclaim, holding up a cowboy boot to examine it then dropping it back into the pile. "Are we going hiking through the mountains? Snowshoeing in three feet deep snow? Walking around a holiday market in the city? That's three very different activities that are all outside."

"I'd go with those cute tie-up winter boots," Avery decides. "They're tall enough that if there's snow involved, you won't end up with wet feet but not too bulky to still be fashionable if you're going into the city."

"Good call." I dig through the closet to find the boots in question then pull them onto my feet. I shove at the pile until I'm able to close the closet door. "Alright then. I should get going. Luke said he was swinging by as soon as he finished up at the station and I still have to grab some things out of my car."

Avery sighs, dreamily. "You guys are so cute."

I snort a laugh. "Needing to grab something from my car is cute?"

"Shut up. You know what I mean." Avery laughs. "I'm just so happy for you both."

For the millionth time over the last week, I smile. "Me too." The past couple weeks have been some of the happiest times in recent memory.

I hang up with Avery and make my way down my apartment steps.

For the first time since Luke and I got together, it feels like we're a real couple. We actually go out to eat instead of ordering takeout and hiding in my apartment. I can kiss him without having to look over my shoulder to make sure no one's looking. I can leave my car parked in his driveway instead of sneaking in through the garage.

It feels...normal. Right.

And to think, we wasted so much time hiding from everyone just for everyone to know about it anyway.

I still can't believe that, by the way.

I might need to talk to Luke about his sneaking abilities. Apparently, he's lost some of his mojo since becoming chief.

Turning the lock on the backdoor, I turn to enter my passcode into the security system on the wall. Once the steady beeping starts, I slide past the door, locking it behind me.

I turn only to come face to face with wild, bloodshot eyes. I try to jump back but a hand snaps forward, wrapping around my wrist before I can get back inside.

"Not so fast, Jolie," Tad Chesterfield purrs, his words slightly slurred. "You're a hard lady to get a hold of."

He looks different than the last time I saw him. His hair is disheveled, his clothes stained and rumpled. He stinks like alcohol and it's barely eleven in the morning.

The change I notice most, though, are his eyes. At the bar that night, I remembered his eyes holding a hint of something scary, almost dangerous. Now, his pupils are blown wide, making me think he's been dipping into more than just booze.

But there's something else. Something...unhinged. Like there was a part of him that had been lurking beneath the surface, waiting for a chance to be unleashed.

By the look of him, I think it's been loose for some time now.

"What're you doing here?" I try to keep my voice calm, though my entire body is on alert. Luke should be here soon. If I can keep Tad talking long enough, maybe Luke will show up in time to save me.

"You know, my life was pretty sweet," he continues as if I hadn't even spoken. "I had a job that let me travel. I went to bars every night and could pick up pussy whenever I had the itch." He laughs maliciously. "And that was often."

Alright. This might not be so hard. He wants to monologue like some low-rent comic book villain? I'll let him talk himself hoarse if it gives Luke enough time to get to me.

"But then I came to this piece of shit hicktown in the middle of bum-fuck-nowhere and offered to pity-fuck your fat friend."

I narrow my eyes, fighting back my temper at his description of Brenna.

Probably a bad idea to piss off the unpredictable junky, Jolie.

"Then I get ambushed by some stupid fucking bitch who doesn't know how to keep her big ass nose out of other people's business."

Okay, rude. I've actually been told my nose is very Cindy Lou Who-esque.

He lets go of my arm to pace in front of me. I take the opportunity to weigh my options. My eyes dart to the back door, trying to determine if I'm fast enough to get my keys out and unlock it before he could catch me. No, that'd take too long. I look behind him. He's blocking the sidewalk that wraps around to the main road. My parking lot is fairly secluded and no one seems to be nearby to see us. My chances at someone hearing us from back here aren't great either.

"Next thing I know," Tad continues, "my boss is firing me for 'inadequate performance' and 'creating a hostile work environment'. But that whore from the second floor knows better than to report me. So I know it's because of you."

He whips his head back to me, his bloodshot eyes glaring at me. My throat constricts with panic. This isn't the calm, ranting man from a moment ago. No, the man before me is as dangerous and unpredictable as a grizzly in the wild.

And his sights are set on me.

"So, what am I supposed to do, sit on my couch and stare at the walls all day? Obviously, I'm going to party. And why shouldn't I hit up my dealers a little more often than usual? Not like I have a job to go to the next day." He runs his hand repeatedly over his head, eyes darting around behind me.

"You wanna know what else I did?" He tilts his head to the side, taking a step toward me. I take a step back. "I started thinking. And I realized something." Another step toward me. I try to step away but my back hits the building wall.

There's nowhere to run.

"This whole thing started because of *you*. My life was fucking *perfect* and then you had to go and fuck it all up!" He screams the last word and I flinch, hunching in on myself.

My heart is tripping over itself, racing so fast it physically hurts. My breathing shallows and I can't get enough air into my lungs.

No, not right now. Don't lose control now. Just a little

bit longer and Luke will be here. Don't let the panic take you under.

But I can feel the darkness coming, pulling at my consciousness.

"So I decide to send you a couple love notes to your email. It was easy to find on your website. Figured I should remind you what happens when you fuck with other people's lives."

His arms brace the wall on either side of my head, effectively caging me in.

Breathe.

Breathe.

In.

Out.

Three things I can hear.

"Then my crook of a landlord decides to kick me out. Couple late bills and I'm out on my ass. That's when I decided to pay you a little visit. Hoped I'd catch you at home. Kinda liked the idea of watching those pretty eyes leaking while I show you what that loud mouth is for."

No. No, no, no.

My breathing is jagged and I can't stop my mind from spinning.

That night. He was inside my studio. Waiting for me. If Luke didn't text me, if I didn't go pick him up, Tad would've...

I squeeze my eyes shut, trying to force the panic away but it's clawing at my throat.

"LOOK AT ME!" Tad screams and I force my eyes open to look into his crazed expression.

The black. It's coming. I can feel it.

Just. A little. Longer.

Luke.

"Maybe after I have some fun with you, I'll go find that fat cunt friend of yours and show her what she missed out on. Think I can fit two of you in my trunk?" he sneers, a sadistic smile peeling over his lips. He thinks he's beat me. He thinks he just delivered the death blow.

But that was his mistake.

The darkness fades and it's no longer black clouding my vision.

It's red.

LUKE

Jolie's gonna kill me. I was supposed to be at her apartment fifteen minutes ago, but five minutes before my shift ended, Millie Loffman decided she needed to report an official complaint against Miss Carla for harassment.

Thirty years those two have been going at it and she decides today of all days to do something about it.

Of course, I talked her off the ledge and convinced her not to file any charges but she warned me if she found kitty litter in her mailbox one more time, she was not responsible for her actions.

Me neither, Millie. Me neither.

I push my gas pedal down a little harder, pushing the speed limit just past what's legal. Any officer who tries to pull me over right now is pulling desk duty for a week.

I swing my truck around the corner of Jolie's building. My eyes glance over the parking lot, expecting to see a seething Jolie waiting for me.

When she's nowhere in sight, I figure she went back into her apartment to wait. I pull further into the parking lot, preparing to grovel.

Something near the building catches my attention. A

dark figure is standing near Jolie's door. My body instantly stiffens, my police brain alert and assessing.

It's then that I see her. Jolie's chestnut hair, barely visible from behind the man. She's pressed against the wall. I can feel her fear from here. Every muscle in my body tenses and my chest tightens. I slam my truck into park and shove the door open with enough force, I'm surprised it doesn't break off its hinges.

My body's only purpose is to get to her.

Now.

I'm going to fucking kill him.

I'm barrelling toward her, ready to tear this scumbag to pieces when a loud *crunch* sounds, followed by a scream. Then the man falls to the ground, one hand covering his bleeding face while the other grips his crotch.

I stop suddenly in surprise, watching as the creep rolls on the ground. Before I can kick my feet back into gear, a body slams into mine. Jolie yelps, arms thrashing as she tries to fight me off.

"Jolie! Jolie! It's me!"

She stops and looks up at me, her eyes lit with fear. "Luke? Oh, thank god." Her arms wrap around my waist and I pull her to me, hugging her tight. She holds me just as firmly.

"You were right. It was Tad. He sent the emails and destroyed my studio. He was waiting for me—he was going to—" Her voice cracks as tears start to flow now that her adrenaline is wearing off.

My hands turn into fists around her back. I know exactly what he was going to do. I want to stomp his face into the pavement for even thinking about touching her.

"Stay here," I growl, starting to take a step away but she tightens her grip.

"No. Please, Luke. Don't." Her panic has me stopping to stare down at her. "Please don't. Just...hold me." Her voice is timid and she's shaking. That's all it takes for me to forget about the piece of shit behind her, still writhing on the ground.

Stepping back to her, I wrap her into my arms and hold her tightly. Without letting her out of my grasp, I pull my cell phone out of my pocket with one hand and dial the station.

Within minutes, three police cruisers fly into the parking lot and five officers run over to where Tad lies on the pavement, still bleeding. They haul him up, cuff him, and toss him into the back of a cruiser.

He's thrashing around in his seat, shouting threats and obscenities. It's then that I get a good look at his face and the damage Jolie inflicted.

I pull back to look down at her. "Where did you learn to fight like that?"

She smiles up at me and my heart lurches at the sight. No matter what he did, he didn't take that spark from her. "I'm an army brat, remember? I've been practicing self-defense since I was nine."

"That's hot." That makes her laugh, just like I hoped it would. Staring down at her, I'm once again amazed that someone like her could ever love a guy like me.

That's all the time we get before two officers come over to take our statements. Hearing Jolie recount the details has my fists tightening at my sides, but I keep my touch around her waist soft. Finally the officers have enough, so I thank them before we turn away.

"Let's go," I say, nodding toward my truck. "I want to show you something."

CHAPTER 53

JOLIE

Luke's truck pulls onto the side of the road. I look out the windshield, not sure why we're stopped on a backroad with nothing but trees and bush around us.

"You know, if you're trying to murder me, let me remind you that I've already kicked one creep's ass today," I say. "I don't mind adding another to my roster."

How I can even joke right now is a testament to the calming effect Luke has on me.

Before Luke pulled up, I could feel myself being dragged into the abyss of another panic attack. My head and my body were already disconnected. It wouldn't have taken much to push me over that edge.

But as soon as Tad mentioned going after Brenna, it's like a switch went off inside me. I clawed my way out of the vortex that was threatening to sweep me away until finally my vision cleared. What I saw before me was a pathetic, self-sabotaging, petulant little child throwing a tantrum.

And threatening one of my best friends.

Yeah, that's not happening.

So, I channeled every ounce of self-defence knowledge that was drilled into me from before I hit puberty and attacked.

Then I ran.

Into the arms of the one man who I knew would always protect me.

The man in question groans from across the truck. "How many times are you going to use that line to your advantage?"

I shrug. "As long as it keeps being true."

He smiles and as it always does, the sight sparks a flutter in my stomach. "Well, for the millionth time, I'm not going to murder you."

I tilt my head as if in thought. "Alright. I won't kick your ass then."

Luke rolls his eyes. "Glad to hear it. Now that we've got that out of the way, follow me."

I shake my head. "Not with manners like that, I won't."

He rolls his eyes again. I wonder if I can make them stay like that permanently. Probably if I tried hard enough.

Challenge accepted.

"*Please* follow me," he bites out.

"Much better," I reply, then push open the door of the truck and hop down onto the road.

Rounding the truck, Luke takes my hand and we walk out into the field beside us. Luckily for us, it hasn't snowed in a few days so there's only a few inches of snow to wade through.

Before long, Luke's pushing aside some branches, revealing a worn path in the trees. He ushers me through then continues down the path.

We don't talk, merely wander along, enjoying the silence. I think Luke was as shaken up by what happened earlier as I was. He's probably blaming himself for being late and not being able to stop Tad from getting to me. But it wouldn't have mattered. Tad had a vendetta against me, blaming me for everything wrong in his life. He wouldn't have gone away nicely without getting a chance at me.

I shudder at the thought and Luke pulls me closer to him.

It takes another ten minutes of walking before we finally stop. Luke turns to me, his face solemn. "Remember the day I pulled you over?"

I smirk. "Which time?"

He pinches my arm and I laugh. "The most recent one." His face turns serious again. "You told me how you drive your grandfather's old car to help you feel closer to him."

I nod. "And you said you understood because you had a special place you went to that reminded you of your dad."

Luke smiles softly. "Yeah, I did." He sweeps his arm forward, pushing back more brush then gestures with his other hand. I duck under his arm to take a few steps until I come out into a clearing. I can't help the gasp that leaves my lips.

It's...stunning is too plain to describe the scene before me. A river winds before me, great towering trees lining each side. The sound of water cascading over some rocks as it makes its way around the bend feels fake, it's so serene. In the distance, mountains stand strong as if protecting the small piece of heaven from wandering eyes.

"This is beautiful," I whisper in awe. "You found this with your dad?"

Luke nods. "I've never been here with anyone but him." He pauses. "Until now."

I spin toward him at the admission. His eyes hold mine,

letting me see every piece of vulnerability, grief and peace inside him.

"Thank you for trusting me."

Luke shakes his head, stepping closer. "It's me who should be thanking you. You pulled me out of the slump I had become far too comfortable in. All I had was my work and my responsibilities. Even when I was meant to be having fun, I saw it as a duty. Something I had to do in order to be a good friend. A good brother. A good neighbor."

He grabs my hands in his. "It wasn't until you that I realized I was living half a life. One night and you'd weaseled your way into that life. You teased, fought, and annoyed me out of the shell I was living in." He lifts my hands to his lips and places a kiss on each one. At this point, my chest is impossibly tight and there's a ball of emotion that has made a permanent place in my throat.

"On paper, we shouldn't work. You thrive in chaos while I need control and order. But maybe that's why we work. You take my hand to help me soar while I keep you from flying too close to the sun.

"I love you, Jolie." He reaches into his coat pocket and pulls out a box. My heart goes from singing to shrieking in seconds. I'm about to turn and run when Luke laughs.

"Stop freaking out. It's not what you think." He pushes the box into my hesitant hands. Cautiously, I open the box, tensing as if a snake might jump out and bite me.

If there's a ring in here, I might prefer the snake.

But instead, inside is a folded up piece of paper. Curious now, I unfold the paper. When I read the words on it, my knees almost give out.

"Plane tickets to Chamonix, France?" I glance up at Luke in shock. "When did you...how did you...what?"

Luke smiles. "They're dated for November of this year.

I figure I can take the time off when it's less busy and we can use the time between now and then to work through your fears."

I stare down at the print out of the tickets. "You remembered?" I croak out.

Just looking at the tickets makes me feel like an idiot. I'm petrified of heights, yet my dream vacation is centered around a glass box at the top of a mountain. But there's something about the idea of it. It seems so thrilling to be so high up with nothing keeping you from falling to your death but some glass and a shit ton of trust.

Kind of like falling in love.

"Of course, I did. I bought these the day after you agreed to date me in secret." He squeezes my hand. "We can start with some small hikes in the mountains and work our way up. You deserve to follow your dreams, Jolie. It doesn't matter if they make sense to anyone else. It only matters if they make sense to you."

How did he know that's what I was thinking?

But at the same time, I'm not surprised that Luke can read me so well. In the short time since we've been together, I've opened up to him more than anyone else in my life. Even my brother.

I would've thought it would be terrifying to let someone see me so wholly and transparently. But it's freeing. To let go of my worries and overthinking and just be me.

Luke's right. On paper, we shouldn't work. We're two very different people—from our jobs to our personalities.

But maybe that's why we work so well. He's the calm in the middle of my storm. I'm the wind that moves his sails. We'd be fine on our own but together, we're so much more.

I look up into the eyes of the man who made me fall in love with him and realize something: I'm not my mother and he's not my father. I will never allow him to control me but he'll never try. He won't keep me down, but lift me up.

We're not them.

We're us.

And given the option, I'd choose us every time.

I lean forward to place a slow, lingering kiss against his lips. "Thank you," I whisper.

"My pleasure, sweetheart."

————-

Luke and I spent the rest of the day exploring the clearing and hiking around some nearby paths. Hours later, Luke suggested grabbing dinner at the steakhouse on the outside of town. We spent the night eating, laughing, and just enjoying each other's company. By the time we get back to my apartment, it's nearly nine o'clock. As we pull up to Main Street, I notice more cars than usual lining the sides of the road.

"Is there something going on in town?" I wonder aloud. "I don't remember hearing anything."

Luke continues humming along to the radio, drumming his thumbs on the steering wheel as he pulls to an open space out front. "Donno."

I narrow my eyes at him. "Luke..."

"Jolie..." he mimics, mirroring my expression.

"What'd you do?"

He shrugs then climbs out of the truck, assuming I'll follow him.

Which I'm obviously going to do because he's acting weird and both my curiosity and defences are simultaneously piqued.

I clamber out of the truck and round the front to his outstretched hand. I eye it cautiously like it's a shark circling me.

He chuckles. "I promise it's nothing bad."

Deciding that I can always make him pay for whatever's about to happen, I follow him toward my dark studio.

Since the break in, I've avoided using the front entrance. The devastation inside just depresses me. My insurance is dragging their feet, giving me every excuse for why they shouldn't have to cover the damages. Unfortunately, I'm too broke to fix it myself, otherwise I would've told them where to stick their policy by now.

Luke reaches for the door and now I'm definitely on high alert. The fact that he didn't even question the studio being locked means he knew it wouldn't be. He pulls open the door and gestures for me to go in first. Eyeing him one last time, I cross the threshold into the dark studio.

The lights suddenly flash on and a resounding cheer of "surprise!" almost knocks me back a step. The room is filled with people from town: Mr. and Mrs. Thompson from the hardware store. Matt and Avery. Brenna and Rhett. Angie and Gavin. Franny and Pete. Jack Henderson from the lumberyard. Sandy, Miss Carla, Maeve, Dottie and her now-husband Harold.

I stare around the room in awe, taking in all the faces who have come to be more like family to me over the past handful of years than my own.

"Wh-what's going on?" I ask, my head swinging to Luke as he steps up beside me.

"Look around," he answers, pointing around the room.

It's then that I notice what's behind the crowd. My studio. It's...fixed. It's even better than before.

The floor to ceiling mirrored wall is perfectly spotless. The drywall is fixed and the walls are painted the same off-white as before, but with a sage green accent wall that I had told Avery I always wanted to add. All new yoga mats line the cubbies on the far wall while new paintings hang from the walls. The poles are cleaned and tucked into the corner. The floors are polished and free of the red paint splatters from Tad's destructive message.

It's beautiful. It's everything I ever wanted the studio to be and more. I have no words. I try multiple times to find them but every time I open my mouth, emotion clogs my throat.

Luke wraps an arm around my shoulder and pulls me into his side as a tear finally escapes down my cheek. I shove at it before it can reach my chin.

"This is...it's too much...I can't..." My voice shakes, trying to form a sentence.

Luke squeezes my shoulder and leans down to press a kiss to my temple. "It's not and you can," he replies. "People wanted to help."

"Well, it was either this or drive to Bakersfield the next time I want to curse with my ass in the air," Dottie comments. I laugh through my tears.

"And I want to practice that spinning upside-down move on the pole some more," Maeve adds.

To my surprise, it's Angie who steps up and takes my hands in hers. "Accepting help isn't easy for women like us. I know. I've fought against it my whole life." She reaches up to brush a tear away from my cheek. "But we need to remember that the people who love us *want* to help. So as hard as it may be, we should let them."

I nod, choking back a sob as she wraps me in a hug. After a moment, I pull back and look around the room.

"Thank you. All of you. I'll never be able to tell you what this means to me." I smile, reaching behind me for Luke's hand. "My heart is so full right now. And it's all thanks to you."

"Alright, alright," Dottie calls. "Enough of the sappy stuff. Who's poppin' the champagne?"

Everyone laughs and Rhett bends over to pull two bottles of champagne from a cooler behind him. Glasses are passed around and someone turns music on the overhead speaker.

I can't help but look around, feeling so damn grateful for every person in this room.

It wasn't long ago that I was just a teenager, broken and searching for my place in this world. It took a while, but I realize now, I was looking for this town. These people.

My family.

Luke wraps his arms around me from behind and I lean into his chest. "I love you," he mumbles and I smile.

"I love you, too."

"So, how many glasses of champagne will it take for you boys to get up on those poles and give us a show? Magic Mike style," Dottie calls while Maeve whistles behind her.

Luke groans while I laugh.

"This fricken' town."

EPILOGUE

JOLIE

"**I**ntroducing for the first time ever: Mr. and Mrs. Brady!"

The wedding guests erupt into cheers and applause as Matt and Avery come dancing into the reception hall hand-in-hand.

Their matching grins are wide as they make their way onto the dance floor. The music slows and when they turn to each other, it's like the roomful of people disappear. The love that they have for each other is plastered on both of their faces from the way they hold each other close to the way they're watching each other.

Matt says something that has Avery laughing and if possible, his grin gets even bigger.

"I swear I could watch those two together all night," Tori croons from her chair beside me. "They're so cute, it's easy to forget that's my same brother who put glitter in my shampoo bottle when I was fifteen."

I laugh. "Wouldn't Matt have been twenty then?"

Tori shoots me a dry look. "You'd think that would've meant he'd matured, but you'd be wrong."

The wedding day has gone off without a hitch. The sun was shining and the last of the snow had melted away just last week. Spring was peeking around the corner and the world was starting to show it.

The venue was stunning. Avery's simple but beautiful décor accentuated the winery's already stunning backdrop. Daisies lined the aisle way as Avery made her grand entrance on Angie's arm. Gavin looked all sorts of handsome standing next to a teary Matt as we watched Avery make her way toward the love of her life.

I only cried three times during the ceremony. The first was when Angie gave Avery away at the altar. The hug they shared and the way Angie looked at both Avery and Matt had my heart exploding in my chest.

The second was when they said their vows. They had written their own and both were heartfelt and emotional. I wasn't sure Matt was going to get through his without losing it, but he managed to only let a few tears slip.

But the log that broke the dam was when Matt finished his vows and turned to Gavin. He got down on one knee and surprised everyone, even Avery, by saying his own vows to Gavin. To love and protect him and be there for him every day for the rest of his life.

There wasn't a dry eye in the place when Gavin threw his arms around Matt and cried into his shoulder.

Avery's makeup stood no chance.

"They look good together," Luke comments as Matt gestures for Gavin to join them. He hoists the first grader into the air, and the three of them sway together. "They're a family now."

"They always were," I reply, unable to tear my eyes away from the trio.

After the first dance, Matt takes Franny for a spin around the dance floor to *Never Grow Up* by Taylor Swift (Franny's idol). When they're done, Luke shocks us all by standing up and reaching a hand out to Avery. The DJ plays *My Wish* by Rascal Flatts while Luke walks Avery out onto the dance floor then takes her hand to sway with her looking every bit the big brother.

They talk as the song continues on and when it ends, he gives her a tight hug and says something that has Avery tearing up and smiling.

God. Every time I think I can't fall any further for this man, he pulls something like this and proves me wrong.

When the traditional dances are done, dinner starts. The meal brings me back to the first weekend Luke and I spent together, sampling the wedding menu and getting to know each other.

Oh, and banging each other's brains out.

"What'd you say we book a weekend at the lodge sometime?" I ask him, leaning in closely and letting my lips graze over his ear. "You know, for old time's sake."

He groans softly then turns his dark eyes on me. "Pick a date and I'm in." He tilts his head to whisper in my ear. "But if you think that means I'm not fucking you against every surface in our hotel room tonight, you're in for a surprise."

I shiver and Luke leans back in his seat, a smug look on his face. Then, as if I wasn't ready to drag him out the door right now to make good on his promise, the bastard *winks*.

RIP, panties. It was nice knowing you.

The music stops suddenly and the DJ hands the microphone over to Matt who stands at the front table beside Avery. They didn't want a formal head table, so it's just the two of them on their own while the rest of the wedding party sits at a nearby table.

"Evening, folks," Matt starts. "Avery and I just wanted to say a quick thank you to everyone for coming out tonight to celebrate with us. It's been a long time coming and I for one am so glad you're all here with us as I finally make Avery mine." Avery smiles up at him, love shining brightly in her eyes.

"They say that the key to a good marriage is to never stop surprising each other. When you've known each other as long as Avery and I have, that can be a little hard to do." He steps away from the table, smirking at a confused Avery. "Freckles, I hope this proves that I'll never stop surprising you."

He points at the DJ and the familiar sound of shaking starts over the speakers.

"No," I stare at Matt in disbelief.

"He didn't," Tori says, half-laughing, half-groaning.

He did. *It's Tricky* by Run-DMC starts to play and to both my horror and delight, Matt starts dancing and lip-syncing to the song.

The whole room is laughing and cheering. Then the second verse starts and Matt points at Rhett, who's sitting across from me.

Or he was. Now he's lip-syncing right along with Matt with all the seriousness of a trained performer. He joins Matt at the center of the dance floor and they start dancing together, perfectly in sync.

I'm howling, unable to believe my eyes but loving every second of this ridiculous dance. Especially when Matt gets on the floor and tries (and fails) to perform the worm, while Rhett raps into an imaginary microphone.

"Oh my god. Can you believe this? Have you ever seen anything so amazing?" I ask Luke, laughing as Matt and Rhett attempt to breakdance.

"Sweetheart, you haven't seen anything yet." Luke smiles devilishly and shocks me by standing from his place beside me. His eyes never leave mine as he starts to sing along to the song.

"What is happening?!" Brenna cries out, laughing.

"This is the best night of my life. Hands down." Tori stands to start recording with her phone.

Luke joins the boys and starts jumping around, rapping and doing what I think is supposed to be dancing. They look ridiculous but the smiles on their faces have me grinning along with them.

But when Gavin joins in, perfectly executing the dance the three men are performing, the entire room loses it. Brenna, Tori and I stand, screaming and yelling like a bunch of groupies in the front row of a concert.

The song finally ends and Matt and Rhett drop to the floor, legs spread in opposite directions with their heads propped on one hand. Luke crouches above them, his arms spread wide in the least gangster-looking pose I've ever seen. And then there's Gavin, his arms crossed over his chest, head tilted up and looking every bit the pop star he is.

Cheers, whistles and applause breaks out, multiple people shouting for an encore. Avery runs over and wraps Gavin in a hug then Matt. She's laughing so hard she has tears running down her face as she pulls his head down to kiss him.

The music changes to a slow song and Luke strolls over to me, smirking. He takes my hand and I let him lead me further onto the dance floor. He pulls me in close and I inhale his scent, so familiar and calming.

"Not bad, eh?" Luke asks, still smirking.

"Not bad for an old guy," I tease. He narrows his eyes then pokes me in the ribs. I laugh, twisting away from his fingers. "I'm kidding. That was amazing. Best thing I've ever seen."

Luke grins down at me, something he's been doing a lot more of lately. These past few months he's been more playful. Calmer. Don't get me wrong, he's still a grumpy asshole, but he balances it out by showing his fun side now, too.

We sway in silence for a while. I glance around the room. Matt is dancing with Angie while Gavin spins Avery around the dance floor. Brenna is talking with Maeve at a nearby table while Dottie sways along with Harold.

To my surprise, Tori and Rhett are dancing near us. She's smiling salaciously up at him, clearly teasing him as he shakes his head, smiling shyly.

Oh, boy. Looks like the interest I saw from Tori at the engagement party hasn't worn off. In fact, I'd say she looks to have set her sights on him. But Rhett won't be easily swayed. He's loyal and honorable. I can't see him compromising his friendships with Matt and Luke over a fling with their little sister who lives three provinces away.

I'm not sure who will win in that test of wills but it'll be fun to watch regardless.

Tori lifts onto her tiptoes and whispers something in Rhett's ear. He looks over his shoulder at Matt, hesitating before giving a small nod. I watch as Tori turns with Rhett's hand in hers and they make their way toward the patio.

Uh oh. That should be interesting.

"What'd you say we make a quick detour to our room while they cut the cake?" Luke wags his eyebrows.

I hum my approval. "You've seen one cake being cut,

you've seen them all." I wrap his tie around my fist and pull him closer. "Besides, I've been thinking about all the fun things I want to do with this tie all night."

Luke swallows hard. "Let's go. Now." He turns and practically drags me toward the hallway while I follow behind him laughing.

Feeling lighter and happier than I've ever been in my life.

THE NEXT MORNING, only after Luke bribed me with bacon to get me out of bed, we make our way down to the dining room for breakfast with the rest of the wedding party.

Avery smiles from her place beside Matt, who has his arm slung over the back of her chair. "I didn't think we'd see you until noon, J."

I place a kiss on the top of her head as I walk by. "Consider this early wake up as my wedding gift to you." She laughs as I take a seat beside her. The conversation picks up again as we trade stories from the previous night.

Mary Benson and Trina Thompson got so drunk that they buried the hatchet on their Jeffrey-the-vagina-man statue. So much so that Mary agreed to buy Jeffrey's matching set.

Dottie and Maeve started a lap-dance competition, where they sat in side-by-side seats and rated lap-dances the drunk guests gave them. Apparently, Miss Carla was the winner by a landslide.

I'm almost sorry I missed that one. But the delicious break I took with Luke in our room more than makes up for it.

There's only one story that isn't shared and it's of the two people who are both noticeably missing from breakfast this morning.

Hmm. Maybe I overestimated Rhett's resistance.

Speak of the devil...

Rhett comes hurrying into the dining hall, frantically searching around the room until his gaze lands on us. Based on the worry still etched onto his face when he sees us, I don't think we were who he was looking for.

He stalks over, stopping just before the table.

"Rhett. Thought you were gonna sleep through breakfast," Matt jokes. "Grab a plate. There's plenty of food left."

"I'm good." He grabs the chair in front of him with both hands. "Hey, has anyone seen Tori yet? She...she asked me for a ride into town, but I can't find her."

Matt stabs a piece of sausage from the serving dish and drops it on his plate. "Yeah, she left already." He cuts it into pieces and pops one into his mouth. "Said she had a work emergency or something and had to leave early."

"She left?" Rhett asks, his brows furrowing in confusion. He looks...disappointed?

Uh oh. That could only mean...

"Yeah, 'bout an hour ago." Matt shrugs. "Guess you're off the hook."

"Might as well grab a plate." Luke offers him an empty one.

Rhett hesitates. "Actually, I should get going, too. I forgot I have a call with a guy about a gig. I'll catch up with you guys later." And with that, he stalks out of the room.

Matt shrugs. "More for me."

I look around the table in shock. Did no one else just see what I saw?

Avery and Brenna are deep in conversation about a new program Avery wants to implement in the bookstore that will benefit the rescue. Matt is more interested in eating his body weight in bacon while Luke obliviously digs into his breakfast.

"Everything good?" he asks, when he realizes I haven't eaten yet.

I'm not about to tell him what I saw, when I'm not even sure I really saw it.

All I know is something happened between Rhett and Tori last night. Enough to have Tori leaving on an earlier flight and Rhett go chasing after her.

This should be fun.

"Everything's good," I assure him with a smile before taking a bite of bacon.

At least, I hope it is.

———

ALSO BY KATIE BECK

Can't get enough of the Haven Bay crew? Follow along on Instagram and TikTok for most up-to-date info.

HAVEN BAY SERIES

Avery and Matt

Jolie and Luke

Brenna and Mike

Tori and Rhett

TORONTO STORM SERIES

Austin and TBD

Chase and TBD